AM   ORM ATION SERVI

Wrong Way Home

Also by Isabelle Grey

Out of Sight
The Bad Mother

DI GRACE FISHER THRILLERS
Good Girls Don't Die
Shot Through the Heart
The Special Girls

Wrong Way Home

ISABELLE GREY

Quercus

First published in Great Britain in 2018 by

Quercus Editions Ltd
Carmelite House
50 Victoria Embankment
London EC4Y 0DZ

An Hachette UK company

'Love Is A Stranger'
Music and Lyrics by Dave Stewart and Ann Lennox
© Copyright 1982 Arnakata Music Limited.
Logo Songs Limited/Universal Music Publishing MGB Limited.

A CIP catalogue record for this book is available
from the British Library

HB ISBN 978 1 78648 647 9

10 9 8 7 6 5 4 3 2 1

Typeset by Jouve (UK), Milton Keynes
Printed and bound in Great Britain by Clays Ltd, St Ives plc

For Brian Smith, with thanks for a great day out in Southend

Rotherham MBC	
B54 025 303 5	
Askews & Holts	23-May-2018
AF	£20.99
MAL	

1

'When beggars die there are no comets seen, The heavens themselves blaze forth the death of princes'.

So said Calpurnia in Shakespeare's *Julius Caesar*.

Today is my twenty-fifth birthday and I've heard my parents speak those words on this day every year for as long as I can remember. Not that I died, and there was no comet, but I'm the boy who was born on the night of the fire. My family has never let go of the idea that somehow that's significant. Maybe it is.

I'm Freddie Craig, and you're listening to *Stories from the Fire*.

On this night, twenty-five years ago, the old Marineland resort in Southend-on-Sea burned to the ground. Built in the 1930s as a seaside leisure complex, its Art Deco theatre, dance hall and bars were once thronged with holiday-makers – until they discovered Spanish package holidays in the 1960s, jetted off to the sun and never really came back. By 1992, with the country in recession, the building was boarded up, awaiting an endlessly postponed refurbishment. Once the fire took hold, it spread in what seemed like seconds. The blaze was, I'm told, an inferno. Even the captain of a passing ship was so alarmed by the distant red glow in the night sky that he contacted the coastguard. It took several hours, a dozen fire engines and hundreds of gallons of water to bring the flames under control. The smell of the fire, it was said, lingered in the air for several weeks.

My mother saw the flames on her journey to the hospital and, throughout her labour, overheard the midwife and nurses whispering about the eerie sights and sounds. After my delivery, she was taken to a ward with windows facing the sea. At dawn she stood, holding her infant son in her arms, watching the sun rise behind a great pall of black smoke drifting slowly eastwards over the mud of the Thames estuary.

It makes a good story. But there's more. Alarmed by such bad omens, my mother was later relieved to hear that, miraculously, not only had no one died in the fire but that it had been the scene of a heroic rescue.

Two teenagers had broken into the empty building, intending to explore its deserted halls. The fire was almost certainly started by their carelessly discarded cigarettes. They quickly found themselves disorientated by the darkness and terrified by the roasting heat. In their rush to escape, one of them fell down some stairs and broke his ankle.

Alerted by their cries, a passer-by managed to smash his way into the smoke-filled building. Carrying the injured teenager on his back, he guided the other one to safety. Two minutes later an almighty explosion rocked the entire cliffside area as a flashover ignited all combustible material. It was a further five long minutes before any of the emergency services arrived. By that time, Marineland was a roaring bonfire.

The boys' saviour was rightly feted. Everyone wanted to tell a story of heroism, survival and, ultimately – after a new shopping mall was built on the site a few years later – renewal.

And this, too, became the story of my birth. I entered this world on the night of the fire, yet, far from seeing it as a portent of fear and destruction, my parents spun it into an augury of a charmed life to follow. After all, the heavens themselves had blazed forth my arrival.

Six weeks after my birth, the Queen's *annus horribilis* culminated with a fire at Windsor Castle. And here are a few other random facts about 1992. *Reservoir Dogs* was released, Bill Clinton was elected President of the USA and DNA fingerprinting was first used to exonerate a prisoner on Death Row.

In Southend, the night of the fire is now remembered for a stranger's rescue of two teenagers, but I have discovered that other, darker events were also taking place in the seaside town. Obscured by the front-page celebration of a local hero, the death of nineteen-year-old Heather Bowyer received little coverage. Yet, just as two bored teenagers were flicking away their smouldering cigarette butts in the derelict Marineland resort, she was being brutally raped and then murdered in a nearby park overlooking the seafront.

Twenty-five years later, that crime remains unsolved. For all we know, Heather's killer may still be living prosperously down the road, a pillar of the local community. He might be the man you drink with in the pub, or even your brother-in-law. Or he could be a drunken vagrant sprawled on a park bench. Nobody knows. Or only one person, and he's not telling.

Heather's life ended as mine began. I can't help feeling that the destinies of all those involved in the dramatic events of that night are intertwined with mine, which is why I've decided to make it my mission to find out everything I can about Heather and the nameless man who has evaded justice for a quarter of a century.

You've been listening to me, Freddie Craig. If you'd like to join me on my journey, then please share and subscribe to hear the next instalment of my podcast, *Stories from the Fire*.

2

Looking around the congregation, Detective Inspector Grace Fisher wondered how many of the people who cried at weddings were shedding tears of disappointed hope rather than joy. Not that this wasn't a lovely wedding – picturesque old church, bright autumnal flower arrangements, uplifting music; and she couldn't be happier for the couple now signing the register – but with the marriage service throwing all kinds of dreams and regrets into sharp relief, she could no longer pretend she wasn't aware of Detective Sergeant Blake Langley sitting two pews behind.

Over the three months since Blake had ended their brief and discreet relationship he had continued to be the wry and supportive colleague she'd, albeit slowly, come to enjoy working with, but he had also scrupulously avoided being alone with her in any non-professional situation. She knew it was probably for the best, yet she yearned for what might have been – and right now felt that ache more keenly than she had previously allowed herself to admit.

Beside her, her boss's wife, Natalie Pitman, took a clean tissue out of her handbag and delicately manoeuvred her hand under the brim of her hat to wipe away a tear. Grace caught her eye and smiled, although she suspected that Natalie's husband,

Colin, a man currently aspiring to be a silver fox, took a rather more pragmatic attitude towards his own wedding vows than might please his wife. The cynical thought reminded Grace not to get sentimental. After all, her own experience of marriage had hardly turned out to be a bed of roses, and no relationship was ever perfect.

The ache, however, did not lessen, and she was glad when the organist switched to more rousing music to accompany the bride and groom as they processed up the aisle with their families, beaming at friends as they went. Although only Grace knew the true reason why it had taken Detective Constable Duncan Gregg years to break his silence, all his friends had guessed long ago that he had a soft spot for Joan, the civilian case manager on the Major Investigation Team in Colchester. Everyone had been delighted when they had finally announced that they were getting married, and – both were pushing forty – as swiftly as possible. Throughout the service Grace had felt that delight filling the air and enveloping Duncan and Joan in an invisible mist of benevolence.

Picking up the basket of confetti at her feet, Grace slipped out of the pew and followed in their wake so that she could find a good position at the side of the church steps, ready to offer confetti to any guest who wanted to shower the happy couple with biodegradable good luck and prosperity. Outside in the watery October sunshine, she enjoyed the spectacle of Joan's four teenage nieces blushing and giggling as they smoothed out their bridesmaid dresses and checked each other's hair, ready for the photographer. When Blake came to stand beside her, Grace saw the eldest bridesmaid also notice the fit, handsome thirty-something, although he appeared oblivious to the flirtatious glances the girl directed at him from under her long lashes.

'Confetti?' Grace proffered her basket.

'Thanks.' He gave her a warm, amused smile and scooped up a handful of dried rose petals and then nodded to where Duncan stood proudly beside his bride. 'Cute, don't you think?'

'Very.'

He was jostled closer as more people came out of the church and crowded round the steps. He looked down at her and smiled once more. Feeling the heat of his body, and sure that he too must be conscious of the heightened emotion of the occasion, she was tempted to say something, although she had no idea precisely what. Maybe it was just as well that, before she could speak, she was side-tracked by several people laughing and reaching for the confetti. As Blake turned aside to speak to someone else, she became aware of her phone vibrating in her clutch bag.

With so many MIT officers present at the wedding, Grace, as senior investigating officer, had volunteered to be on duty. Indicating her phone, she handed Blake her basket and stepped aside into the shelter of a thick stone buttress. She saw that the call was from the team's crime scene manager.

'Hello, Wendy,' she said. 'Aren't you on a course this weekend?'

'I am,' Wendy replied, 'but I thought you'd want to know that we've got a final list from the preliminary search results.'

'And?' said Grace as Wendy paused tantalisingly.

'After applying the filters, there are at least a dozen that merit serious investigation.'

'And?' she repeated, hearing the elation in Wendy's voice.

'Well, if our assumption is correct that the perpetrator is local, then we have one clear front-runner. Deborah Shillingford, charged two years ago with drink-driving.' Wendy paused for effect. 'She's fifty-two and was born and still lives in Southend.'

'So if her father is still alive, or she has brothers or male cousins, they'd all have been around the right age.' Grace felt the first prickle of anticipation.

'It's a good start,' agreed Wendy. 'How's the wedding?'

'Oh, perfect,' said Grace. 'Joan looks beautiful and Duncan can't stop smiling. Will you email me the list?'

'Already have.'

'Great, thanks. See you first thing Monday morning.'

Wendy laughed. 'Don't forget to bring me some cake.'

'I won't. You certainly deserve it.' Grace ended the call, closing her eyes and taking a deep breath. She couldn't imagine a single detective who wouldn't be electrified by such a promising development.

The 1992 rape and murder of Heather Bowyer in Southend-on-Sea was the most serious of the Case Remains Open files that Grace had inherited when she took over as SIO. No serious suspect had ever been in the frame, and previous cold case reviews and even a *Crimewatch* appeal had failed to offer new leads. The crime had taken place twenty-five years ago, not long after the advent of DNA fingerprinting but before the National DNA Database had been set up. At that point DNA could only be retrieved from bodily fluids such as blood or semen, and none had been retrieved at the scene that might identify a possible perpetrator. However, new techniques had been developed over the past decade that made it possible to get results from tiny traces left by physical contact with an object. When crime scene evidence from the Bowyer case was re-examined using these techniques, two DNA profiles had been discovered. One of them was only a partial, from inside a man's leather glove, but the other, from the murder weapon, a kitchen knife, contained a full set of markers. The knife blade, left embedded in the nineteen-year-old victim's back, had found its way between her ribs and perforated her aorta.

The glove hadn't simply been randomly lost: the partial sample from its lining shared enough markers with the profile from the knife to suggest that both could be from the same person. However, if the man had ever committed further crimes, he had escaped arrest, which meant that his DNA was not on the national database. Grace knew that if his profile had been added – a search was run every night to match new samples from those arrested that day to DNA from any previous crime scenes – she would already have been informed.

By the time Grace came to review the Heather Bowyer murder file, other advances in DNA profiling had also made it possible to run a search for a familial match in the hope that a close relative of the unknown offender might be on the national database. While this, if they were lucky, could whittle down the pool of suspects from 'could be anyone' to perhaps a thousand or more who shared the same DNA markers on their Y chromosome, it was expensive. The time-consuming job of tracking down and eliminating the male relatives of each match, possibly spread right across the country, would be prohibitive – unless that number could be meaningfully reduced using filters such as age, ethnicity and geographical location.

Only when Grace learnt from Wendy that her own theory – that the killer was not a weekend visitor – was backed up by the fact that a couple of unusual markers in the DNA profile from the knife suggested he came from a long-standing local family, did the familial search become a gamble worth taking. Grace had then set about convincing Superintendent Pitman to let her argue her case before the deputy chief constable. She'd been thrilled when she'd finally been given the green light.

And now she had a list on which to start work. Not only that, she had one name at the top, around which she could begin to gather intelligence immediately. The thought of the net closing in on a brutal killer who had escaped justice for twenty-five years was spine-tingling. Sometimes, she told herself, she really did have the best job in the world.

She was checking her phone for Wendy's email when Blake came looking for her.

'Anything urgent?' he asked.

'Well, yes and no,' she said. 'It's not a call-out, but Wendy has the results from the familial search on the Heather Bowyer case.'

'Great.'

'Yes, it's fantastic.'

'Duncan's looking for you. He wants you to meet his mother.'

'Oh, yes, of course.' Grace knew that Duncan had been estranged from his family for many years, and that his mother's presence here today meant a great deal to him, but her mind was already off and running along another track. 'I can't wait to get started on this,' she said.

'Twenty-five years, right?' said Blake.

'Yes.'

'So, can it hang on another few hours until the end of the reception?'

She looked up at him. His tone seemed light and teasing, but was that a look of pity in his eyes?

3

The sky was starry and there were very few lights showing in the quiet street by the time Grace opened her front door. Usually she loved coming home to Wivenhoe, ready to slip into the peace and silence of her own space after a busy day, but tonight she felt restless. She had enjoyed the wedding party – dinner and speeches had been followed by dancing to a live band that included Joan's brother-in-law on bass guitar – yet throughout she had felt guilty, secretly longing to leave and make a start on Wendy's information.

She wanted to be well prepared for Monday, when she would have to share some, if not all, of her ideas about how wide-ranging the investigation should be and to make a decision about how far to commit scarce resources. She realised how keen she was to lay her reasoning out privately to Blake before briefing the team. He was shrewd and realistic, and would have few qualms about telling her if he thought she was chasing shadows.

But she knew that the reason she hadn't already involved her detective sergeant in her researches into the Heather Bowyer case wasn't only because she hadn't wanted to waste official resources trying to prove that a private theory had legs. On the drive home, she'd had the unwelcome insight that during the past few months she'd immersed herself in the fine detail of the case as a distraction from how much she wanted Blake back as her lover. Although he had asked her to dance tonight, he'd kept close physical contact to a minimum. And while it was only right and sensible not to indulge in a slow dance with the boss in front of nearly the entire team, his consideration had also made her fear that even if other issues didn't lie between them, he might no longer be interested in resuming their relationship.

It was late, but she knew she wasn't ready to sleep. She put the kettle on and went upstairs to change into more comfortable clothes. As she drew her bedroom curtains she reflected that there was one other person with whom she'd really love to discuss the case. Ivo Sweatman, the only reporter on a national paper to cover the Bowyer murder at the time, was now chief crime correspondent on the *Daily Courier.* She'd learnt to value his opinion, and it might prove incredibly useful to discover if he remembered any additional details that hadn't made it into print. But talking to a journalist, even officially, simply wasn't possible, or not yet, anyway. It wasn't that she didn't trust Ivo. He had helped her several times on past investigations, albeit in highly irregular and unofficial ways, and, whatever his failings, had never let her down. But the last thing she needed was the media getting wind of this latest development. She'd have to wait.

Returning downstairs, Grace brewed a pot of coffee and pulled out her laptop, ready to review her notes. It was all circumstantial and very possibly the result of too much time spent poring over old statements, but she had a very strong hunch that, while Heather Bowyer had been her killer's first murder victim, she had not been the first woman he'd raped. The idea had occurred to her when she'd read the statements given by the friends with whom Heather had spent her last evening. They all said that one minute she'd been there, and the next she was gone. No one had been hanging around them; she'd not gone off with anyone who'd been chatting her up; they'd not been aware of any scuffle or alarm; she'd simply disappeared. That suggested to Grace that the man she was now seeking had already gained experience in taking away a victim.

The original inquiry in Southend had established that there was no link between this case and any other murders in the area. However, Grace had found nothing in the case notes to suggest that Jason Jupp, the detective inspector in charge of the investigation, had looked to see if there might be a connection with other crimes of rape or sexual assault.

After a great deal of digging, Grace had discovered that, over the previous two years, there had been five reported rapes in Southend. The scanty and lackadaisical manner in which these had been recorded made her wonder if there had been others where the victims had been dissuaded from even recording their complaints, let alone taking them further. No physical evidence had been retained – if it was ever retrieved in the first place – making it impossible, twenty-five years later, to do more than hazard a guess as to whether those rape cases might be connected to Heather Bowyer's murder. Certainly, they'd all taken place at the end of a night out, all in local parks and generally on a Friday or Saturday, when the seafront was at its busiest. None of which, it could be argued, necessarily pointed to a single serial offender, given the number of drunk or drugged-up young people out looking for a good time. One tiny detail, however, did. Or might do.

It was something small, random, almost fanciful, and could easily be explained away for other reasons, yet it had lodged in Grace's mind and convinced her – and sufficiently persuaded Wendy – that further digging into potentially linked cases that had never been fully investigated could be productive.

Quite whether she was yet ready to share this more tenuous part of her theory with Blake and the rest of the Major Investigation Team, she wasn't sure. First things first. If by some miracle a male relative of either Deborah Shillingford or one of the other names near the top of Wendy's list proved to be a match to the DNA represented on the murder weapon, then Grace could officially reopen the case and commit proper resources to finding out how many other crimes Heather Bowyer's unknown killer might have committed.

4

Deborah Shillingford's lapse in sobriety, Grace thought, sitting beside Blake as he turned their unmarked car into the cul-de-sac in Thorpe Bay, might be about to have far-reaching and unforeseen consequences. It was half-past eight in the morning, and although some of Mrs Shillingford's neighbours could be forgiven for not yet being up and about, Grace was pretty sure that most of these curtains – if a bit of purple cloth tacked up across a window merited the word – remained closed all day. Like many once-popular coastal resorts, Southend had taken in more than its fair share of social security claimants. Although some tenants had attempted to enhance their jerry-built post-war council houses with new front doors or crazy paving, most of the gardens had been worn down to patches of dirt and concrete littered with broken and discarded furniture, bulging bin bags and sodden cardboard boxes. It was as if a succession of them had been evicted and, once the locks had been changed, simply abandoned their possessions, either too defeated to carry them away or too focused on their next drug fix to care. Even the few parked cars had seen better days and were probably untaxed. But then once you dropped out of this part of Southend, there really wasn't anywhere else to go.

Deborah Shillingford's address two years ago, when she'd been arrested for drink-driving, had been in Leigh-on-Sea, seven miles along the coast to the west. It had only been a small flat above a shop, but it was a world away from here. Grace felt a small pang at the trouble she might be about to bring into this woman's life, but any remorse was quickly swept aside by her rising excitement.

She and Blake had spent most of the past week learning everything they could about the backgrounds of the eight people who, because they were the right age and had a past connection with Essex, topped the list of possible close relatives of the man who had at some point wielded the knife that killed Heather Bowyer. Deborah Shillingford remained the most promising match.

As Blake knocked on her door, Grace noted that at least the curtains were open, and they didn't have to wait long before a woman with dyed reddish hair in a pink Primark dressing gown and oversized slippers opened the door wide enough to peer cautiously out.

'Yes?'

Grace and Blake showed their warrant cards – no use attempting to be discreet: people around here would have instinctively known they were filth the second they saw them get out of the car.

'Mrs Shillingford? I'm Detective Inspector Grace Fisher. This is Detective Sergeant Blake Langley.'

Deborah pulled her dressing gown tight across her chest. 'What have I done now?'

'Nothing, I assure you. We'd like your help. May we come in?'

'I don't know anything about what goes on round here, if that's what you want. I keep to myself.'

'It's nothing to do with your neighbours. We're investigating a serious crime from quite some time ago, and we think you may be able to help. I'd rather not explain it on the doorstep.'

Deborah considered her response and then opened the door wide enough to admit them. They followed her down the narrow hall into a tiny kitchen at the back. The fittings were basic and dilapidated but the room looked clean. A half-smoked cigarette lay in an ashtray on the table next to a mug of instant coffee. A washed-up plate and cutlery were on the draining board. Deborah clearly had a fondness for angels – the pottery soap dish was adorned with a curly-haired cherub, two sparkly Christmas-tree angels hung from the window catch and a row of angelic trinkets and greetings cards filled most of a plate shelf.

There was barely enough space for two chairs, so, as Grace and Deborah sat down, Blake remained standing, leaning against the sink.

Deborah took a drag on her cigarette and then stubbed it out and waved away the smoke. 'Would you like a coffee or anything?'

'No, thanks,' said Grace. 'We're fine.'

'So how can I help?'

Grace suppressed the wave of anticipation that ran through her at the thought that this woman might finally provide the key to such a stone-cold case. 'I believe you were living in Southend twenty-five years ago,' she began.

'Gosh, that far back?' said Deborah. 'Yes, that's when I was married. My two girls would have been in primary school.'

'Do you remember the rape and murder of a young woman called Heather Bowyer? It took place in Cliff Gardens on the first Saturday in October.'

'What, you think I might have known her or something?'

'No, she wasn't from the area. She'd come on a day trip from Chelmsford. Her killer has never been caught, so the police periodically review the case. We have DNA evidence that we have strong reasons to believe is linked to the case. New DNA techniques have allowed us to search for people who might share some of the same DNA characteristics as a possible offender. You may remember that, when you were arrested a couple of years ago, a swab was taken of your saliva so that your DNA could be stored.'

'Probably. I don't remember much about that night,' said Deborah. 'I go to AA now. Haven't had a drink in fourteen months.'

'Congratulations,' said Grace.

'Thanks,' she said. 'All I need now is to pay off my debts and then maybe I can get out of here.'

Grace felt a further stab of regret that she might be about to derail this woman's hard-won recovery along with everything else. She glanced up at Blake, who, apparently thinking the same thing, gave her a small nod of encouragement.

'Well, some of the characteristics of the DNA evidence from this old case match your DNA,' she went on, sticking to the script she had prepared in her mind. 'It raises the possibility that there could be a match to someone related to you. So, we need to trace any male relatives you may have and eliminate them.'

Deborah took a packet of cigarettes and a disposable lighter out of the pocket of her dressing gown and lit up, inhaling deeply before she answered. 'Is mine the only name that came up?'

'No. These kinds of familial searches can throw up hundreds

of matches, more than a thousand, sometimes. At this stage we just want to eliminate those of the right age who had links to Southend.'

Deborah nodded, thinking the information over. 'Well, I've got two younger brothers, and I think there might be a couple of cousins.'

Imagining this was how a hunting animal must feel at the first scent of its prey, Grace tried hard to disguise her mixture of relief and triumph.

'Not sure about my mum's side,' Deborah continued. 'Her lot never stayed in touch.'

'We're only looking at matches through your paternal line,' said Grace, keeping her voice as calm as possible. 'So that means your father and any siblings, uncles or cousins.'

'Something in my dad's genes, then?'

'Yes, if you like.'

Was it Grace's imagination, or did Deborah's frown reveal a slight tremor of anxiety? Deborah quickly turned it into a smile. 'I think I'm right that today's Friday the thirteenth,' she said. 'You sure this isn't a wind-up?'

Grace smiled. 'I'm afraid not. Is your father still alive?'

'I think so. I don't see him,' said Deborah. 'Don't see much of my brothers, either.' She frowned again. 'You said rape and murder?'

'Yes.'

'And you think they might have something to do with it?'

Grace spoke lightly. 'Obviously I can't say for sure, and at this stage we're seeking to eliminate people from our investigation.'

Deborah nodded. 'It was always me who was the black sheep, the troublemaker. Could never do anything right. So it would be kind of funny if it turned out it was one of them up to no good.'

'Can you give us your brothers' names?' asked Grace.

'Reece and Larry Nixon. Not sure where Larry's living now. I'm pretty certain that Reece is still in Colchester. Has his own little business doing garden and landscape maintenance.'

'Do you recall where they were living twenty-five years ago?'

'Larry would've been in Southend. Can't remember exactly when Reece went off and did his own thing, but they both started out working for our dad's taxi company.'

Grace managed to resist looking at Blake. Not only was driving a taxi or mini-cab a perfect occupation for a man on the lookout for potential victims, but she knew that one of the women who had reported being raped had said her attacker was the taxi driver who'd picked her up. She felt a tingle of excitement. Maybe she really could allow herself to hope that they were on the right track.

5

🔊

Welcome back. I'm Freddie Craig, and this is *Stories from the Fire*. I'm walking along one of many paths in the extensive grounds of a cemetery a ten-minute bus ride from the centre of Chelmsford. I'm told that some of the burials here date back to 1887. I'm looking for the grave of Heather Bowyer. She was the young woman who was brutally murdered in Southend-on-Sea on the night that I was born.

I've gone online and paid a fee and been issued with a map marked with the location of Heather's grave. It should be just along here somewhere. I'm very close now. Yes, here it is: 'Heather Bowyer, born 19th August 1973. A beloved daughter, sister and granddaughter, taken from us 3rd October 1992. Never forgotten. Always in our thoughts. Forever in our hearts.' The words, painted in gold, are inscribed on a heart-shaped block of shiny pink granite with two brass flower holders set into the base. They contain white roses that are only just beginning to droop. I'm guessing they were placed here on my birthday, the twenty-fifth anniversary of her death.

There's also a fresh wreath. It's got a card attached. I've read that sometimes murderers can't resist visiting the graves of their victims, that they even risk turning up to watch the funerals. So, I'm going see what's written on the card, just in case. You never know.

'To our darling Heather, love always from Mum and Simon.'

I read an interview with Heather's brother, Simon, in the local paper last weekend. It had a couple of photos of Heather taken on a family holiday and at her eighteenth birthday party. The article said she worked as a hairdresser, and liked clothes and make-up and listening to Bryan Adams and George Michael. There was also a photo of the part of Cliff Gardens where her body was found, taken when it was all cordoned off by police tape and guarded by a uniformed officer.

'Our whole world collapsed when she died,' Simon told the reporter. 'Not a day goes by when we don't still think about her. We're sure there's someone out there who can help us, who remembers something about that night that would help the police. And there's also someone keeping a terrible secret. It's not too late for them to do the right thing and give my mother and me some answers. Heather deserves justice, so please, if you can, please bring this to an end.'

I hope that Heather is resting in peace. This is a lovely spot, green and leafy with birds singing and the trees showing autumn colours. But I can't begin to imagine what it must be like for her family, knowing that her killer is still out there. And what about him? Are you still out there? Maybe you come here occasionally to visit Heather's grave. You might even be here now, watching from beyond those trees.

Do you think you've got away with it? How does it feel to think you'll never be caught? Do you gloat over your dark secret? Maybe you get some sort of sordid thrill out of imagining that one day you might walk right past your victim's family in the street, or even speak to them, and they'd never know. They might be nice to you, share a joke and a laugh or help you out in some way. How does that really make you feel?

Is it really possible that Heather's killer has been able to live an ordinary life, or did that night destroy him in some way, too? I mean, it's been twenty-five years: my entire life.

I can't imagine what it must be like to live in fear that you might give yourself away or that some crucial piece of evidence will fall into place and they'll finally come for you. Or maybe he's not the only one who knows what happened that night. Did he confess to someone who might still one day betray him?

I want to know how it feels to live with the knowledge that every day might finally bring that knock on the door that will expose your whole life as a sham. I really want to meet this man. And I bet I'm not the only one.

I'm Freddie Craig, and you've been listening to *Stories from the Fire*. Come back next time for Episode Three, when I'll take you to visit the scene of the crime.

6

As Grace walked towards Reece Nixon's front door, she caught Blake looking sideways at her shoes. She seldom wore such high heels, let alone to work, but today she had her reasons, and it was those reasons, not the height of the heels, that made her slightly unsteady. Her mouth was dry as she rang the doorbell and waited for the sound of footsteps approaching from inside. A pleasant no-nonsense-looking woman wearing jeans and a fleece opened the door.

'Mrs Kirsty Nixon?' Grace showed her warrant. 'I'm Detective Inspector Grace Fisher. This is Detective Sergeant Langley. It's nothing to worry about, just a routine elimination check, but is your husband at home?'

The woman gripped the edge of the door with a hand that was brown and rough from outdoor work. 'Deb called us,' she said. 'Something about DNA?'

'That's right. If Reece Nixon is here, then we can explain everything to him.'

She gripped tighter, her knuckles white, and then nodded. 'He's in the yard. I'll take you.'

She closed the door behind her and led the way around the side of the house. Three outbuildings flanked an open area where two men were loading fence posts and panels onto a flat-bed truck. The older man looked round when his wife called his name. He, too, was tanned and weather-beaten, yet he went pale and exchanged anxious glances with his wife before turning to the younger man.

'OK, Steve,' he said, 'why don't you run this lot over there and start unloading? I'll join you in a bit.'

Steve looked surprised, then shot a look at Grace and Blake and, obviously recognising them as police officers, curled his lip in contempt. 'See you later, then.'

Reece removed his work gloves and wiped a hand on the back of his jeans before offering it to Grace. 'Reece Nixon. Deb said you'd be coming.'

Grace introduced herself and waited as Steve reversed the van, which bore the logo RN Garden Services, and drove slowly out of the yard. The pause gave her a chance to study Reece: he was slightly taller than her – even in her heels – and muscular. His hair was grey, his eyes greeny-brown and his nose large and straight. Despite an appearance that must have been handsome and imposing when he was younger – she knew that he was now fifty – he looked nervous and uncertain. Neither he nor his wife made any move to invite them indoors. It might be that they were simply used to being outside, or that they were being cautious. She knew that Reece had racked up a minor record in his youth for criminal damage and possession of cannabis and a few ecstasy pills, so maybe that had been enough to leave him with a lifelong aversion to the police. But maybe not.

It was Kirsty who spoke first. 'Can you explain again what all this is about? I don't quite understand what led you to Deborah.'

'Of course,' said Grace. 'We have a DNA profile from an unsolved murder case from twenty-five years ago. It's from the murder weapon, a knife, and can identify the person who handled it. We're now able to search the National DNA Database for anyone who might be related to that individual. It's a process that throws up a lot of familial matches, and your sister is just one of them. Our job is to eliminate her male relatives from our enquiries.'

'It's not just me you want, then?' Reece asked.

'No,' she said. 'We'll also be speaking to your brother and then, depending on the results of those tests, possibly other male relatives.'

Reece nodded slowly while Kirsty watched him anxiously. 'So what can you tell us about what happened, about the original crime?' he asked.

'A young woman named Heather Bowyer was found dead in Cliff Gardens in Southend, killed by two stabs from a knife. You may remember it being reported at the time.'

'It's a long time ago.'

'It is. She'd also been raped.' Grace hoped Blake was observing Kirsty's reaction.

'So the sample you've got, it's, you know, from her being raped, is it?' Reece asked, clearly embarrassed.

'No,' said Grace. 'The suspect left no bodily fluids, but we did find epithelial cells, also known as touch DNA, on the murder weapon.'

'Have you spoken to Larry?'

'Not yet.' Grace smiled, testing to see if the tension would break. 'We're based here in Colchester, so you were nearest.'

Reece did not return her smile.

'I want to reassure you that we'll be making other enquiries, and I'm more than happy to discuss any concerns you might have.'

'If I'm innocent, then this test you want to do will eliminate me, is that right?' he asked.

'That's right. And even if it is a match, you'll have an opportunity to account for why your DNA was present.'

Reece glanced at his wife and then nodded again. 'Well, you'd better get on with it.'

'Perhaps you'd rather do this indoors?'

'We're fine out here,' said Kirsty.

'Very well,' said Grace.

Reece stood with his legs apart, both feet planted firmly on the ground, as Blake pulled on surgical gloves before taking the buccal swab out of its sterile tube. Asking Reece to open his mouth, Blake carefully rubbed and rotated it along the inside of Reece's cheek before replacing it in the tube, which he sealed inside an evidence bag.

'Is that it?' Reece asked, watching Blake label, sign and date the bag.

'That's it for now,' said Grace. 'Thank you very much for your cooperation.'

'When will you have the results?' asked Kirsty.

'Within a week, hopefully less; it depends on how busy the lab is. If there's no match, then in six months' time the sample will be destroyed.' Grace dug in her bag for a card and handed it to Kirsty. 'If either of you have any other questions you can reach me on this number.'

'And Larry?' asked Reece.

'We're hoping to see him later today.'

'OK.' He looked at the ground, scuffing the gravel with his boot.

The couple seemed eager for them to leave. 'Thank you again,' said Grace. 'We'll be in touch.'

She and Blake made their way back to their car. Reece Nixon had not once looked at her shoes.

7

On the drive to Southend, after Blake had hand-delivered the DNA sample to Wendy to send to the lab, Grace tried to draw him out on his reaction to Reece Nixon. She was disappointed that he didn't seem to share her elation that the results of the familial search might crack the case open at last. But then, she reflected, he had not accompanied her on her recent visit to Heather Bowyer's widowed mother, Monica, now in her late sixties, when she'd updated the family on this latest development.

It was a heavy responsibility to accept the trust of shocked and grieving families that the police would finally get to the truth of what had happened to their murdered loved ones. Grace had striven not to raise Monica Bowyer's hopes too high, stressing that although this search technique could dramatically narrow the field of potential suspects, they might still fail to zero in on Heather's killer. But never before had she dealt with a family twenty-five years on, with a mother who remained as devastated now as she had been when the news was first broken to her and who clearly could not rest until her questions were answered. Holding tightly to Grace's hand, Monica had described how her daughter's death had changed her world forever, how all she'd had to hold on to all these years was her broken heart and a grave. Everything else remained unknown.

'You didn't think Reece and his wife were just a bit too leery?' Grace asked Blake. 'I mean, he wasn't very curious. I'd have expected an innocent man to ask a lot more questions.'

Blake frowned. 'I was trying to imagine how I'd feel if someone turned up out of the blue wanting a DNA sample. However virtuous I'd been all my life, I'd still be worried about some freak error or miscarriage of justice. Wouldn't you?'

'I suppose so. But I thought he was trying too hard to appear unconcerned. And he kept looking at his wife. Not sure what that was about.'

'She didn't ask many questions, either,' he said.

'I hope we don't have to wait too long for the results,' said Grace. 'The suspense will kill me.'

Blake laughed. 'You're more nervous than they were!'

'You weren't the one who had to get permission from the deputy chief constable to go ahead with the search.'

'Fair enough,' he said. 'Though I still don't understand why you're so sure the man we want is local. After all, even in the 1990s a million or so tourists visited Southend every year, and goodness knows how many came and went over a weekend.'

Grace hesitated, not sure that she was ready for him to pour scorn on her theory, but then shook herself. If there were holes in it, now was the time to expose them. 'Heather Bowyer was raped,' she said. 'There were also five other reported rapes in Southend over the previous two years. All took place in parks close to the centre of Southend. If they're linked, that suggests the man was either local or had local knowledge.'

'Anything else?'

'Three of the women described being threatened at knife-point by a masked man.'

'OK.'

'One of them said her attacker was the taxi driver who'd picked her up.'

Blake gave a slow nod of reappraisal. 'OK, so what made him escalate to killing his victim?'

Grace couldn't help a smile of relief that he had questioned but not dismissed her reasoning. 'Maybe Heather struggled too hard, or got a look at his face,' she said. 'Maybe someone or something disturbed him in the act.'

'Could be why he left the knife the way he did.'

'And the glove.'

'He panicked, was in a hurry.'

'If he didn't set out to kill her,' she said, 'then maybe that's why the offences stopped afterwards. Murder had never been on his agenda and he wasn't going to risk that again.'

'Could be,' he said, although his tone expressed doubt. 'So have you run a familial search before?'

'No. I've never worked on any case from so long ago. I mean, you and I were at primary school when Heather was killed.'

'The guy could have simply disappeared abroad. For all we know he's dead or emigrated or banged up in a foreign jail somewhere.'

Although she knew Blake was right – after all, he was only echoing her own gentle caveats to Heather's family – his words were an uncomfortable reminder that she might have raised Monica's hopes for nothing.

'Given that the offences stopped, he could be dead,' he went on, his eyes on the road. 'If he never meant to kill, he might not have been able to hack it afterwards. He may have topped himself out of guilt or the terror of being caught.'

'I already checked out any local suicides in the six months after the murder, but there was nothing that stood out,' she said, realising just how much she wanted to offer Heather's family the closure they needed.

They had reached the stretch of the A127 approaching the western outskirts of Southend, and Blake was concentrating on the satnav and watching out for the offices of Larry Nixon's limousine and chauffeur transportation service – weddings, celebrations and executive cars a speciality.

They found Alpha Limos on the edge of a small industrial park in a modern, no-frills unit where a young woman with a hands-free headset looked up from her computer screen long enough to tell them that Mr Nixon was working from home that day. Beyond the other three people also manning phones and computer screens, Grace could see an empty glass-walled section with a desk, a couple of chairs for visitors and, on the wall, a huge framed photograph of a vintage American Cadillac with tail fins, white-wall tyres and wedding streamers – the boss's unoccupied office.

Back in the car, Blake reset the satnav with Larry Nixon's home address and headed towards Chalkwell.

'Were the five previous rapes linked to the murder at the time?' he asked, resuming their earlier discussion.

'No,' said Grace. 'At least not in writing. And the records are so rudimentary, it makes me wonder how seriously the victims' complaints were taken. Two of the women were visitors. They both decided not to proceed.'

'I agree that the similar MOs are striking,' he said, 'but what other factors make a link to Heather Bowyer?'

'Victimology, for a start,' said Grace. 'Like Heather, all the complainants were young women heading home at a weekend after a night's clubbing. Short skirts, low-cut tops, high heels, bit too much to drink.'

'In a town packed with coach-loads of lads looking to get laid,' said Blake. 'That doesn't scream single perpetrator at me.'

'Which appears to be how the police reacted at the time,' she said. 'Whoever dealt with the complaints seemed to reckon that saying the perpetrator had a knife and a mask was taking the piss, that the women were embroidering their stories to make sure the police believed they really had been raped and weren't just making a fuss about a snog that got out of hand.'

'Neanderthals.'

'It only takes one duff officer to be on duty at the wrong time,' said Grace. 'But my point is that Heather was out with friends. Whoever grabbed her did so without any of them noticing. I think he'd done it before. Got it down to a fine art.'

Grace was wondering whether to explain about the shoes when the satnav announced that they had arrived at their destination, a gleaming new seafront apartment building. Blake found a spot right outside and parked facing a carefully tended area of green that partially screened off the main road that ran along an esplanade dotted with incongruous looking palm-trees. The tide was in and, although the day was cloudy with a fresh breeze, there was a clear view south across the water to the Isle of Grain. They entered the lobby and were greeted by a concierge who sat behind a spotless white desk and a large silver computer. Even though the distance between the two was walk-able, Larry Nixon's home felt a world away from his sister's existence in Thorpe Bay.

Without introducing himself as a police officer, Blake gave Larry's name and was told by the concierge that Mr Nixon had gone out half an hour ago. Blake requested that he call up to make sure, and the concierge shrugged, tapped at his keyboard and, after a few moments, shook his head. 'I'm sorry, there's no answer.'

A red-faced man in grey joggers and sweatshirt came out of the lift and, wiping his face with the towel around his neck, hovered behind them, waiting impatiently to speak to the concierge.

'Might he be back soon?' asked Blake. 'Does he usually come and go during the day?'

'I'm really not at liberty to say.'

'It's just that we've come quite a long way and we were told he'd be working from home today.'

'He's a busy man,' said the concierge, dismissing them with a look over Blake's shoulder at the man in the tracksuit. 'Mr Price, how can I help you?'

Blake waited until they were outside. 'You reckon he's deliber-ately avoiding us?' he asked.

'Deborah had told Reece to expect us,' said Grace. 'Either one of them could have tipped Larry off.'

'Interesting that he doesn't want to play ball.'

'DNA results will tell us just *how* interesting,' she said.

'Shall we wait? Try and catch him later?'

'No,' she decided. 'We'll call him to make an appointment. If he misses that, then we can consider putting him under surveillance.'

Only after they'd returned to Colchester and Grace was preparing to pack up and leave the office did she receive a call on her mobile.

'DI Fisher? It's Larry Nixon here. Reece gave me your number. I think you may have been trying to get hold of me today?'

'Hello. Yes, I was. Your brother will have explained why.'

'Absolutely. Only too happy to help. Sorry you had a wasted journey. One of my drivers went AWOL, let down an important client, so I did the job myself.' He sounded genuinely unconcerned about why Grace wanted to see him. 'Got stuck in traffic on the way back from Heathrow. I can see you tomorrow, if that works for you?'

'Thank you, yes, that would be very helpful.'

Grace arranged a time and a place to meet the following day and tried not to think about how disappointed she'd be if the familial search proved to be fruitless.

🔊

8

Welcome back to *Stories from the Fire*. This episode contains descriptions of violence that may be disturbing to some listeners, so please use your discretion.

I'm Freddie Craig. It's late afternoon, and I'm standing at the top of Cliff Gardens in Southend looking down towards the seafront. You've heard in previous episodes how Heather Bowyer was murdered twenty-five years ago. Well, this is where it happened. Or as near enough as I can get. The exact spot no longer exists. Cliff Gardens is a steeply sloping area of twenty-two acres of municipal parkland. Heavy winter rains at the end of 2002 caused a massive landslip that left the whole area unstable. It remained closed to the public for the next ten years.

It's now been made safe and renovated to look much as it did in its heyday. It might look the same, but it's not. We think we know or remember things the way they really were, but we don't. I'm here trying to bring back the past, but even the ground I'm standing on isn't the same.

Less than a quarter of a mile away at about the same time Heather was killed, the fire brigade was bringing the Marineland blaze under control. And, two miles to the north-west, I was being born.

Heather's body lay here undiscovered all night. According to press reports, her corpse, partly hidden by trees and bushes, wasn't found until the park opened in the morning and local people came out to gawp at Marineland's smoking ruins and reminisce about its many attractions. She was lying face down and partially clothed. Gagged with her own pale pink dance-wear cardigan, she had been brutally raped. A large knife was still embedded in her back. The blade had pierced a major artery and the blood from a double stab wound had soaked into the cold, dark earth.

I'm walking along one of the paths that runs between grass and flowerbeds, bushes, dumpy palms and mature trees. There's a view south and west to the mouth of the Thames estuary. The tide is going out and it's mainly mud. A sharp wind is blowing. At my back, a few lights are coming on in the windows of the bay-fronted terraces of Clifftown Parade, and off to my left I can see the long line of lights stretching out along the pier and the candy-coloured neon of the funfair rides. I'm hoping to feel some psychic connection to what happened here. Surely someone who was born as Heather died should be especially sensitive to any lingering atmosphere. Yet, as I walk these paths, I'm not picking up on any echoes of Heather's pain and terror.

Her body lay exposed here for hours. The body that suffered pain and violation, that an unknown man wanted and decided to take against her will, the body that was then probed and dissected for evidence.

Yet even though *her* spirit has gone from here, perhaps some residue of *his* evil remains. Maybe he comes to sit on one of these benches next to the flowerbeds so he can relive his violent sexual actions again and again.

Is he the same man or has he, like the ground on which I'm standing, been reconstituted over the past quarter of a century from new and different materials?

Does he cherish his dreadful secret, or is he filled with guilt and remorse? If he was here now and I could look into his eyes, what would I see?

I've never believed that the truth can be glimpsed in a person's eyes. How would that even happen? Would it be something physical, like eyes that dart away and refuse to meet yours? That's rubbish, isn't it? We go on believing in something like the mark of Cain and yet there were people who employed Fred West as a builder and thought him a good bloke. The truth is that we don't recognise evil when we see it because, if we did, we'd know better than to end up with it in a park at night.

I grew up celebrating my birthday with presents and cake and candles, unaware that it was also the anniversary of Heather's death. Is it just chance who is born and who dies? There are so many things that don't make sense and that we hardly ever bother to think about. Birth and death, a terrible fire and a heroic rescue, good and evil, all happening at the same time. What's the real story? How are these things connected? Are Heather and her killer, and the teenage fire-starters and their rescuer, all part of my life, or are such ideas about fate and destiny meaningless? But the fact remains that an unknown man took a life as mine began. I need to understand the true significance of that. I need to understand *him*.

I feel as if I'm setting off on a journey. Not jumping on a plane to a war zone or to report on an earthquake or a famine. Horror isn't always as far away as you think it is, and I'm venturing into the dark heart of what happened here in this apparently tranquil English park. I'm leaving one world behind and entering another that looks exactly the same, but isn't. I'm embarking on a voyage into the mind of a murderer.

I'm Freddie Craig. Thanks to all of you who have subscribed and are helping spread the word about *Stories from the Fire*.

9

The smell hit Grace as soon as she got out of her car. Acrid, sour, steamy. On one side of the undistinguished house where, when she had visited that morning, there had been a door and windows, there were now gaping black, soot-streaked, dripping holes. Trails of smoke curled up into the night air, lit by the garish lights of the three fire appliances parked in the yard. Men in thick boots, fluorescent jackets and helmets were still busy straightening out and rewinding hoses.

A figure emerged from the apparent chaos and came towards her. 'Are you the duty DI?' he asked.

'Grace Fisher.'

'I'm Paul Arningham, one of the fire investigation officers with the Essex brigade. Thanks for coming.'

All she could see of his face between the raised collar of his jacket and his protective helmet was a pair of dark eyes and cheeks streaked with soot and dirt.

'What have you found?' she asked. 'Why do you need us?'

'Two bodies,' he said. 'One upstairs in bed, the other downstairs. And I'm fairly certain the fire was started at two different sites. We'll bring in a sniffer dog to check for accelerants as soon as it's cooled down a bit, but by my reckoning it's arson. That's why you were called.'

'I was here this morning,' she said. 'I spoke to Reece Nixon and his wife Kirsty. Is that who you've found?'

'I'm told they're the only people living here,' he said, 'but formal identification may take a little longer.'

'Could it be suicide?' Her heart thumped with dread that her mismanagement might have led to this.

'That's what his brother asked, too.'

'His brother?'

'He called the emergency services. Tried to get in and rescue them. He's been taken to hospital with burns and possible smoke inhalation.'

'Larry Nixon was here?'

'That's right.' The fire investigation officer spoke with exaggerated patience.

'Sorry,' said Grace. 'It's a complicated situation.'

'Arson generally is.'

'Was he badly hurt?'

'Looked like he opened the door and got hit by a backdraught.'

'I'll get someone over to the hospital to take a statement.' She looked at her watch: it was after midnight, so she'd have to send whomever was on duty.

Arningham waited while she connected to the MIT office. 'Want me to walk you round the perimeter?' he asked, as she finished the call.

'Yes, please.'

He took her over to his van and kitted her out with protective clothing. The boots were far too big for her, but he insisted.

'I won't take you inside. You can come back tomorrow once we've got forensic boards down. Tonight we'll make it secure and get the bodies moved.'

'Did anyone else call it in?' she asked. She peered into the blackness beyond the lights of the various vehicles, dimly remembering that the house and yard, up a small lane and surrounded by gardens and a couple of scrubby paddocks, had no close neighbours. 'There must have been quite a blaze. Someone must have seen it.'

'Any calls made will be recorded,' he said, 'but I'm pretty certain that the brother's was the first.' He took her round to a back door that led into the kitchen. Pushing it open, he shone the beam of a powerful torch inside. Apart from a trail of footprints across the floor, the room looked miraculously untouched by the fire. He directed the light onto a counter top. 'Can you see what that is?'

'No.'

'Smoke alarm battery. Still in its packaging.'

'Oh.'

Returning round the side of the house, Grace could hear glass cracking under her oversized boots. Arningham shone the light upwards, illuminating the charred rim of an upstairs window frame above the kitchen. Water dripped down from the blackened guttering and broken roof tiles and wisps of greasy-looking smoke dribbled out into the cold night air.

'Bedroom,' he said. 'A body we assume is either Reece or Kirsty Nixon is up there in what remains of the bed.'

'How can that room be so badly burnt when the room below is untouched?' she asked.

'My theory is that whoever set the fire closed most of the

internal doors, but left other doors and windows open so that the passage of air would draw the fire up like a blowtorch.'

'So the bedroom was deliberately targeted?' asked Grace.

Arningham nodded. 'Looks like it.'

'We'll get a full forensic post-mortem,' she said, 'but what's your opinion? Do you think a pathologist needs to examine the bodies in situ?'

He shook his head. 'No. We'll take plenty of video and can answer any queries that get thrown up.'

'OK. But at this stage, it's possible that either Kirsty or Reece Nixon could have set the fire?'

'The brother seemed to think it would be Reece. They spoke on the phone beforehand, apparently.'

Grace filed the information to consider later: right now, there was too much to take in.

Arningham moved forward to a cavernous opening in the side of the house where the smell of smoke was strongest. She could feel the heat still pulsating off the fabric of the building and tried to breathe as shallowly as possible, not wanting the fetid chemical tang of the fire to penetrate her lungs.

'Ready?' he asked.

She nodded, but still yelped when his torch picked out the shape of a human figure lying curled up on the floor among the scorched and melted remains of an ordinary living room.

'People always think they bunch up like that to protect themselves,' he said, 'but it's actually the muscles stiffening and contracting.'

'I had been told that,' she said, taking a deep breath despite herself, 'but it's still a shock when you see it. So you don't know for sure whether that's Reece Nixon?'

'Not until the pathologist confirms it. Should be able to get blood or a muscle sample for DNA.'

To her relief Arningham swung the torch beam away from the body and around the rest of the blackened devastation, picking out piles of debris where the ceiling had collapsed. 'All the furnishings simply combusted once the fire reached flashover point. Combustion creates enormous heat, but doesn't last long, except it blew the window out, creating a fresh source of oxygen to feed the fire. It was the same upstairs. It's not safe to take you inside yet, but the stairwell has burned and the backs of the closed doors are charred while the rest of the house is relatively undamaged.'

'So the aim wasn't to destroy the house so much as to kill the two people in it?'

'We'll sift through everything tomorrow,' he said. 'People imagine that fire destroys evidence, and it often does. What it also does is create evidence of how it started.'

Grace nodded, wondering if this grim scene was Reece's confession – or his wife's retribution – and, if so, how was she going to tell Monica Bowyer that they'd so narrowly lost the chance to question Heather's killer and learn enough to answer her most basic questions?

Was this her fault? Had she bungled it? She'd had no grounds to take Reece Nixon into custody, but should she have placed him under surveillance, or spent longer talking to him and his wife? Had Kirsty known all these years what her husband had done – was that why she, too, was dead? And, if Reece was a serial rapist as well as a murderer, what crucial evidence of those other crimes had also gone up in flames?

10

Detective Constable Carolyn Bromfield was waiting for Grace at the entrance to the Accident & Emergency Department. She was young, and had been transferred from the Domestic Violence Unit to the MIT as cover for Duncan while he was on honeymoon, which was very likely why she'd drawn the short straw and was on night duty. Delicately featured, with blue eyes and dyed and straightened blonde hair, she was dressed in a carefully chosen outfit of tight black jeans and ankle boots, a short black leather jacket and a see-through white lace blouse. It was well after one in the morning, yet her make-up looked recently retouched. Carolyn had only been on the Major Investigation Team a week, but Grace was already finding her eagerness to demonstrate how much she wanted to stay a little trying.

'Larry Nixon has burns to his face, arms and hands,' the younger woman told Grace as she led the way to a curtained cubicle. 'Not deep, thankfully. He won't need skin grafts or anything. The medical staff have just finished with him.'

'What did he say about the fire?' asked Grace. 'Why was he there?'

'He said his brother Reece had phoned him and sounded

upset. He was worried that Reece was about to do something stupid, but when he got there it was too late, the fire was already raging.'

'The fire investigation officer is pretty certain it was arson, which makes this a homicide investigation,' said Grace, 'so we need to tread carefully.'

She took a deep breath before stepping around the blue curtain. A man in a hospital gown, his legs bare except for black socks, sat propped up on an examination couch. His face was red and blistered and his hair and eyebrows were singed. Both of his arms and the backs of his hands were covered in dressings and bandages. 'Mr Nixon?'

Larry Nixon nodded.

'I'm DI Grace Fisher. We spoke on the phone yesterday.'

'Only a few hours ago,' he said.

'That's right. How are you feeling? Are you up to talking?'

'I'm not too bad. They've given me some painkillers.'

'The fire investigation officer said you were trying to get into the house.'

'Was Reece in there?' he asked anxiously. 'What about Kirsty? Does anyone know where she is?'

'I'm very sorry, but they found two bodies in the house.'

Larry groaned and raised a bandaged arm to hide his face. 'He was only fifty,' he said in a hoarse voice.

'Do you think you could take me through the events of the evening?' she asked.

Larry shook his head slowly and, lowering his arm, gave a long sigh. 'They're both dead?'

'They've yet to be formally identified.'

'What about their kids, my niece and nephew? Has anyone

told them? They're in their twenties and I don't know where they're living right now.'

'We'll make sure they're informed,' said Grace, wondering how much of the background to these events she would have to explain to them.

'And I'm pretty certain Kirsty's mum used to live here in Colchester.'

'Please don't worry, Mr Nixon. It'll all be taken care of.'

The man was clearly in a state of shock, but Grace was on tenterhooks to hear how Reece Nixon's death related to her request for a DNA sample. 'You said your brother telephoned you?'

'Yes, I can't believe it. Can't believe what he told me.' Larry seemed to rally himself, trying to order his thoughts and recall events more clearly. 'I think it was around eight o'clock. He'd called earlier in the day, as I said when you and I spoke, to tell me you'd been to see him, so I was surprised that he called a second time. We're not particularly close. We don't speak very often.'

'So what did he want?'

Larry heaved another deep sigh and hung his head again. 'He sounded pretty drunk.'

'But he wanted to talk to you?' she prompted.

Larry nodded. 'He said it was him. The man you're looking for. This cold case you're investigating.'

'What exactly did he say? Can you remember?'

'A woman. He killed a woman. Years ago. Had sex with her, too. Said you'd be coming back for him and he couldn't face it.'

'Did he threaten suicide?' asked Grace.

'Not in so many words,' said Larry, 'but after he hung up I just had a feeling. So I called back, but then he wouldn't pick up. I kept trying and trying and then decided I had to get over there. I was too late. The fire was too much. I couldn't get in.'

'I'm very sorry for your loss,' Grace said helplessly. She caught Carolyn looking at her expectantly, her eyes shining with the drama of the situation. The junior officer's reaction irked her, although she didn't really know why it should – a confession, a murder-suicide, a fire, a cold case solved, this *was* a dramatic situation – but she wished Blake had been on duty tonight instead. She wanted to ask him if they'd failed to pick up any warning signs. Reece had been nervous, certainly, but she didn't think he'd seemed agitated enough to do something so desperate. And why a fire? Why inflict such a death on either himself or his wife?

If Reece Nixon had raped and murdered Heather Bowyer – and perhaps raped other women, too – then few would see his death as a tragedy. Yet, even though Paul Arningham had explained that the curled arrangement of the body on the floor was solely due to the effects of the fire, Grace couldn't help feeling a stab of sympathy, given the impression of vulnerability it had left her with, and was thankful she hadn't been allowed to go up and view the other human remains in the bed upstairs.

Larry reached out for a plastic cup of water on the stand beside him, but, as he drank from it, it slipped through his injured fingers. He rubbed awkwardly with his elbow at where the water had soaked his hospital gown.

'Don't worry,' he said as Carolyn went to his aid, fussing with paper towels from a dispenser on the wall. 'Doesn't matter. My dad's on his way over with some clean things. He'll be here any moment.'

Grace bent to retrieve the plastic cup. Turning her back, some instinct made her wrap it in a clean paper towel and slip it into her bag. As she straightened up she met the gaze of an elderly man standing in the curtained opening to the cubicle, a sports bag in one hand. He looked vigorous for his age and bore a striking resemblance to Reece, although his face was harsh and unyielding in a way that Reece's had not been.

'Who are you?' he demanded.

'Detective Inspector Grace Fisher, Essex Major Investigation Team. And you are?'

'Owen Nixon.' He nodded at Larry. 'His father.'

'I'm very sorry for the loss of your son and daughter-in-law.'

'So Reece is dead, is he?'

'We'll carry out tests tomorrow to confirm the identity of the two bodies.'

Owen Nixon's gaze dropped to her bag where she had concealed the paper cup and then back to meet her eyes, although he made no comment and his expression did not change. He placed the sports bag on the floor beside the bed. 'You all right?' he asked his surviving son.

'Looks worse than it is,' said Larry.

'So you explained to them what happened? All this nonsense about what Reece told you?'

Larry appealed to Grace. 'You know more about it than I do.'

'We're investigating an unsolved murder from twenty-five years ago,' she said, 'and this morning we visited Reece to request a DNA sample for elimination purposes. Until we get the results of our tests I'm afraid there's not much more I can tell you.'

'But you must have new evidence if you're opening an old case back up again?'

'Unsolved murder cases are never closed,' said Grace, 'and there are new developments in forensic science all the time.'

'Whatever Reece said to his brother makes no odds, though, does it? The fire could've been an accident.'

'We'll know more once we have the fire investigation officer's report.'

'If you're not going to tell us anything, I might as well take Larry home,' said Owen. 'Is that allowed?'

'So long as the doctors are happy with him.' Grace turned to Larry. 'We'll leave you to get dressed. And I'll be in touch to arrange a time to take a formal statement. And don't worry about our appointment tomorrow. Get some rest and we'll reschedule it.'

'Thank you,' said Larry.

'Come on,' Owen said to his son, 'let's get you out of here.'

Grace left them to it and walked with Carolyn towards the exit. 'You've done everything you need to here?'

'Yes, I think so, ma'am. I'll go back to the office now and start a case file.'

'OK, good. I'll see you later. I'm going to head home first and put all my clothes in the wash and have a shower. I must reek of smoke.'

They were about to part when Grace remembered the plastic cup in her bag. 'Hang on.' She fished out an evidence bag and, using the paper towel to hold the cup, dropped it inside before scribbling the necessary information on the bag. 'Can you take that for me?' she asked, handing it to the younger woman. 'It's the cup Larry Nixon was drinking from, the one he dropped.'

Carolyn looked surprised. 'Why do you want that?'

'We might still need a DNA sample in the Heather Bowyer

case,' Grace explained. 'Seemed like a useful opportunity to get a back-up in case he refuses to give one.'

'But surely—'

'What?' asked Grace. It had been a long night and she was aggravated by the constable's naivety. 'We have two separate homicide investigations. Until we get the results on Reece Nixon's DNA we rule nothing in and we rule nothing out.'

'Sorry, ma'am.' Carolyn was contrite. 'It's only that I was with Larry Nixon for an hour or so before you got here. He was in a really bad way before the painkillers kicked in. He risked his life to try and save his brother.'

Grace softened, reaching out to touch Carolyn's shoulder. 'I do understand. It's hard to stand by and watch when these awful things happen. But being suspicious goes with the job.'

'I know. Goodnight, ma'am.'

Grace watched her walk away across the car park and, not for the first time, asked herself where the right balance lay between professional cynicism and compassion.

11

The kid claimed they'd met a couple of months back when he was doing an internship at the *Courier*, but Ivo Sweatman wasn't so sure. For one thing, Ivo always did his best to avoid the youngsters who, simply because they'd watched *State of Play* or *Spotlight*, reckoned that by home-time on their first day they'd be telling Woodward and Bernstein how to do their jobs. Or would if they'd ever heard of Watergate.

The kid said he wanted to interview Ivo for a podcast about a story he'd covered twenty-five years ago. According to Freddie Craig, podcasting was now a huge phenomenon, covering everything from politics to sci-fi and fantasy – in homage to the famous Orson Welles radio version of *War of the Worlds*, he said – to true crime to something he described as 'ramble-chats' between celebrities. Ivo sent up a silent prayer that he be saved from ever having to experience a ramble-chat for himself. Anyway, print was dead, apparently, and people now listened to podcasts instead. Ivo had in fact heard of one that the kid had mentioned, 'Serial', although he found his assertion that, world-wide, it had been downloaded two hundred and fifty million times pretty incredible. But at least now he knew what all those commuters were up to, sitting on the Tube with their earphones and vacant looks: amateur jury members soaking up the infinite detail of a murder.

Still, to be fair, the kid was doing his best to make a name for himself. So far as Ivo was aware, none of the work experience kids at the *Courier* had ever been rewarded with so much as a short-term contract, let alone a permanent job – another reason why he kept out of their way. It was a cruel con-trick and he simply couldn't bear the sight of their imploring young faces.

Two hundred and fifty million downloads in a few years. Ivo did a quick tally of the *Courier*'s circulation figures and worked out that, even by the time he retired, his by-line would not have been seen by anywhere near that many readers. Maybe young Freddie's foray into podcasting was actually a pretty smart move. And Ivo did remember the story Freddie wanted to talk to him about. Not that it had generated much heat at the time. The victim wasn't local, and she wasn't the Virgin Mary, just another poor girl in the wrong place at the wrong time. But there'd been a big fire nearby the same night, that had – literally – lent it a lurid glow.

Ivo didn't tell Freddie, but it wasn't the crime that had stuck in his mind so much as his own youthful self. The Heather Bowyer case had been his first story after finally landing the job he wanted in Fleet Street as the *Courier*'s junior crime reporter. He could still remember setting off for Southend with a new notebook, a company phone card, the copy-taker's number and, fool that he was, a song in his heart.

He was already drinking, of course, but in those days he had no idea it was ever going to be a problem. That it already was. He was strong and fit and never had a hangover. And everybody drank – you stood out if you didn't, especially among senior police officers.

The man in charge had been Detective Inspector Jason Jupp – JJ to his mates. There were no communication directorates and media websites in those days. If you wanted the inside track on a case, you found out the name of the local CID pub, got yourself down there and bought a round of drinks. If you were given a scoop, you'd send the detective a case of scotch afterwards – a gesture that nowadays would land you both in court on corruption charges.

Ivo hadn't thought about JJ in a long time. Hadn't wanted to. He'd heard on the grapevine a few years back that he'd died. Hardly surprising. Twenty-five years ago, JJ had been a jovial red-faced bruiser of a man, already coming up for retirement. He'd liked to see his name in the papers, especially if accompanied by a snap of him collaring some villain, and had been amenable to Ivo's eager approaches. If JJ had been disconcerted at Heather Bowyer's killer eluding his clutches, he hadn't let it show. He'd simply deduced that the perp must've been a daytripper who'd legged it off home afterwards and wasn't coming back to drop further clues any time soon. When rumours surfaced that other women in Southend had been raped and the crimes might be linked, JJ had dismissed them as fairy tales. He was old-school, and likely to assume that a woman complaining of rape was just mucking about, especially if she'd been out drinking and was wearing a short skirt. Ivo reckoned there were still one or two coppers like JJ around, although nowadays they'd learnt to keep their opinions to themselves.

Nonetheless, JJ had shown kindness to the junior reporter from the *Courier*, and, off the record, told him a lot more than he should have done about an investigation that had inconveniently hit a brick wall. Their late-night drinking sessions (had they been ramble-chats?) had enabled Ivo to write a story that was full of local colour and had impressed his desk editor back in London enough that, when a juicy kidnap and torture came up in the Midlands the following month, Ivo had been sent off to cover it.

So why shouldn't Ivo, turn and turn about, lend this work-experience kid a helping hand? Freddie had told him he'd done an MA in journalism, plus two or three internships, and yet was still chasing a paid gig, as he called it. Meanwhile, he said, he was stuck out in the middle of nowhere. Unable to afford to rent his own place, his parents had suggested that he live for a while with his widowed grandmother, who'd had a recent hip replacement. That way he could keep an eye on her and economise. Freddie was obviously serious about his chosen career. Ivo doubted he would have been able to find much on the internet about a twenty-five-year-old murder that had never attracted much attention in the first place, so he must have done some good old-fashioned legwork at the newsroom in the British Library or elsewhere to learn that Ivo had reported on the case. And he had then tracked Ivo down by phone which, these days, was no mean feat. The kid had earned his spurs.

Freddie's angle was that, as the case remained unsolved, he, bless him, would take a crack at it himself. He said he'd been to Heather's grave and to the original crime scene, and now he'd like to record an interview with Ivo. Before he rang off he also promised to email links to the earlier podcasts so Ivo could listen to them.

As Ivo put the phone down, a host of unwelcome impressions concerning his younger self threatened to occupy his thoughts. Leading the charge, however, was something that he knew was more recent and that kept snagging at his memory. He was pretty sure it wasn't directly related to Freddie's cold case, but he didn't want it tugging away at him for the rest of the day. Maybe it was something from the morning news feed. He ran through what had come in until he got it. There was a house fire last night, in Colchester, in which a couple died, despite the attempts of the man's brother to rescue them. Ivo was probably just connecting that fire and failed rescue with Freddie mentioning the Marineland fire in Southend – or maybe it was because Colchester made him think of Grace Fisher, his all-time favourite detective – yet still the irritating feeling wouldn't go away. And besides, he'd rather keep picking at that than indulge in any *nostalgie de la boue* to do with JJ.

It was only later, when Ivo was queuing to buy a sandwich at lunchtime, that it came to him: Larry Nixon! The man who had tragically failed to save his brother and sister-in-law in Colchester last night was also the name of the hero who had rescued two teenagers from the fire in Southend twenty-five years ago. It was one of those poignant coincidences that would make a great little follow-up story to last night's incident. Might also be something to tell Freddie Craig so he could podcast about it – if 'podcast' was now a verb. And perhaps even provide an excuse to wangle a little outing to Colchester. He'd just have to see.

12

Entering the mortuary cutting room, Grace found herself grateful to Dr Samit Tripathi, the local Home Office forensic pathologist, for his professional attitude towards the dead. She had just left Michael Nixon and his younger sister, Anne, after persuading them with some difficulty that a visual identification of their parents would be impossible. They were not much older than Grace had been when she had lost her father to heart disease, and they seemed close and supportive of each other. Numb with shock, they had listened closely to her account of the tragedy. Although she shared with them only that the fire had been deliberately set, they remained united in disbelief that their father could have committed suicide or that anyone else could have intentionally harmed either of their parents.

Now, looking at the two curled and charred bodies lying on the stainless-steel autopsy tables, the blackened hands clenched, the knees and elbows bent as if ready to spring into a fight, Grace was glad they had spared themselves such a sight.

Samit began by explaining what seemed obvious, that the bodies were too damaged for any external evidence to have survived that might point towards who had set the fire. 'That evidence,' he said, 'if there is any, will be in the house.'

'The fire investigation officer confirms it was definitely arson,' she told him, consulting the notes of what Paul Arningham had told her on her return visit to the burnt-out house earlier that day. 'There was no sign of forced entry. There are burn patterns upstairs, outside the bedroom, consistent with accelerant having been poured, and they found traces of petrol beneath the wooden floor beside the stairs in the downstairs hall, outside the room where Reece was found. The melted remains of a petrol container were found in the hall, along with its discarded cap. The container matches another full canister in one of the outbuildings, and one of Reece Nixon's employees has confirmed that two canisters were always kept full of petrol for the work vehicles, so that jobs weren't delayed if someone forgot to fill up.'

Samit nodded and then indicated one of the indistinguishable bodies. 'Mr Nixon here was found downstairs, which suggests that, if either of them set the fire, he was responsible.'

'That's what his brother thinks, too. He tried to rescue them, but was too late.'

'If it was neither of them who set the fire, then I'm curious to know why they weren't roused by a smoke alarm going off.'

'There was only one in the house and it had no battery,' she said. 'They'd bought a new one but not yet put it in.'

'A bit odd to buy a new battery if you're planning to torch the place.'

'Maybe it was bought before there was any reason to consider arson.' Grace pivoted involuntarily to look at the second blackened corpse. 'Their two adult kids say they had a good marriage, described both of them as hard-working, quiet and kind. Then I appear out of the blue making enquiries into a rape and murder that took place before either of their kids was born. Yesterday morning Reece Nixon gave us a DNA sample, and by midnight he was dead.'

'They're both dead,' Samit observed.

'I know. And I get that Reece might not have been able to face up to crimes he committed twenty-five years ago, but why kill his wife?'

'Maybe he couldn't bear for her to learn the truth about him.'

'But like this!'

'The bodies are well preserved internally,' he said, 'so I should be able to determine whether either or both of them was alive when the fire started. With any luck Mrs Nixon died painlessly from smoke inhalation without ever waking up.'

'Let's hope so,' Grace said. 'What about other evidence of how they might have died?'

Samit looked at her over his glasses. 'Smashed skulls and broken bones will show up on X-ray, but if either of them had been smothered or strangled or possibly even stabbed, then no, there's not going to be much I can tell you. However, I should be able to find enough blood for toxicological analysis to discover if either of them had been drugged.'

'Larry Nixon said Reece had sounded drunk on the phone,' she said, 'and the fire investigators found the remains of glass beside his body that is probably a bottle.'

'A high alcohol level might be enough to account for why he appears to have been so rapidly overcome by smoke or toxic fumes. And older people die from lower levels of carbon monoxide poisoning than the young and healthy, especially if there's any coronary artery disease present. But even if he had set the fire himself, fully intending to commit suicide, you'd still think it would be human nature, once it took hold, to try and escape.'

Grace shook her head in sorrow. 'He must have been abso-lutely desperate if he saw this as the only way out.'

'It's pretty extreme,' said Samit. 'When will you know whether or not he is your cold case murderer?'

'I've fast-tracked his DNA sample, so another few days, I hope,' she said. 'Meanwhile this certainly looks like an admission of guilt.'

'If it is a murder-suicide,' he agreed. 'I'll get started, then hopefully I can give you a cause of death.'

'Thanks.'

Grace turned to go up to the viewing gallery when Samit called her back.

'Before I forget,' he said, 'you mentioned that the brother tried to rescue them.'

'That was his account, yes.'

'Did he sustain any burns?'

'Yes. His face, hands and arms.'

'Then you should get them examined for elimination purposes.'

'OK,' she said. 'What would I be looking for?'

'I can do the examination, if you like,' said Samit. 'If someone was sloshing petrol about and then set it alight they might have characteristic "flash" burns and almost certainly residue of accelerant on their skin and clothes.'

'I'll organise it, and get his clothes examined.' Grace was annoyed with herself: she should have thought of this before now.

Samit nodded, his thoughts elsewhere. 'Arson's a strange crime,' he said. 'It always fascinates me.'

Grace was surprised. Samit, so level-headed and even-tempered, seldom ventured an opinion beyond what was suggested by the physical evidence.

'I imagine it must be psychologically very satisfying in some all-consuming way,' he continued, indicating the two bodies on their pristine metal beds. 'So theatrical, such a powerful communication of rage or pain.'

Samit's comment hit precisely on what had been bothering her about this whole scenario: fire was indeed an extreme method by which to commit suicide, and seemed out of character for the down-to-earth couple she'd met so briefly. By reducing his life to a pile of ashes, had Reece Nixon finally been able to release the pressure of carrying his secret for twenty-five years? And perhaps even express the intensity of his remorse?

13

Later, as Grace drove back to police HQ, she mulled over the pre-liminary findings from Dr Tripathi's post-mortem. Reece Nixon had soot in his lungs and airways, which suggested he had died from smoke inhalation – Samit had sent blood and tissue samples to get accurate carbon monoxide levels – but Kirsty Nixon's airways were clear, confirming that she was already dead before the fire reached her.

Which meant that Reece Nixon must have killed his wife before he set their home alight.

Samit had not been able to find any signs of physical injury, but couldn't rule out the possibility that Kirsty had been smothered or strangled. Toxicology tests would reveal if she had been drugged.

Grace could imagine a scenario in which Kirsty had gone up to bed while Reece remained downstairs, drinking heavily and working out what the full ramifications of his DNA test were going to be. Needing to confess to someone, he'd called his brother. Maybe the reality of saying the words out loud had been too much, and he'd gone out to the yard, fetched a can of petrol and drunkenly torched the place.

But first he had placed a pillow over Kirsty's sleeping face.

Was it perhaps an act of mercy? Or had he told her everything and they had then fought, ending in her death? He could have put her lifeless body in bed and employed arson as a way of hiding what he'd done, so that their children would never know. Maybe he hadn't intended to kill himself as well, but had misjudged how much he'd had to drink and ended up too intoxicated to escape.

Grace would have to be patient and wait for the results of all the tests.

But her brain kept whirring and, as she parked the car and made her way into the building, she ran through another possibility. What if Kirsty had overheard Reece's phone call to Larry, and that was what had set events in motion? It would explain why, when Larry had called back – too soon yet for Reece to have ignited the fire – he did not pick up. And yet Michael and Anne Nixon had been amazed to learn of their uncle's rescue attempt. They told her that Reece had never got on with Larry. They couldn't understand why Reece would have chosen to confide in him. They had spoken so matter-of-factly that Grace wondered if the full horror of their loss had yet to strike home. All the same, it was odd that, at the hospital, Larry had shown concern for two young people who barely remembered ever meeting him.

She entered the MIT office and, remembering Samit's advice, went straight to Carolyn Bromfield's desk. The detective constable seemed rather flustered by her approach. 'Hello, ma'am,' she said.

'"Grace" or "boss" will do fine,' she said with a smile she hoped was reassuring.

'Yes, sorry, of course, boss.'

'I wanted to check something. Larry Nixon's clothes and shoes from the other night.'

The younger woman's face revealed the truth immediately.

'You did take them?' Grace asked, her heart sinking.

Carolyn swallowed. 'No, ma'am – boss. I didn't realise we'd need them.'

'He was present at an arson attack in which two people lost their lives.'

'I know, but he'd tried to save them.'

Grace became aware that, two desks down, Blake was watching them. 'That's what he told us, and it may be true, but as yet we have nothing to corroborate his story.'

'I'll get on to the hospital right away and find out what they did with them,' said Carolyn, scrabbling among the papers on her desk.

'Please do. If you can find them, we need them back, washed or otherwise.'

'Yes, boss.'

Shaking her head in silent fury, Grace made her way across the office to her cubicle. Blake got up from his desk and followed her.

'What was she thinking?' she said to him. 'How could she be so stupid?'

'She's inexperienced,' he said. 'She's not stupid. I mentored her when she started. She'll do all right.'

'She overlooked vital evidence.' Grace knew she was being unfair. She had been at the hospital and she was the senior officer, so the buck stopped with her.

'She looks up to you,' he said mildly, making her feel worse.

'Well, let's hope she can retrieve the situation.'

Blake's cool look made her wish she'd kept her mouth shut. But then he gave a broad smile. 'Anyway, it probably doesn't matter. Want some good news?'

'Yes.'

'The fire investigation unit have allowed Wendy and the CSIs to make a start on the undamaged areas of Reece Nixon's house. Guess what they found in the attic?'

'Lord Lucan?'

'A file of old newspaper cuttings, not only about Heather's murder, but also a couple of short pieces in the local paper about two of the rapes.'

Grace dropped into her chair, the rush of relief robbing her of strength. 'That's brilliant. So far, Reece Nixon is the only person to have made that connection.'

'Except you.' The warmth was back in Blake's eyes, making Grace more relieved than she cared to admit – and certainly more than was strictly professional.

She couldn't resist making a triumphant clenched-fist victory salute. 'Yes!'

'It corroborates the confession he made to his brother.'

She let out a long sigh of relief. 'Have you told Superintendent Pitman?'

He shook his head. 'I was waiting for you.'

She silently absorbed the significance of the discovery. 'Did Wendy find anything else of interest?'

'Nothing yet, but there's a way to go.'

'All we need now is his DNA and we can tie it all together. I want everything we can find on him,' she said. 'Search his computer, check his credit-card statements for any pornography sites, I want his phone records, and to go back through every statement taken at the time on both the murder and the rapes. If there were any reported witnesses I want to talk to them again. Make sure the team is briefed.'

'Sounds like the original investigations were botched from the start,' said Blake.

'No, I don't think so,' she said. 'Remember that there was no CCTV or mobile-phone data available back then. I don't see very much that I would have done differently, given the more limited tools they had to work with.'

'Larry Nixon's account of that final phone call is going to be key. We should go and take a formal statement while it's still fresh in his mind.'

'Absolutely. We'll need it for the inquest, if nothing else. The post-mortem found that Kirsty was already dead before the fire.'

'She was murdered?'

'Looks that way,' she said. 'We still have to wait for toxicology.'

'What if Reece told her the truth and she took some kind of overdose?'

'We might never know for sure how she died.'

'But if Reece was also a serial rapist,' said Blake, 'you can see why he couldn't bear for his wife to find out. Heather's death on its own he could've spun as some kind of one-off tragic accident, claim that Heather led him on and then went crazy, whatever. He might have *just* managed to persuade Kirsty to forgive him enough to stand by him, visit him in prison, not turn the kids against him, but I doubt she'd have done that once it came out that he'd raped nearly half a dozen other women at knifepoint.'

'Imagine celebrating your silver wedding anniversary and

then finding out something like that about the man you'd married,' she said. 'How would you even begin to live with it?'

'Which might then also explain the fire,' said Blake. 'Although I have to say I'd have found a more straightforward way to commit suicide than burning myself to death.'

Grace agreed. 'Unless Reece's choice was the urge of a guilty man desperate to obliterate his sins.'

'Scorched earth.'

'Pretty much.'

'So you've got your man?' said Blake.

'Looks like it,' she said. 'Come on, I'll let Colin know and then we can tell the team.'

14

The concierge sitting behind the white desk in the lobby of Larry Nixon's seafront apartment building recognised Grace and Blake as soon as they walked in. He gave them a professional smile. 'Good morning,' he said, already tapping at his keyboard. 'Mr Nixon said to expect you. I'll let him know you're on your way up.' He nodded towards the brushed-metal doors of a pair of lifts. 'Floor seven, apartment seventy-one.'

Blake stood back to let Grace enter first and then pressed the button for the seventh floor. Grace was almost unaware of the lift moving before the doors parted smoothly to reveal a hushed internal corridor lit by halogen spots.

'He's done OK for himself,' Blake murmured as they moved towards a pale wooden door with the number 71 on it.

'Well, so far as we know, he's had no wife or kids to support,' she said. 'And his business is luxury cars.' Background checks had shown that Larry Nixon had no criminal convictions, had never come into contact with the police and seemed to have a spotless financial record. His company was up to date with the requisite driver checks and other regulations and had garnered plenty of satisfied customer reviews online.

Larry opened the door as soon as they knocked. Although his

hair had been neatly cut to hide where it had been singed, the raw burns on his face were livid against his pale skin and he winced with pain as he closed the door behind them.

'Have you found out any more about what happened to my brother?' he asked after their initial greetings. 'Do you have his DNA results?'

'Not yet,' said Grace, 'and we're still gathering evidence, but what we have so far supports your apprehensions, that what he said to you could be true.'

Larry sank into an armchair and rested his head in his hands. Grace took the opportunity for a quick look around. The room was large, a single light-filled living space with a sleek, white, fitted kitchen, dining table and seating area all opening on to a wide balcony that overlooked the sea. The view of silver water and sky was stunning. His taste was minimalist, with uncovered wood floors, grey upholstery and a high-tech TV and sound system that must have cost a fortune. Music was playing quietly in the background – Grace recognised an early Eurythmics album – its tone crystal-clear.

'I'm very sorry,' she said. 'I imagine all this has come completely out of the blue.'

For a moment she thought he wasn't going to respond, but then he shook his head. 'Not really.' He let out a groaning sigh. 'There was stuff back then that I could never put my finger on, something that was wrong, you know, a bit off, but you tell yourself your suspicions can't possibly be right. I remember thinking what a sick person I must be even to imagine such things about my own brother.'

'Did you ever speak to him about your misgivings?'

'No, of course not.'

'What about anyone else?'

Larry shook his head. 'I was too scared of what might happen to him, where it would all end up. I was being selfish, really. I didn't want to be responsible for getting him into trouble or to live with the consequences if somehow it emerged that I was right.'

'I can understand that,' said Grace. 'Do you think anyone else shared your anxieties? Like Kirsty, for instance?'

Larry shook his head. 'No, no.'

'Can you give me any example of the kind of thing that troubled you around the time of Heather Bowyer's murder?'

'He just got weird. And that's when he left Southend, or soon afterwards, anyway. Quit working for my dad. Pretty much cut himself off from all of us for a while. We patched things up, but I never really understood why he got like that.'

She was curious about his repeated concern – a concern that certainly hadn't been reciprocated by Reece's children. 'Were you a close family?'

'I wouldn't say that, not recently, but, you know, blood's still thicker than water when all's said and done, isn't it?'

'Reece had worked as a driver for your father's taxi company?'

Larry nodded. 'We both did.'

'So when he called you on Monday,' she said, 'how long had it been since you'd last spoken?'

'Oh, I don't know. A while. We lead different lives.'

'And what did you think about him calling you?'

'I was surprised, to be honest. But I suppose as soon as he told me about your visit and what you wanted, I realised I already knew he'd be the man you were after.' He looked up at them with tear-filled eyes. 'Please, I'm sorry, I haven't even asked you to sit down. Can I get you anything? Coffee or tea?'

'No, thanks, we're fine,' said Grace, moving to sit on the long low sofa opposite Larry. She crossed her legs, letting one high-heeled shoe dangle in his direct line of sight. He glanced at it once and looked away. 'We will, however, need a formal state-ment from you about the fire at Reece's house,' she continued, 'and what passed between you beforehand.'

'Yes, of course.'

'Detective Sergeant Langley will take notes.'

'Sure.'

'Can you please tell me everything you remember of the two conversations you had with him on the day he died?'

'He called the first time around lunchtime to say that the police wanted a DNA sample. I was busy in the office, so didn't pay much attention. Or maybe, as I say, I wasn't ready to face the truth. But when he called again that evening, I knew something was up. And then he said he had to tell someone, that he was the man you were looking for. There was a woman he had sex with in a park and he killed her.'

'Is that all he said about what he'd done?' asked Grace.

'It's all I can remember. I was so shocked.'

'And how did you respond? What did you say to him?'

'I couldn't believe it. I asked if he was sure, which I guess was a stupid question. Anyway, he laughed. I told him prison couldn't be that bad, at least he'd still be able to see his kids, but he said he couldn't face them finding out who he really was. Then he hung up on me.'

'Your brother's phone records confirm his call to you and give us an exact time, which was eight-fifteen,' she said. 'How long after that did you set out to drive to his house?'

'I'm not sure. It wasn't straight away. I tried calling him back first, but he didn't pick up. It took a while for what he'd told me to really sink in.'

'Did you call anyone else?'

'My dad, Owen. He said I must have misunderstood what Reece was saying, to sleep on it and we could speak to Reece in the morning. I suppose I didn't want it to be true.'

'So what changed your mind?'

'I don't know. Finally, it seemed easier just to go over there. I didn't notice what time I left, but it's about an hour's drive.'

'Do you know what time you arrived at his house?'

'No, sorry,' said Larry.

'Your call to the emergency services was logged at twenty-three minutes past ten.'

'Well, there you are.'

'Can you talk us through what happened when you got there?'

'By the way, I hope it's OK, but I sent one of my drivers to fetch my car.' He held up his bandaged arms. 'Not that I'll be driving for a while.'

'That's fine,' said Grace. 'So Reece wasn't expecting you?'

'No, I told you, he wouldn't pick up when I kept calling.'

'I just need a picture of how events unfolded. So you parked in the yard?'

'Yes. There were lights on inside the house and I went to the front door. No one answered and I could see a strange flicker through the glass. I went round the side of the house and saw the smoke and flames immediately. I didn't stop to think, just wanted to get him out of there.'

'Did you go in through the front door?'

'Yes. It wasn't locked, which, I suppose, should have surprised me, but you don't think normally in that kind of situation, do you? Anyway, the instant it opened there was a whoosh and scorching heat, and I couldn't see anything, could hardly breathe. I waited to see if it would subside enough to let me in, but it didn't, so I called 999.'

'You've been in a fire before,' said Grace.

He frowned. 'You saw the *Courier* this morning?'

'Yes.' It had been Carolyn who had brought Ivo's short article to her attention before they left the office. Grace had been alarmed that Ivo might somehow already have picked up on their interest in Reece Nixon, but, going by what he'd written, he appeared oblivious. She hoped it would stay that way.

'How embarrassing.' Larry gave a self-deprecating smile that she imagined had become second nature when reminded of his heroism. 'Their journalist tracked me down yesterday afternoon.'

'You spoke to him?' She prayed that Larry hadn't given Ivo any leads.

'He wouldn't get off the phone until I gave him a comment,' he said. 'But don't worry, I knew not to mention the DNA tests or any cold cases. I don't want the tabloids door-stepping me or my family any more than you do.'

'Good,' she said, relieved. 'I'd be grateful if you'd keep it that way.'

'Although talking to that reporter did make me realise that it was only because of the Marineland fire that I imagined I could simply barge straight into a burning house like that,' said Larry. 'If I'd hesitated long enough to reflect on what the hell I was doing, I'd have called the fire brigade straight away. I guess I just automatically assumed I could do it again. Save them.'

'You were already too late,' she told him gently. 'At least for your sister-in-law. The pathologist says she was already dead.'

His eyes widened in horror. 'He killed Kirsty first? How do you know?'

'It's too soon to say that he killed her, but she wasn't breathing when the fire reached her.'

He seemed genuinely shocked. 'Have you told their kids?'

'We're waiting for the results of further tests.'

Larry got up and went to stand at the floor-to-ceiling window that fronted the balcony and stared out at the misty October vista of sea and sky. Grace took the opportunity to look over at Blake. He gave a little nod of encouragement, his expression serious. As Ivo's article had unwittingly highlighted, the contrast – on the very same night – between one brother's selfless courage and the other's callousness added to the argument that Reece had indeed intended his act of arson to be significant.

Larry spun round, the brightness behind him throwing his face into shadow. 'Could the fire have been a trap to kill me too? I mean, do you think he *meant* for me to go and try to save him?'

'Why would you think that?' she asked, taken aback.

'Forget it. It must be the painkillers talking.'

'Did you have a difficult relationship?'

'Reece always kept me at arm's length. Back when we were young, the Marineland fire got a lot of publicity. I was in the papers, on the telly, only the local news, but strangers would buy me drinks, girls wanted to go out with me. Dad always said Reece was jealous. I don't know if he was, but it definitely got to him.'

'Maybe we'll understand more once we conclude our enquiries,' said Grace. 'Which reminds me' – she tried to make the request sound as relaxed as possible – 'we'll need the clothes and shoes you were wearing on Monday night.'

'Really? What for?'

'This is a case of arson and murder,' she said. 'All material needs to be forensically examined. It's routine. The hospital said they didn't dispose of them, so if you have them here, that would be helpful.'

'I'm afraid my dad took them. I'm sorry if that was the wrong thing to do.'

'Don't worry, we'll speak to him. We'd also like to fix an appointment for the Home Office pathologist to examine your burns. Again, it's just for routine elimination purposes, nothing to worry about.'

'If it's really necessary.' He came to sit down again. 'I can't believe this is happening.'

Grace smiled sympathetically. 'And the last thing' – she nodded to Blake, who had brought the necessary kit – 'we'd still like your permission to take a DNA sample.'

'I don't understand. Are you saying you don't think it was Reece after all?'

'There's other partial DNA from the original crime scene that we need to eliminate.'

'Can you explain? I don't know what I'm supposed to think here. Is my brother a murderer or not?' Larry put a hand over his mouth as if close to tears. 'If there's a chance it wasn't him, that he's innocent, well, that would just be wonderful!'

'I can confirm that we're actively investigating your brother for arson and murder,' said Grace. 'I'm sorry, but that's all I can tell you for now.'

Larry remained silent, making her wonder whether he might refuse to give them a sample. Not that it would matter – they had the plastic cup he'd drunk from which she'd lifted from the hospital – but she'd be curious to know what reasons lay behind his reluctance.

He shook his head in bewilderment. 'You think you know people. It doesn't seem possible that Reece would . . . We weren't close, but . . .'

Grace realised that, unconsciously or not, his gaze was fixed on her feet. As she uncrossed her legs and stood up, she watched his attention snap back to the present.

He smiled wearily. 'They do say you can't choose your relatives, don't they?' he said. 'Of course, you must take the swab.'

15

Owen Nixon lived in Leigh-on-Sea, a leafy, prosperous borough which was only a short detour from Grace and Blake's route back to Colchester. They found him dressed in faded and stained blue overalls, bent under the raised bonnet of a saloon car parked on the stubby driveway of his semi-detached Edwardian house on Oakville Way. Behind the car was a solid brick-built garage, attached on one side to the house. The open doors, which badly needed a fresh coat of paint, revealed a jumble of tools, spare car parts and, Grace noticed, two petrol canisters lined up beside the doors. As they approached Owen straightened up and immediately winced with pain, a hand to his back.

'He's game,' Blake said quietly to Grace. 'He must be heading for eighty if he's a day.'

'Maybe he needs to keep busy after his son's death,' she said, noting that the car bore a taxi light on its roof and the side panels were painted with the blue-and-yellow logo of Owen's firm.

'Detective Inspector Fisher, to what do I owe this honour?' Owen asked by way of greeting.

Surprised by his sarcastic tone, Grace wondered for a second if old age meant he'd forgotten the nature of their investigation. 'We're sorry to distress you further at a difficult time,' she said, 'but your son Larry told us that you took his clothes home from the hospital on Monday night. We'd like to take them for forensic examination as part of the investigation into the fire.'

Owen looked at her shrewdly, wiping his hands on an oily tea-towel. 'You're a bit late.'

'Why's that?'

'They're gone. I burnt them.'

'Burnt them?' Grace heard herself blindly echoing his words.

'They were ruined,' he said. 'All scorched and filthy, and you can never get the smell out. Why do you need them, anyway?'

'For elimination purposes,' she said. 'We're now certain that the fire at Reece's house was arson. We have to investigate fully.'

'Oh well,' said Owen. 'I was making a bonfire in the back garden and pitched them on, so that's that.'

Grace's attention was caught by something over his shoulder. Through the open driver's-side door, she recognised a shape familiar to her from Deborah Shillingford's kitchen. Dangling from the rear-view mirror was a winged, cardboard air freshener bearing the words: 'I'm your guardian angel'. Owen's eyes followed hers. 'Nothing like the yellow glow of a taxi light on a cold wet night, is there?'

He was right, yet his words sent a shiver down her spine as she thought of Heather Bowyer; perhaps she'd climbed into the wrong car in Southend all those years ago.

'Would you mind showing us where you burnt them?' She asked as lightly as she could, but the inference was clear. 'I'm sorry to have to be so thorough, but your son and daughter-in-law are dead, and I'm sure you realise why we have to do this by the book.'

'Suit yourselves.'

Owen led the way down the narrow pathway between the side of his house and the next-door fence. As Grace followed she turned to Blake and was reassured by his answering look that Owen's demeanour was raising his hackles, too. Yet, sure enough, the remains of a recent fire did mar the scrubby patch of ground that must once have been a small back lawn. Along one side of the garden the privet hedge had been recently cut and a few half-burnt twigs remained around the perimeter of the ash pile.

'Happy now?' Owen asked.

'Yes, thank you, Mr Nixon. At some point we may need you to sign a statement confirming what you've told us.'

Owen shrugged and led the way back to his driveway. Grace looked at the surrounding houses, which were well kept, with loft extensions and shiny new cars on the driveways, and wondered how the neighbours felt about the unkempt state of this property.

'Anything else I can help you with?' asked Owen.

'Yes, actually,' said Grace. 'Do you have any photographs of Reece from around 1992?'

Owen leaned back against the car and smiled. 'He was a good-looking boy, I can tell you that.'

'You do understand that we're investigating the murder of Heather Bowyer in 1992?' she asked, still puzzled by his manner.

'I'm not senile,' he said. 'It was Reece. Larry told me.'

'I hope you'll excuse me for saying it, Mr Nixon, but you don't sound very surprised. I can understand you wanting to protect your son, but if there's anything you think we ought to know, we'd like to hear it.'

'Not really,' said Owen. 'He always thought he knew best. Was already in trouble as a teenager. But you'll know all that.'

'I believe he left Southend soon after the murder.'

Owen nodded. 'I threw him out.'

'Can you tell me why?'

'He had no respect. Not like Larry. Larry's done well for himself, but those other two, they'd never listen. They had to do it their own way, and now you can see how that's turned out.'

Grace tried to square what he was saying with the raw sorrow shown by Reece's children. But then, she reminded herself, Reece's children had never suspected their father of harbouring such a terrible secret. 'Might you have any photographs?' she asked once more. 'They would help us to tie up the investigation.'

'I don't know,' said Owen. 'I'd have to look.' He folded his arms, not moving from where he leaned against the front wing of the car.

'I'm sure you'd agree it would be best for everyone involved if we can resolve everything as swiftly as possible.'

'I've lived here forty years,' he said. 'It'd take time to go searching the whole house.'

Blake came forward, holding out a card, which Owen took. 'If you do find the time, Mr Nixon, we'd really appreciate it.'

Owen nodded, looking at Blake appraisingly. He wiped an oil-stained hand against his thigh and held it out to him. 'I'll see what I can do.'

'Thank you,' said Blake.

Owen didn't offer his hand to Grace, who was thankful to remain at a distance. She said goodbye and walked with Blake to their car.

'What was that about?' she asked as they drove away. 'Plain old-fashioned sexism, or what?'

'No,' said Blake. 'I think he just gave me a grip.'

'What do you mean?'

'To let me known he's on the level.'

'I've no idea what you're talking about.'

'He's a Freemason,' said Blake. 'I could be wrong, but I think he may be quite high up, too. I don't know all the variations, but each degree of Masonry is supposed to have its own grip. He could even be the master of a lodge.'

'Does that mean he was expecting a response from you?' she asked. 'Some kind of favour?'

'No idea,' he said, 'I'm not a Mason. I've an uncle who is, and who's always on at me to join. He's taken me along to a few social evenings, so I've learnt some bits and pieces. But Owen Nixon would've known the second I gave him my hand that I'm not part of it.'

'Shame,' she said, 'it might've persuaded him to be more cooperative.'

Blake laughed. 'Not sure it works that way. Once you join, your loyalty is supposedly to the craft.'

They drove for a while in silence as she thought about why Owen's odd manner had seemed so ominous. 'Do you think it's significant that he wanted you to know he's a Mason?'

'Can't see why,' said Blake. 'I guess in a place like Southend the local lodge would carry some weight in terms of doing business, whose firm you employ to do a job, that kind of thing.'

'What does your uncle get out of it?'

'Good dinners, cheap booze, evenings away from my aunt.'

'But then he wouldn't tell you if there was more to it, would he?'

'That's true,' he said, 'but I've never bought into all those conspiracy theories about the police protecting criminals because they're all on the square together.'

Grace frowned, far from sure what to make of Owen's sly approach. 'We still ought to track down a photo of Reece Nixon. At the very least there must be some wedding photographs.'

'Depends on what survived the fire. I'll check with Wendy.'

'Anne or Michael might have copies,' she said. 'If not, then we'll have to ask Kirsty's side of the family.'

'That'll be fun,' said Blake grimly.

16

🔊

Welcome back to *Stories from the Fire*. I'm Freddie Craig, and I've been talking about how, thanks to a simple quirk of fate, the date of my birth connects me to the night of the Marineland fire in Southend, and to the murder of nineteen-year-old Heather Bowyer and the unknown man who ended her life that same night. It's a strange feeling.

I'm trying to find out everything I can about those events, so now I'm sitting in a coffee shop opposite an Art Deco palace originally built for the *Daily Courier*, one of the bastions of what used to be Fleet Street. I'm talking to Ivo Sweatman, the *Courier*'s chief crime correspondent.

Ivo: I can still remember the first time I got a nod of recognition from the uniformed commissionaire as I walked across that bronze and marble entrance lobby. I felt like I'd arrived. Now it's the headquarters of some international accountancy firm.

Freddie: Ivo, twenty-five years ago you were the only reporter on a national newspaper to give Heather Bowyer's murder more than a few column inches. Even then, your story only ran on the inside pages. Why was that?

Ivo: Her death was eclipsed by the Marineland fire. Editors had paid a local snapper a fair whack for his pictures of the hero of the day against a background of smouldering ruins, so no one wanted to run a spoiler.

Freddie: You've recently re-encountered the hero of the day.

Ivo: That's right. Larry Nixon. I interviewed him after he attempted to save his brother and sister-in-law from a house fire. This time he did not succeed. Can you imagine?

Freddie: It's certainly a pretty strange karmic twist. But I believe that even the original fire wasn't such a big story nationally at the time?

Ivo: That's true. As I say, everyone likes a good picture of an inferno, but no one died, and calamity always sells better than good news.

Freddie: Over a long career, you've covered the trials of several notorious killers. What was that like, watching murderers as they sat in the dock day after day and hearing every detail of their sadism and depravity? It must have affected you.

Ivo: Well, not really. You see, I was hanging out with all the other reporters, sometimes from across the world, so in fact there's often a great atmosphere, a lot of black jokes and good-humoured competition. And there's nothing finer than knowing your editor is holding the front page for your copy and that your name is going to be splashed in twenty-four-point bold type. If it bleeds, it leads. The punters love all that 'face of evil' stuff.

Freddie: Do you have a theory as to why the man who raped and murdered Heather Bowyer has never been caught?

Ivo: Forensics and computer records and so on weren't as sophisticated back then, and the police simply didn't have the wealth of investigative data they have nowadays. But most of all, I think the killer had the good sense never to reoffend. If he had, he'd have been caught by now.

Freddie: But something made you dig a bit deeper into Heather's story. Did you ever feel that you were close to finding him? Or guessing who he was, or what he was like?

Ivo: I can't claim that my motives were very noble. To be honest, I was little more than a cub reporter, it was my first assignment for the *Courier* and I simply wanted to spin it out as long as I could.

Freddie: I've read every word you wrote about the case. You tracked down the man who discovered Heather's body. You spoke to her mother and the friends who'd been out with her that night. Got quotes from the detective in charge, DI Jason Jupp. It seems like you got to know him quite well. Do you think he slipped up?

Ivo: You have to remember it was a totally different era. JJ became a detective in the late 1960s. He'd have been taught by coppers who'd seen service in the Second World War. I think he probably did his best.

Freddie: But he can't have liked everyone knowing there was a killer out there thumbing his nose at him, or having local people believe he must have missed some vital clue?

Ivo: There wasn't much to miss. There was no forensic evidence that led anywhere. The friends Heather had been with said she just disappeared into thin air.

Freddie: That was when you spoke to them?

Ivo: Yes. They'd all been at school together, just a group of mates on a night out. No arguments, no undercurrents. They were heading off to catch the last train home and Heather's shoes were hurting – the pathologist confirmed she had blisters on her feet – so she'd lagged behind. She was there one moment, gone the next.

Freddie: Did her friends go looking for her?

Ivo: By the time they realised they'd lost her they couldn't remember when or where they'd last seen her. She'd been trying to persuade them to share a taxi because her feet were sore and they'd teased her about making such a fuss. So they decided she must have flagged down a cab and then, to get back at them, not offered them a ride. They were sure she'd be waiting for them at the station with a big grin on her face. But she wasn't, and by then it was pandemonium because of the fire and they couldn't get anyone to listen to a story about a silly girl who'd got herself lost and missed her train.

Freddie: So maybe, if it hadn't been for the fire, Heather would have been found earlier. Perhaps in time to save her life?

Ivo: That's possible, yes.

Freddie: So it's also fair to say that the fire really helped her assailant, too. The commotion allowed him to escape. Meant that no one paid him any attention.

Ivo: And if anyone did notice something suspicious, they soon forgot about it. After all, the Marineland fire was the biggest thing to happen in Southend for years.

Freddie: Without it, Heather's killer might well have been caught. You could almost say that it pushed his life on to a completely different track, like *Sliding Doors* or parallel universes. Another quirk of fate.

Ivo: One thing I've learnt is that most crime, especially murder, is chaotic. Where you see destiny, I just see mayhem and confusion.

Freddie: The *Courier*'s chief crime correspondent puts on a good show of seen-it-all cynicism, but I reckon he cares much more than he lets on about the victims of crime. But even for Ivo, who spent days talking to people and was on the scene right after it happened, that murder is now just one of thousands he's covered as a reporter. But I feel driven to get to the heart of what really happened and why. Even if I'm the only one who feels like that, I can't let it go.

Which is why I thank you for listening to *Stories from the Fire*. If you have any information about that night, if you were there, or know someone who was, please don't hesitate to get in touch. I'm Freddie Craig. Speak to me.

17

Back in the office, Ivo took out his earbuds and swivelled his chair away from the bank of filing cabinets at which he'd been staring while listening to himself answering Freddie's questions. He'd now listened to all the podcasts in the series. They had a certain odd charm about them, although he suspected that, for all the kid's efforts, he hadn't attracted many listeners yet. With a start, Ivo realised that his section editor was hovering beside his desk and wondered rather uncomfortably how long he'd been there.

'*Listen with Mother*?' the editor enquired.

'Actually, a rather interesting new true-crime podcast,' Ivo replied, 'about a cold case I covered back in the day.'

'Podcast?' the editor echoed. 'Any good?'

'Not bad. It's made by a young graduate who interned for us.'

'Is that so? I keep being told we ought to get more into podcasts. Some of the poncier titles have been doing them for a while.'

Ivo was struck by an agreeable idea. 'I was thinking about running a piece on this one, actually. It's called *Stories from the Fire*.'

'Catchy title.'

'Maybe the *Courier* could sponsor it or something,' Ivo suggested. 'It's a good cause, seeking justice in an unsolved rape and murder.'

His editor nodded. 'Write something up and show it to me.'

Twenty-five minutes later, having won approval to run the piece in Saturday's paper, Ivo texted Freddie to let him know. He was happy to be able to give the kid a break. With a print circulation of over a million and a further two or three million online, the right coverage in the *Courier* would send the number of Freddie's listeners rocketing. It wasn't only that Freddie was struggling to get a job; he'd also confided to Ivo that his relationship was under strain. While he was marooned at his grandmother's on the Dengie Peninsula, keeping tabs on the old girl while trying to save enough money to get the podcast up and running, his girlfriend had got a job and a flat-share in London. They could only see each other at weekends, and she was becoming less and less keen on schlepping out to Essex. Given the real sacrifices Freddie was making for his project, Ivo reckoned he deserved a leg-up. An article would also put Freddie's name under the noses of those at the *Courier* who were in a position to commission work. What happened next was up to him, but Ivo's self-congratulatory glow was gratifying. He could almost see himself getting into this mentoring malarkey.

If he was to persuade the *Courier* to sponsor the podcasts, they'd have to be good. Freddie had pressed Ivo to remember anything he could about the Bowyer case, and Ivo had noted down several colourful stories he could tell him about JJ, including a bizarre evening when JJ had introduced him to the local Masonic lodge. Freddie had also particularly asked for anything to which he could attach sound effects, but Ivo had so far only managed to come up with one suggestion, which was that one of Heather's friends had mentioned hearing a snatch of music from a passing car around the time they lost sight of their friend. It was better than nothing.

He'd already told Freddie he should try interviewing the guy from the fire, Larry Nixon – the tragic irony of a man who had once saved strangers, then failed in the attempt to rescue his own family, was a gift of a story. But Freddie had said he preferred to focus the next few episodes on the cold case rather than the fire. He seemed to think it was only a matter of time before he somehow magically unlocked the mystery. Privately, Ivo reckoned that, by allowing his listeners to expect that kind of revelation, Freddie was simply setting himself up to fail, but had said nothing. The kid had to learn for himself.

It was a long time since Ivo had dwelt in any detail on recollections of his youthful self, and he now found himself struggling with unwanted side effects. These trips down Memory Lane were passing perilously close to certain side alleys that he'd always resisted looking down.

Only with hindsight could he admit how slavishly he'd fallen under JJ's spell. Why had he come to regard the detective as almost a father figure? His actual father was then still living – emotionally stifled, yes, but in other ways a perfectly admirable role model – so why his need to latch on to Jason Jupp, of all people?

JJ had certainly offered a welcome that was warm and boozy and held a whiff of just enough danger and sleaze to be addictively alluring to a crime reporter still wet behind the ears. Ivo had felt as if the older man had opened a door on to a nostalgic era of criminality that Ivo had hitherto known only from tales told by burnt-out hacks around the bar at El Vino's in Fleet Street. It wasn't until long afterwards that Ivo had dared acknowledge that his devil's apprenticeship had had very real consequences, and that JJ had been telling nothing but the truth when, in his cups, he'd boasted about running Southend as his own private fiefdom. Ivo had long ago become adept at swiftly closing down any unnecessary reflection on the part he had played, and had striven to convince himself that JJ's various accommodations with the truth had been driven by the best of intentions – a simple case of 'noble cause corruption'. He knew that sop to conscience was a fantasy, but also that it was far too late to put things right now.

He tore up the notes he'd made about other stories to tell Freddie. Some bits of the past were best forgotten.

18

'Sir?' Grace knocked at the open door to Superintendent Pitman's office. 'We've got a result on Reece Nixon's DNA sample.'

'Already?'

'Wendy leaned on the lab to fast-track it and they managed an extra-speedy turnaround.'

He beckoned impatiently, rolling up the sleeves of his customarily pristine white shirt. 'Well, come in, then. Tell me.'

Grace sat down facing him across his desk. 'Reece Nixon is *not* a match to the DNA profile on the knife used to murder Heather Bowyer.'

'*Not* a match?'

'No.'

'Fuck.' Colin threw himself back in his leather executive chair. 'Excuse my French.'

'We can still put him at the scene,' she said, trying to make light of her own frustration. 'He is a match to a partial profile from inside the glove, where there was a mixture of DNA.'

'So what?' he sighed heavily. 'Gets us nowhere.'

'It brings us an awful lot closer to Heather's killer than we've ever been before.'

He sat forward again. 'Fair enough. At least I can inform the chief constable that the familial search wasn't a waste of time.'

'And you could argue,' she said, 'that if the perpetrator was wearing gloves, then we wouldn't expect to find a full profile on the knife.'

'Remind me how many angels can dance on the head of a pin?'

'The profile on the knife is touch DNA,' she reminded him. 'All that tells us is that we might be able to identify someone who handled it. It doesn't tell us when or how the DNA was deposited. But we know that the glove and the knife are forensically connected because some of the other DNA markers found in the glove also match the profile on the knife. They suggest we're looking at first-order relatives. And it's a kitchen knife. At the time of Heather's murder Reece Nixon was living at home with his father and his brother Larry. The DNA on the knife might well belong to someone he had shared a kitchen with.'

'You've got DNA samples from the other family members?' asked Colin.

'We took one from Larry yesterday. It'll be early next week before we can expect the results.'

'But you still think Reece Nixon killed Heather Bowyer?'

'If he wasn't guilty, why would he kill himself on the very day that we turn up?' said Grace. 'Dr Tripathi is going to be examining Larry Nixon's injuries from the fire for evidence of flash burns later today. Unfortunately his father destroyed the clothes he was wearing. But in any case, there's nothing to contradict the assumption that it was Reece who killed his wife before setting fire to his house.'

'He might've thought to leave us a signed confession.'

Grace smiled. 'He did have the foresight to leave the news-paper cuttings in his attic.'

'True.'

'Even if we had Reece Nixon as a live suspect, we'd still have to present corroborative evidence.'

'If he was alive, we'd also be charging him with arson and the murder of his wife,' Colin said tartly.

'Yes, but we'd still need to close the Bowyer case.' She took a deep breath, knowing that her boss would not like what she was about to say. 'Reece Nixon kept cuttings about Heather's murder and also about two reported rapes that had taken place in South-end some months before. Not even the original investigation linked these crimes, so why did he?'

'I expect you're about to tell me,' said Colin.

'He kept no cuttings about other crimes, which suggests that, for him, there was a connection. I think our clearest line of enquiry will be to link Reece to these two rapes.'

Colin frowned, and Grace guessed that he would be looking for reasons to say no.

'Reece didn't mention any further offences when he made his confession to his brother,' he said. 'If he was already considering suicide, he had no reason not to.'

'Shame?' she suggested. 'Thinking about his kids?'

'Maybe,' said Colin. 'Is there any forensic evidence from the original investigations into those two rapes that we can use?'

'Nothing was retained,' she said. 'Southend had no rape suite or specialist officers. The women were expected to go to the local hospital for examination. Initial statements were taken but there was no follow-up.'

'Then I'm afraid it doesn't look very promising,' he said. 'And I don't want to blow the budget on a deceased offender.'

'There were three other reported rapes that, in terms of geographical profiling and other similarities, I believe might also be linked to Heather's case. Now that we have a suspect, we might get something useful from one of the women.'

'After twenty-five years?'

'Rape is the most serious survivable crime, sir.'

He nodded, but she could see that he was still casting around for a counter-argument. She stayed silent, hoping he wouldn't find one, and was saved by the phone on his desk ringing.

Colin picked up the receiver. 'Superintendent Pitman.' He glanced at Grace. 'Yes, Hilary, she's with me now, why don't you join us?' He hung up. 'She's on her way. You may not have seen this morning's *Courier*.'

'No, sir,' she said, trying to stifle a wave of anxiety that Ivo had, after all, somehow got wind of Reece Nixon's link to the cold case.

'Apparently there's an article about some young man who's podcasting about the Heather Bowyer case,' he said. 'Hilary says the profile is by the same journalist who ran yesterday's piece about Larry Nixon being the hero of the Marineland fire.'

'Ivo Sweatman,' said Grace, relieved that the media had not yet cottoned on to her investigation. 'I know him. He also wrote most of the original coverage of the Bowyer murder that we found in Reece Nixon's attic.'

'Did he now? Well then, he's definitely getting a bit too close for comfort.' He looked up as Hilary Burnett tapped on his door. 'Ah, good. Come in.'

The communications director smiled at Grace as she took the

chair beside her, smoothing her skirt and neatly crossing her legs as she sat down. Her hair and make-up were as flawless and professional-looking as ever. It had been Hilary's friendship with Grace's stepmother when they'd worked together in PR for the beauty industry that had first led Grace to apply for the job in Essex. Since then she'd learnt to trust Hilary's agile mind as well as her discretion. Although Hilary knew more than most about the extent of Ivo and Grace's unofficial collaborations in the past, Grace had always tried to compromise the older woman's position as little as possible.

'So how much does this podcaster know?' asked Colin.

'So far only what's always been in the public domain,' said Hilary. 'He's called Freddie Craig and his podcast is called *Stories from the Fire.* His original link to the murder is that he was born the same night. I'll send you the link so you can listen.'

'Thanks,' said Grace.

'The last episode was an interview with Ivo Sweatman,' Hilary continued, 'so Freddie Craig knows there's a link between the Marineland fire and the arson at Reece Nixon's house.'

'That's already been in the *Courier*,' Grace pointed out.

'Yes,' said Hilary, 'but I'm concerned that it will be only a matter of time before either Ivo or this podcaster finds out about the prior police interest in Reece Nixon.'

'We need to stay in control of the narrative,' said Colin, stating the obvious.

Hilary turned to Grace. 'We need to make a statement about the Heather Bowyer case. How much can you give me?'

'It's all circumstantial so far,' she said.

'We don't want this story dribbled out in bits and pieces,' said Colin. 'I think it's time to take a view.'

'I'd like to put out a media statement today, if possible,' Hilary agreed.

'I must keep Monica Bowyer informed,' said Grace, thinking fast. 'Warn her that she might get door-stepped.'

'Yes, of course,' said Hilary. 'Tell her to call me if she needs any support. Are we positively identifying Reece Nixon as Heather's killer?'

'We have his partial DNA in a glove found at the scene, his confession to his brother, the contemporary newspaper coverage he kept and his suicide,' said Colin. 'Seems to me that's sufficient evidence to register a recorded crime outcome.'

'I'm fine with identifying Reece as a person of interest, but I'd rather delay anything more definite until we've made further enquiries,' said Grace.

'When will that be?' asked Hilary.

Grace held up her hands. 'End of next week?'

Hilary shook her head. 'My advice is to issue as firm a statement as we can today.'

Grace saw a hole in the fence and bolted through it. 'What if we say that we're widening the scope of our enquiries? That gives us room to manoeuvre and an opportunity to appeal for information.' Grace briefly explained about the earlier rapes and was relieved when Hilary readily accepted her theory.

'Closing the book on a serial rapist would certainly paint Essex Police in a positive light,' Hilary said. 'The media tends to give very favourable coverage to the resolution of serious cold cases, especially if they can report them without worrying about *sub judice*.'

Grace turned to Colin. 'And the publicity should help to bring forward new information.'

'Freddie Craig is also trawling for witnesses,' Hilary told Colin. 'We need to be one step ahead of him here.'

'You're right,' he said. 'I don't want any fresh evidence going to some amateur sleuth and not to us. An appeal will speed things up and may also keep the costs down.'

'I'll draft something to put out in time for the early evening news,' said Hilary. She turned to Grace. 'Will that give you enough time to brief the families?'

'Just about,' said Grace. 'Thanks, Hilary.'

Colin also turned to her. 'Very well, go ahead and make further enquiries about those cases. But don't go overboard.'

'No, sir.' She tried to hide her grin. 'Thank you very much.'

19

As Grace crossed the MIT office, she beckoned to Blake to join her. She registered as she passed that he was leaning down to speak to Carolyn, his hand on the back of her chair and, when he entered Grace's cubicle, Carolyn was hovering meekly behind him. Irritated by the young woman's presence, Grace looked forward to Duncan's return from honeymoon when the constable could go back to the DVU whence she'd come.

However, the reason for Carolyn's diffidence immediately became clear. 'Sergeant Langley told me about Larry Nixon's clothes,' she said. 'I'm sorry, I know it's entirely my fault we didn't secure them in time.'

Remembering Blake's earlier admonition, and striving to remember her younger self in the early stages of her own career, Grace spoke kindly. 'Not entirely. I was there, too. All the same, it's a useful lesson about seizing evidence.'

'Yes, boss.'

'Anyway, the good news is that Superintendent Pitman has given the green light to pursue a connection between the Southend rapes and the Bowyer murder.'

'Excellent!' Blake pulled out the spare chair, only to offer it to Carolyn, as he went quickly to fetch another for himself from the main office. Grace could hardly tell a junior team member she wasn't wanted, and silently blamed her tetchiness on Carolyn's over-eagerness to please.

'Right,' said Grace when Blake had returned and sat down. She clapped her hands together in a gesture that immediately reminded her of her least favourite teacher at school. 'I have to go to see Monica Bowyer and explain the implications of the DNA result, but I want the team to get started on further enquiries. First off, we need photographs of Reece Nixon as he looked twenty-five years ago.'

'We will have to ask family members,' said Blake. 'Wendy found no family albums or snaps in the house.'

'Isn't that a bit strange?' asked Carolyn.

'Not really,' he answered. 'Everything in the living room went up in smoke.'

'I'll also be speaking to Michael and Anne Nixon to warn them there'll be a media statement,' said Grace, 'so I can ask them if they have any.'

'Sorry, boss,' said Carolyn, 'but why are photographs important?'

'I'm hoping a photograph may jog memories. Although three of the rape complainants said their attacker was masked, one said she was assaulted by the taxi driver who picked her up. Reece was a local driver, and one of the women might have come across him previously.'

Blake nodded. 'It shouldn't be too difficult to track down at least a couple of the original complainants.'

Grace nodded. 'Two were visitors, like Heather, but three were local, so let's start with them.'

'Carolyn's been working on a profile of Reece Nixon

twenty-five years ago,' said Blake, nodding at the young woman to read out her notes.

'He was twenty-five, living at his father's house in Southend and working as a driver for his father's taxi company,' said Carolyn. 'His then girlfriend, Kirsty, was pregnant. They got married and moved to Colchester in November 1992 and their first child, Michael, was born the following March.'

'When Larry mentioned Reece moving away,' said Grace, frowning, 'he said Reece got weird and cut himself off, and Owen said he threw him out. But getting married and having a baby seems to me like a perfectly normal reason for a fresh start.'

'Settling down and starting a family could also have been what made him stop offending,' Blake pointed out.

'Especially if he never meant to kill,' said Grace, 'and the shock of it brought him to his senses.'

'He has juvenile drug offences, but no record of violence against women,' said Carolyn. 'He's never come to police notice as a kerb-crawler and no pornography was found in his house or business premises or on his computers. And, apart from a few tricky financial patches in his business, that's it. A model citizen.'

'If he's our man,' said Blake, 'then you'd expect him to make sure he kept his nose clean.'

'That's true,' said Grace. 'You wouldn't want to open the door to an unnecessary police investigation, would you?'

'So, what are we looking for from the rape complainants?' asked Blake.

'Well, firstly, all the usual things,' said Grace. 'An identification, any distinguishing marks, more detail on his MO, anything on the car he used, victimology. But there's also one other aspect we haven't discussed, something I think could be really important. Heather Bowyer's clothes were retained as evidence, but one of her shoes is missing. According to the senior investigating officer's notes, it was assumed that it came off during the attack and the search team then missed it.'

'How do you miss a shoe at a murder scene?' asked Blake.

'I thought it was rather unlikely,' agreed Grace, hoping he'd be prepared to take her theory seriously. 'The notes conveniently suggest that maybe some random person picked it up and took it away or that it had been lost earlier when Heather's killer was transporting her to Cliff Gardens.'

Carolyn looked puzzled. 'How does this link to the rapes?'

'Three of the women who made a complaint of rape mentioned losing a shoe.'

'*That's* a bit more than coincidence,' said Blake.

'Maybe he took one away in order to slow his victim down,' said Carolyn. 'Gave himself an opportunity to escape before she was able to find help.'

'Could be,' agreed Grace. 'Heather's shoe was a pink slingback with a high heel. I'd like to know what style the other missing shoes were.'

'He may have singled out women in high heels because it would be more difficult for them to run fast,' said Carolyn.

'That's also possible.' In spite of herself, Grace was impressed by the constable's clear thinking.

'What did investigating officers at the time make of the missing shoes?' asked Blake.

'Nothing. It looks as though it was only recorded either in passing or because the woman in question insisted. Reading between the lines, the officers thought they were all drunk or dozy or both.'

'Essex girls,' said Carolyn.

Grace smiled. 'Afraid so.'

' "Why does an Essex girl wear knickers?" ' asked Carolyn. ' "To keep her ankles warm." "What do Essex girls use for protection during sex?" "Bus shelters." "What's the difference between an Essex girl and the *Titanic*?" "You know how many men went down on the *Titanic*." I heard them all when I was growing up. Can you imagine trying to report that you'd been raped on a Saturday night in Southend twenty-five years ago?'

'I haven't heard the punchline to that one,' said Blake.

'Precisely,' said Carolyn grimly.

'So you can imagine how it would play out if one of these women had dared to suggest that their attacker might have had a thing about shoes,' said Grace.

'Aha!' exclaimed Blake. 'So that's why you've taken to wearing high heels. You think our man has a shoe fetish!'

'Yes,' she admitted. 'I wanted to see if either Reece or Larry Nixon betrayed any kind of involuntary reaction.'

'And did they?'

'No,' she said. 'Reece was either oblivious or studiously not looking, and although I did catch Larry looking at them, I couldn't read anything into it.'

'Any other similarities about the shoes?' he asked. 'Colour, left or right shoe?'

'No detail was recorded in the statements,' said Grace. 'But I'm hoping the complainants might remember.'

'Say Reece did take a shoe from each of the women he raped because that was his fetish object,' said Blake, 'he'd have wanted to keep them, wouldn't he?'

'They'd certainly be precious to him,' she agreed.

'Maybe that was another reason for the fire,' said Carolyn. 'He wanted to take his precious trophies with him, couldn't bear anyone else to touch them.'

Grace nodded agreement. Pleased yet again by the young woman's insight, she was ready to retract her earlier misgivings about Carolyn's ability to fit into the team. 'I asked Wendy to look out for women's shoes,' she said, 'hoping that Kirsty's wardrobe would reveal tastes that might suggest she'd gone along with her husband's fantasies – which might also explain why he stopped his attacks – but there was nothing.'

'Their bedroom was destroyed in the fire, though, wasn't it?' asked Blake.

'Yes,' said Grace. 'But while most high heels are made of plastic, some contain metal, which would be more likely to survive a fire. All Wendy found was Kirsty's gardening boots by the back door.'

'Perhaps he hid them elsewhere,' Blake suggested.

'Be nice to find them,' said Carolyn. 'That would wrap this case up perfectly.'

Grace smiled, relieved that they had accepted the evidence of the missing shoes as a valid line of enquiry. 'Yes,' she said, 'and if we do, there's every chance we'd also retrieve DNA belonging to the women who wore them. That would be pretty much a slam-dunk.'

20

The square sitting room in Monica Bowyer's post-war terraced house in Chelmsford was suffocatingly hot. Her son Simon had left work early to join them, alerted by his mother that, for the first time in twenty-five years, the police seemed to have real news. Grace had visited twice before and knew not to sit directly opposite the glass-fronted cabinet that held silver-framed photographs of both Heather and Monica's late husband, who had died never knowing who was responsible for his daughter's death. Heather had not been naturally beautiful, but had worked out how to make the best of herself through attention to her hair and make-up, and, while never the one pushing herself to the centre of any group shots, she appeared to enjoy life. In among the photographs were a pair of baby shoes, a diminutive school cup and the certificate the teenager had earned on her hairdressing course. Not much to show for a life cut short.

Grace thought of her own younger sister, Alison, who was coming to stay that night on a rare visit. Grace hadn't yet made up the spare bed or shopped for an evening meal, but any consideration of such chores felt like a luxury when set against the poignancy of Monica's shrine to her daughter.

'You'll remember that I explained how we were running a

search for familial DNA that would match DNA retrieved from the scene?' Grace began.

Monica and Simon both nodded solemnly, not taking their eyes off her face.

'Well, we received results this morning that show a partial match.'

'You've caught him?' exclaimed Simon, jumping to his feet.

'Not exactly.' It was unbearable to disappoint them. Grace knew that, this time, they had allowed themselves to believe there would be real progress. 'The individual is not a match to the full DNA profile on the weapon, but can be matched to partial DNA found on another item recovered from the scene. It's not enough to say for sure that this man ever came into contact with Heather.'

'So what *are* you saying?' asked Simon, sitting back down.

Monica said nothing. She remained perfectly still, apart from repeatedly rubbing her hands together.

'What we do know is that the familial search has narrowed down our field of suspects to a very few individuals. We believe we've found the man we're looking for, but we need to make further enquiries to confirm it. We'll be releasing a statement to the media to that effect later today.'

'What further enquiries?' asked Simon. 'What else can there possibly be left to find out now?'

'We think there's a strong possibility that the man who killed Heather had previously attacked other women. We're going to be speaking to them.'

'But you've got him locked up, right?'

Grace took a deep breath and shook her head. 'Our suspect is dead. There'll have to be an inquest, but we believe that he committed suicide the same day we approached him for a DNA sample.'

'How could you let that happen?' demanded Simon. 'We've waited years for this, and you let him get away!'

'We had dozens of potential matches to investigate and at that point there was nothing to indicate that he ought to be of particular interest to us. But I'm very sorry. I realise how crushing this must be for you.'

Simon stared at her with a mixture of confusion and hostility, unable to find the words to express his frustration.

'Who was he?' Monica spoke for the first time.

'We're not going to release his name until we've completed our enquiries. When we do, you'll be the first to know. Again, I'm so sorry that his death has cheated you of the chance to see justice done.'

'What's he been doing all this time?' Monica asked softly.

Grace recalled her encounter with Reece and Kirsty in the yard of his landscape gardening business: a down-to-earth, hard-working, unremarkable couple. They had been understandably cautious in dealing with police officers, but there had been absolutely nothing to set any of Grace's alarm bells ringing. And yet hours later their house was on fire, a house where evidence of his interest in long-ago crimes lay hidden in the attic, and they were both dead. 'Just leading an apparently normal life,' she answered.

Monica nodded, her face a blank.

Simon spoke for them all when he spat out a single word. 'Bastard!'

'I'm sorry,' Grace repeated helplessly.

'Some guy called Freddie Craig has been calling,' said Simon.

'Says he wants to tell our story on his podcast. I told him to get lost.'

'Just refer anything that like that to our communications director. She can deal with it for you.'

'That's not the point,' he said. 'What right has he got to talk about Heather like that? He's even been to her grave. If you can't nail the guy, then what's to stop people like him raking it up again and again?'

Grace could only apologise once more and, after some discussion of media tactics should the reaction to the story become overwhelming, was guiltily relieved to leave the house. She looked at her watch. When she'd spoken earlier to Michael Nixon he'd said that he and Anne would both leave work early and make the journey to Colchester to hear in person what new revelations the police had to make about their parents, and she needed to get a move on.

Even though it seemed farcical to worry about banalities like food shopping in the midst of doling out such life-altering news, the fact remained that at some point today she had to get to a supermarket if she wanted to cook something special for her sister's visit. She knew she'd pass a store on the return journey and double-checked that she'd brought her list of the ingredients she needed.

Twenty minutes later she was thinking how much she hated shopping in unfamiliar supermarkets, especially one this big, where she couldn't just automatically grab the usual items from the shelves. She was trying to locate a tin of coconut milk when her phone rang. It was Dr Tripathi, who explained that Larry had turned up promptly for his appointment, but that it had not been possible to examine the burns on his hands and arms or take samples for evidence of petrol residue because the burns had become badly infected. Samit had been unwilling to uncover them as Larry had already been running a fever. He said he'd sent him back to the hospital for more effective antibiotics.

'He seemed fine when Sergeant Langley and I visited him yesterday,' she said, frowning.

'With burns an infection can take hold very rapidly,' Samit said. 'He did look fairly unwell to me.'

Grace thought uncomfortably of the loss of Larry's clothes and her failure to oversee a new member of her team. 'So there's nothing you can tell me?'

'I observed two things, neither of which are conclusive.'

'I'll take anything I can get.'

Samit laughed. 'OK, so he has no burns to the palms of his hands and he has a "crow's-foot" pattern around his eyes – the place where any facial lines remain unaffected by fire or scorching. Both are often characteristic of the kind of flash burns sustained when igniting a flammable liquid such as petrol.'

'Hang on. You're saying Larry Nixon might have started the fire?'

'I'm saying I can't rule it out. But it's also possible that being beaten back by a ball of flame when he opened the front door could account for the pattern around his eyes, if not entirely for the lack of general injury to his hands.'

'But we should consider the possibility that Reece Nixon didn't set the fire?'

'You know the adage: "The absence of evidence is not evidence of absence".'

'One of the least helpful maxims I know. But tell me what you made of Larry Nixon,' she said, curious to hear Samit's opinion.

'Apart from the pleasant change of having a living person to talk to, you mean?' He considered his reply. 'I thought he was plausible.'

'Plausible?' she echoed. 'That doesn't sound like a ringing endorsement.'

'I've dealt with a lot of grieving relatives over the years,' he said. 'They usually want to know if their loved one suffered, what kind of death they had. Larry Nixon didn't ask me a single thing about his brother.'

'They weren't close.'

'There you are, then. I found him very plausible.'

Grace thanked him and ended the call. A woman pushed past, tut-tutting that Grace was blocking her way, to reach for something on a high shelf nearby. Grace moved aside, mulling over Samit's words. The pathologist was right: everything so far about Larry Nixon had been entirely plausible. But was it *too* plausible?

She looked, unseeing, at the shopping list in her hand, and then clicked back to the present. Where was the damn coconut milk?

21

Michael and Anne Nixon, sitting side by side, looked up at Grace expectantly as she entered the soft interview room at Colchester Police HQ. They appeared exhausted and bewildered. In the week since their parents' deaths the cares of the world had been heaped upon their young shoulders, and now she was about to deliver further shattering blows. She was glad she'd asked Blake to sit in on the meeting with her. She'd told him what Samit had said about Larry Nixon's burns, but Blake hadn't shared her alarm that they might be looking at the evidence the wrong way. She clung to his confidence as she began to explain to Michael and Anne that it was very likely it was their father who had torched their family home. She then went on carefully to outline his probable motive for doing so.

'That's impossible.' Michael gave a laugh of disbelief. 'Dad could never have murdered anyone, especially not like that. There's no way. It has to be a mistake.'

'I'm very sorry.'

'No, no, no,' he said, smiling and shaking his head. 'It's just not possible.' He turned to his sister for affirmation.

'Michael's right,' she said. 'Dad was totally against violence. Hated any kind of bullying. Mum gave us the odd slap on the leg when we were little, but never Dad. Besides, Mum would never have stuck with him if he'd done something like that. She'd have gone straight to the police.'

'She might not have known,' said Grace, aware she'd have to force herself to keep saying the words that would demolish brick by brick every belief they'd ever had in their father. 'In his attic we found old newspaper cuttings relating to the murder. And other crimes.'

'No,' Anne said decisively. 'He was the gentlest, sweetest man. You can ask any of the people he worked with. They always said the business suffered because sometimes he was too much of a soft touch.'

'He phoned his brother Larry and confessed to the murder before setting fire to the house.'

'He wouldn't call Larry,' exclaimed Michael. 'He wouldn't give him the time of day!'

Grace turned to Blake, hoping that a second voice would help them to process the information.

'We checked both their phone records and confirmed that the calls took place between them exactly as Larry Nixon described,' he said.

'And, although your father is not a match to the full DNA profile found on the murder weapon,' said Grace, 'he is linked to the crime scene by partial DNA on another item found there.'

'So whose DNA *is* on the weapon?' asked Anne. 'Why aren't you looking for them?'

'We believe it to be from a family member who had previously handled the kitchen knife at home.'

'You mean Larry?' Michael asked bitterly.

In the brief silence that followed Grace summoned up her last reserve of emotional strength to resume her task. 'Your mother was already dead before the fire reached her. We're waiting on tests to see if she was drugged, otherwise it's likely that she was smothered.'

'Not by Dad!' Anne cried. 'He wouldn't have hurt a hair of her head.'

'There's no other explanation. If it helps, we think it's likely that your father had a great deal to drink that night.'

Anne stood up abruptly. She was slight and pale, with dark shadows under her eyes, but she thrust her chin up defiantly. 'I don't care what you say, you're wrong. He'd never hurt Mum. And Mum would never let him!'

It took an effort for Grace to remain seated while they vented their outrage.

'He couldn't have done that,' said Michael. 'He'd never lay a finger on her. Even if he was afraid that he was somehow going to be fitted up for this murder, he still wouldn't harm her. They always talked things over when they had problems. She'd have made him see sense.'

Hating herself, Grace continued to the end. 'The murder victim, Heather Bowyer, was raped before she was killed.'

'Not by Dad,' said Michael, showing the first signs of real, cold anger. 'Never.'

'There's no way Mum would've stood for that,' added his sister as she sat reluctantly back down.

'We think that whoever murdered Heather had previously raped several other women in Southend.'

Michael laughed once more in disbelief. 'This is nonsense. Not only that, it's disgusting.'

'I realise how hard it must be to believe such things,' said

Grace. 'And people change, I know that. I'm quite prepared to accept that the man you loved was not the same person who did these things.'

'Have you taken Larry's DNA too?' demanded Michael.

'He's given us a sample,' said Blake, 'but we've not yet had the results.'

'Even if his DNA is present, it doesn't change anything,' said Grace.

'Why not?'

'Well, for one thing,' said Blake, 'we know where he was on the night of Heather Bowyer's murder: rescuing two lads from a fire at the leisure complex.'

'What about his father?' asked Anne.

'Owen?'

'Yes. Is he still alive?'

'Yes. But he has different mitochondrial DNA,' said Grace. 'We know it has to be someone who shares DNA with your father's sister, Deborah Shillingford.'

Anne shook her head in perplexity. 'I'm not sure we've ever met her either.'

'I don't care what your evidence is, you need to look again at Larry,' Michael said stubbornly. 'He'd turn up from time to time, but Dad never trusted him an inch. And Dad hated his own father.'

'I'm very sorry to be the bearer of such difficult news. But I wanted you to know now because we're putting out a media statement later today saying that we have a significant new lead in the Heather Bowyer murder case and that we are pursuing further related enquiries. We're hoping that these further enquiries will give us the conclusive evidence we need to close the case.'

'Naming Dad?' asked Michael.

'He remains our primary suspect.'

'No,' said Anne, rising to her feet once again. 'It can't have been Dad. Not in a million years. You didn't know him. We did.'

Leaving Blake to show them out of the station, Grace leaned against the wall in the corridor and shut her eyes. She tried to remember the excitement she'd felt on Duncan's wedding day when Wendy had rung to tell her they had the results of the familial search. What she'd failed to take into account, after twenty-five years, was the collateral damage that would inevitably follow a successful investigation. She had just ruined two young lives. Barely coping with their parents' deaths, how did she expect them to absorb the accusations now levelled against their father? And how was she supposed to balance that against the scant comfort she could offer Monica and Simon Bowyer?

'That was tough.'

She opened her eyes to find that Blake had come back. She managed a shaky smile. 'It was.'

'You OK?' He reached out to touch her arm.

She nodded. 'I'm glad you were there.'

'Any time.'

'I hope we're right,' she said. 'We're staking a lot on the assumption that Larry Nixon's telling us the truth.'

'We can only go on the evidence we have.'

'But we're missing the evidence that would validate his account of the fire.'

Blake's expression tightened. 'We'll have his DNA back next week. That might shed new light.'

'I'm not blaming Carolyn,' she said. 'She seems to be finding her feet OK now. I'm just stating facts.'

Blake relaxed. 'Everything Michael and Anne said, about their father hating violence, that could be disgust at what he'd done, an attempt to wash away the past.'

'Yes, I know.'

'Then we turn up, ready to undo every good and decent act of the past twenty-five years.'

'You're probably right.' His words didn't make her feel any better.

'Hey, look,' he said, 'we're not responsible for what we find out about the past. If Reece was the Southend rapist, then whatever his family has to suffer is on his head, not yours.'

'I know.' She sighed and then managed a smile. 'Thanks, Blake.'

'You want to go and get a drink?'

Her heart lifted, but then she looked at her watch, remembering Alison's visit. 'I can't, sorry. In fact, I really need to run.'

'OK. Take care, boss. See you tomorrow.'

Grace hesitated, wanting to end their conversation differently but not sure how. Instead she hurried away, fighting the urge to spin round and look back.

22

On the drive home to Wivenhoe Grace told herself repeatedly how much she was looking forward to her sister's visit, but, when the doorbell rang while she was still unpacking the shopping – forty minutes earlier than Alison had estimated she would be – her heart sank. She knew that Alison would seize on her unreadiness as due, not to her own premature arrival, but Grace's lack of domesticity. No matter how many times Grace reminded herself that the tacit point-scoring said more about Alison's insecurity over giving up work to look after her two young sons, it still always left her feeling wrong-footed and resentful.

Before she opened the door, she took a deep breath and reminded herself how lucky she was to have any family at all. Alison was her only sibling; their mother had died giving birth to her and their beloved father had died when they were students. They'd been grateful to their stepmother for pitching in, but they'd been a bit too old when she'd first come on the scene to feel it was fair to lean on her much. And so, during the few years until Alison had married and produced her babies, it had really been just the two of them.

With this in mind Grace welcomed her sister with genuine

warmth and was almost able to overlook the quick appraising glance Alison cast over the less-than-tidy open-plan living space.

'You must've made good time,' Grace said. 'I've not been home very long.'

'The journey was much easier than I expected.' Alison hugged her tight. 'It's so good to see you. It's been ages. Why don't we see more of you?'

Grace knew her sister's answer to that: Alison took it for granted that, since she had a husband and two small children, it was up to Grace to make the journey to visit them in Winchester.

'It's been a busy year,' said Grace.

'You'd hardly recognise Joe and Alfie, they've grown so much.'

'Let me give you a glass of wine while I sort out your room.'

'Don't be silly,' said Alison, picking up her overnight bag. 'I'll come and give you a hand.'

By the time they'd shaken out the duvet cover and plumped the pillows up, the tensions were gone. Grace decided that, instead of making the meal for which she'd shopped, they should make the most of an opportunity to recapture some of the irresponsibility of their youth. It was quick and easy to take the train from Wivenhoe into Colchester, and they could have a night out together before getting a cab home. Alison was delighted by the suggestion and, after ringing home to check on her boys, put on fresh lipstick and was ready to go.

Once in Colchester some impulse led Grace to the little bar where Blake had taken her in the summer. Over cocktails, she asked Alison lots of questions about the three-day course at the University of Essex that had brought her to Colchester, her plans to go back to teaching once Alfie had started school and her anxieties over juggling childcare at the same time as re-entering the job market. Seeing how torn Alison was between excitement at escaping family life for the weekend and missing its warm cocoon, Grace could feel the stirrings of her own buried regrets, not so much about her divorce – she never wanted to see Trev again, thank you very much – but about the loss of the hopes and plans that had been an integral part of her marriage.

She caught her sister looking at her shrewdly. 'I wish you hadn't kept quiet about what Trev did to you,' said Alison. 'You should have told me.'

Grace sighed, aware that she couldn't keep putting off this conversation. At the time, she'd never given her sister the true reason for her divorce or for her abrupt departure from her former job in Maidstone, and, later, Alison had been dreadfully upset to learn from a newspaper article that Grace had taken Trev to court for assault after he'd beaten her up, and that this had earned her the bullying contempt of their colleagues for ending his career as a police officer. When Alison found out, they'd had bitter words and had since avoided the topic.

'I know you were hurt,' said Grace, 'and I'm sorry. I wasn't able to think straight, and then, after I came here, I just wanted to leave it all behind.'

Alison reached across the table to touch Grace's hand. 'I might've been able to help.'

'Of course you would've helped,' said Grace, remembering how desperately she'd longed for her father, yet hadn't felt deserving enough to summon her sister away from a new baby and a demanding toddler. 'That's not the reason I didn't tell you. I suppose I just crawled into a hole and hid away.' She took a deep breath. 'I was like a wounded animal. I would've bitten anyone who came near me.'

'And now?' asked Alison. 'Are you over it?'

'Yes, pretty much. I certainly think it's made me better at what I do.' She smiled wryly. 'I learnt a lot about being a victim.'

'Sometimes I think you find it easier to face criminals than your own family!'

'That's not fair.' Grace laughed, but the words stung.

'But are you over it?' asked Alison. 'Do you feel ready for another relationship?'

'Yes, I think so.'

Alison's eyes lit up. 'Does that mean you're seeing someone? Tell me!'

Grace wished she hadn't chosen this bar with its memories of the first time she and Blake had slept together. 'The job doesn't make it easy,' she said. 'Shall we go and get something to eat?'

Alison laughed. 'You're not palming me off that easily! Come on, tell me. There is someone, isn't there?'

'Maybe, but there are professional issues. I promise I'll tell you if we manage to work things out.'

'You don't want to wait too long,' said Alison. 'Not if you're getting broody, anyway.'

Grace tried not to resent the intrusion. In some ways she and Alison were very close, but at the same time they didn't really understand enough about one another's lives to go poking into such private feelings. 'I'm not broody,' she told her firmly. 'Not yet, anyway. And right now, wild horses wouldn't make me give up my job.'

To head off further questions, Grace launched into the edited highlights of the search for Heather Bowyer's killer. She couldn't help being pleased when Alison's eyes widened in astonishment, and maybe also a little envy, at how Grace got to be right at the heart of such dramatic events.

'Wow,' said Alison when Grace finished. 'When will it be on the news?'

'A statement went out today, but we're trying to keep it low-key,' she said, already regretting that she'd spoken. 'And I'd rather you kept what I've just told you off the record.'

'Yes, of course.' Alison shook her head in bafflement. 'I still don't understand how you deal with this stuff day in and day out. I mean, it's brilliant, and I can see the fascination, but aren't you worried it'll, I don't know—'

'Contaminate me?'

'I guess so. After all, it is a bit gruesome and grisly.'

'Sure, sometimes, but that's irrelevant against being able to offer some answers to the victims' families.' Grace spoke awkwardly, aware of how she'd just hijacked Monica's grief in order to boast to her sister. 'The work is never glamorous once you've dealt with a victim's family.' Yet, even as she said the words, something in her rebelled against being made to feel at fault. The work might not be glamorous, but it could be addictive. So yes, she'd been stung by the pitying look Blake had given her outside the church, but she still stood by the reckless sense she'd had then of not caring if everything else in her life took second place to following up a new lead on a cold case. Did that reaction make her unnatural? That seemed to be what her sister was implying.

'You won't do this forever, will you?' asked Alison. 'All this horror and grief. I'm sure that what you do must put a lot of men off. That's what Edward thinks.'

Grace wanted to hit back, say she didn't care what Alison's husband thought, that she didn't want the kind of life her sister had, but she merely stared into her empty glass.

Alison did not let up. 'Promise me you'll eventually move to something a bit less dark and odd?'

Grace forced herself to smile. 'Right now, I'd like to move to some place where we can eat. I'm starving.'

Alison conceded and led the way out. She insisted on paying the bill and, while Grace waited, she took deep breaths and reminded herself once again that Alison meant well and was the only family she had. She looked around the now packed bar. All the seats were taken and the floor area was jammed. When a group moved to take over the booth she and Alison had just vacated, a space opened up and Grace spotted Blake sitting with his back to her on a stool at the far end of the bar. She'd been sitting facing away from the entrance and, in this crowd, he was unlikely to have seen her on his way in. She considered going over to say hello, but acknowledged her reluctance to introduce her sister, given the third degree Alison might submit him to and would certainly later submit *her* to. Then Blake leaned forward, reaching for his drink, and she was able to see who was with him. It was Carolyn Bromfield. They were sitting close together in order to hear one another above the din and, as Grace watched, Blake threw back his head in laughter while the younger woman smiled at him in admiration.

23

🔊))

Welcome back to *Stories from the Fire*. I'm Freddie Craig, and this episode truly is the story from the fire. Not only that, but it contains an extraordinary revelation, one that justifies my belief that my birth really does connect me in some mysterious way to the events of that night.

But first, let's go back twenty-five years, to the fire at the old Marineland resort in Southend-on-Sea.

Larry: I'd been there many times as a kid, and occasionally when I was older, too, although it was pretty run-down by then. Somehow, even in the dark, I just seemed able to find my way around.

Freddie: That's Larry Nixon, the man who ran into a burning building to rescue strangers. Now a successful businessman in his late forties, he's tall and looks like he keeps fit. I'm sure he won't mind me saying that he doesn't have film-star good looks – he's not someone you'd especially notice in a crowd – but he's a hero, nonetheless. A hero who saved the lives of the two teenage boys whose discarded cigarettes accidentally started the fire. He still insists he did nothing special, only what anyone would have done.

So, Larry, tell me what happened that night.

Larry: I was working, driving for my dad's taxi company. It'd been busy, so I was taking a breather and dawdling along the top road before heading back down to the esplanade. As a taxi driver you get used to keeping an ear out for people hailing you, and I must've registered someone shouting. When I looked to see where it was coming from, I noticed smoke pouring out of the building and I guess I just put two and two together.

Freddie: A lot of people would have gone off in search of a telephone box to call the fire brigade. You didn't.

Larry: I could see one of them. He was banging desperately on a broken window. I could picture exactly where they were inside the complex, could visualise a route to that spot. And also I'd stopped right beside where they must've got in, where the fencing had been pushed aside. To follow them in just seemed like a total no-brainer at the time.

Freddie: You carried one of them out on your back because he'd injured his ankle. Minutes after you got clear of the building there was a mammoth explosion. Any later and you'd all have been killed.

Larry: I didn't think about it. Still don't. And I had no idea how fast a fire can spread, how furious it can become. Believe me, if I'd realised, I would never have gone in.

Freddie: Are you still in contact with the young men you rescued?

Larry: One of them always sends me a Christmas card. The other, I don't know.

Freddie: But they're alive because of you.

Larry: Oh well, I don't know about that.

Freddie: Which makes the events of last week all the more tragic. You lost your only brother in a house fire. You've said you don't object to my asking you about what happened. You were there and tried to rescue him.

Larry: And my sister-in-law. She's the real victim here. The police have admitted that it was arson, but you see, it's very much more complicated than that.

Freddie: Larry Nixon falls silent. I wait for a few seconds before encouraging him to speak again. I have no idea what he's about to tell me.

Larry: You've been speculating in these podcasts about the man who murdered Heather Bowyer all those years ago. Well, I can answer that. It's not easy, but it's right that I should be the one to speak. It was my older brother, Reece Nixon.

Freddie: I'm speechless. I was born the night Heather died, and now I'm the channel through which the identity of her killer has finally been revealed.

Larry: Reece phoned me that evening. Told me he'd had a visit from the police. They'd wanted a DNA sample to see if he was linked to the attack on Heather. He told me everything. I could hardly understand what he was saying, and yet at the same time so many things simply clicked into place. When he confessed to killing her, I knew he was telling the truth.

Freddie: And Essex Police know all this?

Larry: Of course.

Freddie: Yesterday they announced an important new lead in the case. Why didn't they name your brother?

Larry: I've no idea. Some kind of legal red tape, I suppose. But it's one of my family who did this. We have to own this. I wish I had saved him. He should have faced up to what he did, but instead he took his own life. Not only that, his wife, my sister-in-law, Kirsty, also lost her life in the fire he started.

Freddie: What can you tell me about Reece Nixon? What kind of man was your brother?

Larry: Just normal, respectable. But then we hadn't been close for some time. He kept himself to himself.

Freddie: You said how things clicked into place once he confessed to having murdered Heather Bowyer.

Larry: Well, I always thought he had secrets, things that troubled him. The way he cut himself off from us, from the rest of the family. I had no way of knowing the real reason at the time, but looking back I can see that he was clearly very disturbed about something. Now I realise it must have been right after he'd killed her.

Freddie: So you think it ate away at him, what he'd done?

Larry: You could hardly forget a thing like that, could you?

Freddie: The police also mentioned further related enquiries. Do you know what they are?

Larry: My fear is that it's to do with how my sister-in-law died. I'm not going to speculate. It's all dreadful enough without imagining anything worse.

Freddie: Yet he managed to live an apparently normal life all these years.

Larry: Apparently. I wish I'd had the guts to speak to him when we were younger, ask him outright what was wrong. Perhaps if I had, he and Kirsty would still be alive. I blame myself.

Freddie: Larry Nixon's grief and regret highlights how many victims there are in this case. And now the truth is out. You heard it here first on *Stories from the Fire*. We know the identity of Heather Bowyer's killer – an apparently ordinary husband, father and brother, a real person, not a monster.

But some mysteries remain. It was DNA evidence that led

Reece Nixon to make his final confession, DNA that he shares with Larry. It still seems incredible to me how one of these young men could risk his life to save two strangers while, less than a mile away, the other was so brutally taking a life. What makes two brothers so different? Some alignment of the stars when they were born? Solving this case raises as many questions as it answers.

I'll continue to respond to events as they unfold. Anyone with information can get in touch with me. Make sure you come back soon for more *Stories from the Fire*.

24

Grace did not feel ready for the day ahead. She'd slept badly after an ill-digested dinner. During the evening she'd been too distracted to pay proper attention to her sister and there'd been no time in the morning to make amends – or for her usual morning run, which would have restored her spirits. She'd waved Alison off to the university where she'd be staying for the two nights of her course, promising to see her again on Sunday for a late lunch. During the short drive to work Grace regretted wasting their precious time together and lectured herself on what a further waste it would be to spend the next few hours dissecting every look that might pass between Blake and Carolyn.

Before she'd noticed them sitting at the bar, she'd been ready to acknowledge that Alison was right – she ought to make room in her life for more than work – so it had been bitter to discover that she might have left her change of heart too late. Even worse was the fear that struck as sleep eluded her in the small hours of the night that, for Blake, their brief relationship had never been more than a fling.

She knew she was over-thinking the situation – her sister's visit had stirred up too many buried emotions – and that Blake and Carolyn had almost certainly been merely colleagues having a casual after-work drink. After all, Blake had invited her first, and she had declined. And if Carolyn's expression had strongly suggested otherwise, then all Grace could hope was that, among all the other pillow-talk, Blake wouldn't tell the young detective constable that he'd also slept with their boss. That suspicion was unfair – she had every reason to trust in Blake's discretion – but nonetheless she walked into the MIT office feeling both foolish and cruelly exposed.

Blake greeted her with an easy smile. 'Hey, boss. We're start-ing to get some traction on yesterday's media statement,' he said, waving some sheets of paper at her. 'BBC Radio Essex ran with it, and Hilary says a couple of local papers have picked it up. We're starting to get a few random calls already.'

'Good,' said Grace, relieved to have some immediate distrac-tion. 'Anything so far I should know about?'

'One call that could be interesting,' he said, following her to her cubicle. 'A woman who says she was a police constable in Southend at the time of the murder. She left the job a year or so afterwards and isn't offering any specific intelligence, but seems keen to speak to someone.'

Grace pulled a face. 'You're sure she's not someone who feels like she deserves to join in the action just because she was once in the job? I don't want to waste time on rubber-neckers.'

'Carolyn thought she sounded too sharp for that,' said Blake. 'Plus she offered to come here.'

'Carolyn took the call?'

'Yes.' His expression didn't change. 'It might be worthwhile. We've not yet spoken to anyone in a position to shed light on the investigative thinking.'

Grace remained doubtful. 'But if she was only a PC—'

'Still a WPC back then,' noted Blake. 'And that's the point.

Carolyn thinks a woman might have noticed different things and taken a separate view of how enquiries were handled.'

'OK.'

'I think she's right.' A slight frown gathered when she did not immediately respond. 'Don't you, boss?'

'Yes, of course,' said Grace, admonishing herself. 'Good thinking. Let me know when the woman arrives. If I'm free I'll speak to her myself.'

'Will do.'

'Where have we got to on tracking down the current whereabouts of the rape complainants?' she asked.

'We've located one of them,' he said. 'Cara Chalkley. She's still in Southend. And we're awaiting confirmation on two others.'

'Great. Get in touch with Ms Chalkley and set up a time to interview her. The sooner the better.'

'I'm on it, boss.'

She watched him go back to his desk, noting that he didn't look over at Carolyn, who remained intent on her computer screen. Grace was relieved that if he had spotted her with Alison in the bar last night, he clearly wasn't going to mention it. Best not to hear any explanations or, even worse, evasions. She concentrated on her own screen and fired off a couple of emails, first to Dr Tripathi to ask when they could expect the toxicology results on Reece and Kirsty Nixon, and then to Wendy to check they were up to date with everything from the fire investigators and to make sure that all possible pressure was being put on the lab to deliver Larry Nixon's DNA result as soon as possible.

She was tempted to make contact with Ivo so she could get his take on Larry Nixon, whom he had interviewed after both fires. She trusted his instincts about people, and had every justification to speak to him on an official basis. Before she could decide, she was side-tracked by an incoming email from Wendy, who had replied almost immediately. The crime scene manager's only new information was that the fingerprints on the unopened smoke alarm battery left in the kitchen matched those found elsewhere in the house: it was almost certainly Kirsty Nixon who had purchased it. Grace tried to imagine Reece Nixon placing a pillow over his wife's sleeping face. Had she threatened to call the police when he told her the truth? Or maybe it had been a suicide pact, and she'd stared up at him, willing him to do it. Was that why he'd sat downstairs after-wards, drinking and waiting for the flames of hell to swallow him up?

But would either of them have done that to their children? And not even have left a note?

Her train of thought was interrupted by the sight of Hilary entering the main office and making straight for Superintend-ent Pitman's door. As Hilary knocked and was about to go in, she caught Grace's eye and beckoned for her to join them.

'Have you heard the new podcast?' Hilary began with no pre-amble. 'An interview with Larry Nixon. He's named Reece Nixon as Heather's killer.'

'Shit!' said Colin. 'I said we should have run with the whole story ourselves when we had the chance.'

'Who is this Freddie Craig anyway?' Grace asked angrily, recalling the care she had taken *not* to reveal Reece's name, not even to Monica Bowyer.

'He's got an MA in journalism,' said Hilary. 'Just trying to make a name for himself.'

'Well he's certainly done that,' said Colin.

'This scoop will send his listener numbers sky high,' Hilary agreed.

Sponsored, Grace thought angrily, by Ivo Sweatman. She was glad she'd been diverted before she was able to seek the chief crime correspondent's help.

'All we can do now is concentrate on damage limitation,' Hilary continued. 'We'll have to put a face to this, hold a media conference.'

'It's Grace's baby,' said Colin. 'She applied for the familial search and set the whole ball rolling.'

'She should certainly be there, but I think this requires a more senior level,' said Hilary. 'Either you or you plus the deputy chief constable.'

The superintendent didn't hide his disgruntlement. 'I don't think we need to drag the DCC into this.'

'Whatever you judge best,' said Hilary. 'The immediate question is, how much of Reece's confession are we prepared to corroborate?'

'I'm *not*.' Grace surprised even herself. She paused to try and work out why that had been her instant gut reaction. She couldn't really offer a good reason, and yet suddenly she was convinced she should have taken her earlier doubts far more seriously. 'I don't like that Larry Nixon has forced our hand,' she said, knowing how weak it sounded.

'No one's arguing with you about that,' said Colin. 'But we need to seize back the initiative here.'

'But why has Larry done this?' Grace persisted. 'He's far from stupid. He didn't have to, and he must know how disruptive it would be for our investigation.'

'Maybe he likes the limelight,' said Colin. 'After being such a hero maybe he's developed a taste for it.'

Grace shook her head. 'He's not been straight with us from the start.'

'About what?' The superintendent leaned forward, observing her sharply.

'Nothing major, but lots of little things that add up, like he managed to delay giving us a DNA sample, and made out he was much closer to Reece and his family than he is.'

'Maybe that's understandable in the circumstances,' Hilary suggested gently.

'He didn't need to lie,' said Grace. 'It feels manipulative. Reece's son said his father never trusted Larry. And, while we have no evidence, we can't rule out the possibility that he set the fire at his brother's house.'

'Hasn't Dr Tripathi examined his burns yet?' asked her boss.

'He wasn't able to,' she said, relieved that Colin was taking her seriously. 'Larry had developed an infection. Samit said he was running a fever, so he didn't want to uncover them unnecessarily.'

'He obviously felt well enough to give an interview to the podcaster,' Colin said drily. 'Shame we don't have his clothes from that night.'

'That's my fault, sir. I take full responsibility. I should have considered him more strongly as a suspect from the beginning.' She thought uncomfortably of Michael telling her to look again at Larry. What if she had got all this horribly wrong? Had Larry – the chilling notion struck her with full force – murdered his brother and sister-in-law in order to fake Reece's confession and save his own skin?

If so, then Larry Nixon had just played her for an absolute fool.

25

Grace sighed when Blake informed her that Melanie Riggs, the former WPC from Southend, had insisted on driving over immediately to see her at Colchester Police HQ. She was desperate to seek his opinion on Larry Nixon, but hadn't yet found an opportunity.

'I hope she's not going to be some drama queen,' she said as they made their way downstairs to the soft interview room. 'We've got enough to do.'

'We'll soon see,' he said soothingly.

She knew she was on edge, but right now Blake's kindness wasn't helping.

Melanie Riggs was no diva. In her early fifties, she was slim and business-like in tailored trousers and a matching jacket. She wore good jewellery, although not much of it, minimal make-up and her hair had been expensively cut and coloured. She shook both their hands, explaining succinctly once they had all sat down that she'd left the police to train as a paralegal and then married the senior partner in the London law firm where she'd worked; that had enabled her to take a law degree and she was now a partner herself. 'Part of the reason I left the police,' she concluded, 'was the handling of the Heather Bowyer case.'

'Please go on,' said Grace, intrigued by the woman's determination.

'The short report I heard on the radio mentioned further enquiries,' said Melanie. 'Is that correct?'

'Yes,' said Grace.

'Into other rapes that were reported over the previous year or two?'

'Before I confirm that I'd like to hear what you have to say.'

'Of course,' said Melanie. 'I understand.' She fiddled with her diamond ring before speaking. 'I dealt with two of the women who reported that they'd been raped. There were clear links between their cases and other assaults, but Detective Inspector Jupp refused to listen. On the other hand, he was only too happy to let a WPC knock herself out dealing with sexual crimes. He thought women were all a waste of time – both female officers and rape victims.'

'Was he just a dinosaur?' asked Grace. 'Or was there another agenda?'

'Both,' Melanie answered promptly. 'You needed wing mirrors to work with JJ.'

'You think he was corrupt?'

'I've absolutely no proof that he was. He was too clever for that. But it was the supergrass era, remember? You put someone down in the cells to sweat for a bit and then, in return for intelligence, offered them a letter to the judge in the hope of getting a more lenient sentence. If they were useful enough, they got signed up as a registered informant and were paid out of a dedicated police budget. After that, they became untouchable and meanwhile senior detectives like DI Jupp could organise raids and arrests based on information received without ever having to leave the pub.'

'I realise it was a system that left itself open to abuse,' said Grace, wondering what this history had to do with her investigation. 'But to be fair, intelligence-led policing was all the rage at the time.'

'It was, until the opportunities for blackmail or conspiracy became clear,' said Melanie. 'Once I became a lawyer I saw how many major criminal cases simply crumbled in court. Officers' testimony was tainted, criminals were settling old scores, money was flying around like confetti.'

'So what happened in Southend?' Grace asked, trying to get the conversation back on track.

Melanie pulled a face. 'Let's say that JJ liked to play both sides against the middle.'

'But how does this affect the Heather Bowyer case?'

'OK, so a big part of JJ not pursuing a proper investigation into the various rape allegations was pure misogyny. He simply couldn't be bothered. If young women wanted a night out in Southend then that's what they'd get, with bells and whistles on it. And if I wanted to take these women seriously, he was happy to let me get on with it, although I wasn't to expect any manly help. Then, suddenly, that all changed.'

'Why, what happened?'

'I wanted to speak to a local taxi firm,' said Melanie. 'I thought it was pretty routine. One of the women I dealt with mentioned seeing a taxi driving past soon after she'd been attacked. When I looked up the other statements, she wasn't the only one. Another woman had said the same thing, and they both described the same blue-and-yellow taxi logo. I thought it was worth asking the drivers if they'd seen anything, like the perpetrator leaving the scene, or whether maybe one of them had even picked him up. But it turned out that the owner of the taxi company, Owen Nixon, was a registered police informant, and I wasn't to go anywhere near him or his drivers, even though I was looking at them as potential witnesses.'

Grace looked at Blake, whose shock equalled hers. 'There was no mention of a taxi, let alone a specific logo, in your official notes,' she said.

'No,' Melanie said drily.

'You never suspected that one of Owen Nixon's drivers might be responsible for the assaults?'

'Not until another woman was attacked by a cab driver in almost identical circumstances. She either couldn't identify the company logo or, if she did, it wasn't recorded.' Melanie clapped her hands on her thighs as if marking a conclusion to their discussion. 'Anyway, I've told you, for what it's worth. You don't have to believe me, but I thought you should know.'

'Do you think there was a deliberate cover-up?' Grace asked.

Melanie shrugged her shoulders and played with her ring again. 'When DI Jupp warned me off, he said it was because he was protecting an informant.'

'DNA evidence links the Nixon family to items found at the scene of Heather Bowyer's murder,' Grace told her quietly. 'Whether or not DI Jupp actually knew the further damage he was doing, he shielded a killer.'

Melanie's cheeks paled beneath her make-up. 'I should have pushed harder. I should have done more. To think there might've been a chance to stop him before—'

'You're here now,' said Grace. 'And we are actively pursuing the other rape allegations and locating as many of the original complainants as possible. Anything more you can remember would be very helpful, especially anything that might help confirm that we've identified the right people.'

'Of course,' she said. 'I did my best to record everything that I could, but I wasn't on duty when the other women came forward, and I know that at least two of them withdrew their complaints – or were persuaded to.' For the first time she looked embarrassed. 'I also tipped off the local paper. I would never have dreamt of doing such a thing, but this man was a danger to women and we were failing in our duty. I resigned soon after.'

'I don't blame you,' said Grace. 'One last question. It's recorded in your notes, without any comment, that each woman had lost a shoe. I wonder if you can fill in any more detail?'

Melanie frowned. 'The first woman I dealt with was anxious that I write it down, but she wouldn't explain why. I thought it was because he'd used a shoe to— You know, as an aggravated assault. So when I noticed that the second woman had also lost one of her shoes, I made a note of it.'

'Did you ask either of them what happened to their shoes?'

'I tried, but they were both in such a terrible state and I didn't want to make it worse.'

'What about whether the shoes were similar in any way?'

'I don't remember. I suppose I should have recorded it. Look, I'm not making excuses, but I had no training and Southend nick on a Saturday night was hardly the ideal place to win the trust of a woman who'd just been raped at knifepoint. I suppose I was relying on the medical examination and a later interview, but I wasn't allowed to accompany them to the hospital and we never heard from them again.'

Melanie rose to her feet. 'I know you need evidence, and I've not given you much more than gossip,' she said, 'but it's been on my mind for a long time.'

'You've been more helpful than you know,' said Grace. 'Thank you for coming in.'

As Blake showed Melanie out, Grace sat back down in the soft interview room, glad of a little space and time to herself. She tried to think through everything in order from the beginning. A familial DNA match linked a member of Deborah Shillingford's family to the knife found embedded in Heather Bowyer's back. Her brother Reece's DNA was a partial match to the mixed DNA retrieved from the man's leather glove also found at the scene, but not to the full profile on the murder weapon. But if Reece had been wearing gloves, then his DNA might not have transferred to the knife. And, even if Larry Nixon's DNA proved to be an exact match to the knife, that could be because Larry had previously handled it in the family kitchen.

Could the opposite also be true? That Larry had worn gloves previously worn by his brother? He might have known to wipe away any fingerprints on the knife, but – justifiably ignorant of future advances in the science of DNA – unknowingly deposited his own epithelial cells there as he did so.

So far, the existence of a glove found at the scene of Heather's murder had not been revealed to either the media or the Nixon family. Making sense of the DNA evidence was complicated, especially given how recent the science was, and she doubted that Larry's grasp of the subject would be crystal-clear. It would be interesting to see how he reacted to the information that Reece's partial DNA match wasn't conclusive of guilt.

But she was getting ahead of herself: they wouldn't have

Larry's own DNA results until after the weekend, and he might not even be a match to the profile on the knife.

She realised, with a sinking heart, that while finding a familial DNA match had indeed spectacularly narrowed down the search for a needle in a haystack, the DNA evidence alone was not going to rule either brother in or out. She had discovered not one, but two needles in her haystack.

26

The drive to Southend offered Grace a useful stretch of time in which to take soundings from Blake about Larry Nixon. She was unsure how to begin without it appearing that she continued to blame Carolyn for the loss of what was now clearly – to her, anyway – vital evidence: the clothes Larry had been wearing the night his brother and sister-in-law had died. Although she felt she had every right to be annoyed at the junior officer for failing to do her job properly, she also knew that she was no longer able to disentangle that from her feelings about what she'd glimpsed – or thought she'd glimpsed – the other night. *Jealousy*, she told herself, that's what she'd felt. She had to own it for what it was.

She glanced at Blake behind the wheel. He gave her a brief smile before looking back at the road.

'Have we missed a trick?' she asked. 'Could Larry, not Reece, be our man?'

'Not much use speculating until we get the DNA results, is there?' he said. 'What's made you suspect Larry all of a sudden?'

She ran through her arguments – that Larry could have invented Reece's confession, set the fire at Reece's house himself and conveniently got rid of his fire-damaged clothes.

'So what you're suggesting,' Blake responded, 'is that, as a young man, Larry was a serial rapist and a murderer and now, to escape arrest for those crimes, he's also committed arson and fratricide?'

'Don't forget the murder of Kirsty Nixon.'

'He's kept it together pretty well over the intervening years.'

'You could argue that if he's narcissistic, controlled and calculating, then self-preservation would come high on his list.'

'Which doesn't exactly square with dashing impulsively into a burning building to rescue two strangers on the night of the Bowyer murder,' Blake reminded her.

'So you don't buy it?'

'If we get a match on the DNA it'll be enough for an arrest,' he said, 'then we can interview him under caution, search his flat, comb through his entire life. If we turf something up, fine, otherwise I'm inclined to stick with Reece being a rapist who never meant to kill Heather Bowyer, and who spent his life doing his best to atone for it. Why else did he have those press cuttings in his attic and sit there with a bottle of whatever while his house burned down around him? And it accounts for why Kirsty was dead before the fire – he didn't want her to suffer. I don't see Larry bothering to risk killing her beforehand if she was already asleep in bed.'

Grace frowned. She knew Blake's reasoning was right. She'd only met Reece Nixon for a few minutes, and yet every instinct screamed that Larry, not Reece, might be their man. 'What if Reece had kept the cuttings because he'd always suspected Larry?' she asked.

'I think you're stretching things to fit a theory,' he said. 'Stick to facts.'

'What about this media conference later?' she asked. 'We have to give some response to that bloody nuisance of a podcast.'

'Invite Larry to take part,' Blake said promptly.

She laughed. 'Of course! That's so brilliant. See if he dares to shed crocodile tears in front of the national media! I'll call Hilary and ask her to suggest it to Colin.'

Blake drove in silence while she spoke first to Hilary, and then to Colin, and then to Hilary once more. She looked up to find that they had arrived at their destination, an anonymous office block on the outskirts of Southend where Cara Chalkley worked as a claims negotiator for a large insurance company.

Grace let out a breath. 'Right,' she said, 'let's see what was missed at the time about the reported rapes.'

As they entered the building and were directed to a lift to take them to the third floor, she felt a mix of emotions: anxiety on behalf of the woman about to be asked to relive an unresolved trauma, but also an adrenalin rush at the hope that this meeting might clarify the ambiguities at the heart of her investigation.

Cara Chalkley was waiting by the lifts as they emerged and greeted them matter-of-factly, explaining that she'd cleared it with her line manager to take as much time as they needed. In her mid-forties, with a tired face and unloved hair, she wore sensible shoes and looked as if she'd put on weight since buying the navy skirt and jacket that had probably cost a tenth of the smart business suit Melanie Riggs had been wearing. She led the way briskly to a small meeting room and appeared so completely unfazed by the reason for their visit that Grace almost wondered if they'd identified the wrong woman.

'No, I remember it as if it was yesterday,' Cara said as soon as they had settled around the bland office table. 'It doesn't upset me any more. It's more like I'm watching a film of it happening to someone else, yet I can see it all absolutely clearly.'

'Do you think you'd be able to recognise your assailant?' Grace asked. 'We have some photographs we'd like to show you.'

Michael and Anne had only been able to produce a couple of images of their father when he was in his twenties, one of them a wedding photograph from which the technical people reproduced a digital headshot. They'd done the same with a photograph of Larry Nixon from the contemporary newspaper coverage of his role in the Marineland fire. Both images had been compiled into a page of headshots with other men of similar age. The two brothers, at twenty-five and twenty-three, had been strikingly similar, and Grace wasn't hopeful that, after all this time, anyone who hadn't known them would be able to choose between them in a line-up.

Blake laid the sheet in front of Cara, who scanned the rows of faces, biting her lip nervously, but then shook her head. 'Sorry, no. What I see in my "film" is only what I registered at the time. I know I must have seen his face when I got into the taxi, but you just see a face, don't you, not a person? I think he was youngish, white, and I don't remember anything else, not even whether he had long hair or a beard. By the time I'd realised we weren't going the right way he'd put on a hood, like a balaclava. And I'd had a lot to drink.'

Grace watched Blake note down the details. The statement taken by a different police officer – not Melanie Riggs – when Cara reported the attack had been sketchy, but what Cara was describing could so easily have been Heather Bowyer's experience also.

'Can you remember anything about the car?' asked Grace, as Blake put the headshots aside. 'Colour, make, company logo?' She held her breath, hoping against hope that Cara would identify one of Owen Nixon's taxicabs.

'No, sorry.'

Grace hid her disappointment. 'Where did he take you?' she asked.

'Southchurch Park. He had a knife. Dragged me out of the car and kept it at my throat.'

'Can you describe the knife?'

'Like a big kitchen knife.'

'Like this?' asked Blake, showing her a photograph of the knife used to murder Heather Bowyer.

Cara nodded and then pressed her lips together and looked away quickly. Blake placed the photograph back out of sight in the file from which he'd taken it.

'We're sorry to have to inflict this on you,' said Grace, 'but we hope we're getting close to identifying the man who raped you.'

'How? After so long? Why are you even bothering? No one did at the time.'

'We think the assault you reported may be linked to a murder inquiry,' said Grace.

Cara nodded, her silence a sign of how hard she was trying to hold on to her carapace of competence and efficiency. 'You want to know what happened?'

'Please, if it's not too distressing.'

'I was nineteen,' she began after a pause. 'Had a row with my boyfriend and walked off, hailed a cab. I wasn't thinking about what route we were taking, barely realised we'd stopped until he'd opened the door and grabbed me. He already had this black hood on and a big knife at my throat. Bent my arm up behind my back. It hurt so much I thought he was going to break it. He dragged me some way into the park, threw me down on my front and knelt on my back while he pulled off my shirt. When I yelled, he knelt harder. He shoved my shirt into my mouth and tied it around the back of my head and yanked up my arms and somehow wrapped it around my wrists, too. I don't know how he did it. It was only loosely tied, but I was too frightened to move anyway. Then he rolled me over onto my back. That really hurt. My shoulder was sore for weeks. He showed me the knife, then did a few little jabs with it at my throat, here' – she touched a spot beneath her right ear – 'then he reached down and took off my shoes and then my pants.'

Barely any of this detail had made it into the official statement, yet Grace couldn't believe this wasn't the story told to the police at the time: evidence, perhaps, if Melanie Riggs was right, of DI Jupp's pernicious influence.

'Did he wear a condom?' Grace asked.

'I don't know. Maybe. I couldn't see what he was doing.'

'In your statement you mentioned losing a shoe.'

'I didn't lose it,' Cara said vehemently. 'He took it. That's why I insisted that the officer who questioned me wrote it down.'

Grace couldn't help glancing at Blake, but tried to hide her elation. 'Can you tell me any more?'

'After he got my pants off he put one of my shoes on the ground right next to my head. Kept repositioning it so it was exactly where he wanted it. Looked at it the whole time he—'

'Did you see him take it afterwards?'

'No,' said Cara. 'He'd rolled me back over so my face was pushed into the ground. I was too scared to move. It wasn't that hard to untangle myself, but I was afraid he was going to kill me.'

'Did you hear him leave?'

Cara shook her head. 'I waited ages to make sure he wasn't still hanging around.'

'Did he ever speak?'

'He must have done when I got in the cab, but I don't remember a voice.'

'What about a smell? Or what he was wearing?'

Cara shook her head once more. 'No, sorry, I don't remember.'

'And the shoe?'

'Gone. The other one was there, so I looked for it because it would've made it easier to get out of there. It was late and I didn't have the courage to go banging on doors around the park and wake people up. He may have thrown it into the bushes or something, but I'm convinced he took it. All the time he was— He never took his eyes off it. He hardly looked at me.'

'What was the shoe like?'

'White, only cheap plastic but a classic stiletto.'

'Was it the left or right one that you couldn't find?'

Cara thought for a moment. 'Left.' She cupped her mouth and gave a gulping, wailing sob. Her eyes filled with tears and she looked away, fighting to regain control. After a couple of deep breaths, she looked from Grace to Blake and back. 'You actually believe me,' she said flatly. 'You really do, don't you?'

'We don't think you were the only woman he attacked,' said Grace.

Cara's face puckered and big tears rolled down her cheeks. 'It was like no one ever believed me.'

Grace dug in her bag, found a clean tissue and handed it over.

'The policeman I spoke to laughed when I told him about the shoe,' Cara continued. 'Said now I was gilding the lily. Even my boyfriend said I must've gone along with it, that I went off with a taxi driver just to spite him.'

'Were you medically examined?'

'They sent me to the hospital. I had to sit in A&E with all the Saturday-night drunks. I'd had enough by then. I know I should have stuck it out, but all I wanted was to go home, lock the door and have a hot bath. When I went back to the police the next day they said that proved I'd been lying all along.'

'I'm so sorry you didn't receive proper respect and support,' said Grace. 'It's inexcusable.'

Cara took a deep breath and sat up straight. 'Not being believed, that was almost worse. Like being raped all over again. I can't tell you what it means to see in your eyes that you don't think I'm lying.'

'I'm glad to hear that,' said Grace. 'As a detective in these situations, I'm always concerned that all we're doing is making things worse.'

Cara shook her head firmly. 'You haven't, I promise.'

'One last question before we go,' said Grace. 'Can you recall if he was wearing gloves?'

Cara thought about it and then made an expression of surprise. 'He was! I'd forgotten I knew that, but yes, he was.'

'You're sure?' asked Grace. 'I don't want to put ideas in your head if you're not certain.'

'Black gloves. Maybe leather.' She shuddered. 'I can remember the feel of them.'

'OK, thank you.' Grace rose to her feet and handed Cara her card. 'If you remember anything else, however insignificant, do please get in touch. And again, I can only apologise for how inconsiderately you were treated at the time.'

Cara walked them out. A lift arrived promptly and, as Grace and Blake went in, Cara held her hand across the open doors. 'By the way,' she said, 'I don't know if it's helpful or not, but it was like the only proof I had – for me, anyway – that I hadn't made it all up, so I never threw away the other shoe.'

Cara took her hand away and the lift doors began to close. Grace jabbed at the buttons, eager to tell Cara that they would want to take the shoe away for forensic examination as soon as possible.

'I'm not sure exactly where it'll be,' Cara said doubtfully, 'but I'll have put it somewhere. I'll search my cupboards and give you a call.'

Grace thanked her, crossing her fingers that the shoe would be easily found, and was about to press the button to close the doors when Cara once again held them back. 'You will let me know, won't you?' she asked. 'As soon as you catch him?'

Grace promised and, as the lift descended, turned to Blake, her eyes shining. 'If she finds that shoe, it might not mean anything for the investigation, but somehow it makes me feel like we're getting close, can almost reach out and touch him.'

'We'll nail this, whatever it takes.' He smiled and raised his hand. For a split second she thought he was about to caress her cheek, but, as the lift stopped and the doors opened, all he did was lightly touch her shoulder to usher her out before him.

27

Grace took her seat between Superintendent Pitman and Larry Nixon at the table set up in front of a large panel bearing the Essex Police crest and the logo 'Protecting and Serving Essex'. Scanning the gathering of reporters, she saw at least one cameraman, and crossed her fingers that this would not become one of those media events endlessly played and replayed once the supposedly grieving relative appealing for help had been unmasked as the scheming perpetrator.

She also couldn't fail to notice Ivo sitting in the front row. He smiled at her, but, with so many eyes upon her, she could only give a polite nod in return. Beside him, perched right on the edge of his chair and looking around expectantly, sat a much younger man whom she didn't recognise. Was this Freddie Craig? Hilary had told them that Freddie's podcast interview with Larry Nixon was already going viral and, while Grace had no real right to condemn Ivo for doing his job, she couldn't help being annoyed that he had assisted this novice to torpedo her investigation. Larry's revelations in the podcast interview had placed the police and the media firmly back on opposing sides. However much she longed to ask Ivo if he could shed any light on what Melanie Riggs had said about DI Jason Jupp, she'd have to maintain clear and solid boundaries.

Hilary introduced everyone and then Colin made a brief statement that Grace knew had taken nearly an hour to get exactly right. His primary concern had been damage limitation for the force's reputation (by which he meant his own), while hers had been to appeal directly to anyone who might have information. Hilary had managed to steer a delicate line between the two, as well as including a tribute to the courage of Heather Bowyer's family.

The beauty of having Larry there in person – thanks to Blake's inspired suggestion – was that his account of Reece's confession could be reprised without the police needing to confirm or deny it themselves. Their explanation that, while new DNA evidence connecting Reece Nixon to the scene was a genuine break-through in the case, it was not conclusive, tacitly suggested that Larry's evidence, too, remained questionable.

It immediately became clear that the media were only inter-ested in Larry, besieging him with questions about what Reece had been like, whether he had suffered remorse, about Larry's earliest suspicions, and whether he thought his brother had ever told anyone the truth.

'How do you feel now that the truth is out?' was Ivo's question.

'Gutted,' Larry replied. 'Most of all that I couldn't save him, and that I hadn't been able to help him when he clearly felt so cornered, so desperate. I was too slow to react, too shocked by what he'd told me on the phone.'

'And if he was here now,' Ivo continued, 'what would you say to him?'

'That, whatever he'd done, his family would stand by him. That it's never too late to be sorry and ask forgiveness.'

Grace was sitting beside Larry, his knee almost touching hers. She fought to remain still, not to shift further away or allow her face to reveal her turmoil. Was it possible that a man who had cold-bloodedly murdered his own brother in order to evade justice could really look so calmly into a camera and talk such cant about forgiveness? What level of wickedness did that require? She strove to hear some ring of inauthenticity in his voice, but, if this man was a liar, then he was one of the best she'd ever encountered. Or he was innocent, and it was *she* who should be condemned for her dark suspicions.

The young man whom Grace assumed was Freddie Craig raised a hand. Larry nodded and waited for his question.

'You were hurt in your attempt to save your brother and sister-in-law from the fire at their house. Can you show us the extent of your injuries?'

Until now Larry had kept his bandaged hands and arms more or less out of sight beneath the table, but now he raised them in response to the question. Several people lifted cameras and smartphones to take photographs, and Larry remained with his arms up, twisting his head slowly from one side of the room to the other until everyone had their picture. Grace found the composure of his gestures troubling. In the footage she'd seen of those media interviews in which a killer had trembled and wept and pleaded for their missing stepchild to come home or for the public to help catch a monster, it had seemed clear, in hindsight, that those criminals were shedding crocodile tears. Maybe Larry had seen the same footage and knew better than to overdo his performance. It was impossible to tell.

As Hilary took over, thanking Larry and preparing the way for Grace to make her request for information, he turned to

Grace and gave a helpless little shrug, as if to say, *What else could I do?* Could this really be the same man who, wearing a balaclava, had dragged Cara Chalkley out of his taxi at knifepoint? She shuddered, and could only hope that he didn't notice her reaction.

Hilary had finished speaking, and it was time for Grace to look into the camera lens and make the little speech that Colin had reluctantly agreed to include.

'Thanks to modern forensic science,' she said, 'we are closer than we have ever been to closing this case. However, there is one other avenue of investigation that may help bring this inquiry to a conclusion. Heather Bowyer was raped before she was killed. We believe that there may be other women who suffered a sexual assault in Southend in the years around 1990 to 1992, who, for whatever reason, did not report it to the police at the time. I appeal to them to come forward and speak to us now. We'd also like to hear from women who did report it, but who perhaps feel that more could have been done. I realise how difficult this may be, but you can talk to a female officer and, should you wish, any contact with us can remain confidential. Thank you.'

Was it her imagination or, as she was speaking, had she sensed Larry stiffen beside her like an animal sensing danger?

28

Ivo awoke from a nightmare in which the walls of a prison cell were closing in around him. Or was it one of the spartan dormitories of his prep school where he'd slept for four years from the age of nine? A wave of regret engulfed him. He had plenty to choose from – his mother, who died when he was ten; his distant father, also dead; two failed marriages; a grown-up daughter he hadn't spoken to in years and countless other nameless griefs and fuck-ups. Yet most immediately upsetting, if he was honest, was the fact that Grace Fisher had pretty much blanked him at yesterday's presser.

Of course he understood why. Officially, they were barely supposed to know one another. And, with Freddie stuck to him like glue, he wouldn't have approached her anyway. But it had been good to see her again. Somehow he always felt like he was a slightly better person when he was around her. When they'd first met, he'd dubbed her the Ice Maiden, but, after witnessing her dogged passion for justice, he'd changed his mind. All the same, watching her walk off at the end of the media conference without any kind of personal acknowledgement had been like waving to his parents as they drove away and left him at the start of term. He simply hadn't expected to feel so bereft.

It was still dark, but not so early that he couldn't get up and start the day rather than lie sleepless in bed. He put the kettle on for coffee and stared out across damp autumnal gardens to the patchwork of windows spread across the back of the Victorian terrace opposite. There were always one or two lights left burning – to reassure young children, he assumed – plus, in some, the tiny, eerie red or green glow of LED standby indicators. It would be another hour or so before daylight, but there was enough murky light in the sky to make out the movement of a wood pigeon huffing up its feathers in the branches of an ivy-clad sycamore.

Ivo knew very well what had provoked his bad dream, so depressingly banal in its use of stock nightmare imagery. He'd been genuinely delighted that Freddie had got his scoop – the best way for the kid to make a name for himself was to stir up trouble – but maybe it had been a mistake to give him so much of a helping hand. Ivo hoped it wasn't merely because of the flattery that he'd taken a liking to the kid. OK, so sometimes Freddie had laid it on a bit thick, begging for more and more tall tales of Ivo's youth, but schmoozing the punter was a vital part of the job and it was quite nice to be on the receiving end for a change. All the same, telling those stories had churned up old memories and disturbed one or two of the slimier bottom-feeders that were now enjoying a good thrash around in his subconscious.

To distract himself, he wondered if he had been like Freddie at that age. The kid was eager and appreciative, sharp-witted and enterprising, but with a spiky chip on his shoulder that accentuated his immaturity. Although Ivo had been equally immature, there'd been no chip on his shoulder – or not towards the world he'd wormed his way into, anyway. A motherless only child, he'd had his issues, but nothing a few beers followed by a double gin wouldn't dispel. No, he'd been thrilled to be accepted into the newsroom, first on a local paper and then in Fleet Street. Too thrilled, perhaps. He could see now how his own youthful eagerness had made him an easy mark for an old hand like DI Jason Jupp.

To begin with, like Freddie, he'd simply wanted to be part of the club, hanging out with the veteran reporters and listening to their yarns. And later, by the time the last national paper had left Fleet Street and the tabloid world had become more vicious, his drinking was occupying most of his time and ingenuity.

As the kettle boiled he tried to think how his younger self would pass judgement on the shipwreck he'd become . . . *Shit happens, get over it*, probably. But then that had been the joy of being twenty-five. You believed you were rust-proof, that the slow corrosion of shame and regret would never catch up with you. He couldn't remember when he'd last allowed himself to revisit any memory in which he'd felt hopeful and optimistic. Those were the memories he took the most care to avoid.

He poured water over the granules and stirred them into a semblance of coffee. No good feeling sorry for himself. Each of the blank windows staring back across the autumnal gardens hid a story. His was no different. Being an alcoholic didn't make him special.

Freddie still imagined that taking a life had made Heather Bowyer's killer different, had singled him out and marked him as forever damned. But Ivo wasn't so sure. Freddie had asked him about all the murderers he'd watched as they sat in the dock day after day. Truth was that, during long trials full of dull legal arguments, even the worst of them had nearly dozed off. Like them, Reece Nixon was more likely to have simply shrugged off what he'd done and carried on, preoccupied not with the dark reaches of his soul, but with the same daily chores as everybody else.

All that Ivo had so far managed to discover about Reece Nixon's life seemed to support that: a business just managing to stay afloat; a wife and two veg; looking forward to getting his mortgage paid off. Maybe he'd atoned in whatever way he could, reinvented himself as a boy scout who helped old ladies across the road. After all, there was no shortage of stories about lifers who appeared genuinely changed, filled with special sweetness and wisdom. In the end, most murderers were like everybody else, both good and bad.

So why the dramatic exit after the police came calling? Maybe Reece had been one step away from topping himself for years, and the knock on his door had finally freed him to check out. Most people would assume it was from fear of exposure or of the punishment to follow, but Ivo had a different theory. He knew a thing or two about punishment – about doling it out to the hapless miscreants he wrote about, and his own visceral need to feel punished. Not that it alleviated the pain for long, at best tipping the scales and balancing the books for a while, but it offered some meaning to his existence. It was probably why he'd so ferociously embraced the merciless front-page deluge of blame and shame, because deep down he knew that such a scourging was what he himself deserved. Handing out such inhumanity to others in order to feed his readers' desire for justice of the flogging and hanging kind helped to cut off any retreat into accepting kindness or forgiveness for himself.

No, Ivo reckoned he understood Reece Nixon's suicide better than most. Punishment was far easier to accept than understanding and compassion.

Especially if you hadn't yet admitted to yourself what you'd done.

29

🔊

Welcome back to *Stories from the Fire*. I'm Freddie Craig, and I'm here in Southend retracing nineteen-year-old Heather Bowyer's last steps – which means I'm also walking in the footsteps of Reece Nixon, the man whom even his own brother believes raped and killed her.

Reece Nixon was working as a taxi driver at the time of Heather's murder, but we're not sure whether that night he was in a car or on foot. Nor do we know if Heather's abduction was a spur-of-the-moment decision or whether he had been watching her all evening. Was she his first victim? Or had he already stalked and raped other women before?

We do know that Heather arrived with friends by train from her home in Chelmsford and spent the evening drinking and dancing in various pubs and clubs along the seafront close to Southend's famous pleasure pier – the longest in the world.

This wasn't date-rape. Heather's friends didn't notice anyone paying her particular attention: no one bought her a drink and she didn't flirt with anyone. She hadn't been 'asking for it', hadn't brushed Reece off and hurt his feelings, or left him thinking he was owed a shag. He was a stranger who came out of the darkness with a knife, a man who set out that night with the desire to hurt a woman.

Perhaps Reece had spent the evening cruising the streets, playing music on his car stereo and picking up fares while also waiting to spot the right victim. One of Heather's friends said he caught the strains of this song you're hearing from a passing car as they walked back to the station shortly before she disappeared.

We now also know that the police are widening their investigation of this cold case to include other sexual assaults. It seems that unlucky Heather might not have been his first victim, although she appears to have been his last.

What was it about Heather that made him pounce? Was he specifically looking for someone like her? Had she triggered something in him, or would any woman have served his purpose that early autumn night?

How do you decide to rape a woman? When I was at university, I'll hold my hands up and admit there were times when I went on a night out thinking it would be nice to end up in bed with someone. Who doesn't? But my aim was to hook up with a woman who also fancied having sex with me. To be honest, it's how I first got together with my girlfriend, and we've been together for two years.

Right now, I'm in a phone box near the Kursaal casino and amusement arcade, close to where Heather and her friends would have walked. It's plastered with tart-cards advertising the services of local prostitutes. Some have drawings or photographs of semi-naked women, nearly all with large breasts and many wearing black leather. Other cards are merely names and phone numbers. Calling one of these numbers is the nearest I can get to imagining having sex with a woman who hasn't chosen whether or not it's me she wants to have sex with.

I don't find large breasts or black leather erotic. But maybe that doesn't matter because they're just shorthand, a semiotics of sex signalling that I can have whatever I want.

Is that how it starts? Having the power to choose, being in control, doing whatever I want regardless of what she might prefer? Even to do something to her that she actively doesn't want or like but is prepared to go along with in return for cash? Something that hurts or humiliates her and makes me feel dominant? I can put a coin into this pay phone, punch out a number, end up in a bedroom with a woman where I can play out any fantasy I want. She'll fall in love with me. She'll beg me to do the thing my girlfriend doesn't like. She'll be in awe of my sexual prowess. I can make her afraid of me.

And afterwards? I think maybe the realisation that it was just business and I'd paid not to be rejected would make me angry and resentful. Next time I'd really want to show her who's boss.

I'm not a rapist or a murderer but I'm trying hard to understand what it was like to drag Heather at knifepoint into Cliff Gardens. I'm trying to put myself inside Reece's head. You were aroused not by lust, but by the excitement of power and absolute control. Planning your attack must have been an intellectual challenge worthy of your unrecognised abilities. You enjoyed it when she struggled, got off on her fear and her desperation to escape with her life. Lucky Heather, you thought, she's the one who finally gets to understand who I really am.

And then you killed her.

And after that? Did you really just go home? How do you do

that? Did you catch the football results and go to bed, with your secret still tingling inside you? And not just on that night but for the next twenty-five years?

They say Reece Nixon led a blameless life, but I think that his kind of secret, told to no one, suspected by no one, must have been empowering. You're not who everybody thinks you are. You're the killer next door, and they don't even begin to have a clue. Only your brother, Larry, had his suspicions, and you avoided him.

RN Garden Services. All those times when you were putting up a fence or laying a patio or cutting back a hedge, and some nice woman brought you out a mug of tea with never a care in the world about what might be in your head. By way of thanks, were you watching her through windows, up a ladder peeping into her bathroom or bedroom? Fantasising about what you could do if only you chose, because you *knew* you could – you'd done it before. When you smiled and asked for two sugars, were you really picturing what you'd done to Heather that night in Cliff Gardens?

Twenty-five years is a long time, but I don't believe you ever forgot a single detail.

RN Garden Services. If you have employed the services of Reece Nixon and have a story to tell, you can get in touch through the contact details on the webpage.

I'm Freddie Craig. Thank you for listening to *Stories from the Fire*, brought to you with support from the *Daily Courier*, Britain's favourite newspaper.

30

Grace's sister was dropping in for lunch in Wivenhoe before heading home after her course, and, as Grace prepared vegetables for soup, she caught up with Freddie Craig's latest podcast. In the background of this episode he played a song she recognised as 'Love Is A Stranger' by the Eurythmics. A shiver ran down her spine as she listened to Annie Lennox's velvety voice singing about how desire and obsession felt like being tempted into an open car and driven helplessly away. Adjusting the heat under a pan of gently frying pancetta, she listened more closely. According to Freddie – and she supposed he'd learnt it from Ivo as there was nothing about it in the police files – one of Heather's friends had caught the strains of this music from a car that passed them on their way to the station.

It was always possible that Heather's friend *had* mentioned it to an officer who'd considered it irrelevant and not recorded it. Regardless of whether, at the time, it would have linked up to something else of significance, the lyrics unquestionably made a haunting background to Freddie's weird speculations about how Heather had been snatched off the street.

Freddie had assumed with absolute conviction that Reece Nixon was her killer – Grace supposed he was hardly likely to start casting doubt on his own scoop – but the very creepiness of the young man's voyeurism only reinforced her instinct that the disturbed predator he described had not been the hardworking family man she'd met so briefly. Even the weekend newspapers, which had been full of stories about him, had been unable to dish up any real dirt on him.

'Love is a stranger, in an open car . . .'

Was it Reece or Larry who had played that music in his car? Reece had been about to marry Kirsty, who was already pregnant with Michael, a son who described his father as a kind, sweet man. Grace wasn't especially familiar with the Eurythmics' music – slightly before her time – but, as she pushed leeks, celery and shallots off the chopping board into the pan, she recalled having heard it recently. Where had that been?

On Larry Nixon's silky-smooth sound system.

Her grip on the kitchen knife tightened involuntarily. She found herself staring at her own whitened knuckles around the handle of the sharp blade. However hard it would be to convince others, she was more and more certain that Larry Nixon, successful businessman and owner of a sleek, minimalist apartment, the hero of the Marineland fire, with photographs of his bandaged arms plastered across the weekend tabloids, was capable not only of multiple rape and murder, but also of burning his brother and sister-in-law to death and of standing by and waiting for the flames to engulf the house before he called the fire brigade.

Or was she being ridiculous? It was only a pop song! For all she knew, Freddie Craig had hijacked it merely because the lyrics were so spookily apt. She would have to find a way to ask Ivo. And even if Heather's friend *had* heard the music that night, dozens of cars must have driven past while they were walking to the station. Reece and Larry were of a similar age; they might both have continued to enjoy listening to a duo popular when they'd been teenagers.

She had to get this right. She owed it to Heather's family, to Michael and Anne Nixon and to Heather.

Annie Lennox sang on, repeating the lines about wanting, about obsession . . .

And then there were the shoes. Reece had been oblivious to the high heels she had worn, but she had caught Larry staring at them. Cara Chalkley had called the day before to say that she had found the shoe she'd kept all these years, the pair to the one she claimed had been taken by the man who raped her. Grace had immediately dispatched an officer to collect it, log it as evidence and deliver it to the forensics team. Cara's attacker had worn gloves, but the lab might still retrieve some fingerprint or DNA evidence. And if he'd taken its pair, Grace was certain he'd have kept it. Wendy and her team had thoroughly searched Reece's outbuildings and what was left of his house, but found nothing. Would they find Cara Chalkley's matching shoe concealed somewhere in Larry's apartment?

Grace had checked in with the office earlier that morning. Calls had been coming in steadily since Friday's media conference, nothing significant so far, but various snippets that all helped to paint a picture of people and events twenty-five years ago. She started to jot down notes, making mind-maps around any promising leads, considering ways to build on the information they were gathering.

The doorbell rang. Grace welcomed Alison with a mixture of frustration and guilt. She wanted to be a good sister, but she also wanted to focus on the scattered jigsaw pieces of this case. Reminding herself that nothing could really fall into place until they had Larry Nixon's DNA results, she went to check on the soup and was pleased to see that the addition of pearl barley had thickened it up nicely. Alison proved to be full of lively chat about her course and the other people on it, and they parted after lunch with a warm hug. Grace stood on the doorstep to wave her off and felt a pang of loss, along with a rush of pleasure that, for an hour or so at least, she seemed to have got the balance of life right.

31

Grace arrived at work on Monday morning to find the whole team welcoming Joan and Duncan back from their honeymoon. She added her greetings to the rest, delighted to see Duncan looking happier and more relaxed than she could ever remember seeing him. Joan, too, was glowing with health and contentment. Marriage was clearly going to suit them both. And Grace had a private reason to celebrate her detective constable's return to duty: it meant she could send Carolyn Bromfield back to the DVU. To be fair, there was no reason to suppose that Carolyn wouldn't develop into a useful member of the team, but her secondment was never intended to be permanent. And besides, if Carolyn and Blake were now pursuing a relationship outside work, then it was up to their boss to minimise its impact on their colleagues. Grace told herself it wasn't personal, it was good practice.

At her desk she worked through the list she'd made the day before, starting with a call to Wendy to make sure that work on Cara Chalkley's shoe would be fast-tracked. She also asked the crime scene manager if it was possible for someone to have planted the file of newspaper cuttings in Reece Nixon's attic. Disappointingly Wendy said that, while they hadn't been able to lift any fingerprints, the file had been covered in undisturbed dust. It hadn't been moved in years. She added, however, that the lab had promised to send Larry Nixon's DNA results to her later that day.

Grace then rang Dr Tripathi, who had left a message to say that he now had the toxicology reports on Reece and Kirsty Nixon.

'There was nothing more than very low blood alcohol in Kirsty Nixon,' he told her, 'so the most likely assumption is that her death was due to suffocation, from being either smothered or possibly strangled. Reece Nixon did, however, have very high blood alcohol.'

'Which is what we expected,' she said.

'Yes. It wasn't in lethal range, but enough to have incapacitated his reactions and his ability to escape from the fire. No other toxins were found.'

'So there's nothing to contradict Larry Nixon's story?' she asked.

'No,' he said. 'Nothing.'

'OK, thanks, Samit.' She hung up and stared out of her window. She felt like all she could see in this case were confusing shards of light darting in too many directions at once. Plausibility, a familiar strain of music, a glance at her high-heeled shoe, Larry's body language at the media conference: it wasn't anywhere near enough to accuse a man of murder. Damn Carolyn and those missing clothes!

A thought struck her, and she called Samit's number again. 'Sorry to bother you, but can I ask what might be a stupid question?'

'Fire away.'

'Is it possible that Larry Nixon's burns could have been deliberately infected to stop you examining them?'

There was a long pause at the other end of the line as Samit considered his reply. 'They were more badly infected than one might expect,' he said finally. 'But he must have realised that a serious infection can lead to blood poisoning. You can die from septicaemia.'

'If he's guilty, then he's facing life imprisonment,' she argued. 'At his age he could very well expect to die in jail.'

'It's still a pretty big risk for an uncertain outcome,' he said. 'And it must hurt like hell.'

'OK, well, thanks anyway.' Making sense of her suspicions felt like trying to distinguish a solid shape beneath a glittering reflective surface. 'I warned you it was a stupid question.'

'On the other hand,' Samit said as she was about to hang up, 'once the infection has healed it won't be possible to interpret the burns to any degree of legal accuracy. I have to admit it would be a very clever thing for an arsonist to do.'

'So you wouldn't entirely rule it out?'

'I'd keep an open mind, but there's no final answer.'

'Thanks, Samit.'

As she ended the call the internal phone on her desk rang. She picked it up. 'DI Fisher.'

It was the front desk. 'There's a woman here that one of your team might want to speak to, ma'am. In connection with other offences in Southend in 1992.'

'Right, thank you. I'll get someone down there.'

She looked out into the main office, where everybody seemed to be already busy on the phone or diligently typing. Keen to take some kind of positive action, she decided to go downstairs herself and hear what the woman wanted to say.

When Grace saw the figure sitting in the waiting area she

was moved to pity. Painfully thin, in child-size black jeans with fashionable rips at the knees and a ratty fur gilet probably purchased in a charity shop, the woman looked as if, for far too long, she had been spending her money on drugs instead of food. From the half-inch of grey along the parting in her hair, Grace guessed she was only in her mid-forties, but she could easily have been mistaken for sixty. She stood up as Grace came towards her, hugging a flimsy blue-and-white-striped carrier bag to her chest.

'I saw you on the TV,' she said, her smile revealing a missing tooth.

'That's right.' Grace gave an answering smile. 'I'm Grace Fisher. Can I get you a cup of tea or coffee?'

'No, you're all right.' She jittered from one foot to the other. 'Got to be somewhere soon, you know?'

'Then I won't keep you,' said Grace. 'Come in here where we can talk.'

She showed the woman into a soft interview room and offered her a chair. 'May I have your name?'

'Rather not, if you don't mind. That's OK, isn't it?'

'It's up to you,' said Grace. 'The important thing is that you're here. Do you live locally? I hope you've not had to come far.'

'Been in Colchester a few months. Probably move on again soon.'

'Well, thank you for coming in. What is it you'd like to tell us?'

'The guy next sitting to you on the telly,' she said. 'I'd heard him on the news before, like years ago. I recognised his voice.'

'Larry Nixon?'

The woman shrugged. 'I don't know. But I know his voice. Never forgot his voice.'

Grace felt the skin on the nape of her neck tingle. 'Why not?'

'He raped me.' She sniffed and wiped the back of her hand across her nose. 'In Cliff Gardens when I was eighteen.'

'It must be hard for you to tell me that, so thank you. Do you mind me asking how old you are now?'

'Forty-three.'

'Did you report the assault to the police at the time?'

The woman gave a rasping laugh. 'Why would I bother? I had a caution for soliciting. They'd have said it was an occupational hazard. Though it wasn't like that. He wasn't a client. He just grabbed me out of nowhere.'

'I'm sorry you didn't feel the police would have listened. We'll try and do better for you this time.'

'Nah, I don't want it followed up. Don't have the time for courts and what-not, you know?' She put her hands on the table to push herself to her feet. 'Just thought you should know. Up to you to nail the bastard.'

'Wait, please, just a few more questions,' said Grace. 'You only recognised his voice, not his face. Why was that?'

'He had like a mask. And a knife. But then, a few months later, he was on the local radio, to do with that big fire in South-end. And right away I knew that voice. I saw his picture and his name in the paper, but I only recognised the voice.'

'You still didn't feel able to report the assault?'

'He was like the big hero already. I was a working girl.' This time she did rise to her feet. 'Look, I've really got to go now. Sorry.'

'Wait, your shoes. Was he interested in your shoes? Did he take one?'

'What? No. I don't think so. Maybe. I don't remember.' She

picked up her plastic bag, the cans in it clunking together, and edged towards the door.

'Did you see any kind of car nearby, or going past before or afterwards?'

'Nah, look, I need to go now.'

'May I have some contact details in case we want to get back in touch?' asked Grace.

'No, not my scene. Sorry. Can you show me out?'

'Yes, of course,' said Grace, going to open the door. 'Thank you for telling me this. It's invaluable information. If you reconsider, please come back, or call me. I can always come and meet you if that's easier.'

The woman took the card Grace handed her then, head down, made straight for the exit and disappeared outside. Grace thanked the civilian on the front desk and ran up the stairs back to the MIT office. An anonymous identification was not evidence that she could take to court, but it was proof enough to convince her that she was right. And it was yet another allegation of rape. No wonder Larry had limited Reece's supposed confession to a single event and been careful not to open the door to a wider investigation.

Blake got to his feet as soon as she walked in. 'Boss? DNA results are back. Larry Nixon's an exact match to the trace DNA on the knife.'

'That's good enough to arrest him,' she said. 'And to search any premises under his control. Let's get on it.'

32

As Grace got out of the car in Southend at five minutes to seven the following morning, she felt slightly dizzy from the adrenalin rush of excitement and apprehension. The sun was up, but only just, and a brisk wind blew in off the sea across the road from Larry Nixon's apartment block. She had spent the previous day planning the arrest and interview strategy and it struck her now that Larry lived right at the heart of the map she'd made of where the crimes she was about to accuse him of had been committed. Perhaps Freddie Craig's speculations about Heather's gloating killer getting a buzz out of his physical proximity to the locations of his assaults were not so far-fetched after all.

She looked across at Blake as he locked the car. He nodded back, unable to suppress a grin. Duncan, who was leading the search team, pulled into the parking space beside them. A second search team would be arriving simultaneously at Larry's business premises. There was no real need for Grace to be here at all except that she wanted to witness Larry's reaction first-hand. She had little expectation of being able to charge him any time soon, but she wanted to use the shock value of a full-on arrest to add to the pressure of his having to answer questions under caution.

The night porter was handing over to the daytime concierge as they all entered the lobby. Blake had a quick word and then they crammed into the lift together, pushing the button for the seventh floor.

The first expression on Larry Nixon's face as he opened his door in response to Blake's pounding was one of anger. Grace watched closely as it changed swiftly to alarm and then to something more interesting: a mixture of hurt and resignation that she was sure was entirely fake.

Blake did not respond to Larry's exclamations and stood aside for Grace to step forward and make the arrest. 'Larry Nixon, we're here to tell you that the results of your DNA test confirm that your DNA profile is an exact match to the DNA found on the knife used to kill Heather Bowyer in 1992. I am therefore arresting you on suspicion of the murder of Heather Bowyer. We will also be asking questions related to the deaths of Kirsty Nixon and Reece Nixon. I must caution you that you do not have to say anything. But it may harm your defence if you do not mention, when questioned, something which you later rely on in court. Anything you do say may be given in evidence.'

Larry shook his head in apparent bewilderment as she handed him a piece of paper. 'We have a warrant to search this address. We have also been granted a warrant to search the offices of your business, Alpha Limos.'

'What on earth are you hoping to find?' he asked. 'You're wasting your time.'

'Sergeant Langley will accompany you while you get dressed,' she said, 'and then you'll be taken to police headquarters in Colchester for questioning.'

'You know what I've got to say!'

'Sergeant Langley?'

Blake placed a hand on Larry's arm, urging him to do as Grace had said. Larry looked down at his black Calvin Klein sleep pants and top and, shaking his head one more time, consented to go with Blake. By the time he emerged from his bedroom, dressed in a dark business suit and a grey linen collarless shirt, Duncan and the two other members of the search team had pulled on blue protective gloves and started work on the storage units that lined the wall behind the dining table. Seeing Larry glance at what they were doing, Grace hoped he felt an appropriate level of invasion and interference.

Coming out of the lift, Blake took hold of Larry's arm while Grace walked on his other side, well aware that the concierge was scrutinising their exit. They drove in silence to Colchester, with Blake driving and Grace sitting beside Larry in the back. As the custody sergeant booked him in and he responded politely and laughed on cue when the sergeant made a small joke, she observed with satisfaction from the thin line of his mouth and his clenched fingers that his anger was beginning to build. She instructed the gaoler to offer him a hot drink and a microwaved breakfast and then leave him to kick his heels in a cell for half an hour.

'So far so good,' she said to Blake, as they made their way upstairs in search of coffee.

'Yes,' said Blake, 'but he's had twenty-five years to come up with a good story, remember.'

'That's what I'm banking on,' she replied. 'That he'll offer far more detail than he needs to. Detail that we can check and hopefully disprove.'

'He didn't want a lawyer,' Blake observed. 'Shows how confident he must feel.'

'Yet if he was innocent, and genuinely thought the DNA evidence was going to trap him into some nightmarish miscarriage of justice, you'd imagine he'd be screaming for a good lawyer to come and sort it all out, wouldn't you?'

'I certainly would,' he agreed.

They had reached the MIT kitchen area and Grace, desperate for caffeine after their early start, reached immediately for the kettle. Blake leaned against the worktop beside her, folding his arms and watching absently as she shook ground coffee into a filter. 'We're going to be busy, right, boss?'

'Looks like it.'

'So will you be keeping DC Bromfield on?'

'Not now Duncan's back,' she said, trying not to sound sharp. 'I need to keep an eye on the budget.'

'But you can find some wiggle-room, can't you? We're going to need all the bodies we can get.'

'We'll manage.'

'Look, Grace, Carolyn knows how badly she messed up, but she's really keen to stay part of the team.'

I bet she is! Grace strove to hide her desperation. 'Let's wait and see. Any word from Wendy on when we can expect the forensics on Cara Chalkley's shoe?'

'I'll text her.'

She was relieved when Blake shifted his attention to his phone. She lifted the kettle, blinking angrily, and concentrated on pouring boiling water onto the coffee grounds with a shaky hand, no longer able to kid herself that she was capable of taking a dispassionate decision about Carolyn's future.

They took their coffee to her cubicle, where they could run through her strategy notes before the interview. Grace resented her loss of focus and found it hard not to blame Blake for championing the younger woman. Larry was going to be a tricky enough customer without her wasting energy being upset about something that was no longer any of her business.

She'd seen how some suspects could be highly sensitive to the mood of the interviewing officer. She expected that Larry might be one of them, and she didn't want him gaining an advantage by letting him pick up on the fact that she was rattled by something. But then an idea struck her: he knew nothing of the extent of their investigation and, rather than demolish his confidence, it might be far more effective to build on it in the hope of leading him into making detailed statements, on record, that she could then test and disprove. Sometimes a detective had to be a good actor, and if she could make him think she was now regretting his arrest and fearing it was a bad mistake for which she'd be held to account, that might play to her advantage.

'Change of plan,' she told Blake. 'You can monitor the interview on the video feed. I want Carolyn in with me.'

He frowned. 'She's not done any interview training.'

'I don't care. She won't have to say anything. Come on, let's get her prepped.'

33

Grace took her seat opposite Larry Nixon. She spread various bits of paperwork out in front of her, leaving DC Carolyn Bromfield, wearing lipstick, hastily applied red nail polish and a borrowed pair of high-heeled shoes, little choice but to place herself next to him.

After they had all named themselves so that their identities were recorded on tape, and Grace had informed Larry that the interview was being remotely monitored, she began. 'You're here because your DNA sample matched the profile found on the knife used to kill Heather Bowyer in Southend in 1992. I will therefore be asking you about the events of that night. I will also be asking you about the deaths of Reece and Kirsty Nixon.' She leaned back with an anxious smile. 'I'm sure you can see my problem. If it can be shown that you, and not your brother, murdered Heather Bowyer, then a scenario in which he confessed before committing suicide no longer seems credible.'

Larry shook his head in sorrow. 'I haven't killed anyone.'

'But you understand why we need to establish exactly what happened on the night that your brother died?'

'I'd like to know, too,' he said, glancing at Carolyn, who nodded encouragingly.

'Good,' said Grace. 'But first, please begin by telling me every-thing you can remember about the events leading up to the Marineland fire. At what time did you leave home?'

Grace led him courteously through his movements, wanting to know what he was wearing, the car he was driving, what fares he picked up, who else he spoke to, what and when he ate and when he relieved himself. She then moved on to the fire at Reece Nixon's home. As the questions became more and more specific, Carolyn crossed and uncrossed her legs and jiggled her foot up and down. Once, as Grace asked the same question for a third time, Carolyn cast up her eyes and shot Larry an embarrassed smile. Intercept-ing the look, Grace shuffled her papers apologetically and said that it was her responsibility to establish all the relevant facts.

As Larry Nixon relaxed he seemed almost to enjoy retelling the stories of the two fires in which he had featured as the hero. It seemed to Grace, listening carefully, that his current narra-tions differed very little from those she had heard before. However gently she pushed, he had added nothing new and offered no superfluous detail. It made some sense that maybe he had spoken about the Marineland fire so often over the past twenty-five years that the telling had become a fixed narrative, but that could hardly be the case for the recent traumatic and chaotic events at his brother's home.

'I still can't believe that Reece is dead,' he ended. 'It's a tragedy.'

'Have you been in touch with his son or daughter?' she asked.

'No, I didn't like to intrude.'

'You've said that you and Reece weren't close, but what about in 1992, when you were both still living at home? Did you hang out with each other much?'

'We were working pretty hard, helping Dad build up the business.'

'And when you weren't working? Did you spend much time at home together?'

'We had different friends. We didn't socialise together much.'

'Did you watch television? Eat together? Who did the cooking, for instance?'

For the first time Larry looked uncomfortable, making Grace wonder if he was trying to work out what answer would best account for his DNA on the knife.

'Once Mum had gone Dad used to get girls in to help out. Otherwise it was the microwave or fry-ups.'

'Are you handy with a frying pan?'

'You can get away with junk food when you're young. I try to work out and eat a bit healthier now.'

'You and Reece were quite close in age; did you ever borrow each other's clothes?'

'I was younger, and money was tight, so yes, there were always hand-me-downs. But, look, I don't understand. You already said you have DNA that connects Reece to the murder, but now you're saying it's mine. So how does that work?'

'We have a full DNA profile from the murder weapon which matches your DNA but not your brother's. However, we also have mixed and partial DNA from a glove recovered from the scene.'

'A glove?'

'Yes.' Grace could all but see his mind whirring, but wanted to keep the temperature low. 'Reece was a match to the partial DNA recovered from the glove, which also includes genetic markers that you both share.'

'But if I didn't kill anyone, how could you find my DNA on the knife?'

'The DNA is what's known as trace DNA. Because it's now possible to analyse very small and also invisible fragments of skin cells or sweat, we can now show who could have touched or handled an object.'

'It so complicated, I'm not sure I always understand it,' said Carolyn, right on cue.

Larry smiled at her and sat back. 'Well, there you are. I could easily have handled a knife that Reece took from the kitchen.'

'And that remains a possibility,' said Grace. 'But you can see our difficulty, why we need to be so thorough?'

'Everyone knows where I was that night,' he said. 'Dozens of people saw me. I couldn't have killed Heather, so why would I want to kill Reece?'

'Let's explore an alternative version of events based on the premise that you did kill Heather Bowyer in Cliff Gardens shortly before making your way along the road towards the Marineland resort.' Grace allowed a note of hesitation to creep into her voice. 'Your brother had some reason at the time to suspect you of the crime. That's why he moved away and kept contact to a minimum. Nonetheless, after we called to ask him for a DNA sample, he decided to speak to you, either to warn you or to beg you to tell us the truth. Maybe he threatened to share whatever he knew with us. When he wouldn't answer your repeated calls, you drove to his house. He let you in, which is why you didn't need a key.'

Larry was looking down at his hands, clasped between his knees, and now he shook his head in silent denial.

'Either he was already fairly drunk or the two of you sat

talking and drinking together while Kirsty went to bed,' Grace went on. 'He wouldn't back down, or you simply felt he was too much of a liability, so you kept topping up his glass until he'd pretty much passed out.'

Larry raised his arms to show the dressings that covered his burns. 'I wanted to save him. I called the emergency services.'

'You slipped up to their bedroom and smothered Kirsty with a pillow. Your business is cars, and you both learned from your father to keep spare petrol at hand so that a vehicle low on fuel would never delay a job. It was easy for you to guess that you'd find petrol in one of Reece's outbuildings. You used it to set fire to the house, targeting the rooms where Reece and Kirsty were already passed out or dead. The rest we know.'

Larry shook his head in mute distress.

'Do you have any response to that scenario, Mr Nixon? Now is the time to speak. I should remind you of the caution you were given, that it may harm your defence if you do not mention when questioned something which you later rely on in court.'

'That's not what happened. What else can I say?'

'You have nothing further to add concerning any of these events, that you brought about your brother's death in order to cover up your part in the murder of Heather Bowyer?'

'I'm sorry, but no, of course I don't. You have your killer. My poor brother, Reece.'

'Very well. Interview suspended at ten fourteen.' Grace clicked off the recording equipment and gathered up her papers.

'What happens now?' asked Larry.

'You'll be taken back to your cell.'

'And after that?'

'We'll let you know.'

As Larry remained seated, absorbing his immediate future, Grace stood up, keeping her gaze away from Carolyn, who also pushed back her chair and got to her feet. As she did so, she stumbled as the heel of her left shoe scraped sideways and her ankle folded. Gripping the table she lifted her stockinged foot out of the shoe and, tottering in an ungainly way on the other high-heel, grimaced in pain and rubbed her leg.

Larry Nixon bent down and solicitously picked up the discarded shoe, his fingers cupping it as if it were a precious jewel. As he handed it back to Carolyn, who laughed and apologised for being so clumsy, he slipped one finger inside the rim. Grace only just caught his fleeting look of ecstasy.

34

'I didn't think he'd buy it,' said Carolyn, as soon as they were out of earshot of the custody area.

'I didn't either.' Grace was shaking with shock and relief. 'You played a blinder. Thank you.'

'That was so cool!' Carolyn's eyes shone with delight. 'Blake told me you were brilliant, and you are!'

'Sadly, it's not evidence.'

'No, but we saw why there was only one shoe found with Heather Bowyer's body.'

'It's still meaningless to anyone else.'

Colin and Blake were waiting for them in the superintendent's office. Grace knew that they had both been watching the video feed of the interview, but she wasn't sure whether they would have been able to catch the way Larry had handled the high-heeled shoe.

'Did you see?' Carolyn asked excitedly.

'Only that he picked it up,' said Blake. 'What did we miss?'

'It meant something to him,' said Grace.

'It was creepy,' said Carolyn.

Grace gave her a warning look to make her pipe down. Larry Nixon's reaction *had* been creepy, but it was important that they took his fetish seriously, and the last thing Grace wanted was a junior officer making silly remarks in front of their boss. She turned to Blake. 'Has the search of Larry's flat unearthed anything of interest?'

'No. Some fairly vanilla adult porn. His passport shows visas for a couple of trips a year to Thailand, which could be sex tourism. We took a quick look at his computer. Straight after our first contact he made several searches for DNA evidence and DNA science, but then so did Reece.'

'And so would I if the police arrived out of the blue asking me for a DNA sample,' said Colin.

'Exactly,' Blake agreed. 'He does, however, have nearly every Eurythmics album ever made.'

'You can't bang a man up for his musical tastes,' said Colin.

Grace laughed politely. 'What about the forensics on Cara Chalkley's shoe?'

Blake shook his head. 'Nothing found. No fingerprints or DNA other than hers.'

'Damn! Even a partial would have given us a way in,' she said. 'We need something to shake his confidence.'

'He's had years in which to prepare himself for this,' said Colin. 'Seems to me he's been very canny so far about not saying anything that he couldn't have learned from media reports. We need to take him off-piste, send him down a black run and see if he trips himself up.'

'I've been researching shoe fetishists,' said Grace. 'There are two types, apparently. One kind may be inadequate, with poor social skills and possible masochistic tendencies. For them the fetish object is a way of avoiding a feared rejection or humiliation if they were to approach a woman.'

'Doesn't sound like Larry,' said Blake.

'Could fit Reece Nixon, though,' said Colin. He raised his hands in surrender at the others' reactions. 'Just playing devil's advocate here. The crimes stopped when he got married and had a kid. Found a woman who accepted him for who he was.'

'That's possible,' said Grace. 'The other type of paraphiliac is an obsessive who is into power and domination. He will be prepared to steal or even to assault a woman in order to acquire the shoes, which he may then slash or burn. For both types, sexual arousal may become impossible without the fetish object.'

Carolyn grimaced. 'If you'd *seen* the look on his face when he rubbed the inside of the shoe I was wearing. I'm glad I only borrowed it. I'd never be able to wear it again!'

'The second type is the right profile fit for the man who carried out the multiple rapes in Southend,' said Grace. 'I've seen nothing so far to rule Larry out.'

'So what made him stop?' asked Colin.

'I have a theory about that,' said Grace. 'Those podcasts gave me the idea, going on about fate and destiny. If Larry killed Heather Bowyer, then he did so right before running into a burning building and rescuing those two boys. It gave him the perfect alibi. Would have disguised any of Heather's blood on his clothes. Maybe it gave him an outlet for whatever heightened emotions he was experiencing, especially if he hadn't set out to kill her. But it also made him famous, too famous, perhaps, to risk reoffending, at least on his home turf. Most of all – and this is my theory – it turned him into a hero, gave him a new identity. If he's into power and domination, then maybe this new persona gratified those desires in some way, fed into his grandiosity. Maybe that's why he was so sure he could get away with last week's arson and could justify to himself the need to murder his brother and sister-in-law.'

Colin nodded. 'I don't dispute your psychology, Grace,' he said, 'but we need some hard evidence from somewhere to back it up.'

'I know.'

'Larry Nixon has no live-in partner and has never been married,' said Blake. 'If he's stopped offending, then where is he getting his kicks? I know we don't want to go public yet about the shoes, but we could ask around among the local sex workers about men with special tastes. See if any of them know him.'

'Good idea,' said Colin.

'And I want to go back over all the coverage of the Marineland fire,' said Grace. 'So far no one's tested Larry Nixon's alibi for the night of Heather's murder. We've always assumed that he couldn't have been in two places at once, but we don't know precisely when she died. We need to establish a proper timeline and plot Larry's movements immediately before the fire.'

'And how do you plan to do that a quarter of a century down the line?' asked Colin.

'We'll just have to use old-fashioned methods,' she said. 'Spend some time in Southend, ask around, jog memories. I'm hoping that people who remember the fire will also remember where they were and what they saw.'

'Hilary can put you in touch with the local paper,' said Colin. 'I'm sure they'd run an appeal for people to come forward.'

'Larry was driving his cab that night. People would be reasonably familiar with the firm's cars and drivers. Someone might remember seeing him.'

'Or Reece.' Colin's tone sounded a warning note.

'Or Reece,' Grace conceded.

'We're still tracking down the original rape complainants,' said Blake. 'Now we have photographs of two potential suspects to show them, we might get a positive identification.'

'And now?' said Colin. 'Do you want to carry on with a second interview, or do we release Larry Nixon on police bail?'

'I say we let him go pending further enquiries,' said Grace. 'Let him think we were just covering our backs and that we still buy into his story that it was Reece.'

'He'll have to surrender his passport if he gets bail,' said Blake, 'so at least he won't be able to scarper off to some palm-fringed resort with no extradition treaty while we make further enquiries.'

'I'm not sure he would anyway,' she said. 'Fleeing the country would be tantamount to an admission of guilt, and I'm not sure Larry Nixon will allow himself to admit to what he's done. Besides, we'll keep eyes on him.'

'Bail him to return in a week,' said Colin. 'I can't allow this to drag on too long. We only have limited manpower and resources.'

His reminder was superfluous, and Grace suspected that the superintendent's true concern – which, God knows, she shared – was that they might have come so tantalisingly close to solving the case – now in full view of the media – only to face the possibility of leaving empty-handed. She guessed that Colin was also considering the impact on his career. She didn't entirely blame him, but then he wasn't the one who would eventually have to break it to Monica Bowyer that they had come this far, only to fail.

Her boss's self-interest shone an uncomfortable light on her own desire to send Carolyn back to DVU. 'Sir,' she said, before she could have second thoughts. 'I'd like to keep DC Brom-field on the Major Investigation Team for a little longer. I realise that resources are tight, but she's proved her value to the investigation.'

Carolyn went pink with pleasure, holding her breath for Colin's reply.

'Very well,' he said. 'Two more weeks and then we can review it.' He swung his chair to face his computer screen. They were dismissed.

'Thank you, boss!' Carolyn said as soon as they'd left the superintendent's office.

'So long as you're not afraid of hard work,' Grace said awkwardly.

'Of course not! Thank you.'

Behind her, Blake also gave Grace a warm smile. His gratitude was almost more than she could bear.

35

Hello and welcome back to *Stories from the Fire*. I'm Freddie Craig, and I've been thinking a lot about sex. I should also warn you that this episode discusses subjects that may be offensive to some listeners, so please use your discretion.

Have you noticed how, once your attention is snagged by something you've never given much thought to before, you then can't escape it? You realise it surrounds you constantly, that your world is saturated by it. So I've been thinking about sex, specifically about buying it, and suddenly it's there for the asking. Everywhere. A massage parlour in the high street; a girl on the street corner; even a card in a newsagent's window.

An online search for personal, adult or escort services will offer pretty much whatever you want and at a wide range of prices. It becomes clear to me that in residential streets all over England, mixed in beside the local primary school, GPs' surgery, supermarket and municipal park, there are ordinary-looking pebble-dashed terraced houses that are brothels. For many men they're clearly just another normal local amenity, conveniently situated between the pub and the kebab shop.

You might have to enter by a back gate so as not to annoy the neighbours. A maid lets you in and it's up the stairs and into one of the tatty little bedrooms. A bed, a sink and a couple of mir-rors. Drawn curtains and some rosy lighting disguise a reality that wouldn't look very arousing in daylight. The woman whose services you're paying for – so much for hand relief, more for full sex – will be of almost any nationality. Some are young, trafficked from Eastern Europe; others are middle-aged and choose to fly in from EU countries to work for a couple of weeks a month. Many of the women, of course, grew up in a nearby street, went to that local primary school and were offered their first taste of drugs hanging around the swings in the park.

I make my excuses and leave.

Besides, I think that kind of set-up was too safe and domestic for Heather Bowyer's killer. I think Reece Nixon would have pre-ferred an element of the hunt. In Southend that meant exploring east of the pier, the area around Southchurch Park. Ambleside Drive is a haunt of street prostitutes and, until the car park was fenced off and better lighting installed, the park was where the girls did business. Was that where he liked to go, either watch-ing or taking part? Or was paying for sex too easy, like shooting fish in a barrel?

Nowadays of course you can submerge yourself in online porn, but not back in 1992. Then the world-wide web was only getting started – not that it took long for people to see its poten-tial for sexual encounters. Now more than ten per cent of all content on the internet is pornographic – billions of dollars' worth – and the menu is encyclopedic, all tastes catered for. It's normal to watch porn online, right? But that's not our guy, either. Heather's killer wanted the knife at her throat, the smell of her fear and the thrill of jeopardy – that he might be caught in the act.

So I go stalking.

I start on the corner of Royal Parade, by the hotel where Lady Hamilton once threw a ball for Lord Nelson. I have a good view from here, up the pedestrianised shopping street towards the train station and down towards the gaudy lights of Adventure Island and the pier. I need a woman on her own, or one like Heather, who looks as if I could easily separate her from the group she's with. Within minutes, I realise that I am looking at the young women who walk past with new eyes, judging them by criteria I have never considered before. I'm looking for a woman who will be the perfect victim.

I'm Freddie Craig, and you've been listening to *Stories from the Fire*.

36

With its pleasing horizontal lines, flat roof and nautical blue-and-white facade, Southend's police station was a perfect example of optimistic early 1960s architecture. As Grace and Blake approached the front entrance, she smiled and drew his attention to the nice retro touch of a blue police lamp mounted on one side of the zigzag portico.

Blake had called ahead and agreed a time to speak to Inspector Dave Clements, the officer in charge of community policing, yet twenty-five minutes later they were still kicking their heels in the recently refurbished reception area. Under the eye of the civilian at the front desk they didn't want to show any irritation, but the intention was clear: to put the visitors from the Major Investigation Team in their place. The tacit hostility left Grace reluctant to discuss the case if it meant disclosing details she didn't want overheard, so, as the hands of the wall clock ticked past the half-hour, she sat beside Blake in silence, giving her plenty of time in which to regret the loss of their old easy intimacy.

She was well aware that the unaccustomed stiffness between them originated with her, but, over the course of the hour-long drive to Southend, her self-consciousness had communicated itself to him and they had completed the journey in silence.

She was relieved when Dave Clements finally arrived to greet them. He was full of affable apology, although he gave no reason for their long wait. He led them up to his small first-floor office, where they declined his offer of tea or coffee.

Determined not to react to the delay, Grace did her best to appear oblivious. 'I hope we're not here on a wild-goose chase,' she began, 'but as you know, we've reopened a cold case here on your patch, although it was long before your time.'

'The Heather Bowyer murder,' said the inspector.

'Yes. We have new DNA evidence, but it's inconclusive.'

'But you're looking at Reece Nixon?'

'And his brother Larry. DNA links both of them to the crime.'

'You're not suggesting they acted together?'

'No, not at all,' she said, 'but, if possible, we'd like to eliminate Larry by closing the time gap between Heather's murder and the Marineland fire.'

Clements laughed. 'You're optimistic!'

'We've got some old TV film coverage of the aftermath of the fire,' said Grace. 'We're asking the local BBC news to run it alongside an appeal. I'm hoping people will remember where they were, what they saw.'

Clements gave her an appraising look. 'So where do *we* come in?'

'Local knowledge,' she said. 'Any officers still around who were serving back then? Do they know of people who had businesses open on a Saturday night – pubs, places to eat, amusement arcades – anyone who was regularly out and about?

The Nixon brothers were both taxi drivers, so it would be helpful to speak to any other cab drivers working in 1992.'

Clements frowned. 'You're still looking at Reece as your primary suspect, right?'

As Grace met his eyes she recalled Melanie Riggs's revelation that Owen Nixon had once been a registered police informant. 'Would it be a problem if Larry Nixon was in the frame?'

'Of course not,' Clements said promptly. 'Although I'd be pretty surprised. He's always very supportive of my officers. His limo company offers generous police federation discounts, and I've attended several weddings where he's provided not only the cars, but excellent service.'

'Does he offer that because his father was a registered police informant?' she asked.

'I have no knowledge of that,' said Clements.

Grace didn't believe him. 'So you don't know if Owen Nixon is still an informant?'

'We don't have much call for that kind of intelligence-led work any more,' he said. 'Anything bigger than antisocial behaviour and persistent offenders, we hand over to your lot.'

Grace saw Blake trying to catch her eye. When she did, he looked down at his hands, where he was making the ghost of a handshake. She gave him a tiny nod of assent.

'We went to talk to Owen Nixon last week,' Blake said. 'He's a Freemason, isn't he?'

'No idea,' said Clements, barely hiding his irritation. 'I don't mix in those circles. But look, it's thanks to Larry Nixon that I didn't have to go to the funerals of two of my school friends when I was fifteen. I was with Kevin Barnes and Phil Langstone that night, the two lads who broke into the old Marineland complex.'

'You were there?'

'Yes. Only I didn't have the bottle to go roaming around that huge empty place with them in the dark.'

'So what did you do?' asked Grace, comprehending better now where his opposition might be coming from.

'I hung around for a while, waiting for them to come out, and then set off home. I ran back there as soon as I saw the fire engines.'

'Which way was home?'

'My parents lived in Westcliff.'

Grace looked at Blake, disappointed: Cliff Gardens was in the opposite direction. 'You didn't happen to see which direction Larry had come from?' she asked.

'I only saw him when he brought them both out.'

'Did you notice a Nixon taxi pass you as you were walking away?'

'I'm not sure I would have registered it if I had.'

'But you don't remember seeing one?'

'No.' Clements must have sensed the importance of the question, for he clearly disliked being pressed to offer information that might somehow incriminate Larry Nixon.

'Can you remember what time Kevin and Phil entered the building?' Blake asked. 'Or how long they were inside before the fire took hold?'

'I can't give you a timeline,' said Clements, 'but I hung around for maybe ten or fifteen minutes. And then I must've walked for about another ten minutes before all the commotion started.'

'Are you still in touch with either of them?' asked Grace.

'Phil's still around, but Kevin and his family moved away a long time ago. I don't know what Phil can tell you other than that Larry saved his life.'

'He may have noticed something that would never have seemed significant,' said Grace, 'something that would now be useful.'

'About Larry?' Clements asked sharply.

'Yes, about Larry.'

The inspector studied his fingernails. 'You're here because you want local knowledge,' he said at last, 'so let me give you some. Three stops on the train from here the line ends. After Shoeburyness you can choose between sea or marsh. There's nowhere else to go. So we look out for one another. You can take that however you like, but I was there that night, and believe me, Larry Nixon was a hero.'

'And if he turns out also to be a multiple rapist and a murderer?' Grace asked.

'You show me the evidence and I'll cuff him for you,' he said. 'Southend might be a dead end, but it isn't the Wild West.'

'What about when DI Jupp was in charge?' she asked. 'From what I've heard he liked to think he was the law in this town.'

'So what? He's dead,' said the inspector.

'Whoever killed Heather Bowyer was a serial rapist,' she said. 'Something DI Jupp appeared to overlook. Do you have a view on that?'

'I can't help you,' said Clements. 'I was a schoolboy when Jupp was running things.'

'So what is DI Jupp's posthumous reputation around here? Could he have been corrupt, or was he just incompetent?'

The hostility in the inspector's eyes was clear, but Grace no longer cared. Clements looked pointedly at his watch. 'If you don't mind, DI Fisher, I don't have time for ancient history. Tell me what help you want and we'll get right on it.'

Exasperated at his stonewalling, Grace let Blake answer. 'We'd like to talk to local sex workers,' he said. 'We're looking for a client who has very specific requirements.'

'We're not exactly their favourite people right now,' said Clements. 'We've just completed an initiative, cautioning kerb-crawlers and handing out community protection notices to the girls. A lot of them need money for drugs, which means they breach the notices the same day they're issued and then they land up in court. Doesn't make them happy.'

'We'd still like to talk to them,' said Blake.

'I'll see what I can do.'

Grace got to her feet. 'We can pursue this inquiry independently if we have to. But if we end up treading on toes or upsetting local sensibilities, don't say we didn't approach you first.'

'We're overstretched as it is,' said Clements, also standing up. 'If you lot over in Colchester can afford the luxury of reopening ancient cases that everyone else has forgotten, then knock yourselves out.'

Grace had had enough. 'Inspector Clements, you seem to think that we've come swanning into your nick merely because we like throwing our weight about, but I can give you a whole list of people who have most certainly not forgotten these crimes, and they're the reason I'm here. I get why you'd be pissed off with how the force has been restructured, and how you might feel pushed aside, but if I find at any point that you or your officers have been deliberately obstructive, believe me, I will bury you.'

Clements blanked her. 'A pleasure meeting you too, DI Fisher. Let me walk you out.'

Back under the zigzag portico Grace clenched her fists, too angry to speak. Blake raised an eyebrow. 'So that went well, boss.'

His smile made her laugh. 'I just blew up the bridge there, didn't I?'

He grinned. 'Sky-high.'

37

Far more leaves littered the car park than remained on the surrounding trees, and rain dripped from the denuded branches onto the roof of the car. At eight forty-five it had only been fully light for an hour. Anne and Michael Nixon had secured the first slot of the day for their parents' burial service, a wise move in Grace's opinion, given the thankfully small group of press photographers already huddled together where they could keep watch on the entrance. She was pretty sure she'd spotted Ivo among them. It would be very useful to have a private chat with him, but, with Blake beside her in the driver's seat, she'd have to wait until she could peel Ivo away by himself.

Determined to protect Blake from any possible fallout from her previous dealings with Ivo, she'd kept her unconventional friendship with the reporter secret. But Blake had sensed that she was keeping something from him, and it had been her refusal to explain that had led him to end their budding relationship. At the time, he'd felt keenly that she didn't trust him enough to tell the truth, but that hadn't been the reason. She'd needed Ivo's help to solve a case, yet if it had come out that she'd shared information with a journalist, she'd have been subject to disciplinary action, if not outright dismissal. And, if she'd told

Blake and expected *him* to keep quiet, she'd have made him complicit. She had simply been too afraid of dragging him into trouble. But it was no good regretting all that now.

She looked out of the car window at the modern red-brick crematorium chapel. She hated this kind of duty, but right now even the smallest insight they could gain into the Nixon family could only be helpful. She was pleased for Anne and Michael's sake that the coroner had acted without delay, opening and then adjourning the inquest so the bodies could be released. She only wished that she could offer them the certainty they craved about what had happened to their parents.

There weren't many cars in the car park, and most of the people she and Blake had seen making their way to the sheltered entrance where the hearses would draw up had been in their twenties, no doubt friends of the children rather than the parents. It was a miserable situation, no doubt about it.

A large black Mercedes with dark-glazed privacy windows slid into a space nearer to the crematorium. The driver and front passenger doors opened, and Larry and Owen Nixon climbed out. Owen wore a black overcoat and an old-fashioned Homburg hat; Larry a tailor-made black suit with a white shirt and black tie. Keeping their heads down, they made their way side by side into the chapel.

'I can't imagine they're going to be very welcome,' said Blake.

'No,' she agreed. 'Maybe it's time we went in too.'

The carpet and drapes were in comforting shades of purple and rose-pink, with matching upholstery on the wooden chairs. They took seats at the back, with quite a few empty rows separating them from the dozen or so mourners at the front. Grace saw that Owen and Larry occupied one side of the front row with the other half left empty for Anne and Michael, who would presumably be arriving any minute with the funeral cortège. Grace had learnt from the coroner's officer that the family had opted for burial, and assumed that after this service there would be a short graveside committal. She hoped for their sakes that the rain would clear up by then.

Behind them the doors opened to admit the two coffins carried by undertakers and topped with white flowers. Grace couldn't help recalling the curled, charred remains of Reece and Kirsty on Samit's autopsy tables and tried hard not to think about what the coffins contained. Anne and Michael, both in black, walked behind. Grace watched as they took their seats. They appeared not to notice their uncle or grandfather until Larry leaned across the aisle, offering Michael his hand. Michael gave a quick shake of his head and nudged his sister to move further along the line of chairs, away from their uncle. A young woman sitting behind Michael laid a comforting hand on his shoulder and he twisted round to give her a tense but grateful smile.

The service began with a hymn, the voices hesitant with the unfamiliar music. As the singing began to grow more confident, it was interrupted by a commotion at the entrance. Grace and Blake both looked round to see who the late arrival was and recognised Deborah Shillingford. She had tried her best to dress appropriately in a black jacket two sizes too big for her, but, red-faced and out of breath, had succeeded only in looking messy. Faced with other people turning to stare, Deborah looked around wildly and, recognising Grace, slumped in relief onto the empty chair beside her.

'I can never understand why these places have to be in the middle of nowhere,' Deborah whispered.

'Don't worry, we're still on the first hymn,' Grace replied reassuringly.

Deborah patted the large angel brooch pinned to the lapel of her jacket and picked up a hymn book. Once she had found her place, she began to sing in a clear and rather beautiful contralto.

The rest of the service was not too long drawn-out. Neither Michael nor his sister spoke, but an older man who looked vaguely familiar – Blake whispered to Grace that he thought it was Steve, who'd worked for Reece Nixon and had been in the yard the day they'd gone to ask for a DNA sample – read a short eulogy. It made no mention of the manner of Reece and Kirsty's deaths, but stressed their kindness, fairness and devotion to one another.

As the mourners filed out at the end, Anne glanced curiously at Deborah, but did not respond to her nervous smile. Grace wondered if Anne even had any idea that this woman was her aunt, raising the question of what had really taken place within this family to make its members so resolutely separate from one another.

Grace and Blake were the last to leave the chapel, but Michael was clearly watching out for them and approached immediately.

'Thanks to you, our grandmother isn't here to bury her daughter,' he began, without waiting to hear Grace's condolences. 'She didn't want them buried together because she believed in your crap, that Dad killed Mum. We know that's not true, and that Mum and Dad should be together, so we had to go against her and then she refused to come at all. She's an old woman, grieving, and it seems to us that you're doing everything you can to make it worse.'

'I'm very sorry,' Grace began. 'We're doing—'

'How long are you going to let this go on?' Michael cut in. 'You must know by now that Dad never hurt anyone!'

He looked over to where the undertakers were placing his parents' coffins back in the hearses for the short journey across the cemetery to the burial plot. Grace followed his gaze and met that of Owen Nixon. The look in his eyes wasn't grief for his son, yet almost as soon as she'd glimpsed it, it was gone, replaced by a look of concern for Deborah, who hovered behind Grace's shoulder.

'Deb,' he said, stepping forward. 'There you are. I wondered where you'd got to.'

'Dad.' Deborah shifted from foot to foot, keeping her head down like a kid outside the head teacher's office.

Owen laughed and held out his hands. 'Well, aren't you going to give your old Dad a hug?'

Grace observed Michael watching with a mixture of curiosity and disgust as Deborah stepped forward, keeping her arms by her sides and twisting her head away from her father's unwelcome embrace.

'And a hug for your brother, too,' said Owen.

Larry patted his sister's arm by way of greeting.

'So, where have you been hiding all this time?' Owen asked. 'Not cleverly enough to avoid the breathalyser, though. Silly girl, causing all this trouble.'

'What are you talking about?' Michael demanded of him. 'What are you even doing here?'

Owen turned to face him. 'Burying my son,' he said sorrowfully. 'I am very sorry for your loss. And that must be my granddaughter.' He looked over to where Anne was being comforted by Steve and two of her friends.

'You weren't welcome in my parents' house when they were alive,' said Michael, 'and you're not welcome here now.' He pivoted to Larry. 'And as for you—'

Grace stepped in front of Michael as Blake moved to head off Owen and Larry. 'Now is not the time,' she told him firmly. 'I know how you must feel, but—'

'No, you don't!' He struggled out of her grasp and tried to push past Blake, who was blocking Larry. 'You killed my parents!'

'I tried to save them,' said Larry.

'You murderer!' shouted Michael. 'You liar!'

Out of the corner of her eye, Grace saw the press photographers on the far side of the turning circle where the hearses were waiting. Their lenses were trained on the confrontation and they were all clicking away. She could also see that, despite their professionally blank expressions, the undertakers waiting beside the cars were watching avidly.

'Don't do this, Michael,' said Grace, attempting to pull him back. 'Not here, not in public.'

As Michael threw her off, Anne, in tears, came and grabbed at his other arm. 'Stop it, please. I can't bear it!'

Larry must also have noticed the cameras, for he dodged around Blake and walked calmly over to them, holding up his hands in surrender. 'Hey guys,' he called. 'Knock it off, OK? You can see how my poor young niece and nephew are almost out of their minds with everything that's happened. Just give them a break, can't you?'

One or two of the photographers continued to take pictures. Beyond them, Grace spotted Ivo. In that instant she couldn't help hating the tabloid reporter for everything he represented.

Michael appealed to Grace, his eyes not on the photographers, but on Owen. 'Are you going to stand for this? Can't you get rid of them?'

'We've done nothing wrong,' said Owen loudly, before Grace could reply. 'No one's going to tell me I don't have a right to be at my son's funeral.'

'You've paid your respects,' said Grace firmly. 'It would be better if you left now.' She addressed Michael and Anne. 'The car is waiting to take you over to where the burial service will he beld. I suggest you go. We'll deal with things here.'

Blake positioned himself in front of Owen, screening him from sight, as Grace tried to walk Michael backwards towards the cars. Anne, in tears, pulled at his arm. 'Please, Michael. Let's go. Mum and Dad are waiting.'

Michael hesitated, but then allowed Anne to lead him away. As they reached the cars, Larry, waiting beside the press pack, entreated them, 'I tried my best.'

'I know what you did to my parents,' Michael responded. 'And I hope you rot in hell for it!'

38

The Ice Maiden was living up to her name, thought Ivo, as Grace walked briskly towards him across the cemetery car park. Judging from her frosty expression, they weren't about to enjoy their usual cosy chat. Instead, she looked angry, and he had the distinct impression that it wasn't only because of the family shouting match that had erupted in full view of the snappers. If she was angry with him, then he wasn't entirely sure what he'd done to deserve it. He wasn't responsible for any Nixon family feuds. All the same, he was glad now that he'd dissuaded Freddie from coming along. Ivo hadn't wanted him earwigging on any conversation he might manage to have with the detective. It hadn't been difficult to shake Freddie off. The kid was in a state because, after his girlfriend had expressed strong objections to the tenor of his latest podcast (Ivo's editor had also voiced misgivings), she had, unsurprisingly, dumped him. Not that Freddie's romantic mishaps would prevent him being pissed off once he learnt he'd missed such an interesting fracas.

'Mr Sweatman, I wonder if you could spare me a moment?' She spoke loudly enough to signal that this encounter was going to be official.

'DI Fisher. I always have time for you.'

It was a hopeful sign at least that she'd left her sergeant in the car. Ivo knew she'd been working with DS Langley since the Merrick case in the summer. He'd watched them earlier walking into the chapel together, and reckoned there was something in the way the young man moved so easily beside her suggested he, too, had a soft spot for her. Ivo was probably reading far too much into the sergeant's manner, but he liked the idea of Grace having someone to look out for her, despite the sharp stab of envy he couldn't entirely suppress.

'This is strictly off the record,' she began. She'd never felt the need to issue that warning to him before, and it stung.

'Of course,' he told her.

'You covered Heather Bowyer's murder at the time,' she continued. 'I've read all your coverage. I wanted to ask if there was anything else you could tell me that you didn't print?'

For a second, Ivo had a clear mental image of JJ in the pub, raising a glass of Scotch to his lips with a teasing grin. There was plenty he could tell her if he chose to, but the long shadow cast by those ancient events in Southend made him uneasy. 'Depends what you're looking for,' he said.

She gave him a dusty look and he felt it shrivel what was left of his soul.

'I've been listening to *Stories from the Fire*,' she said. 'One of the episodes had some background music. Was that something you told Freddie Craig about?'

'Yes,' said Ivo, happy to be able to give her what she wanted. 'Freddie asked for something moody that would break up the words. I remembered that one of Heather's friends told me he'd heard it playing in a passing car right around the time she disappeared.'

'And the friend definitely said it was that track?' asked Grace. 'A Eurythmics song?'

'Yes, because afterwards the lyrics seemed so unbelievably apt and creepy. That's why I remembered it.'

Grace gave him another look. 'So why didn't you use it yourself?'

'My editor simply didn't believe it, thought I'd made it up, so it got subbed out.'

'Did Heather's friend say what kind of car? Was it a taxi?'

'I can't remember, sorry.'

'None of this is in any of the statements her friends gave to the police.'

'No, well, I got a bit more out of them than they were prepared to say to the police,' said Ivo. 'Thing is, part of the reason this friend of Heather's went to Southend was to score a few dozen ecstasy pills to sell to his mates back home in Chelmsford. It made him leery of having the local plod come and visit his house to ask questions.'

She frowned. 'As far as I'm aware there was no MDMA found in Heather's body. I'll have to check again what toxicology tests were done. But if she was off her face, it might explain how she could be taken off the street so easily.'

'It is the love drug,' he agreed. 'Never tried it myself, but I'm told it can make you feel very warm and fluffy towards strangers.'

'Do you think it undermines her friends' testimony about when they lost sight of her?' she asked. 'How long it was, really, before they noticed she'd gone? And whether they would have paid full attention if she had been talking to someone earlier?'

'He said they were all coming down from the drugs by the time they were heading for the station, but who knows?'

'I wonder if it's a factor in the other cases as well.' Grace seemed to be speaking to herself more than to him, but his ears pricked up.

'The sexual assaults you're investigating?'

Her cool grey eyes assessed him frankly, and then she smiled. OK so it was a rather tight little smile, not her usual warm glow, but it was a smile nonetheless.

'You saw what just happened here,' she said. 'And obviously it'll be all over the papers tomorrow. But you can see the hell that family is going through, never mind Heather Bowyer's. The thing is, the DNA puts both Reece and Larry Nixon in the frame. The only way to narrow it down is to investigate the other assaults. So if you can give me anything from 1992, even if it doesn't mean much to you, I'd be extremely grateful.'

Ivo thought hard. He didn't want to open up a box of snakes and then not be able to get the lid back on. But he also wanted to help Grace Fisher. 'The ecstasy angle might be worth pursuing,' he said finally.

'OK, thanks. There's something else I want to look at, and this really is as off the record as it can be.'

Ivo held up a hand in a three-fingered salute. 'Dib-dib-dib.'

'You, a boy scout!' She laughed, her face softening at last. 'So it's this: a WPC who tried to investigate the previous rapes was warned off even talking to anyone at Owen Nixon's taxi firm. She said it was because Owen was a registered police informant.'

Ivo felt those snakes writhing in his stomach. This was something he hadn't known.

'Did you have many dealings with DI Jason Jupp when you were in Southend back then?' she asked. 'Did he ever mention using informants?'

He tasted bile. 'Let's just say that you shouldn't put too much faith in the police record,' he said. 'DI Jupp policed Southend strictly for his own purposes and advantage.'

She didn't look surprised. He'd give a lot to learn exactly what else she already knew.

'You sound bitter,' she said. 'What else can you tell me?'

He shook his head in reply, sorry now that he'd said anything at all.

'I've already been told that DI Jupp wasn't too bothered about some silly girl from out of town getting herself killed,' Grace said. 'Waste of resources so far as he was concerned, apparently. But are you suggesting something worse? An actual cover-up? Could it have been to protect a member of the Nixon family?'

'I don't know,' he said. 'JJ was a Freemason, so that might've come into it. But as far as his lack of diligence in the Bowyer case is concerned, my money would be on simple old-fashioned sexism.'

'Why?'

Ivo thought of all the AA meetings he'd attended where it had been drummed into him that he must admit his wrongs and make amends. He looked down at the scuffed toes of his shoes. 'JJ's focus lay elsewhere.'

Grace's patient silence felt like torture. 'I didn't hear anything about Owen Nixon being an informant,' he said at last, 'but I did know about a big bust at an ecstasy factory in Southend. That's far more likely to be the reason why JJ took his eye off the ball on the Bowyer case.'

'Go on.'

She was giving him that clear, direct look of hers, and he couldn't resist. But it would be OK, he assured himself, he could tell her about this, but just not the rest of it. Never about the rest, not to anyone.

'You have to remember that this was the height of the rave scene,' he said. 'Acid house meant there was enormous demand for pills in all the clubs in Southend. Apparently, some bad stuff had been coming in from Russia with nasty side effects, so when a local conman met a chemistry graduate who needed to fund his PhD, they set up in business to make a cleaner product.'

'Sounds like *Breaking Bad*,' she said, raising a sceptical eyebrow.

'I know,' said Ivo, 'but that's how it really did operate back then. Those two imported a tableting machine and MDMA powder from Holland and began churning out thousands and thousands of pills. Called them "White Lightning" and sold them in the pubs and clubs for ten to fifteen pounds apiece, all in cash. So when JJ got a tip-off and raided the place, he found over half a million in used notes just stuffed into supermarket bags. He and a few of his closest pals split most of it among themselves.'

'Did JJ tell you this?'

'Bits of it. He liked to brag when he was in his cups. Some I heard from a girl I'd been talking to as background for the Heather Bowyer murder. The rest I pieced together myself.'

'But you never printed it?'

'No.'

To his relief she didn't ask why.

'No wonder JJ could afford to take early retirement,' was her only comment.

Ivo still felt an urge to explain everything, to vindicate himself in her eyes. 'You needed sharp elbows and sharper wits around old JJ,' he said. 'Everything had to be a deal, something in it for him, preferably cash in a brown envelope. I was a lot wetter behind the ears then than I liked to think. Looking back, I can see that I let him run rings round me.'

But she was following a different train of thought. 'Taxi drivers must overhear a lot in the back of their cabs,' she said. 'And get asked for things, too. If Owen Nixon tipped JJ off about the pill factory, and then that kind of money fell into JJ's lap, no wonder he owed Owen a favour.'

'Makes sense.'

'Did DI Jupp ever mention Owen Nixon at the time?' she asked. 'Did you ever meet him?'

'No,' he said. 'And I'd the remember the name.'

She reached out and touched his arm. 'You've been incredibly helpful, Ivo, thanks.'

Feeling as if a weight had lifted from his shoulders, he looked around and realised that the next funeral of the day was already making its way past them into the chapel. He watched the coffin on its precarious progress atop the undertakers' shoulders. Seize the day, he told himself. What else was there?

39

When Grace got back to the car, she found Deborah Shillingford hovering beside Blake and sucking on a cigarette.

'I said we'd give Ms Shillingford a lift to the train station,' he told Grace. 'It's on our way.'

'Of course,' she said, pleased at his foresight. She was longing to ask Deborah the burning question: which of her brothers did she think was the most likely to be a killer? It was impossible, of course, yet some insight might still be gleaned during a short car journey.

'I was hiding in the Ladies,' Deborah offered. 'Waiting 'til they'd all gone.'

As Blake held open the rear passenger door she took a last drag then, her hand shaking, flicked the stub onto the grass verge. 'Seeing him again was just too fucking much,' she muttered as she clambered in.

Grace sat in the front beside Blake and twisted round to face Deborah. 'Do you mean Larry or your father?' she asked.

'My dad. I thought I'd got him out of my head and now he's back, crawling all over the inside of my skull.'

'I'm sorry for your brother's death,' said Grace. 'And the way you've been thrust into the middle of this investigation. What happened just now can't have been easy.'

'No,' Deborah said. 'But he's right. It is all my fault. It always is.'

'What is?' asked Grace.

'Everything. If I hadn't got pissed and tried to drive a car, you wouldn't have my DNA and Reece would still be alive.'

'You can't let yourself think like that,' said Grace.

'True, though, isn't it? Can I smoke in here?'

'No, I'm sorry.'

'Then can you put on the blues and twos or something, and get us there faster?' Deborah aimed for a joke.

Blake did his best to laugh. 'We're only about ten minutes away.'

'Jesus, but I could do with a drink.'

'You go to meetings, don't you?' he asked. 'If you want to find out where and when the next one is around Colchester, we can drop you there instead.'

'No, don't worry. I'll call my sponsor when I get in.'

Grace recalled the pang of guilt she'd had outside Deborah's house on their first visit, and remembered the excitement she'd felt then. How conveniently she'd quashed the concern she should have for a vulnerable woman. But she'd had a job to do, and she still did. She had to make the most of this chance to find out more about the Nixon siblings' childhood.

'What happened to your mother?' she asked. 'Is she still alive?'

'No, she died,' said Deborah. 'Cancer.'

'When was that?'

'Summer of '82. She was only thirty-three. It was very quick.

Or maybe it was just what they said to kids in those days. Anyway, I left home soon after.'

'Where did you go?'

'I met a bloke and got pregnant. Couldn't wait to get away, if I'm honest. Never went back, or not if I could help it. But I can't help wondering if things would've turned out different if I'd stuck around to keep an eye on them.'

'Your brothers?'

'Yeah. They were both still at school. I felt bad leaving them.'

'Why was that?' asked Grace.

'Dad.'

'Was he violent?'

'Not often. He didn't have to be. A look was enough. He'd just, I don't know, needle away at you all the time, until you couldn't think straight.'

'Was he equally hard on all three of you?'

'I always felt he hated me most, either because I was the eldest or because I was the girl. Don't think he likes women much.'

'And your brothers?'

'Reece learned to keep his head down, and then he got out, too. Larry stayed, but then he was always the blue-eyed boy.'

'Were you close to your brothers?'

'Not really. But I always liked Reece, which is why it's so hard to get my head around what he did. Anyway, I don't really get why you're bothering, especially now he's dead. And even if he wasn't, he'd led a blameless life for twenty-five years. What purpose would it serve to lock him up now? Or is it that you get Brownie points for every case you solve?'

'It's not as simple as you think,' said Grace. 'Reece might not have been responsible for Heather Bowyer's death.'

'Then why did he kill himself?'

Grace chose not to address that question head on. 'The DNA evidence we have from the crime scene suggests that Heather's killer could be either one of your brothers.'

'Fuck me!' Deborah gave a frightened laugh. 'You're not suggesting it was Larry? He always was a cunning little bastard.'

As Blake steered into the approach road to the station, Grace caught his eye. But as they drew up, before Blake even killed the engine, Deborah was already tugging at the handle to get out. Realising that, desperate for nicotine, their passenger wasn't going to sit and answer any more questions, Grace went to open the rear door from the outside. Deborah climbed out, already fumbling with a pack of cigarettes and a lighter.

'Thanks for the lift,' she said. 'Appreciate it.'

'No problem,' said Grace. As Deborah lit up Grace once again noticed the angel brooch on her lapel. She couldn't help finding the image trite and a little tacky, but its significance to Deborah struck her as desperately poignant.

Deborah caught her looking at her and smiled, but with an odd twist to her lips. 'Don't waste your sympathy on me. Dad would laugh his guts out if he caught you feeling sorry for any of us.'

'None of this is your fault,' said Grace.

Content to take her time now that she could smoke, Deborah shook her head. 'So you still think Reece killed himself?'

'We don't know for sure,' said Grace. 'But if there's anything you can tell us about your family or your childhood that would help us make sense of this case, we'd be very grateful.'

Deborah looked at her oddly as she inhaled deeply and blew out a long stream of smoke. 'I've got two daughters,' she said.

'They don't want to know me. To hear their story, I'm the worst mother in the world. People can only do their best, right? I'm not going to speak against my family.'

Grace decided the time had come for some straight talking. 'Not even if one of your brothers took a woman he'd never met off the streets and then raped and killed her?'

'You're only here because I fucked up. I'm not digging myself in any deeper.' Deborah took a last drag, ground out the half-smoked cigarette under her foot. 'Besides, if you lot had done your job properly at the time, we wouldn't be in this mess.' Raising a hand behind her in farewell, she walked off into the station.

40

🔊

I am a stalker. I am your nightmare. I am Freddie Craig, and this is *Stories from the Fire*, brought to you with support from the *Daily Courier*, Britain's favourite newspaper.

I'm out searching for the perfect victim. Today I've stationed myself beside a wide store entrance halfway along the main pedestrianised shopping street in Southend. From here I can observe people going in or out, passing by, hanging about waiting for friends or stopping to check their phones. It's easy to feel invisible, but I'm not so sure the hunt is going to be as simple as I expected.

I'm discovering that there's an art to watching people, and to watching women in particular. They're more tolerant of being looked at because they're used to it, but they're also far more aware of me doing it. And I'm also learning that, while men either don't really notice or aren't that bothered if I casually observe them, they catch on pretty quick if I target a woman they consider theirs.

I need to stay under the radar. I don't want anyone remembering me later and giving the police a description. That's how I have to think. If I was seriously going to do this, I'd have given thought to my clothes. I saw once on a TV documentary that if I wear clothes from Gap or M&S, stuff that loads of people wear, it'd be harder for the police to track me down from any fibres I might leave at the scene. And I'd have to plan for what equipment I'd need. Heather Bowyer's killer was masked and had a knife.

I can see how the planning stage can become a big part of the event. Addictive, almost. Calculating, solving problems, anticipating how it's going to be. Acting it out in my imagination over and over again so I get it right and don't overlook anything, but also because I start to relish the rehearsing and refining until it becomes a ritual, not to be rushed, but to be savoured. And that's when I realise that not any woman will do. She'll have to be the right one.

Quite early on I spot one who looks like she'd be easy to pick off. Just like the weak animal at the edge of the herd that the leopard singles out for attack. She's fidgeting at the periphery of a group that obviously doesn't really care whether she's there or not – and wouldn't notice if she vanished. She's laughing along with them, but isn't part of what's going down. At one point she catches my eye, and then a little later glances slyly back, to see if I'm still looking. I am and she likes it. I'm sure I could coax her into peeling off and coming away with me.

But I don't want her.

And that's when I realise: it's not about preying on the vulnerable and defenceless, or even about whether she's pretty or blonde or got a nice rack. It's about finding what I want. It's all about me. I have to zero in on my own pure line of desire because that's the only thing that's going to drive me to see this thing through to the end.

Now I've appreciated that, I'm amazed that I never understood it before. It's not about her and what she's like. It's only about me and how I feel. I've carefully planned it *this* way because *this* is what I want. And recognising what I want and realising that I have a plan and can go and get it feels powerful, almost erotic.

I always thought that, like almost everyone else, I'd have a moral safety switch, that there'd be places I wouldn't go, not even secretly in my mind. Yet there's something in that endless rehearsal, that ritualising of what I might do and how I would do it, that strokes and smoothes the brief objections of moral outrage out of the way. What remains is my growing desire to do this, to get it done.

And that's what defines my perfect victim. A woman onto whom I can project what I want. I can get my own back for being hurt and rejected. I can get back on top. A switch clicks on in my head and I understand that I can have what I want just for the taking.

So when I see a woman who stands out from the crowd, walking alone down the street, I follow her. It feels instinctive, that sense that she's the one. She walks with purpose. She has somewhere to go. Her confidence means she's not going to notice me, and it's her confidence that makes me want to take her down.

She wears tight black jeans with high-heeled ankle boots and a short black leather jacket that accentuates her waist. Her straightened blonde hair swings as she walks. As she arrives within sight of the sea she takes a left and continues, sure-footed, towards Southchurch Park. It's an intriguing destination for a woman like this. She doesn't look like a prostitute, but then what would I know? I like watching her. And I'm in no rush. It doesn't even matter if I take this further with her or not.

I'm the one in control here. And I can always lock her image up inside my mind to take home and play with later.

I'm beginning to see inside the mind of a stalker, to understand how Heather Bowyer's killer started out on his journey, and why. It's quite a ride.

I'm Freddie Craig, and you're listening to *Stories from the Fire*. Stick around for the rest of the trip because this is where we get closer to the dark heart of this true crime.

41

Grace and Blake sat at a window table in a seafront ice-cream parlour as they waited for Carolyn to join them. The morning's rain and cloud had cleared away and Grace was glad of the blue-and-white striped awnings that shaded their eyes from the low sun glittering off the water on the far side of the road. As she stirred her coffee, she caught Blake eyeing up the extravagant sundae a young waitress had placed in front of a child sitting nearby. The little boy picked up a long spoon and, wide-eyed, dug down through the whipped cream while his grandparents looked on indulgently.

'You can order one if you want,' she teased Blake. 'I won't tell.'

'Yeah, right!'

Blake's eyes met hers with their former easy warmth, and for a moment Grace felt as if everything was falling back into place. Perhaps now would be a good moment to explain to him about Ivo. But, just as she began to formulate the words, the waitress came over to their table. 'I've spoken to the owner,' she told them. 'She says her grandfather would remember the fire.' She handed them a slip of paper. 'That's his home number.'

Grace took the paper. 'Thanks.'

'Can I get you anything else?'

Grace looked questioningly at Blake, who grinned but shook his head, thanking the waitress.

The two of them had spent the afternoon traipsing around the town centre, working their way through a list that Duncan had produced of Southend businesses that, since the night of the fire, had remained in the ownership of the same people or their families. They had flashed their warrant cards and asked for memories, descriptions, photographs, anything that could help to build a picture of how events had unfolded. They'd also shown photographs of Reece and Larry and found that several of those they spoke to who had lived in Southend for years were immediately familiar with Owen Nixon's boys. But, so far, they had gained no significant new details.

They had already discovered from trawling through every available media image what clothes Larry had been wearing and where he'd left his taxi with its distinctive blue-and-yellow company logo, but they were still missing any eyewitnesses to the crucial half-hour before he dashed into the burning building. Duncan had told Grace that Wendy had a nifty computer program that could build a three-dimensional map of the area between Cliff Gardens and the old Marineland complex, onto which they could plot every piece of information that came in, as well as being able to place people where they said they'd been standing, what direction they were looking in and where photos had been taken. They could then 'walk' around the model and work out what else people might have noticed, but not actively remembered.

Grace had been delighted to put Duncan back to work. He loved detail, and if anything was going to crack this case, it was going to be detail, detail, detail. But so far, although they'd come across several people who'd readily recalled that night, it was clear that the young podcaster had been right. The pandemonium of the fire had so engulfed the events of Heather's murder that no one would have paid the slightest attention to her killer escaping the scene.

Grace knew that the afternoon had, in truth, been a waste of a senior detective's time – there was plenty she should be getting on with back in the office – but this case had got under her skin and the idea of Larry Nixon thumbing his nose at justice and slipping free a second time was more than she could bear. If she had to micro-manage to ensure that no vital clue was missed, then so be it.

She had also given Duncan the job of tracking down the other rape complainants. Melanie Riggs had managed to recall just enough minor personal details about the two women she had dealt with for Grace to be confident they would be making an approach to the right people.

Across the water the sun was going down. Outside passers-by were buttoning their coats and wrapping scarves more tightly around themselves. Inside, people were leaving and the queue at the counter for ice cream had thinned. Carolyn ought to be here soon. Grace had decided that, with her recent experience in the domestic violence unit, Carolyn would be the best officer to canvass the sex workers for any talk on the street about Larry Nixon. But the girls wouldn't want a cop hanging around once it got dark and punters started cruising past on their way home from work. In a red-light district even the very best cop always stuck out a mile.

Sooner or later Grace was going to have to share with Blake and the rest of the team what Ivo had told her that morning, that DI Jason Jupp had been corrupt and that Owen Nixon might have been involved. It would certainly help make sense of the frosty welcome they'd been offered at Southend nick. Even though Jupp was dead, it was still his manor and, as she knew all too well, either old loyalties died hard or there was the simple matter of upholding the honour of a tight-knit local nick.

The door opened and Carolyn came in. She looked chilled to the bone and Grace beckoned to the waitress to order her a hot drink.

'Sorry I kept you waiting, boss,' said Carolyn as she sat down beside Blake. 'The strangest thing, I could have sworn someone was following me.'

'Not Larry Nixon?' Blake asked sharply.

'No. I caught sight of the guy. It was someone smaller and younger.'

'I don't like the idea that Larry may have fixated on you because of your shoe,' said Blake. 'You need to be careful.'

'Could he have been a pimp who didn't like you hanging around?' asked Grace.

Carolyn shook her head. 'I'm pretty sure he was behind me earlier on, before I started talking to any of the women. Anyway, it doesn't matter. Probably just coincidence that he was walking the same way as me.'

'You must report it if it happens again,' said Blake.

Carolyn smiled up at him. 'I will.'

'So how did you get on?' asked Grace, trying to subdue the acid rising in her throat.

'No one admitted knowing Larry,' said Carolyn. 'And the only one who described a client having anything like a shoe fetish said her client was Asian. Several of them, however, talked about Owen Nixon.'

'He's a client?' Grace asked eagerly.

'Not sure, boss. They were a bit cagey about that. But a couple of them described him as a friend. He offers lifts, sometimes for free if the weather's bad. Sometimes he lets girls stay with him in return for cooking and housework.'

'Housework?' asked Blake. 'That all?'

'So they say. And not just working girls, either. One said she'd heard stories of him offering women a bed for the night if he saw them wandering the streets late at night with no way to get home.'

'No strings attached? Really?'

Carolyn shrugged. 'They have a nickname for him. The "Guardian Angel".'

Nothing like the yellow glow of a taxi light on a cold wet night, thought Grace. She wondered if it had been one of the girls who had given him the cardboard air freshener that hung from the rear-view mirror in his taxi.

'I only met him briefly at the hospital,' said Carolyn, 'but if I ended up in his house, I'd make bloody sure my door was locked.'

'What sort of age were the women you spoke to?' Grace asked. 'I don't suppose they were old enough to remember the fire twenty-five years ago?'

'Some looked it,' said Carolyn, 'though it's hard to tell. No one showed any interest when I asked about it.'

'Owen's wife died when his sons were teenagers,' said Blake. 'If he was in the habit of picking up random women and bringing them home for sex, maybe that's where one of the boys learned his warped ideas.'

'Larry did make some comment about Owen finding girls to help out in the house, didn't he?' said Grace. 'He didn't seem to say it with any heat behind it and he didn't have to mention it at all if it risked revealing private stuff.'

'Perhaps Owen is on the side of the angels after all,' said Blake, 'and that's why he was also a police informant.'

'Not if his handler was bent,' said Grace. 'Ivo Sweatman, the reporter I was talking to at the cemetery this morning, he told me how DI Jupp walked off with carrier bags full of cash from a raid on an ecstasy factory. Over half a million quid.'

Blake whistled through his teeth.

'Let's just say it was Owen who tipped Jupp off – that would explain why Jupp ordered a young WPC not to approach Owen, even as a potential witness,' she continued.

'It's also a possible reason for the DI to stifle any investigation of Owen's sons,' said Carolyn.

'It doesn't even need to be about outright corruption,' said Grace. 'Ivo also mentioned that Jupp was a Freemason, like Owen.'

'And a journalist simply volunteered all this?' Blake didn't hide his scepticism.

'Ivo and I have some history,' she said shortly. She couldn't begin to explain herself in front of Carolyn. And perhaps, with Carolyn beside him, Blake wouldn't care now anyway.

'If that stacks up,' said Blake, his thoughts on the case, 'then how far did the cover-up go? Is that why there was so little forensic evidence, for instance?'

'There's no way to unravel any conspiracies now,' said Grace. 'We just have to keep going with what we've got.'

The young waitress came and laid a saucer on the table with the bill on it. Grace looked around. While they'd been talking it had grown dark outside and they were the last ones there.

42

Grace was glad to close her own front door behind her in Wiven-hoe. It had been a long day. She kicked off her shoes and went to put on some music and root out the opened bottle of white wine she'd left in the fridge. She felt an unaccustomed pang of loneli-ness and realised it wasn't only her passing impression of reconnection with Blake, it was also to do with Ivo Sweatman. He had once again proved himself loyal and yet the ambivalence she'd felt about seeing him again hadn't dissipated. She knew it was unfair. Unworthy, even. Ivo had freely offered his help and she had been glad to take it. It wasn't his fault that she had lost Blake.

She had, however, sensed that Ivo could have told her more about DI Jupp if she'd pressed him. She should have done. Why hadn't she? Had it been her awareness of Blake waiting nearby and her unwillingness to open a dialogue with Ivo that would distance her even more from him? And, if so, did that mean she was prepared to put her own private life ahead of the possibil-ity, however faint, of a much-needed break in this case?

She curled up on her sofa with her glass of wine and con-sidered her conversations with Alison. Her sister's concern was genuine, and Grace accepted she was probably right. She mustn't leave it too late to establish a life outside of work. But did that have to mean compromising on winning justice for victims of crime, whether living or dead?

There had to be another way to solve this case. The yellow legal pad on which she scribbled notes and ideas lay on the coffee table where she'd left it. She picked it up and turned to a fresh sheet. What had they learnt so far?

The Southend rapist drove a taxi and perhaps liked the Eurythmics. One of the victims recognised Larry Nixon's voice when he was interviewed not long afterwards. Larry appeared to be aroused by high heels. His DNA was an exact match to the trace DNA found on the murder weapon. He had opportunity and motive to murder his brother and sister-in-law, and it could be significant that physical evidence which might have shown him to be an arsonist had been destroyed or effectively masked.

It was all circumstantial, yet it might be enough to put before a jury – except for one thing. Reece could not be ruled out as a suspect – and that would be Larry's defence. A judge would have to advise that that fact constituted reasonable doubt.

Was that why Larry had volunteered to be interviewed by Freddie Craig, to make sure that his version of events was out there? If he'd delayed until he'd been charged with the crimes, the entire matter would be *sub judice* until the trial was over and he'd no longer be able to peddle his alternative narrative. Grace wondered if it had been Larry who'd tipped off the media about Reece's funeral that morning, hoping they'd run with pictures of the grieving hero of the Marineland fire. Maybe Ivo would know.

She'd have to convince a jury that Reece wasn't the Southend rapist and the killer of Heather Bowyer. But how? She couldn't. The person most likely to alibi Reece was Kirsty, and she was dead. Other family members with whom he'd been living – Larry and his father – had little reason to tell the truth now. And after twenty-five years, it simply wasn't going to be possible to prove a negative – that Reece *hadn't* done it.

Grace wondered what part Owen Nixon was really playing. She could understand that, with Reece dead, he would strive to save his surviving son from imprisonment for crimes commit-ted so long ago, but would he seriously protect Larry if he believed Larry had so callously murdered Reece and Kirsty?

Could Owen really have known what he was doing when he destroyed Larry's fire-damaged clothes? It was more likely, surely, that he simply hadn't questioned Larry's request either to dispose of them for him or to fib to the police about the fact that Larry had done so himself.

But then maybe Owen had known from the beginning what Larry had done, and, all those years ago, had leveraged his knowledge of DI Jupp's corruption to shield his son from investigation.

Or was that all just too far-fetched?

Carolyn believed she'd been shadowed by a man as she'd talked to the working girls along York Road and Riviera Drive. Grace couldn't silence an apprehension that Blake's concern might prove to be justified. In retrospect, perhaps the stunt with the high-heeled shoe had been foolish but not, she hoped, dangerous. Nonetheless the risk that she had baited Larry too far underlined her sense that she was dealing with more than she fully understood.

She looked at the time. Not too late to call Wendy and once

more run through the possibility that some potential evidence retrieved from the fire at Reece Nixon's house had been overlooked.

The crime scene manager didn't seem too put out by being disturbed at home and admitted that she, too, had remained sufficiently uneasy about the case to keep picking away at it in her mind. She was happy to spare the time to talk it all through again.

'There may possibly be one further test we can do,' Wendy told Grace eventually. 'It's not cheap and may not yield any results at all.'

'We're desperate for something,' said Grace. 'Tell me more.'

'Well, there's a technique that should be able to retrieve any fingerprints from the cap of the petrol container – if there are any.'

'I thought the canister was completely melted?'

'The can was, yes, but not the cap, which was found separately and is made of a more robust type of plastic. It'll be an extremely slow, arduous process, chemically lifting away layer after layer of the sooty deposits until we get back to the original surface, but I've seen it done.'

'Wouldn't that also remove any fingerprints?' asked Grace.

'Not if you're clever.'

'Fair enough!'

'But we may do all that only to find that he wore gloves,' Wendy warned.

'He threw the can into the fire,' argued Grace. 'He can't have imagined any of it would survive. It has to be worth a go, if only to see his face when we tell him there's a possibility we can get fingerprints from where he unscrewed the cap.'

'OK, leave it with me. I'll email you an accurate costing tomorrow and you can decide if you want to go ahead.'

Grace thanked her and ended the call, relieved to have identified a practical task on which to pin her hopes, however slim they might be.

It hurt as much as if he was probing an exquisitely painful dental abscess with the tip of his tongue, but Ivo knew it had to be done. He'd awoken from another central casting nightmare and he simply couldn't take any more of the dreadful clichés his unconscious was employing to prod him into confronting his past.

Ivo had never shied away from his sins – apart from this one exception. In fact, as he'd come to realise once he stopped drinking, he'd almost begun to define himself by the failed relationships, the alimony, the mornings after the nights before. When he was drinking he'd told himself all the mess and chaos just made him a Jack the lad, a free spirit, what the fuck anyhow. Now he asked himself how much of the chaos he'd created had been fuelled by the urgent need not to look back or examine what he'd done.

Not that he ever really knew precisely *what* he had done. He'd saved himself that. JJ had merely asked him for a small favour and Ivo had agreed to it. The favour hadn't even required him to do anything. That was the most insidious part of it. He could tell himself that he'd never carried out a wrongful action so there was no reason to repent. He'd done nothing. Which was precisely what JJ had asked of him.

But doing nothing had grown into something that occupied an awful lot of space, something that took up more and more of the air around him. Here he was, back in his kitchen again at four in the morning. It was the time – or so he'd been told – when all the signs of life are at their lowest and the breath can simply give out. As he waited for the kettle to boil and looked out over the autumnal gloom of the adjoining London gardens, he felt acutely aware of the coming and going of his own shallow breath and relived the panic that arose whenever he looked back at that defining moment in a Southend pub with JJ.

At the time it hadn't seemed like very much at all, and JJ had certainly never required Ivo to know why he was asking this particular favour. And Ivo had been happy to take the hint and not enquire. But unwanted comprehension had eventually come anyway, arriving in dribs and drabs over the years via news reports of a trial, a lifer's two failed attempts to appeal against conviction, and then the premature death of a man who had consistently asserted his innocence. The man whom JJ had casually asked Ivo not to mention seeing in the pub on a particular afternoon.

Damon Smith had been his name. A habitual petty criminal, but not a murderer. By the time his second appeal was turned down, JJ was dead and there'd been no reason for Ivo not to give his evidence at last. Nothing except a shame so overwhelming that any kind of utterance was inconceivable. And then it was too late. Damon Smith developed cancer and died in prison.

Ivo had seen him in the pub on the afternoon a pregnant girl was kicked to death, so knew that Damon Smith was innocent. He'd never been told why JJ had wanted him to keep quiet, nor whether JJ had any inkling of who had in fact committed the crime. Ivo had always assumed – or conveniently let himself assume – that JJ had good reason not to offer Damon Smith an alibi, and that this was one of those cases of so-called 'noble cause corruption' that seemed almost fashionable at the time.

He had read in a magazine that around a quarter of wrongful convictions involve false confessions. The majority involve a mistaken eyewitness, scientific fraud or junk science, or suppression of evidence by police. They were American statistics, but Ivo had done his bit to boost that final category.

He poured boiling water on top of the instant coffee granules and stirred. A light went on across the gardens and the shadow of a figure moved against a drawn blind. He had never felt more like an outcast. Affairs, unpaid bills, unaccounted absences, special occasions missed or ruined by drunken scenes – all that might be forgiven. But sending an innocent man to prison for life?

Yet even if he could atone, he'd left it too late. Damon Smith was beyond help and JJ was past being held to account. Except, what if JJ's motives linked up somehow with Grace Fisher's investigation? She'd floated the idea that maybe JJ, in his turn, had owed favours to other people. For all Ivo knew, the malevolent presence that he had empowered by his silence all those years ago was Owen Nixon. He should tell her everything. Finally unburden himself. Let her decide whether or not an old injustice could still somehow be righted. Maybe it could even provide the clincher in the Heather Bowyer case.

He had almost made up his mind to call Grace at a civilised hour and offer up his confession when he saw in his mind's eye her look of disappointment and contempt and knew that he could never bring himself to tell her, of all people, the truth.

When Grace arrived for work she found a yellow sticker on her computer to say that a Philip Langstone was waiting downstairs to see her. It took a few seconds for the name to register. Phil Langstone and Kevin Barnes had, as teenagers, accidentally started the Marineland fire.

She found him sitting in the reception area by the main entrance. A man of middle height in a sharp blue suit, white shirt and narrow tie, he sprang to his feet as soon as he saw her, bouncing lightly on his toes as he introduced himself. 'Dave Clements told me you were asking about Larry Nixon,' he said, 'and I just had to come over right away and tell you what I know about him.'

Grace found his energy and sincerity endearing. She smiled and showed him into an interview room. 'I'm glad you came,' she told him. 'It will be very helpful to have your account of that night.'

'The fire?' he said. 'I wouldn't be here if it wasn't for him. He carried Kevin out on his back. I'd totally panicked, didn't know what to do. We'd have died if it wasn't for Larry Nixon.'

'Can you tell me what happened?'

Langstone shook his head more in wonder than bewilderment.

'We couldn't believe it. We thought we were goners, and then he appeared out of nowhere. Seemed to know his way around. Kevin couldn't walk. We found out later he'd broken his ankle. I helped him grab hold of Larry's shoulders and climb up in a piggy-back, and then I clung onto the tail of Kevin's jacket so I wouldn't get lost in the smoke.'

'What was Larry wearing, do you remember?'

'Dark clothes, I think.' His frown cleared away. 'He took his jacket off, threw it down, before we hoisted Kevin up.'

'So his jacket got left behind?' she asked.

'I guess so.'

'Do you remember what kind of jacket?'

'Leather, I think. You know, the kind with zip-up pockets.' He laughed. 'So strange what comes back if someone jogs your memory. I never realised I knew that, but I can see it quite plainly now!'

'Why do you think he took it off?'

Langstone shook his head. 'Must've freed up his movements or something. Made it easier for Kevin to take hold.'

Grace asked herself whether a balaclava and a single blood-stained leather glove had been zipped up in the jacket pockets. If Larry had assumed he'd safely destroyed them then that would explain his surprise when he'd been told that a glove had been found at the scene. 'It didn't seem strange to you?' she asked.

Langstone's expression darkened. 'Dave Clements said you had the idea that Larry had something to do with that poor girl's death, but you couldn't be more wrong.'

'We have DNA evidence that links him to the murder weapon,' Grace said mildly. 'We have to follow that up and see where it leads.'

Langstone shook his head firmly. 'Then you're talking to the wrong guy here. That night turned our lives around. Kevin, he was heading for trouble, but that second chance straightened him out, made him start working for his exams. He moved with his family to Australia soon after, but the last I heard he was in medical school there, training to be a doctor. Who knows how many lives he's saved? I wasn't brainy like him, but I focused on my running, got as far as the national squad. Now I'm a sports physio and I've been all over the world working with elite athletes. I have two kids who wouldn't exist if it wasn't for Larry Nixon. I'm telling you, he was our saviour.'

'I can understand why you hold him in such high esteem,' she said, 'but I can't simply ignore the scientific evidence. Did he ever mention anything to you about how he came to be passing the Marineland complex or noticed that there was a fire?'

'Only about how lucky it was that he did. I can't believe how modest he was afterwards. He never looked for the limelight, had to be badgered into giving interviews.'

Grace realised she'd probably gleaned everything she could from his recollection of that night and, taking a note of his contact details, thanked him for taking the time and trouble to come in.

'No worries,' he said, 'it wasn't far out of my way. But seriously, if you think he's a suspect for anything so appalling, you're barking up the wrong tree.'

Grace saw him out and climbed the stairs to the MIT office, mulling over how one of Kevin Barnes's patients might feel if they were told that they owed some life-saving diagnosis or treatment to a chain of events connecting them to a multiple rapist. Would they care? Did it matter? Did a subsequent good contribute in any way towards cancelling or diminishing an earlier evil? These were certainly not questions a police detective had to answer, yet they intrigued her.

As Grace entered the office, Carolyn looked up. 'Can I have a word, boss?'

'Of course.'

The constable followed Grace to her desk and remained standing. 'Have you heard the latest podcast, boss?'

'No, not yet,' said Grace. 'Should I?'

'Well, you know I thought someone was following me yesterday?'

Grace went on the alert. 'Yes.'

'I think it was him,' said Carolyn. 'Freddie Craig. He obviously has no idea who I am, but he describes stalking a woman in Southend. I followed the same route and was wearing the clothes he describes.'

Given her misgivings of the night before, Grace's immediate reaction was relief that Carolyn's stalker was definitely not Larry Nixon, but she was infuriated that Freddie Craig was continuing to insert himself into her investigation. 'That's not on,' she told Carolyn. 'I'll listen, and if necessary ask Hilary to have a word with him. It'll be less heavy-handed if it comes from her. Are you worried by it?'

'I don't think so. I mean, it's difficult to say how much he's doing for effect, to create a more visceral response, and how much might be real. I've listened to quite a few of the well-known true-crime podcasts. I think they're great. And they do try to make stuff sound weird and scary. He might just be being clever and spooking his listeners into believing that he's actually losing the plot and turning into a stalker.'

'Or?' asked Grace.

'Or he's actually turning into a stalker.'

'Leave it with me,' said Grace. 'But if you're following up with any of the women you spoke to in Southend, don't go alone, OK?'

'Sure. Thanks, boss.'

Grace expected Carolyn to go, but she hovered in front of her desk. 'Is there something else?' she asked.

'Yes, boss. I would've mentioned this, but I wanted to follow it up before talking to you.'

'And?'

'A couple of the sex workers I spoke to asked if we were looking into the missing girls. So I did some digging, and Southend does seem to have had more than its fair share of young women reported missing.'

'Did the sex workers see this as connected to the 1992 rapes?'

'No. It's all much later.'

'Are they saying the young women who went missing are linked to each other in some way?'

'No.'

'So then what's your thinking about why it sheds light on our investigation?'

'I don't really know, but I thought it was worth looking into.'

Grace bit back her impatience. It was good that Carolyn was both thorough and prepared to act to some degree on her own initiative, but right now their priority had to be uncovering the evidence required to charge Larry Nixon. She made an effort to speak kindly. 'Firstly, there's no reason to suppose that missing persons aren't adequately dealt with at Southend nick,' she said, 'and I seriously don't want to tread on their toes any more than

I have to. And secondly, we simply don't have time to go chasing up leads that can't be justified strategically.'

'Sorry, boss.'

'Make a note in the strategy file, but please concentrate on the work in hand.'

'Yes, boss.'

'OK, thanks.'

Grace reviewed what Carolyn had said about Freddie Craig. She couldn't see how he could have known that Carolyn was a detective – unless his stalking behaviour was more insidious than it appeared, in which case he would definitely have to be warned off. But even if his pursuit of one of her officers had been inadvertent, his intrusion was a gratuitous sideshow and an unwelcome distraction.

She decided to listen to the podcast without delay. Freddie's 'ride' was coming to an end when Blake tapped on the partition of her cubicle and waited until she had removed her earbuds.

'So you've heard it?' he asked.

'Yes,' she said. 'I'm inclined to go with Carolyn's assessment, that it's amateur dramatics.'

'He talks about wanting to take her down,' said Blake indignantly.

'He makes it plain it's all in his head. He's committed no crime.' She observed the stubborn line of his mouth. 'I've told her not to go back to Southend on her own, and I'll make sure Hilary knows.'

'OK.' He sounded a little mollified. 'I've just had Owen Nixon on the phone.'

'What does he want?'

'You're not going to believe this one.'

'So Freddie Craig isn't the only one stretching his imagination?'

'No,' he said. 'Owen Nixon is now claiming that he completely forgot to mention that he might have another son.'

'*What?*'

'He says that he caught his wife messing around with another man, and then she discovered she was pregnant. She insisted it was Owen's child, but he refused to have it in the house. Says he told her to get it adopted. He insists it was a boy, but can't remember when the child was born or the other man's name.'

'It's a blatant red herring,' she said angrily.

'Of course it is,' said Blake, 'but he knows we'll have to check it out because otherwise it could derail a trial.'

'He's wasting his time. It's Larry's DNA on the knife, and only a twin will have the same DNA as Larry.'

'Except he wouldn't have to be a match to the knife,' Blake reminded her. 'A match to the mixed DNA in the glove would be sufficient. After all, we'd have been willing to run with that if we'd stuck with Reece as our prime suspect. The mere existence of a mysterious brother is enough to introduce reasonable doubt.'

'It's bullshit!' she said. 'He's playing games. How quickly can we knock this on the head?'

'We can try his in-laws,' he said, 'although Owen said he hasn't been in touch with any of his wife's family for years. Her name was Theresa, known as Terri, that's all he'd give me.'

'Deborah said her mother had died in 1982, not long before she left home. Put Duncan on to it. If anyone can get to the bottom of it, he will.'

'Will do.' Blake turned to go.

'Wait a second. Did Owen specifically ask to speak to you?'

'He came through on my direct line. But then I did give him my card that day at his house.'

'Do you think his contacting you directly has anything to do with the funny handshake?' she asked.

'How so?'

'If there was some kind of corrupt relationship between Owen and DI Jupp back in the day, maybe he still imagines the police are open to negotiation.'

'That I might make him an offer, you mean? Come to some arrangement to make it all go away?'

'At the very least he's supplied us with a plausible excuse to back off if we choose to,' she said. 'What do you think?'

'I wouldn't put anything past him,' said Blake. 'Should I play along? Perhaps I can get the evidence to charge him with attempting to pervert the course of justice?'

'We should hang fire until Duncan's had a chance to check out his story,' she said. 'And then we can see how far Owen pushes it.'

'Right you are, boss.'

'Thanks, Blake.'

With a smile, he made a mock salute and went off to speak to Duncan.

Grace swivelled her chair so she could look out of her window. The day was blustery, the wind blowing dead leaves from the trees down onto the road where they spun around in the wake of passing cars. Owen's diversionary tactic surely meant only one thing: that he knew Reece had been innocent because he knew not only what Larry had done all those years ago, but also that it was Larry who had set the fire at Reece's house. Owen's attempt to cover up for his surviving son, his blue-eyed boy, was tantamount to an admission of Larry's guilt.

She opened her email and scanned down the list of new messages until she found the one she wanted. Wendy's estimate of the cost of the forensic test on the cap of the petrol canister was eye-watering. Never mind. She wasn't going to risk Colin telling her it was too much, so typed a quick response, telling Wendy to go ahead.

45

🔊

It's an obsession. I get that now. Twenty-five years ago, taxi driver Reece Nixon drove around Southend looking to tempt a girl into his car so he could drive her far away. He played the Eurythmics song 'Love Is A Stranger'. It's that beat, that repetitive rhythm of wanting, wanting, wanting, that made what was coming – the rape and murder of nineteen-year-old Heather Bowyer – inevitable.

I'm Freddie Craig. Welcome back to *Stories from the Fire*.

I said I wanted to go inside the mind of a murderer, and now I really feel like that's where I am. I've talked about fate and destiny as if a killer and his victim were star-crossed lovers. That was because I'd read Shakespeare and Dostoyevsky when I was at uni, and imagined that great forces of guilt and evil and innocence had to be at play. But I was wrong. It's nothing like that. It's simply an earworm that won't let you go. The beat of a song that says 'I want you' until you can't resist and it becomes like the beat of your heart in a world where you can no longer imagine this not happening. You reach a point where you acknowledge that you can't – or won't – stop yourself, that you're going to cross a line, go too far, do the thing that, even an hour ago, you told yourself was only a fantasy, an idea to toy with on a dull night cruising around Southend.

It's no longer even about those thoughts that brought me here. All the hurt and anger and resentment have been reduced to an insistent voice that keeps telling me this is what I want, so do it. This is what I want, so do it. It's an obsession.

I've already found my victim. But she's not what's important to me any more. Making my selection, that was an earlier phase. It's gone now and I've moved on to the next level. That makes this sound like it's some kind of online game. Believe me, it's not. This is so much better. This is vivid and real, my very own personal game that I can play any way I like. And it's rigged in my favour.

I've followed her home, my blonde-haired woman in her tight black jeans. She can strut her stuff as much as she likes, but she's not going to win. It's not about what she wants or thinks or expects me to do. She can't walk out on me. Can't change her mind about being with me. Doesn't get to tell me what's happening. I'm in charge here.

I'm outside her house now, watching her move about behind the blind that covers her kitchen window. She's on her own. There's nothing she can do to stop me watching. She doesn't even know I'm here. And it'll stay that way until I decide to change the rules. My rules.

Somewhere in her life I'll find a weak spot, a place where I can step in and tempt her far away. And then the beat goes on. The things I want to do. The pumping rhythm of my heart. I want it, I want it, I want it. An incessant beat that will carry me over the line. I can't wait.

And I get to carry my secret with me all the time. No one else knows I'm a superhero. I realise how great it can be to possess a secret. To *be* a secret. Part of me wishes that other people could sense it, feel that I'm not who they think I am, that I'm so much more scary and in control than they realise. But that would dilute the power of being alone with my knowledge.

How on earth could Reece Nixon give all this up? He had tasted this power, exercised this incredible potential within himself, and yet left it behind and went off to run a landscape gardening business. Seriously, how did he not go mad with frustration? Or did the secret knowledge of what he'd done keep him going, even when annoying customers complained or the bank wouldn't extend his overdraft and his wife nagged at him?

You'd think that, when he was finally going to be unmasked, he'd have longed for everybody to understand who he really was, how badly they'd underestimated him all these years. That should have been his moment of glory.

But then, maybe it was. After all, he chose his own end and went out in a blaze of glory. Maybe arson was his way of demonstrating that he'd remained true to his vision right to the end.

I'm Freddie Craig. Thank you for accompanying me on this journey and listening to *Stories from the Fire*.

46

Grace played the latest podcast on her journey to work in the morning. Freddie's insinuating voice gave her such creeps that, finding Carolyn wasn't yet in the office, she felt a sudden spike of anxiety. She looked around, but the rest of the team seemed to be at their desks – all except Blake. Unbidden, all the regret and jealousy she'd struggled to push aside since seeing them in the bar returned like a tidal wave.

She retreated to her cubicle, from where she could keep an eye on the door. Five minutes later Blake and Carolyn came in together. They were laughing, and Blake touched her lightly on the arm as they separated. Blake stashed the sports bag he was carrying under his desk. Was it an overnight bag? Grace felt sick with misery, but swiftly ordered herself not to be railroaded by disappointment over something that was her own stupid fault. She rose to her feet and made herself walk calmly over to where Carolyn sat.

'I was worried about you.' She spoke as lightly as she could manage. 'I don't like the tone of that last podcast one little bit.'

Carolyn smiled. 'Yes, I heard it too,' she said. 'But don't worry, I live in an attic flat, and there's no blind on my kitchen window.'

'Well, that's a relief,' said Grace, noticing Blake glance over attentively. 'Except that he's stalking someone, even if it isn't you.'

'I doubt it, boss,' said Carolyn, 'I reckon he's making it all up.'

'Why would he do that?'

'He's playing to his audience,' she said. 'Ever since the *Courier* wrote about him, the podcasts have been all over social media. I've seen lots of chatroom speculation and online comment. Most of it is the usual trolls egging him on, so I reckon he's just giving them what they want. The more outrageous he is, the more the podcast will be talked about and the more followers he'll get.'

Grace still didn't like it. 'But what if another woman is in danger?'

Carolyn shook her head. 'It was me he was following the other day. There was definitely a man behind me, and in that podcast he described exactly what I was wearing and the route I took.'

'Should someone have a word with him, boss?' asked Blake.

'Hilary was going to anyway,' said Grace, conflicted that she should find his chivalry so painful merely because it was directed towards another woman. 'She said she might raise it with the *Courier*, too, if they're supporting him. But I still want you to watch your back,' she told Carolyn, 'just in case.'

'Understood. And thanks. But I honestly don't think any of it is serious.'

Grace turned with relief to Duncan, taking refuge in the pressing needs of work. 'Any progress on the two rape complainants?'

'Yes, boss. Unfortunately it looks like Jodie Miller may have passed away.'

'That's a shame.'

Duncan nodded. 'But I found Rhona Geary on Facebook and have left her a message vague enough to hope she'll get back to us.'

'Great,' she said. 'And the search for Owen Nixon's phantom offspring?'

'No births registered to Owen Nixon's wife other than the three children we know about.'

'Hardly a surprise,' she said.

'Terri Nixon was barely sixteen when she had Deborah, her first child,' said Duncan, 'and there wasn't much of a gap between her and the next two babies, so if there was another son, it's more likely he was born after Larry. That was 1969, and then Terri died in 1982.'

'Plus, if he's to be a credible suspect, he had to be old enough in 1992 to drive a car,' said Grace.

'And strong enough to overpower his victims,' said Blake.

'So he had to be born between 1969 and 1975 at the latest,' said Duncan. 'Not too big a window. I'll keep searching, boss.'

'Good, thanks. It's important that we can show a judge that we've done all we reasonably can to follow this up.'

Grace went to sit at her own desk. While it was aggravating to have to waste precious resources on Owen Nixon's brazen attempt to muddy the waters over the DNA evidence, she was glad of the distraction. She felt ambushed by a regret she had never fully allowed herself to feel. The sight of Blake and Carolyn arriving together, relaxed and laughing, and of him stashing away his overnight bag, confirmed the fear that until now she'd promised herself wasn't real. But it was. He'd moved on. There was no chance of Grace resuming their affair. Why had she let him go? Why had she not seen what she was truly giving up?

She checked herself. She wasn't some broken-hearted school-girl. She was the senior investigating officer in what was turning out to be one of the most significant cases of her career.

She forced her mind back to Owen Nixon's arrogant power play. They would have to hope that, if Duncan's searches produced nothing, and Owen – as he surely must – failed to come up with any convincing proof of his assertion, then no judge could instruct a jury to take into account an unidentifiable sibling whose DNA might in theory be a match to the crime scene evidence.

Yet a niggle of doubt lingered. She mustn't allow herself to be side-tracked by it. She had a complex investigation on her hands that was in danger of stalling. Clear the ground beneath your feet, that's what she'd tell another SIO to do, so why wasn't she taking her own advice? If she didn't come up with something soon that would lock down the case against Larry Nixon, then Colin would pressurise her to wind up the cold case inquiry. Worst-case scenario, he'd dismiss the flimsy evidence against Larry and ask her to accept Larry's account of Reece's confession and declare Reece Nixon a Deceased Offender.

She recalled how hard it had been to persuade Colin of the cost-effectiveness of the original familial DNA search. That initial discussion felt like a very long time ago, and her original projection of how the case would develop if they were to find a match now seemed ridiculously simple and optimistic. If only she could stall him long enough for the results of Wendy's forensic tests to come through.

'Boss?'

She looked up to see Duncan trying to catch her attention. 'Sorry, I was miles away.'

'I just had a reply already from Rhona Geary,' he said, clearly delighted.

'That's quick. And brilliant, thanks.'

'She lives in Northumberland, but she's agreed to a Skype interview.'

'And she's OK with that? She knows what we want to discuss?'

'I didn't totally spell it out, but I said it was regarding a complaint she'd made to the police in Southend in 1992.'

'If she was one of the victims, then she'll realise what it's about,' said Grace. 'Set up the call for whenever suits her.'

'I'll let you know.'

Rhona Geary seemed all too keen to speak, and replied that she'd be free in an hour's time, giving Grace long enough to set up a computer screen in an interview room where the conversation could be recorded. She hated having to use Skype. It would be almost more effective with voice contact alone than attempting to create a meaningful connection with a stranger with patchy streaming and eye contact that kept flicking between the screen and the camera. But it was Rhona Geary's choice, and Grace was impatient to hear what she might have to tell them.

Rhona, however, had questions of her own. 'Why are you looking into this now?' she asked, once Grace had introduced herself. 'It's the last thing on earth I expected after all these years.'

'You understand what I want to talk to you about?' said Grace. Although the screen angle made the other woman appear slightly distorted, Grace saw a pretty face with short dark hair and dangly earrings, and guessed that, beneath the anxiety of the situation, lay a natural animation and confidence.

'You want to talk about when I was attacked in Southend,' said Rhona. 'Please, whatever you want to ask, just get on with it. I can't – I don't understand how you tracked me down, what you could possibly want to know from me now?'

'We have new DNA evidence from the rape and murder of a young woman that we have strong reason to believe was linked to the sexual assault you reported.'

'You've caught him?'

Hearing the eagerness in Rhona's voice, Grace's sense of failure cut deep. 'Not yet,' she answered carefully. 'But it might help if you could bear to tell me whatever you remember most clearly.'

'I can't describe the whole thing,' said Rhona. 'I can't go through it again. I can maybe answer some questions, but I can't put myself back there.'

'We have your original statement,' said Grace. 'But maybe in hindsight something stands out, or you can add something to what you reported at the time?'

'You say he killed someone?'

'A young woman was murdered a few months after you were assaulted.'

'I thought he was going to kill me, except it wasn't about me. I didn't understand it at the time, but now I'm older it makes a bit more sense.'

'Can you explain?'

Rhona shifted her head so that her face all but disappeared from Grace's screen, leaving her with a partial view of a sitting-room fireplace with shelves to one side crammed with a jumble of books.

'I just want it to be over. I want to be able to stop looking over my shoulder. That would be so wonderful. Is anything I tell you really likely to make a difference?'

'I know it's hard,' said Grace, 'and I'm enormously grateful to you for your courage in agreeing to speak to me. The more information we have, the more likely it is that we'll be able to bring charges and hopefully put the right man behind bars where he belongs.'

Rhona nodded, her chin dipping so all Grace could see was the top of her head. 'It was my shoes. That's the only thing worth telling you. It wasn't really me he had sex with. He only had eyes for one of my shoes. It's partly why I've been able to put it behind me. In the end all he really took from me was that shoe.' She managed a curdled laugh. 'I've never worn high heels since.'

'Are you able to describe the shoe?' asked Grace.

Rhona sighed. 'I was kind of going for the supermodel look. Pale pink, with a heel I could barely walk in, and like a decal, a medallion, across the front. They weren't cheap, either.'

'What did he do with it afterwards?'

Rhona fell silent, staring at Grace's image on her screen before she spoke again. 'This is actually making sense to you, isn't it?'

'It's extremely helpful.'

Rhona laughed again. 'Thank God! I hope you get him. He took it away with him. He cradled it like it was some precious object.'

Just like he had with the borrowed shoe Carolyn had worn in the interview room. 'How did he leave?' asked Grace. 'Did he have a car?'

'I was by myself when he grabbed me. My own stupid fault. I was a bit drunk and desperate for a pee, so I went into a park across the road from where we were walking. Told my mates I'd catch them up.'

'You didn't notice any kind of car nearby either before or afterwards?'

'No, sorry.'

'If we're able to bring this to court, as I hope, how would you feel about giving evidence?'

Rhona thought it over. 'Maybe. If it would help to put him away, then yes.'

'Thank you.'

'I'd like to go now.'

'Of course.'

'But you'll let me know, won't you?' Rhona asked. 'The minute he's charged, I want to know.'

As Grace agreed and ended the connection, she thought about the other promises she had made, not only to Cara Chalkley, but also to Monica Bowyer and her son. She could not let them down.

Rhona's description of her attacker cradling her shoe had been uncanny. There was no doubt left in Grace's mind that Larry Nixon had raped Rhona, Cara, Heather and the evidently drug-addicted woman who wouldn't give her name, as well as the other women they hadn't managed to trace and any who had never reported the crimes against them. Grace was also more convinced than ever that Larry would still possess the collection of shoes he had taken from his victims. But where?

The police had been keeping tabs on his movements since his arrest, but so far he'd failed to lead them to a convenient lock-up or storage facility. It was possible that he had stored them at his father's house – he had called Owen after speaking to

Reece – but she had no cause to apply for a search warrant and anyway couldn't believe that Larry would share something so deeply personal with his father. But until they came up with new evidence, they couldn't even continue interviewing him.

She hated the idea that, through his possession of the shoes, Larry could perpetuate his feeling of control over the women he'd attacked. The thought made her even more determined to find his treasures, if only to rob him of them.

47

The kid looked even worse than he'd sounded on the phone. Freddie had been desperate for someone to talk to but, when Ivo suggested he come to London, admitted that he was too skint. Ivo had taken pity on him and agreed to meet in Burnham-on-Crouch. After all, it was only an hour on the train, and Ivo had nothing else to do on a rainy end-of-October Saturday.

From Freddie's descriptions of the remote village where he was lodging with his grandmother, Ivo had imagined the Dengie Peninsula as a wilderness but, even in the rain, the quaint little town was much prettier than he'd expected. Freddie met him at the station and they walked the short distance to a rather flash Essex gastro-pub that served fancy coffee. If anyone looked as if they didn't belong here, it was Freddie. His hair was lank and his clothes looked crumpled and unwashed. If Ivo's editor were to see him now, there would be absolutely no remaining hope of persuading him to change his mind about cutting the *Courier*'s support for the lad's podcasts.

As Ivo expected, that was what Freddie wanted to talk about, begging him to do his best to get his sponsorship reinstated.

'Look, it's not about the money,' said Ivo for the fourth time. 'What they were paying you was a drop in the ocean as far as the paper's concerned. It's this stalker scenario you're acting out. It's gone too far.'

'But the punters love it,' Freddie insisted yet again. 'You should see the threads on Reddit, the Twitter traffic.'

Ivo had no idea what Reddit might be, but someone at the *Courier* was clearly up to speed. 'It's the tone of all that which the paper doesn't like,' he said.

'But that's the clickbait, don't you see? It's working.'

'For all the wrong reasons,' Ivo warned. 'The only way I can get them to keep you on board is if you change direction.'

'I can't risk that,' said Freddie, 'not when it's really starting to take off. It could be huge.'

'You don't want to make an enemy of the *Courier*.'

'This is my one chance,' said Freddie. 'If I can make my name with *Stories from the Fire* then all kinds of doors could open to me. Not just journalism, but maybe radio and television, too.'

'Freddie, this isn't journalism. Pretending you're going to abduct someone and then encouraging your listeners to egg you on to do it is at best fiction and at worst a lurid misogynistic fantasy. Believe it or not, the *Courier* likes to think of itself as a family newspaper. It can't be part of this in any way.'

Freddie shook his head despairingly. 'I'm twenty-five. I've got a good degree and an MA in journalism, but I'm staying with my granny, have no girlfriend and now I'm having to borrow cash from my parents if I want to go and see my friends. This is all I have.'

Ivo sat back on the slippery cream-leather banquette. Rain was now streaking the leaded windows of the centuries-old pub. Why the fuck had he come? He looked across the table. Freddie had his head in his hands, his unwashed hair in danger of falling into the beer that Ivo had bought him.

'Chin up, kid,' he said, marvelling at what a soft touch he could sometimes be. 'You'd better talk me through it. Maybe we're all just being dinosaurs and not understanding what you're aiming for. Your vision – that's what all your generation have to have these days, isn't it, a vision you're passionate about?'

His lame joke worked, for Freddie raised his head and even managed a faint smile. He swallowed a mouthful of beer. 'It's all just shades of truth, isn't it, the difference between fact and fiction?' he said. 'Take that media conference we went to, for instance. There was a lot the police weren't telling us, right? So you could say that was merely a performance designed to put across the story they want to tell and keep back the facts that aren't yet part of it.'

'They might have sound operational or legal reasons for that,' said Ivo.

'But no one accuses them of lying,' said Freddie. 'So OK, what about a courtroom? A trial is pure theatre. Each witness tells their story, then the barristers bend the evidence to suit which side they're on and the jury have to decide which story they're going to believe.'

Ivo felt sick. He knew the truth of Freddie's argument better than anyone. Tell one story and the wrong man goes to jail; tell another and he doesn't. 'I don't see how this takes you to being a pretend stalker and rapist,' he said, needing to steer Freddie away from shark-infested waters. 'How does it get to the truth of who killed Heather Bowyer?'

'You have to make the story matter.' Freddie was starting to perk up, already looking better as he warmed to his theme. 'The lines between factual journalism and escapist entertainment were blurred a long time ago. I think my audience understands that. Sure, one or two of them are sick trolls who need to crawl out from under their rocks, but I think the majority are like me, people who want to make up their own minds about what's fake and what's true.'

Ivo was only half-listening. He was thinking about a different story, one where there could be no alternate ending. A woman had been kicked to death, five months pregnant and little more than a kid herself, and whoever had done that had walked free while an innocent man had gone to prison and died there.

'Responding to events in real time becomes part of the story.' Freddie was still speaking. 'I have to make things happen in order to move the story forward and make it dynamic.'

Ivo shook himself back into the present. 'And once the police have enough evidence to close the case, where do you take your story then?'

'If it's gained enough momentum, then I can let the audience decide,' said Freddie. 'That's why I have to keep going, why I need your help. If you could just write about it one more time. Please, Ivo. I could tone down the stalker angle if I have to, intro-duce some new thread to investigate. I can easily do that. It doesn't even have to be real. Taking wrong turns and changing direction can all be part of the journey.'

Ivo looked at Freddie. His eyes were red-rimmed and over-bright, his unshaven cheeks thin and pale. It had been Ivo's vanity at wanting to rediscover something of his younger self in this kid that had prompted his encouragement, his article that had been the catalyst to send *Stories from the Fire* viral. He had to own some responsibility for the state the kid was in. This pretend stalking business could land Freddie in real trouble. Seeing his unhinged state, Ivo worried about what stupid lengths Freddie might go to in order to keep his podcasts alive.

'If you really want to make your mark,' Ivo said, 'you have to find a true story, something real, and get stuck into that.'

'Like what?'

'I don't know. Like a miscarriage of justice, maybe.'

'That would be great,' said Freddie. 'I don't mind the research. I love it. But how do I go about finding a case worth pursuing? If you can help me, that would be awesome.'

Ivo heard the words spoken aloud as if they were issuing from someone else's mouth. 'Don't bring me into it, but you could try taking a look at Damon Smith.'

48

Vincent Rondini, a rotund eighty-seven-year-old, was a good head shorter than Grace. He wore an open-necked white shirt, tan trousers pulled halfway up his chest, huge old-fashioned glasses and several pieces of gold jewellery. He was genial and garrulous, and Grace imagined he must miss the sociability of the seafront ice cream parlour he had founded. A side-table had been laid with an ornate tea set and a plate of fancy biscuits, and she hoped that he had agreed to see them because he had something of value to share and not because he was lonely. As if reading her thoughts, he gave her a sly look and an imp-ish grin.

'You're not here to humour an old man,' he said. 'But take a seat.' He dropped heavily backwards into an armchair. 'Help yourself to anything you want.' He waved an arthritic hand towards the cups and saucers.

'It's very kind of you to see us.'

'So you spoke to my granddaughter?'

'Yes,' said Grace, as she and Blake sat together on the tasselled sofa.

'I hope she didn't charge you for the ice cream!'

Grace smiled, instinctively liking him. 'She was very helpful.'

'Good,' he said. 'She tells me you want to know about the night the old Marineland building burnt down.'

'That's right.'

'Lovely place it was when I was young. Used to get all spruced up and go dancing there. So what can I tell you?'

'Let's start with where you were on the night of the fire,' she said.

'Taking the dog for a walk,' he said. 'I always used to take him down along Westcliff Parade before turning in.'

Grace exchanged glances with Blake. 'Westcliff Parade runs along the top of Cliff Gardens, doesn't it?'

'That's right. Nowadays, if you carry on, you get to that shoddy little shopping centre they plonked on the site. Anyway, that night the wind must have been blowing out to sea, because I could smell the smoke quite strongly. Couldn't see where it was coming from at first, but then – it was scary how fast it all happened.'

'Did you notice anyone else nearby at that point?'

'I did. I saw it all, how that man went in to rescue those two boys. Owen Nixon's boy, Larry, wasn't it?'

'Yes.'

'I only found that out later,' said Rondini. 'The place was boarded up, but kids were always breaking in. It was only a matter of time before there was some kind of trouble. Didn't expect it to burn to the ground, though.'

'So where was the man you saw when you first noticed him?' asked Grace. She was tingling with anticipation that they might finally have their first sighting of Larry before the fire.

'He came out of Cliff Gardens and ran off. There was a taxi parked up ahead and I thought he was dashing to try and catch it, but then I saw it was parked because he opened the driver's door. Then he must have seen or smelled the smoke, too, because he slammed the door again and ran off towards Marineland.'

'Do you remember if the taxi had a logo?' asked Grace.

'Well, once I knew who it was I assumed it was one of Owen Nixon's cars, but I can't say now whether I realised that at the time or put two and two together later on.'

Grace was pleased that Rondini was so scrupulous. If he was being so careful not to embroider, then they might safely rely on his testimony. 'Can we show you some photographs?' she asked.

Blake opened the file he had brought with him. Both local radio and the Southend *Echo* had carried Grace's appeal for photographs or people's memories of the fire and been rewarded with both. Blake now handed Rondini copies of a couple of colour photos that had captured a Nixon taxi parked in the background.

'Is that where the taxi you noticed would have been parked?' she asked.

Rondini lifted up his glasses and, holding the images inches away from his milky eyes, examined them closely. 'Yes,' he said, replacing his glasses and handing back the photographs.

Grace hid her elation: Larry had said in an interview – and publicly on Freddie Craig's podcast – that he had been *driving* past when he had spotted smoke coming out of the building. Catching him out in one lie would make it easier to unravel the others.

'And you saw him enter the building?' she asked. 'It was definitely the man you saw running out of Cliff Gardens who then went in and rescued those boys?'

'He was ahead of me the whole time. He scrambled through a hole in the fence the contractors had put up around the building and disappeared. I stood there like an idiot, trying to think where the nearest phone box was, and then someone else came running up and pointed to a call box right there on the corner. He went and called the fire brigade.'

'Can you say precisely where you were when you saw him come out of Cliff Gardens?'

'Just coming up to the point where I usually stop and head back,' he said. 'He must have come out of the westernmost gate.'

'Can you remember anything about him?' she asked. 'What he was wearing, for instance?'

'That's not the sort of thing I notice, I'm afraid. I've always worn what my late wife told me to wear.'

'It was a chilly night,' she said. 'Might you have noticed if he was only wearing a T-shirt, for example?'

'All I can say is that nothing stood out.'

'Was he carrying anything?'

Rondini frowned. 'You know, I think maybe he was. He was in front of me, but when I picture his movements, I can see him put something in the car. It can't have been anything bulky or heavy, though.'

'But you didn't see what it was?'

He shook his head. 'If I'd had X-ray vision, maybe.'

Grace laughed. 'Any idea what he might have been doing in the park?'

'I imagined he'd been relieving himself. I thought afterwards that that's why he was running, to get back to work.'

'And, later on, when you heard about the murder?'

'What murder?'

'A nineteen-year-old called Heather Bowyer.' She glanced at Blake, hoping that they hadn't overestimated the old man's mental capacity. 'It was reported at the time.'

'That same night?' he asked.

'Yes, in Cliff Gardens.'

'So that's why you're here, not about the fire?'

'That's right. Your granddaughter didn't explain?'

'Maybe she did.' Rondini removed his glasses and rubbed his eyes. Replacing his spectacles, he shook his head as if distressed. 'He was running hell for leather. I just thought he was chasing the taxi.'

'You described Larry as Owen Nixon's boy,' Grace said. 'I imagine you're a few years older than Owen, but not by much. You grew your businesses at the same time, in the 1960s and 1970s.'

He nodded. 'Before the package holidays nearly finished us off. We couldn't sell ice cream fast enough in those days.'

'Were you friends?'

'With that snake? No.'

'Why do you call him that?'

Rondini pursed his lips in distaste. 'My late wife never took to him. I always listened to her. Sixty years we were married, God rest her soul.'

'You must miss her a great deal.'

As Rondini sank further down into his chair, exhausted, Grace realised what an effort he'd been making for them. 'We won't keep you much longer,' she said.

'I don't remember ever hearing about a murder. Not in relation to the fire, anyway. We always went home at the end of the summer season, back to Italy for a month to see my wife's parents. If I'd known—'

'Don't worry about that, Mr Rondini,' she said. 'It's not your responsibility.' It worried her that, even twenty-five years later, it hadn't taken much old-fashioned legwork to find this witness. What was the real reason DI Jupp had failed? 'Just to finish off your memories of that night,' she continued, 'how long did you remain in the vicinity?'

'The dog got frightened by the fire and all the commotion,' he said. 'We were only in everyone's way, so we went home.'

'Any idea what time you would have set out on your walk?'

'Probably about a quarter to ten. With a business to run, you stick to a routine.'

Grace knew from contemporary newspaper reports that the first call to the emergency services had been at seven minutes past ten, corroborating the timeline of Vincent Rondini's testimony. He would make a convincing witness. At last, they were getting somewhere. And, finally, they had the new information they needed to be allowed to reinterview Larry Nixon officially, under caution.

49

As soon as Larry Nixon turned up at Colchester Police Station the following day, according to the conditions of his bail, and was told that he would be reinterviewed, the clock would begin ticking once more on how long he could be held in custody. Grace was eager to have everything she wanted to put to him – timeline, maps, photographs, witness statements – meticulously prepared. She and Blake ate sandwiches at her desk as they worked out their strategy and the order in which they would disclose the details of their case. They had always worked well together – and Grace was grateful to the pressure of work that pushed all other private considerations aside.

They disagreed on only one thing: Cara Chalkley's shoe. Blake reasoned that the shock value of producing the pair to a shoe Larry had stolen, plus the humiliating risk of his erotic fantasies being made public, might destabilise him enough for him to slip up and make a mistake.

But Grace strongly believed that Larry would hold onto his trophies as long as he could, and feared that revealing how much they knew about the missing shoes would leave him with no choice but to destroy the only remaining physical evidence that could tie him to any of his crimes.

Although Blake countered that Larry was far too smart not to have got rid of such incriminating evidence long ago, Grace remained convinced that the hold these fetish objects had over him would still be too strong for him to do so.

They were still arguing when Duncan appeared at the entrance to her cubicle, a deep frown on his face. 'Boss?'

'Yes?'

'I realise we're already up to our eyes,' he said, 'but something odd has come up.'

'What is it?'

'You know me, belt and braces – I wanted to tie up all the loose ends – so I requested a copy of Terri Nixon's death certificate.'

'And?' Grace asked, as he paused dramatically.

'Theresa Elizabeth Nixon, née Walker, born sixth of November 1949. There's no record of her death.'

'But her daughter told us she'd died of cancer.'

'Well, there's no death certificate,' said Duncan. 'I checked to see if she'd divorced, remarried, changed her name, anything that might account for it, but there's nothing.'

Grace had never had reason to doubt Duncan's diligence. 'How strange,' she said. 'Could it be some kind of admin error? You could try asking the hospital if they still have any records of her treatment.'

'I already did, boss. The main records department at the hospital in Southend has nothing on file. They suggested I speak to oncology, who usually keep their own records for research purposes. Nothing. They couldn't rule out her records being mislaid, but they thought it more likely that she'd never been treated there for cancer.'

'Even stranger,' said Grace.

'I asked if she might have been treated elsewhere, but, even if she'd gone privately, which seems unlikely, her GP should still have some notice of her referral. Again, no suggestion of cancer or any other terminal illness. No cremation certificate and no coroner's inquest.'

'So she could still be alive?'

'I can run the usual missing person checks if you want, boss,' said Duncan.

'Yes, please.'

'If Terri ran away because Owen was abusive,' said Blake, 'she'd have made damn sure no one could find her.'

'And then what?' Grace asked. 'Rather than admit the truth, Owen made up the story that she'd died?'

'Saving face, perhaps,' Blake suggested. 'Anyway, if you do manage to track her down, Duncan, then at least you can ask her to vouch for how many sons she has.'

As Duncan went back to his desk, Grace turned to Blake. 'Do you think Deborah believes her mother is dead?'

'She said it was very quick. That makes for an easy story.'

Grace stared out of the window, remembering how, when her father died, it had been necessary to produce a seemingly end-less stream of paperwork in order to tie up his affairs. 'Deborah was old enough to leave home soon afterwards,' she said. 'Old enough to grasp what was really going on if her mother did run away.'

'Maybe she wanted to protect her,' said Blake. 'You saw the state Deborah was in at the funeral, the way she hid from her father. She was scared of him.'

'So she might have accepted a convenient fiction to make

sure her mother could stay safely lost.' Grace thought of Deborah patting the angel brooch on her jacket, and then of the air freshener hanging in Owen Nixon's taxi. Even though Deborah's loyalty was to a family that had failed her, when pressed she had refused to speak out against them.

'Why don't we just ask her what she really thinks happened?' he said.

'Later,' she said. 'Right now, we've enough to get on with. All the same, I wish I understood a bit more about what kind of family we're dealing with before we interview Larry.'

'What makes a rapist, you mean?' he asked. 'Nature or nurture?'

'Nurture?' Grace echoed. 'Not a word I'd readily apply to Owen Nixon.'

50

🔊

Welcome back to *Stories from the Fire*. I'm Freddie Craig, and in this episode I'm going to be looking into another murderous crime that took place twenty-five years ago in Southend.

The circumstances of this crime may be distressing to some listeners, so please use your discretion.

In the same month that Heather Bowyer met her death in Cliff Gardens, another young woman, sixteen-year-old April Irwin, was brutally beaten to death along with her unborn child. Officially, at least, this is not an unsolved crime. Forty-five-year-old Damon Smith was swiftly apprehended, convicted of her murder and sentenced to life imprisonment. However, from the moment of his arrest until his death in prison twelve years ago, he persisted in protesting his innocence.

A new and unnamed source, someone who has never spoken before, has told me that Damon Smith may have been telling the truth.

I've been talking to you recently about how a predator chooses his victim; about what makes a good victim. If you're after vulnerability, someone unlikely to put up a fight or to be missed afterwards, then from what I've been able to discover so far about April Irwin, she was the perfect candidate. Shortly before her sixteenth birthday she ran away from home in Romford after repeated rows with her mother's new boyfriend. She couch-surfed with friends for a few weeks until their patience ran out, and at some point arrived in Southend just as the summer season was getting underway. In a single phone call to her mum after she'd left, she said she'd found a job of sorts and somewhere to stay, but refused to say more. Her mother made no attempt to find her.

A couple of months later April became pregnant. The police never discovered the identity of the father, but it wasn't the man convicted of her murder, the man whose floor she'd been sleeping on for the previous four nights.

She'd been punched in the face. Once she had fallen to the floor, she was kicked in the head and torso, breaking several of her ribs and causing internal damage. Her attacker then stamped repeatedly on her stomach. She was nearly five months pregnant. She had broken fingers on both hands as a result of trying to protect her unborn child. Later, one of the jurors at Damon Smith's trial became so upset by the photographs of her injuries that he had to be excused.

The story of Damon's childhood and teenage years is strikingly similar. Perhaps that's why he offered April sanctuary in his cramped bedsit. He came from a traveller family, but parted ways with his community after a falling-out. He never fitted in anywhere else and, functionally illiterate, drifted from hand-to-mouth jobs to burglary, theft and petty fraud. A probation officer, his only character witness at the trial, said he missed his close-knit family and would often make up for it by helping people he considered down on their luck.

According to the account Damon gave at his trial, he came

home after an afternoon in the pub to find April's battered body on the floor of his rented room. He panicked and ran. He didn't run far and it didn't take the police long to pick him up. He was still wearing the same unwashed clothes stained with April's blood from where, he said, he'd knelt beside her to check whether she was still breathing.

He had no prior convictions for violence and no motive was ever put forward as to why he should have directed such violence towards April's unborn child. They weren't in any kind of relationship. Damon barely knew her and had merely offered her shelter because, he said, she'd been desperate.

He maintained through thick and thin – police questioning, a trial and two attempts to mount an appeal against his conviction – that he'd spent that afternoon in the pub. His problem was that, when first interviewed by the police, he was a little hazy as to which pub and, when he did finally regain some clarity, was unable to name or describe the other handful of drinkers present. The barman insisted Damon had not been there that day.

'When beggars die there are no comets seen, The heavens themselves blaze forth the death of princes'. I quoted those lines from Shakespeare's *Julius Caesar* when I first started talking to you. I never thought they'd come to carry such meaning, but, when I think about it, April and Damon were pretty much modern-day beggars. They certainly weren't princes.

My parents saw the fire on the night of my birth as a good omen. Now I'm not so sure. The more I investigate the events surrounding it, the more I see the inferno, the pall of black smoke and ash and the lingering smell as grim portents of the realities of life.

The Marineland fire was not a sign of great things to come.

They built a shopping mall on its ashes, now filled with cheap chain stores struggling to survive. The fire wasn't a comet, it was a conflagration. If it celebrates anything, let it celebrate the death of beggars.

April's body – and presumably that of the baby she was carrying – was cremated. I could find no record of any memorial. Her mother applied for financial compensation for her daughter's death under the criminal injuries scheme.

Damon Smith died in prison of a previously undiagnosed cancer. He was fifty-eight and had been protesting his innocence for nearly thirteen years.

I once heard a prison officer jeer that, to hear the inmates tell it, prisons are full of innocent men. Maybe Damon Smith was just another one of them, career criminals who declare 'I never' and give 'No comment' interviews. But what if he wasn't?

If my birth on the night of the fire can do any good at all, then it is this: I want find out what really happened on the afternoon that April Irwin died. It's of no use now to Damon for me to clear his name, but there are other people out there who know what happened, who have never told the truth, who may even be guilty.

I want you to help me. If you're out there and know anything about April Irwin, please get in touch via the website. Did you know her either before or during the few months she spent in Southend? Were you the father of her child? Do you have any ideas about who killed her, or why? Or were you one of the four other men in the pub with Damon that afternoon? If so, then talk to me. Walk down this road with me, be part of the journey. I'm Freddie Craig, and you've been listening to *Stories from the Fire*.

51

Larry Nixon looked up when Grace and Blake entered the interview room. 'I was given to understand that coming here today to answer my bail would be just a formality,' he said, 'but they've taken my phone and only allowed me one call.' He looked at his expensive watch. 'Right now, I'm letting down important clients.'

'I'm sorry about that, Mr Nixon,' said Grace blandly, 'but we do have important matters to discuss.'

He smiled wearily, but said nothing. Although he had once more declined to have a solicitor present – Grace imagined he must believe this would somehow project his innocence more powerfully – she was certain he would have previously taken careful legal advice.

'When we spoke to you last week,' she began, 'you gave us your account of your movements prior to the Marineland fire. We now have three witnesses whose statements differ significantly from yours.'

He gave a soft laugh and shook his head. 'From twenty-five years ago?'

'The fire was a memorable event.' Grace made a show of looking at her notes. 'You told us that you approached the Marineland complex from the west, is that correct?'

'So far as I remember, yes.'

'Along the most direct route from Westcliff to the Marineland complex?'

'Yes.'

'And you were in one of the six cars belonging to your father's taxi company?'

'Yes, I'd been working all evening.'

'You were driving when you heard shouting and saw smoke pouring from the building?'

'Yes. I was dawdling along, taking a breather, otherwise I wouldn't have noticed.'

'I am showing Mr Nixon a contemporary map of the area around the old Marineland complex,' said Grace. 'Please can you show me as precisely as possible where you parked your vehicle.'

Larry pointed to where he had indeed left the taxi.

'I am marking the position here in red,' she said. 'Please can you confirm for the tape that this is where you indicated that you left your car?'

'Yes, that's it. I remember driving on a few yards so that it would be away from the fire and not be a further hazard.'

'Thank you. I am entering this map into evidence as exhibit LN eight.' Grace passed the map to Blake, who slid it into an evidence bag which he then sealed and signed.

'So you were driving away from Westcliff when you passed the Marineland complex, saw the smoke and drove on a few yards, leaving the vehicle just to the east of the building?'

'That's right.'

'I am now showing Mr Nixon exhibit LN two, a copy of a black-and-white photograph printed in the afternoon edition of the Southend *Echo* on the fourth of October 1992, the day after the fire. Behind the fire engines, can you make out the taxi that is parked pretty much on the spot you just marked on the map?'

Grace let the silence extend as Larry stared at the photograph in which a taxi with the Nixon company logo was parked facing the camera. 'It's certainly one of my father's fleet of cars,' he said.

'Is it the car you were driving that night?'

'I don't know exactly when this photograph was taken, but it's obviously once the fire was already being brought under control. One of the other drivers may have stopped there to watch what was happening.'

'That's perfectly possible,' she agreed. 'But if so, then where in this photograph is the taxi *you* had been driving?'

'Maybe someone moved it,' Larry said. 'I was taken to hospital to be checked out. I don't know what happened to the car.'

'But you agree that the taxi belonging to your father's firm in this photograph where you said you parked is facing west?' Grace asked. 'Not east, as it would be if your account of your movements prior to the fire is correct.'

Larry said nothing.

'Mr Nixon?'

'Maybe I swung round before I parked. You can't expect me to remember.'

'You turned the car before parking, even though you've already said publicly that you had seen one of the trapped boys banging desperately on a window?'

'People do all sorts of things in extreme situations, don't they?'

'We've spoken to someone who was walking along the road towards Westcliff precisely when you would have had to pass him. He has no memory of seeing a taxi.'

'People never notice taxis until they need one,' said Larry. 'They just become part of the landscape.'

'We have a second witness who was behind you as you approached and entered the Marineland building,' said Grace. 'He says you were on foot and that your taxi was already parked in this spot exactly where it is on this photograph. Would you care to comment on that?'

Larry leaned back and crossed his arms. 'Your witness is mistaken.' He must have realised how defensive his posture appeared, for he casually uncrossed his arms and made an effort to relax his facial muscles. 'Back then I drove around Southend all day, every day. It all fades into a blur.'

'So you're saying you might have approached from the east?'

'In the car, yes, I suppose it's possible.'

'So what brought the fire to your attention if you hadn't yet reached the building?'

'You see? That's why I know I was coming from the west,' he said, smiling at the apparent hopelessness of her exactitude. 'Twenty-five years is a long time!'

'The witness who was walking behind you saw you come out of Cliff Gardens and then go to open the driver's door of a taxi parked in this position. Did you open the door and put something into the car?'

'No.'

'You didn't go into Cliff Gardens, in order to relieve yourself, perhaps, and then pick something up that you placed in your car?'

'No.'

'Can you account for why a witness would say that you did?'

'No, I can't,' said Larry, 'because it didn't happen, or not with me, anyway. Maybe there was another of my dad's drivers there,' said Larry. 'Like my brother Reece, for instance.'

'The witness who observed the man coming out of Cliff Gardens also saw smoke coming from Marineland. He watched the same man go through the gap in the security fence and enter the building. The man he saw rescued the two boys. He saw you, Mr Nixon.'

'This is your opportunity to clear up any discrepancies or misunderstandings about the evidence we're putting to you,' said Blake. 'I should remind you that you're still under caution.'

'OK, so maybe I didn't remember accurately what happened before the fire. As I say, night after night of driving around the same town all blurs into one. Maybe I did pop into one of the parks for a call of nature.'

'Right around the time when, according to you, your brother Reece was raping and murdering Heather Bowyer in the same park?' Grace was openly sarcastic. 'That's a bit of a coincidence, don't you think?'

'A tragic coincidence, yes,' said Larry, his eyes blazing.

Grace couldn't decide whether his uncharacteristic revelation of emotion was merely pretend anger at his brother's deeds or a genuine response to the net finally closing around him. Either way, she was pleased. They were getting to him.

'Let's move on,' she said, as Blake, on cue, handed her more photographs. 'You told us in your first interview what you were wearing on the night of the fire. In fact, you described precisely what you can be seen wearing in photographs taken at the scene after you had rescued Kevin Barnes and Phil Langstone. For the tape, I am showing Mr Nixon exhibits LN five, LN six and LN seven.'

She allowed time for Larry to glance at the photographs, which she assumed must be familiar to him, and to ask himself where her questions were leading.

'You told us that your jacket was in your car, that the car was warm enough not to wear it, is that correct?'

Larry looked at her suspiciously. 'Yes.'

'We've spoken to Phil Langstone, who has a clear memory of you wearing a leather jacket, but taking it off and discarding it before lifting Kevin Barnes onto your back. Could that be correct?'

'I suppose so. In the circumstances, whether or not I'd been wearing my jacket was hardly at the front of my mind.'

'So you might have taken it off and left it in the fire?'

'If that's what Phil remembers, then yes.'

'Did you do that because the jacket was bloodstained?'

'What? No!'

'Because you realised that, if you got out safely and were hailed as a hero, someone might notice Heather's blood?'

'No.'

'Here in this photograph, which unfortunately is black and white, there are noticeable stains on your T-shirt.'

'From the fire.'

'Heather Bowyer was stabbed twice, both wounds piercing her aorta. A single wound might not leave significant marks on her attacker, but, in removing the knife before plunging it back in, small droplets from the blade will be spattered within a short radius. We've had these photographs analysed by a forensic expert and the pattern of blood spatter on your T-shirt is consistent with such an attack. These specific marks are not consistent with the smudges and smears one might expect from a fire situation.'

Larry made an exclamation of contempt and pushed the photographs back across the desk. 'You're clutching at straws.'

'I'm happy to leave that for the CPS to decide,' she said, gathering up the photographs and handing them back to Blake. 'We will be seeking advice on whether or not we can charge you today.'

'Reece killed that girl, not me.'

'Is that why you also murdered your brother and his wife, to provide you with that alibi?'

'No,' said Larry. 'You're wrong. I would never have harmed my brother.'

'We're awaiting the results of forensic tests on the cap of the petrol canister found discarded in your brother's house after the fire,' she said, watching his reaction carefully. 'There's a very good chance that we'll be able to retrieve fingerprints from it.'

He shifted uncomfortably. It was the first time he'd betrayed any real unease. 'I didn't kill that girl,' he said. 'Reece did. You have his DNA at the scene, a car that could have been the taxi he was driving that night parked near Cliff Gardens, and you have proof that he phoned me shortly before committing suicide, a call in which he made a full confession.'

This was no bluff. And Larry didn't even yet know about the press cuttings found in his brother's attic. When this came to trial – if it got that far – Larry's arguments would be enough to raise reasonable doubt. The very thought of a jury acquitting him made Grace feel almost sick with anger. Reece could no longer speak for himself, but *she* could. It was time to fight back, and try to use Larry's own self-assurance against him.

'Are you aware that your father has introduced the possibility that your mother may have given birth to another male sibling who might also fit the DNA profile?'

'No,' said Larry, 'that's news to me.'

She suspected his answer was rehearsed, but it didn't matter. 'We have, of course, investigated fully, but have so far found no record of such a birth,' she said. 'I was wondering what light you could shed on your mother's life.'

'I was only about twelve when she died.'

'You weren't aware of any other pregnancy?'

'No, but then I wouldn't, if it was before I was born or not yet old enough to understand.'

'But you remember her death?'

'Of course.'

'I'm sorry if it brings back painful memories,' she said, 'but can you tell us about the circumstances of her death?'

'What do you mean?'

She could read absolutely nothing from his expression. 'Did you visit her in hospital?'

'I don't remember.'

'Did you go to her funeral?'

'Dad said we weren't to go. We were just kids.'

'But you've visited her grave? You know where she's buried?'

'What's this got to do with whether or not she had another son?'

'I'm just trying to paint a picture of her life, of her life with your father, of how she might have managed to have a child without recording its birth. Was your home life such that you could imagine that happening?'

'Dad took care of us. He helped me set up my business.'

'If your mother had had another child, do you think she'd have found it easy to give him up for adoption?'

'How would I know?'

'Well, what was she like?'

Larry gave a sneering smile. 'I hadn't realised the police offered free psychotherapy sessions.'

'Then let's go back to my earlier question: do you know where your mother is buried?'

'No, of course I don't!' Larry pushed back his chair and was about to stand up. He was trembling but, as it dawned on him how strange his reply must have sounded, he forced a smile and sat back down. 'I'm sorry. It's a shock. I just haven't thought about these things for a long time. You see, my dad did his best to protect us. It might not be the way things are done nowadays, but he told us to forget all about her. Not her, I mean, it, the cancer, the way she died.'

Grace wondered what his brief self-exposure signified. Somehow it didn't ring true as being the distress of a twelve-year-old boy whose mother had suddenly vanished from his life. The swift mastery of his feelings had been driven by some bigger imperative. She kept up the pressure. 'You've never visited her grave, not even as an adult?'

'I wouldn't want to upset my dad by asking about it.'

Although Grace could hardly imagine Owen Nixon being affected by such tender emotions, it was curious that Larry, a successful man in his late forties, would admit to feeling unable to ask questions his father might find unwelcome.

Unless – the idea struck her – he was protecting his father from something more serious than the dent to his pride from having a runaway wife. Feeling a sudden chill, she looked at

Blake. His answering gaze suggested he was having similar thoughts.

'Have you ever considered the possibility that your mother might still be alive?' she asked.

Larry laughed in exasperation. 'Why would I do that?'

'Because the local hospital has no record of treating her and there's no death certificate.'

He didn't argue, merely looked at her appraisingly as if they were adversaries in a game of poker. 'If you say so.'

'Might she have left your father? Or had reason to want to disappear?'

'I was twelve,' he said coolly. 'How would I know?'

How indeed? Maybe she should feel compassion for a boy who might have suspected or even witnessed some alarming occurrence related to his mother's disappearance, yet all Grace could think as she met Larry's eyes across the table was that whatever had gone on in his childhood had created an exceptionally controlled and dangerous man.

Colin Pitman, who had been observing the interview on the video feed, waylaid Grace and Blake as soon as they returned to the MIT office. 'It's time this cat-and-mouse game had an end in sight,' he said, sitting down behind his desk without indicating for either of them to take a seat. 'Have we nothing more we can throw at him? Because otherwise we're going to have to let him go. Again.'

'We're waiting on the forensics on the cap from the petrol canister retrieved from the fire at Reece Nixon's house,' said Grace. 'But it's a slow process, and the results will be another day or so yet.'

The superintendent shook his head. 'Well, at this rate, we might as well send him home until we get them.'

'We've still got the witness statements about the missing shoes to put to him.'

'Words alone aren't going to budge him. We just saw that.' Colin flexed a shoulder, wincing in pain. Grace thought perhaps this small injury was what was making him testier than usual. He caught her eye. 'Overdid it with the weight training yesterday evening.'

Imagining how her boss's vanity would lead him to compete

with much younger men at the gym, she had scant sympathy. 'We do have more than words, sir,' she said. 'We have Cara Chalkley's shoe. You didn't see how he reacted to the high-heeled shoe that DC Bromfield wore in the previous interview.'

She looked to Blake to explain the argument he had earlier put to her.

'We think the sight of the mirror image of a shoe he's likely to have treasured must carry some impact,' he said. 'It should be familiar to him. He might not even immediately realise it's not the one he took. The shock value might have a useful effect.'

'So why haven't you shown it to him already?'

Grace stifled a sigh. Colin had already signed off on their interview strategy the day before. 'We haven't yet said anything to him about the rape victims' shoes. Once we do that, we run the risk that he will destroy the only physical evidence that might still exist.'

'So, keep eyes on him,' said Colin, making no attempt to hide his irritability. 'Put a tracker on his car. Blow the budget! If the man's guilty, I want him charged.'

'And if his father decides to have another bonfire in his back garden?' asked Blake. 'Other than using a drone, we've no way of seeing what Owen gets up to.'

'Owen Nixon has already destroyed Larry's fire-damaged clothes for him,' Grace reminded her boss.

'So arrest the father for conspiracy!'

'We can't do that until we're in a position to charge Larry with arson,' she said patiently.

'Then you'd better find those shoes!'

There was no point arguing when Colin was in this kind of

mood, and besides, she refused to make excuses for herself or her team.

Colin read her silence as a surrender. 'Let him kick his heels for a bit and then show him our shoe.' He swung his chair around to face his computer screen. It was a discourteous dismissal.

Blake followed Grace to her cubicle. 'Maybe he'll calm down once he's taken a couple of paracetamol,' he said.

She smiled. 'He is so going to hate getting old. But he's right. We've searched everywhere we can think of and come up blank. We'll never get a conviction unless we can find those shoes.'

'He'll have hidden them well.'

'Colin's right,' she admitted. 'You're right. We should use what we've got.'

'I think it could work,' said Blake. 'You could see Larry didn't like being confronted with the reality of the photographs, not after decades of being in total control of the narrative. One more visceral reminder of his crimes might just pierce his armour.'

'Maybe.' Her feeling of hopelessness was nudged aside by the nagging and incongruous image of her boss lifting weights. As she pushed aside the painful image of the sports bag that Blake had stashed out of sight – evidence perhaps of an affair with a junior colleague that, at some point, as their senior officer, she might have to address – another fleeting image dropped into her mind. It was of a red-faced man in a grey tracksuit coming out of a lift. Where had she seen that? For what reason had she recalled it now?

'Hang on,' she called, as Blake prepared to go. 'What's the name of Larry's apartment building?'

She waited with fingers poised over her keyboard as he brought it to mind. She typed in the name and, scrolling down the search results, came to the website of the estate agents who had originally marketed the newly built flats. 'Yes!' She beat the air with a fist.

'What?' asked Blake. 'What have you found?'

'It's probably nothing, and it's my stupid fault for not realising sooner, but Larry Nixon's apartment building has a basement gym. It's private, residents only. We never searched it, did we?'

'No,' he said, 'but if Larry uses it, he'll have a locker.'

'He looks pretty fit to me,' she said. 'And he's paying for the use of it, anyway, through his service charge. Get your coat.'

The hour-long journey to Southend seemed to stretch on forever. Grace was only too aware of how the clock was ticking on Larry Nixon's period in custody. If they returned empty-handed, she would have wasted precious time.

Although the concierge recognised them, he was initially reluctant to allow them access to the private gym, let alone to a resident's personal locker. Blake explained politely that, with Larry Nixon under arrest and currently in custody, they had a legal right to search any property occupied or controlled by him, which included any personal storage area to which he held the key. The young man consulted a list on his computer that supplied Larry Nixon's locker number and then accompanied them down in the lift. It opened on to a small lobby where a glass partition fronted an exercise area heavy on industrial chic, with bare concrete walls and exposed metal pipework across the ceiling. Various pieces of black equipment – weights bench, treadmill, cross-trainer and rowing machine – faced floor-length mirrors on the opposite wall. An elderly man plugging away on an exercise bike nodded to the concierge and watched curiously as he led the visitors into the male changing room.

It was not a big area and had few amenities other than simple bathroom facilities and a wall of blond wooden locker doors sitting above a wide slatted bench. The concierge identified the locker at the far end as belonging to Mr Nixon of apartment 71 and, once he realised that Blake would otherwise force entry, nervously handed over the master key.

Blake pulled on a pair of nitrile gloves and then unlocked the tall wooden door. Grace held her breath and crossed her fingers tightly behind her back as he opened it wide. A quick glance showed exactly what she would have expected: towels, shorts, several singlets, discarded sweat bands and a pair of well-worn trainers. The disappointment was painful. But then she followed Blake's blue-gloved hand up to the top shelf where a black sports bag had been stashed into a space only just big enough to contain it.

He lifted it down carefully. It was bulky but did not appear to be heavy. He placed it on the bench and stood back. The zip fastening was padlocked. Grace met Blake's gaze, feeling herself go cold with anticipation. Was this it? Why else would a bag left down here be padlocked? Would it contain all the evidence they needed to put Larry Nixon away for life?

She watched Blake run his hand tentatively over the stiff fabric, feeling for the contours of the objects inside. They appeared to shift about relatively freely inside the bag and he looked at her, his eyes shining.

'Could be,' he said.

'Let's get it straight to the lab.'

The drive back to Colchester with their precious cargo bagged up on the back seat felt even more tortuous than the journey down. Intensely aware of the aura given off by whatever lay sealed inside the bag, Grace was certain that the malign spell the mysterious contents cast over Larry Nixon was nothing compared to the powerful charge they were exerting right now over her.

53

Grace stood watching beside Blake as Wendy swabbed and taped the padlock on the black sports bag before cutting through the flimsy bolt. They were all wearing forensic suits and masks so as not to contaminate any DNA evidence the bag might contain, and the air seemed almost static with expectation. Grace had a flash of doubt, suddenly convinced that her hunch had been a foolish waste of time and the bag would be crammed with mouldering gym-wear. Wishing the ground would open and swallow her up, she held her breath as Wendy unzipped the bag. She and Blake both leaned forward to peer inside and saw the soft nap of beige, white and pale blue drawstring bags. Shoe bags. Her heart leapt. It was over, she'd been right, they had him!

'Open one,' she begged Wendy.

Wendy smiled. 'You'll have to be patient.'

Wendy stood back to allow the forensic photographer a better angle on the interior of the sports bag and only then lifted out the first fabric pouch. She took it over to a separate bench where she placed it on a piece of blanking paper, laid a scale beside it and waited for the photographer to record it. Grace was on tenterhooks as Wendy requested close-ups of how the drawstring had been tied.

'Sometimes a knot can offer important evidence,' she said by way of apology for making them wait. She snipped the string and removed the intact knot, bagging it up separately. Finally, she slipped a gloved hand into the opened bag and pulled out a black patent-leather shoe with a high, tapered heel. The sole was worn and the inside stained with what looked like sweat. It was for the left foot. As Wendy turned it over for the photographer Grace could make out the size number stamped on the inside. She'd expected to feel exhilaration, but it was one of the saddest sights she had ever seen.

Blake put a hand on her shoulder and squeezed, looking at her in excitement. She didn't trust herself to speak. Triumph, exhaustion, pity, relief; she wasn't sure which one was uppermost.

Wendy swabbed and taped the inside and outside of the shoe before examining it under different wavelengths of light. Finding a faint glow on the inner sole, she delicately removed it and then, warning them that such findings were not conclusive, scraped an area of its surface for an enzymatic test for seminal fluid. When that showed a positive reaction, she cut away a small portion from which a slide would be prepared for confirmation prior to DNA testing.

Wendy slowly unburdened the black sports bag of ten further single high-heeled shoes, taking her time to examine and then bag each of them in turn. Each was in its own cloth bag, none was new and all were for the left foot. Grace was able immediately to identify three of them: one had belonged to Cara Chalkley (white plastic), another to Rhona Geary (pale pink with an imitation metal-embossed decal) and the one which had been worn by Heather Bowyer (a pink sling-back). Heather's shoe, the pair to which had been gathering dust in a police property store for twenty-five years, still bore a faded and half-torn-off price sticker on the unworn instep, a sharp reminder of a life unlived.

Eleven pieces of evidence, each in its numbered evidence bag. *Eleven* women. It seemed safe to assume that, in addition to Heather's, five of the shoes would belong to the women who had reported being raped to the police at the time of their assault, and one probably to the poor wretch whom Grace had met and who hadn't wanted to give her name, but that still left four other women who had suffered in silence. Grace dreaded the task of tracking them down. Although she hoped a conviction would bring some measure of closure, she wouldn't be surprised if, after so many years, the unidentified women who had owned these shoes chose never to come forward.

She realised how little, when she'd first grasped the possible significance of the missing shoes, she had prepared herself for this sight, and hoped that the twelve eventual jury members flipping through the photographs in their evidence books would fully understand the pain, terror and ongoing trauma that each of these ordinary and inoffensive objects represented.

'How quickly can we get DNA?' she asked.

'I assume you only need a match to him and one of the victims to charge him,' said Wendy. 'We can fast-track for those and take our time with the rest.'

'So tomorrow or the next day?' The clock was ticking, but Grace was confident she would now be granted a thirty-six-hour extension to the time they could hold Larry Nixon in custody for questioning.

'We'll do our best,' said Wendy. 'Which one do you want us to process first?'

'Heather Bowyer's pink sling-back,' said Grace. 'An initial charge of rape and murder should quash any argument about remand.'

'And being able to disprove his account of Reece's "confession" opens the door to charging Larry with arson and a further double murder,' said Blake.

'We're making good progress on that petrol cap, by the way,' said Wendy. 'If there's anything to find, we should have it for you in the next day or two.'

'Brilliant.' This welcome news didn't stop Grace experiencing another flash of anxiety. She looked at the shoes. 'We will be able to find his DNA, won't we?'

Wendy grinned. 'If he's been doing what I think he's been doing with them, we'll have more than enough.'

Grace laughed from the relief finally coursing through her veins. 'Can you imagine the nicknames they're going to give him in prison?'

'His violent, grubby little secret is going to be on the front page of every newspaper.' Blake's tone was unforgiving. 'He's not going to like that one bit.'

'No,' Grace agreed. 'He's going to hate us.'

She was right. A couple of hours later, as soon as Larry Nixon fully recognised what they were showing him, he turned so pale, shivery and clammy-looking that Grace considered putting him back in his cell and calling a doctor. However, he quickly made what was evidently a huge effort to pull himself together and the colour returned slowly to his cheeks. Re-assured that he wasn't about to faint or be sick, she placed in front of him, sealed in its evidence bag, the first of the three shoes they had identified.

'Did you take this shoe from Heather Bowyer?'

Larry stared down between his knees at the floor. 'No comment.'

'Did you, on the third of October 1992, in Cliff Gardens, Southend, rape Heather Bowyer and, furthermore, stab her in the back with a kitchen knife, resulting in her death?'

'No comment.'

'Did you take this shoe from Cara Chalkley?'

'No comment.'

'Did you, on the fifth of June 1992, in Southchurch Park, Southend, rape Cara Chalkley?'

'No comment.'

'Did you take this shoe from Rhona Geary?'

'No comment.'

'Did you, on the eighteenth of July 1992, in Cliff Gardens, Southend, rape Rhona Geary?'

'No comment.'

As Blake removed each shoe and placed another in front of Larry, Grace observed what torture it was for him to endure the sight of another man handling his treasures. Barely attending to her questions, his gaze followed each shoe as Blake placed it aside. As Blake put away Rhona's expensive pink shoe, Larry stretched out a hand towards it and looked around and under the table as if searching for the rest. Far worse than the dawning realisation that they knew his secrets, that he was never going back to his light-filled apartment and that he was going to prison, possibly for the rest of his life, was the loss of these precious objects. He could never touch any of them again. They had passed beyond his control. He had lost everything.

Larry Nixon began to weep. The urbane and meticulous businessman they had previously encountered crumbled before their eyes as his intense private world fell apart.

Grace had what she needed for now and ended the interview, telling him that he would be held in custody overnight – she had already been granted an extension. As Larry was led back to his cell, she warned the custody sergeant to keep him on suicide watch.

She was exhausted. Colin had been over the moon when informed that, hopefully within the next twenty-four hours, they were likely to have the DNA evidence that, this time, would be enough to convict Heather Bowyer's killer. Colin had congratulated her in front of the entire team, who were all equally jubilant. Duncan had said he was glad he got back in time to play his part, and Carolyn that she couldn't believe her luck at getting to work on the investigation. Grace knew she had gambled on the original familial DNA search and won. She ought to be as thrilled as everyone else, but now, after the interview with Larry, she couldn't face going for a drink with them all. She just wanted to be on her own.

She managed to slip away without anyone noticing. Outside in the car park it seemed later than it was. The clocks had changed at the weekend and she was not yet used to the earlier darkness. Driving home, she saw bunches of kids with painted faces roaming the streets dressed as black-hatted witches, skeletons and Frankenstein monsters bandaged with toilet paper, and she passed several front gardens that sported glowing pumpkins carved with jagged, leering faces. She had forgotten that tonight was Halloween.

It all seemed laughably theatrical compared to the banal yet potent evil of the man locked up in a cell in the basement of Colchester Police HQ. Tomorrow Grace would also have to visit Monica Bowyer and explain to her that her beautiful daughter had died so that Larry Nixon could toss himself off into one of her shoes. She wasn't going to phrase it so crudely, but that was the depressing truth. Maybe it would be easier if rapists and murderers did actually look like monsters, but she knew all too well that true evil was never as simple as that.

54

🔊))

Welcome back to *Stories from the Fire*. I'm Freddie Craig, and I've been investigating a second brutal murder that took place in Southend around the time I was born, that of sixteen-year-old April Irwin. Her death is not connected with the rape and murder of nineteen-year-old Heather Bowyer. Or not in the obvious ways. But we'll get to that later.

Right now, I'm speaking to a woman I'll call 'Jane'. That's not her real name but, well, you'll see why she's nervous about identifying herself.

So, 'Jane', explain why you got in touch after hearing the most recent episode of *Stories from the Fire*.

Jane: I was at school with April.

Freddie: That was in Romford?

Jane: Yes. I wasn't her best friend. That was a girl I'm going to call 'Hayley'.

Freddie: Jane has also asked me not to make Hayley's real name public either.

Jane: I remember when April ran away. At school we talked about nothing else for weeks. To begin with no one knew where she was. And then 'Hayley' started getting letters from her.

Freddie: Letters?

Jane: She would bring them to school and read bits out, about why April had left, about her mum's horrible new boyfriend, about how lonely and miserable she was. April used to cover the letters in kisses and stuff, saying how much she missed her mates. That was until she met someone, anyway.

Freddie: Did she say who? Did she give a name?

Jane: I'm sure she must have done, but there's no way I'd remember it now. Too much water under the bridge since those days. And April was never my closest friend.

Freddie: But it was a boyfriend she wrote to about, very possibly the father of her child?

Jane: Oh yes, definitely. She was on cloud nine. Although after April met this guy, her best friend, 'Hayley', would only show us tiny bits of her letters. Used to put her hand over parts she didn't want us to see. I think she got a kick out of making like they were too personal to share with anyone else, and that she was the gatekeeper. Made her feel important.

Freddie: So if April had named the father of her child in these letters, why didn't the police speak to him? Why were April's letters never mentioned at the trial?

Jane: Because by the time we found out that April was dead the police had caught someone. It never occurred to us that they wouldn't have got the right man.

Freddie: You didn't hear about her murder when it happened?

Jane: The nearest thing to newspapers that we read were *Smash Hits* and *Just Seventeen*. And most of us were leaving school, getting jobs. I guess it didn't take long for us to forget about poor April.

Freddie: Did she ever mention the name of Damon Smith, the man convicted of her murder?

Jane: Not that I can recall now.

Freddie: So what happened to April's new romance? Something must have gone badly wrong for her to end up sleeping on a stranger's floor.

Jane: I don't know. To be honest, the main thing I remember is us all crowding around 'Hayley' and her showing us these pieces of paper with big loopy handwriting and, as I say, lots of hearts and flowers and long lines of kisses. She loved the attention.

Freddie: You're not in touch with her now?

Jane: No.

Freddie: Well then, that's my job, to track down April Irwin's best friend. She might be more likely to remember the name of April's new boyfriend. She might even have April's letters still in her possession.

Any fresh leads they might reveal are too late now to be of any help to Damon Smith, who died in prison, but they might raise interesting questions around why the police were so quick to charge him. And why the father of April's unborn child never came forward at the time.

So, if you're listening now, or if you're someone who can put me in touch with April's best friend at school, or maybe even knows the name of the man who fathered April's unborn child, you can contact me through the website. I'm Freddie Craig, and this is *Stories from the Fire*.

As I said earlier, April Irwin's murder is not connected in any obvious way to that of Heather Bowyer. The two young women never met, and I'm not suggesting that the same person is responsible for both slayings. But there is a connection and, if you think about it, it might spread even further than these two crimes.

Two unrelated and possibly unsolved murders in the same small town within a month of each other. I'm not saying there's an ongoing conspiracy. But Damon Smith, the man perhaps wrongly convicted of April's murder, died protesting his innocence. And it's taken twenty-five years for the police to get anywhere near catching Heather Bowyer's killer. As I speak, still no one has yet been charged. Why not? What do the police have to hide?

Maybe you can begin to understand why 'Jane' chooses not to reveal her real name, or that of April's best friend.

Maybe there are innocent explanations for all the questions I'm trying to raise. Either way, you can help me to find the answers. Spread the word, get in touch, let me know what you think. I'm Freddie Craig. Thank you for listening to *Stories from the Fire*.

55

The morning ground slowly on as the whole of the Major Investigation Team waited for news of the first DNA results from Heather Bowyer's pink sling-back shoe. People pretended to be working, but Grace could see how often they glanced up at the clock or, like meerkats, pivoted in unison to look towards a ringing phone. She was no better. With each hour that passed she reminded herself that it might be the next day before the results came back, and yet, with each hour, her insecurity grew that somehow Larry would yet again slide from their grasp.

She distracted herself by considering how best to proceed with the troubling update Duncan had given her about Terri Nixon. Terri had been fifteen when she got pregnant with Deborah. It appeared that either her family had cut her off – at no stage had she ever been reported missing – or Owen, who was ten years older, had deliberately isolated her from them. By the time she was twenty she had three young children. She had a National Insurance number, and had claimed child benefits, but did not appear to have worked outside the home, and her NI number had not been linked to any current address since the 1980s. She had not otherwise generated any kind of official identity that had needed to be dismantled after her death – no bank account, credit card or any household bills in her name. But then perhaps it wasn't so unusual for a woman married at sixteen in the mid-1960s to leave all financial matters to her older husband, and Grace could easily imagine Owen choosing to retain complete control.

It was possible that Terri Nixon had been sophisticated enough to run away and then cover her tracks, but it seemed unlikely. And she had never applied for a passport, so it was also unlikely that she was now living abroad. According to Larry, her children had not attended their mother's funeral and he seemed to consider it normal that he should have no idea where she was buried. His lack of curiosity about her fate, now that he was an adult, was striking.

Did both Larry and Deborah possess an obedience to their father so ingrained that neither would even question the cover story he'd invented for a wife who had fled from him and her children? Or was it something worse? Was it that neither Deborah or Larry dared risk finding out what had really happened to their mother?

Had Reece Nixon felt the same? Owen claimed he'd thrown Reece out because he had no respect. Was that because he'd been asking awkward questions? Grace would have loved to be able to ask Anne and Michael whether their father had ever talked about his mother. She also looked forward to assuring them that Reece had had no hand in Kirsty's death and had been totally exonerated of the other, older crimes. They could now make peace with their grandmother. However, until she had the DNA results from the shoes and could tell them officially that Larry had been charged, she was loath to disturb them with further dark speculations about their grandfather.

She could, however, arrange to speak once more to Deborah Shillingford.

Grace had just got off the phone when she saw Wendy enter the main office, a broad smile on her face. Grace hurried to greet her as the rest of the team crowded round.

'Thought I'd bring the news in person,' said Wendy.

'Well, go on then!'

'DNA inside Heather Bowyer's shoe is a match to the DNA profile from a blood sample taken from her body. Other DNA present is a match to the sample given voluntarily by Larry Nixon two weeks ago.'

'Yes!' A huge cheer went up. Grace looked around at beaming faces as members of the team slapped her on the back or came up to shake her hand.

'You did it, boss!'

'Got him!'

'We nailed the bastard!'

Colin came out of his office. 'It's done?'

'It's done,' she said. 'We'll match as many of the other shoes as we can to their owners, but it's done.'

'Congratulations, DI Fisher,' Colin said formally. 'Excellent work.'

'Thank you, sir. Larry Nixon is a very dangerous man. It'll be a pleasure to see him behind bars.'

'It was you who first made the connection between the rapist and the missing shoes,' said Blake. 'We wouldn't have him if it wasn't for that.'

'We have him,' she said, pleased. 'That's all that counts.'

As the others milled around, not yet ready to put their euphoria aside and get back to work, Grace retreated to her desk.

She wasn't sure why, but she felt more relief than elation, and wished she could share in her team's sense of jubilation. She looked up as the crime scene manager approached her desk.

'Thanks for all your hard work on this, Wendy,' she said. 'I would never have started down this road if it weren't for you.'

'You were the one sticking your neck out,' said Wendy. 'Though you might not be too pleased with the rest of my news.'

'You'd better hit me with it then.'

'We managed to find one amazingly clear fingerprint on the cap of the petrol canister from the Nixon fire.'

'But that's good, isn't it?'

'Yes, except it doesn't belong to Larry Nixon,' said Wendy, 'or to anyone on the IDENT1 database. We also ran them against the prints we lifted from the house for Reece and Kirsty Nixon: *nada*. I'm afraid you blew the budget for nothing.'

Grace frowned. 'Can't be helped. And it was always a long shot. So maybe Larry Nixon wore gloves. This doesn't rule him out. The prints probably belong to one of the guys who worked for Reece. I'll get it checked out.'

'Sorry not to put the cherry on your cake,' said Wendy, 'but great work all the same.'

As Wendy returned to join in the chat in the main office, Grace shifted her chair to look out of the window. Larry was the only person with a motive to kill Reece, and they still had Dr Tripathi's opinion that his injuries from the fire could have been the distinctive flash burns of an arsonist. She wondered what had really passed between Reece and Larry that night. Had Reece called Larry to warn him about the DNA tests and begged him to turn himself in? The press cuttings in the attic suggested that Reece had suspected his brother for a very long time.

Was that why Larry had stopped offending after Heather's death, because Reece had threatened to go to the police if he didn't? Until now, Grace had imagined that it was something to do with the grandiosity of being the hero of the Marineland fire, a chance juxtaposition only minutes after taking a life that offered a potent promise of redemption. But maybe, all along, it had been Reece who was the silent hero, who had found the determination to exert control over his younger brother while retaining enough family loyalty not to go running to the police. If so, then he and his wife and children had paid a terrible price for that loyalty.

56

The body of the young man lay face down in the mud. The back of his padded jacket had two slashing tears in it and, despite the seawater, was heavily bloodstained. It was only just light, but Inspector Dave Clements advised Grace that the tide had turned and she needed to get the body photographed and then moved as quickly as possible. There was not enough time to call Dr Tripathi down here, and in any case the body had probably been carried here by a swelling or retreating tide, depending on the time and place it went into the water, which could be anywhere along Southend's coastal strip.

Grace thought it likely that the time of death would be late the previous night or in the early hours of the morning – the usual time when young men got into fights and knives caused mayhem and tragedy. Once this young man's body had been identified they would no doubt be able to piece together an all-too-common tale of drink, rivalry and misplaced bravado. She was back to business as usual.

She looked at her watch. Another couple of hours and Larry Nixon would be put in front of the magistrates in Colchester, who, unless he had found an extremely clever lawyer, would place him on remand. He had been formally charged the previous afternoon with the rape and murder of Heather Bowyer, the rape of Cara Chalkley and Rhona Geary, and with arson and the murder of Kirsty and Reece Nixon. Further charges would follow once the owners of all the other shoes had been identified, a task that Grace hoped they'd be able to accomplish fully.

When asked by the custody sergeant if he had anything to say in response to the charges, Larry had answered quietly that he was not responsible for his brother's death. Grace didn't believe him. She had seen before how the most brazen offenders would, out of some obscure shame, baulk at admitting to what might even be some small and seemingly insignificant detail of their crimes. Fratricide was hardly a small thing, and it didn't surprise her that Larry couldn't bring himself to accept that this was what he had done. Or maybe, she thought, he was too in love with the image of himself as the would-be rescuer dashing into the inferno to confess the truth.

Blake would represent Grace in court, but she would have liked to stand beside her team to watch Larry leave the station in Colchester. It was the completion of a job well done.

The easterly wind was biting cold and Grace was grateful that Dave Clements had suggested on the phone that she wrap up warm and bring welly boots. The cold hadn't, however, stopped a small group of curious dog-walkers and runners from gathering on the path that ran along the shore. She hoped the mortuary van would arrive soon and they could get the investigation underway. Someone, somewhere would be wondering why this young man had not come home last night.

Her visit to Monica and Simon Bowyer the previous afternoon was fresh in her mind, along with her calls to Cara Chalkley and Rhona Geary. She knew that the end of her inquiry was only the beginning of a new phase in how each of them separately dealt with the past.

Dave Clements returned from speaking to his uniform officers, asking them to move the rubber-neckers along. He sniffed as if the freezing air was making his nose run. 'I saw on the news last night that you've charged Larry Nixon,' he said grudgingly.

So far they had been meticulously polite to one another, and neither had mentioned their earlier meeting. 'Yes,' she said. 'We have definitive evidence linking him to a series of crimes, and, although he's not made any admission, he's not denying it, either.'

'I have to be honest with you, DI Fisher, I've never been more gobsmacked in my life. I don't know the man well, but I've chatted with him, shared a joke. I mean, I've asked him to drive my wife and kids on a couple of occasions. It's thrown me completely.'

'I can imagine,' she said. 'In our job you always think you have the right antennae.'

'I never saw it,' he said. 'Never.'

Seeing his sincerity, she decided to push a little to discover if there was more he would tell her. 'We might not be done with the family yet,' she said. 'Our inquiry has thrown up an anomaly we need to straighten out.'

He nodded, showing none of the antagonism she'd faced when they'd met before.

'Larry's mother, Terri Nixon, appears to have vanished off the face of the earth around 1982.'

Clements frowned and shook his head. 'I never heard any-thing about her. Was she reported missing?'

'No,' she said. 'Owen Nixon told his kids she was dead.'

'Southend is full of transients,' he said. 'Poverty-on-Sea. People drift in for the summer. A few become fixtures, but most move on and occasionally take new friends along with them. Have you spoken to Owen?'

'Not yet,' she said. 'Did you know that the working girls around Southchurch Park call him the "Guardian Angel"?'

Clements laughed. 'I think you'll find they were pulling your leg.'

'What makes you say that?'

Before Clements could answer, both the forensic photog-rapher and the mortuary van arrived, and Grace wanted to pay attention to the body as it was moved. Once it had been rolled over all she could see was a face plastered in mud, the wet hair sticking to the scalp, yet there was something about the shape of the jaw that seemed familiar. It was only later, at the mortu-ary, after he had been undressed and cleaned up, that she recognised the young man as Freddie Craig.

57

When Ivo saw it on the *Courier*'s news feed his hands started to shake the way they had when he'd first quit drinking, and all he could think about was how desperately he wanted someone to hand him a bottle of gin. He'd killed Freddie. First he'd sent an innocent man to jail, and now he'd got Freddie killed for doing what he should have had the guts to do himself.

He knew that if he tried to remain at his desk and pursue a normal day, he would end up in one of the trendy wine bars that had replaced the local pubs. It had been five years since he'd last experienced such an urgent desire to feel the unfettering effects of alcohol hit his brain, and he recognised that he wouldn't be able to fight it for long.

The *Courier* could hardly ignore the murder of the podcaster they'd championed and then dropped, and, after the usual grumbling, his editor was happy enough to let him head off to Southend in pursuit of the story. At Liverpool Street Ivo bought a ticket to Colchester and called DI Fisher from the train. She was the only person he wanted to see. The thought of her was his only redemption, and he clung to the sound of her voice on the phone like a drowning man to a lifebuoy.

He took a taxi straight to the police station. The woman on

the front desk had been told that DI Fisher was expecting him and showed him into a windowless little room that tried its best not to look like a padded cell. Ivo hoped he wouldn't have to wait there on his own for long. He wasn't sure he'd be able to hold his nerve.

He got up eagerly when she opened the door, but was immediately disappointed to see that she had someone with her, a younger woman whom Grace introduced as DC Carolyn Bromfield. Grace shook hands without much of a smile and then invited him in a formal manner to sit down.

'You asked to speak to us because you have information you believe might be relevant to the death of Freddie Craig, is that correct?' she asked, every inch the Ice Maiden of old.

Ivo hung his head, avoiding her cool grey eyes. This might not be the offer of redemption he had envisaged, but beggars can't be choosers. 'I told him to look into the murder of April Irwin. I think that's why he was killed.' He took a deep breath. 'It should have been me. I should never have sent a boy to do a man's job.'

'You'll have to explain,' she said.

He looked up and hoped he wasn't wrong about the encouraging hint of warmth he read into her steady gaze. 'It all goes back to DI Jason Jupp.' He stopped. Could he say the words aloud? Admit to the most shameful thing he'd ever done? He knew he had to, if only to save himself. If he didn't tell her everything right now, his only hope would be to get drunk and stay drunk. He kept his eyes on Grace, doing his best to ignore the presence of the other detective. 'JJ knew from the off that Damon Smith never killed April Irwin.'

The world did not stop turning. The two women merely waited calmly for him to say more.

'JJ knew because I'd told him I'd been drinking in the same pub as Damon Smith all afternoon. JJ told me to go back to London and forget all about it.'

Her silence was unbearable. He couldn't look at her. He'd give a king's ransom for a slug of gin.

'And did you?' she asked finally.

'Yes.' He wasn't going to make excuses for himself. Besides, he didn't have any, apart from being stupid and naive enough to fall for JJ's reptilian charm.

'Do you know why DI Jupp asked you to do that?'

'He never said, but he led me to believe it was to protect an informant.'

'An informant who'd kicked a pregnant girl to death?'

The chill in her voice was like a slap. He deserved every bit of scorn and contempt she could muster. He was a journalist. He could have discovered JJ's reasons in five minutes flat if he'd really wanted to.

'The woman Freddie interviewed in his final podcast,' he said, 'The one he called "Jane", have you spoken to her?' She paused just that bit too long. 'I'm here to tell you everything I know,' he pleaded. 'Totally off the record, whatever I can do to help.'

She thought it over and then nodded. ' "Jane" doesn't exist.'

He saw the younger detective look at Grace in surprise. From the manner in which DC Bromfield immediately tried to mask her reaction, her boss must have committed a massive indiscretion. Ivo thanked all the gods he could think of, silently promising to light candles, pour votive oil or kill fatted calves, whatever it took to express his overwhelming gratitude that he hadn't entirely forfeited Grace's trust.

'So who was Freddie talking to?' he asked.

'The woman whose voice we heard on that last podcast came forward as soon as she heard about Freddie's death,' said Grace. 'She owns a hairdressing salon in Southminster, which is where Freddie's been staying with his grandmother. "Jane" is a leading light in the local am-dram society and says he asked her to do it and gave her a script.'

Ivo was stunned. The kid had made it up! He was more creative than Ivo had given him credit for.

'We have Freddie's phone and computer. No school friend of April Irwin ever made contact through his website.'

'So there are no letters to "Hayley" either?' he asked.

Grace glanced at DC Bromfield. 'We had an idea that he might have been fictionalising events for a while now,' she said. 'Do you know why he'd do that?'

'He was a nice kid,' Ivo told her, 'but he was desperate. He was skint and had been dumped by his girlfriend. All he wanted was to be a journalist, and he viewed this podcast as his last chance to catch a break. He must've decided to sex it up.'

'And you think this stunt got him killed?'

'If the man who did murder April Irwin believed Freddie was about to get hold of letters that would name him as the father of her child, then yes,' said Ivo. 'Whoever he is, he had the clout back then to make JJ risk a cover-up for him.'

'Perhaps someone who knew enough about Jupp to blackmail him?' she asked.

'That would do the trick.'

'I don't know how long the star of the show in Southminster will be able to keep it to herself,' said Grace, 'but if at all possible I don't want anyone else finding out that the letters were never real.'

'You have my word.'

'What about you?' she asked. 'Do you want police protection?'

'Me?' The thought hadn't occurred to him.

'This man might know that DI Jupp suborned your silence.' She stated it matter-of-factly, and he was grateful that she hadn't attempted to whitewash it.

'If I'd had the balls to tell the truth in the first place, Freddie would still be alive,' he said. 'I never warned him, never told him the full story, just sent him out into no man's land without so much as a white flag.' The enormity of the kid's death hit him with full force and he rubbed a hand over his face. 'You've spoken to his parents?'

'His father came this afternoon to identify the body.'

Ivo tried to picture the daughter he hadn't seen since she was a little girl. Emily would be about the same age as Freddie. What was wrong with him? What kind of piss-poor excuse for a human being was he?

'You should arrest me,' he said. He longed for her to agree, for an external agency of justice to offer him a means to atone. 'I knew Damon Smith was innocent and I said nothing.'

'Did you lie under oath?'

'No. I never said anything. JJ told me to keep my mouth shut and I did.'

'Then it's not perjury.'

'But I had a pretty good idea of the consequences of what I was doing.'

She gave him a look that almost broke his heart. 'Unfortunately, inaction in such circumstances does not qualify as an offence,' she said. 'You'll have to deal with your conscience in your own way.'

He got to his feet. 'Then you'll excuse me while I go and find the nearest AA meeting.' Finding the nerve to look Grace Fisher in the eye as she held the door open for him was one of the hardest things he'd ever done.

58

After a long talk with Wendy, Grace called her team together and asked for everything they had so far on the murder of Freddie Craig. Dr Tripathi had confirmed that he died from two upward stab wounds to the back, one of which had perforated his heart. In Samit's opinion they were likely to have been administered at close range, with the attacker securing his victim around the neck with his free arm. Freddie might well have been taken by surprise and would have had little opportunity to struggle or fight back.

Duncan had tracked Freddie's journey from his grandmother's house in Southminster by train to Southend, and was coordinating a search of all available CCTV footage between Southend Victoria station and the seafront. So far it had not been possible with any accuracy to pinpoint when or where Freddie's body had entered the water.

There was nothing among the comments on the podcast website to explain why Freddie had travelled to Southend that evening. The only clue Blake had found was a three-minute call received little more than an hour before Freddie purchased his train ticket at Southminster station. Given that there had been no previous contact between Freddie and this number – which

Blake had traced to a pay-as-you-go SIM card that was now unobtainable – he was curious as to how the mysterious caller had obtained Freddie's mobile number.

Blake had also spoken to his grandmother – a seventy-two-year-old who made it clear she wasn't going to give in to shock or grief in front of strangers – who said that Freddie had originally intended to stay at home with her that evening but, after receiving a phone call, had changed his plans and seemed quite excited about whatever it was he was rushing off to do. She felt responsible for not knowing his plans or who had called, and for not reporting him missing when he didn't come back that night, but insisted he was a perfectly capable young man who needed his freedom and she'd tried not to fuss over him.

Grace now added in Ivo Sweatman's belief that Freddie might have been killed because someone believed his invention about the existence of letters naming the father of April Irwin's unborn child. She had been shaken by Ivo's explanation as to why he was so certain it was not Damon Smith who had killed April and why he believed that her actual killer was still at large. Grace had grown fond of the old rogue and knew she owed him a debt for past assistance and support, but, all the same, she had not expected to feel quite so shocked by his revelations. Past loyalty made her reluctant to spell out the details of his collusion to the whole team, but there was no skirting around the fact that he had helped a corrupt detective frame an innocent man.

She glanced over at Blake sitting with his arms folded beside Carolyn, who leaned on the table twiddling a pen, her straight blonde hair falling forward and half-hiding her face. Grace's recollection of how her own protective silence over Ivo had forfeited

Blake's trust made her all the more bitter about the reporter's betrayal of her faith in him.

As if reading her thoughts, Blake voiced his own doubts. 'How far should we trust this Sweatman character?'

'On this we can,' she answered briskly.

Carolyn kept her head down, prompting Grace to wonder if she had confided in Blake her doubts about the wisdom of their boss sharing confidential information with a tabloid reporter. Grace had to accept that Carolyn's doubts had been justified, yet the fact remained that Ivo had chosen to come to her today to offer his confession, regardless of the cost to himself.

'I think we should also trust his opinion on why DI Jupp might have risked covering up the truth of such a brutal and vicious crime,' she continued. 'That it was to protect an informant.'

'That's what I don't get, boss,' said Duncan. 'Why would an informant be worth the risk of losing his career, his pension and even his freedom?'

'Ivo Sweatman thinks it was because Jupp's previous corruption had left him open to blackmail,' she responded. 'It may be that he had very little choice. Jupp apparently boasted about trousering around half a million in cash thanks to a tip-off from an informant about a factory in Southend churning out ecstasy pills. Jupp claimed to have shared the booty with a couple of fellow officers, so they'd all have good reason to keep their informant happy. It was the supergrass era, remember. If the informant found himself arrested he was likely to turn Queen's evidence and spill the beans on internal corruption in Southend.'

Grace paused to look at each of her assembled team. 'According to Melanie Riggs, a former police constable,' she continued, 'one of Jupp's main informants at that time was Owen Nixon.'

She waited for the quiver of reaction to pass around the room. 'So the important question is whether the background to the murder of April Irwin was a credible enough motive to have killed Freddie Craig twenty-five years later. If so, then we have to take a very close look at Owen Nixon.'

'The working girls I spoke to in Southend said he sometimes offers girls free lifts or a bed for the night,' said Carolyn. 'He might have met April that way.'

'And Larry Nixon said in interview that his father had girls staying who helped with the housework,' said Grace.

Blake frowned. 'How old would Owen have been at the time?'

'Fifty-two.'

'And April was barely sixteen.'

'Yes, but so was Terri Nixon when she became pregnant with Owen's first child.'

'Terri Nixon who is missing, presumed dead,' said Blake.

'Precisely,' she said.

'Or it could have been one of his sons who was the father of April's unborn child,' Carolyn pointed out. 'And, therefore, also her killer.'

Grace nodded. 'We know from Melanie Riggs that Owen had already used his clout with DI Jupp to steer the rape investigation away from Larry.'

'So we'd need to place April in Owen's house in the months before her death,' said Blake dubiously. 'I'm concerned that we're putting an awful lot of faith on the say-so of a tabloid reporter. I mean, who gave Freddie Craig the story about April Irwin in the first place?'

'Ivo did,' said Grace.

'So it could all be some kind of wind-up or distraction.'

Grace had to accept that Blake's caution was right and sensible. 'Except that now Freddie is dead,' she said. 'And besides, there should be a relatively quick and easy way to establish whether there's any link between April and the Nixon family. Wendy says that a DNA profile will almost certainly still be available in the archived case file from blood samples taken from the child that April was carrying when she was killed. Once we have that, we can establish whether or not the father was a Nixon.'

'Larry was in custody last night,' said Duncan. 'Would Owen bother killing Freddie unless it was to protect himself?'

'It's Owen who brings young girls home,' said Grace.

'I don't see someone of Owen's age listening to a true-crime podcast, though,' said Carolyn. 'And how would he get hold of Freddie Craig's mobile number?'

Blake tapped a pen against his teeth. 'Freddie interviewed Larry Nixon for one of the podcast episodes. So he'd probably have Freddie's phone number, right?'

'Yes, but Larry was in already custody when Freddie's final episode about the letters went online,' said Grace. 'Too late for him to pass Freddie's number on to his father.'

'But Larry wasn't in custody when the first podcast about Damon Smith and a miscarriage of justice went live,' said Blake.

'But why would that have set alarm bells ringing for Larry unless he already knew about April Irwin?' asked Carolyn.

'Larry would still have been living at home with his father when April became pregnant,' said Blake. 'So if she *was* one of the girls who helped out with the cooking and cleaning, then

Larry was highly likely to have heard about what happened to her, even if none of the Nixon family had anything to do with her death.'

'Maybe enough to know what had made her desperate enough to sleep on Damon Smith's floor,' said Grace. 'Enough to warn his father that Freddie was digging up trouble. I know it's all fairly tenuous and circumstantial until we get the DNA, but it does all fit together pretty neatly. It has to be worth looking at.'

The only question that remained was whether a pensioner could really have overpowered a young man. Grace recalled her first encounter with Owen Nixon in the hospital and the unyielding way he had looked at her. Whatever his age, he certainly didn't lack unflinching determination or strength of will.

59

Although on the phone Deborah Shillingford had seemed resigned to Grace's request to visit her in Thorpe Bay, she opened her front door with tightly crossed arms, her gaze averted. Grace sympathised with her antagonism. They all knew the presence of the detectives could only result in further trouble being heaped upon her shoulders.

Deborah led Grace and Blake into the kitchen, where, as before, a burning cigarette and a half-drunk mug of instant coffee awaited her. As Grace sat down she had the impression that the number of gift-shop angels dotted around the tiny room had multiplied since their first visit.

'How are you feeling, Mrs Shillingford?' she asked. 'This has been a pretty difficult time for you.'

Deborah nodded. 'I don't understand what more you can want from me,' she said. 'It's all over now, surely?'

'Your brother Larry has been sent for trial, yes.'

'That'll be months away, won't it?'

'I expect so.'

'So, what do you want?'

Grace glanced at Blake, who stood leaning against the worktop, clearly feeling as uncomfortable as she did. 'Some other matters have arisen as a result of our investigation,' she said. 'You might be able to help us clear them up.'

Deborah turned her head to stare out of the window. Grace followed her gaze: an unkempt patch of grass, a dilapidated fence and a grey sky didn't offer much comfort. Grace waited until Deborah looked back into the room and nodded. 'Go on then,' she said.

'It's about your mother, Theresa Nixon.'

'She died of cancer.'

'Did you visit her in hospital?'

'No,' said Deborah. 'I wasn't living at home much then.'

'Did you go to her funeral?' Grace asked.

Deborah shook her head. 'Dad thought we'd be too upset.'

'What about your mother's family?' Grace continued doggedly, hating every word. 'Did they attend her funeral?'

'I never met them. They never came near us.'

'But you've visited her grave?'

'No. Thing is, Dad never told us much, just that she'd got ill but it was too late to do anything and she passed away. We didn't want to upset him, so we let him deal with it in his own way.'

'The problem is that there's no evidence your mother was ever treated for cancer,' said Grace, 'and there's no record of her death.'

Deborah lit a fresh cigarette with a shaky hand. 'So what are you saying?'

'You have no memories of her going to hospital?'

'She always was stick-thin.'

'Or of her funeral?'

'Dad told me I had to come over and keep an eye on the boys. He put on a black suit and went out, then he said it was best if we never mentioned her again.'

Grace looked at Blake, whose set face conveyed his revulsion at such a father, even if the preposterous story had been true.

'Do you have any reason to suppose she might still be alive?' Grace asked.

Deborah drew on her cigarette and then busied herself rounding off the ash on the edge of the ashtray. 'No.'

'If your mother had reasons to want to disappear, she wouldn't be in any trouble,' Grace assured her. 'We just want to know what happened to her.' She waited until it was clear that Deborah wasn't going to speak. 'Can you think of any reason why your father would have told you that she'd died when she hadn't?'

'No.' Deborah took a sip of cold coffee, avoiding having to look at either of them.

'What sort of relationship did your parents have? Was it volatile? Did they have rows? Was either of them ever violent?'

Deborah was unable to suppress a laugh. 'I told you before, didn't I? Dad never needs to hit anyone. He just has a way of making you do what he wants.'

'And if you refuse?'

Deborah pressed her lips together and once again stared out of the window. Grace caught Blake's eye and sent a silent appeal for help. He shifted slightly, attracting Deborah's attention.

'Do you have any photographs of your mother?' he asked gently.

'No,' said Deborah, showing the first signs of regret. 'I don't think I ever had one. And besides, so much of my stuff has got lost along the way. I left the last place with nothing but a couple of bin bags. I don't even have photos of my kids from when they were little.'

Her gaze panned slowly round her display of angels in what appeared to Grace to be a familiar meditation. It seemed to strengthen her, for she shifted in her seat to face Blake directly. 'You probably think I'm a total fuck-up,' she said. 'But sometimes, you know, given what my life's been like, I think I'm doing quite well.'

'I think you are, too,' he said. 'All the grief that our investigations have brought to your door, I'm not sure I would have coped as well.'

She gave a wan smile. 'Thanks.' She fiddled with her cigarette lighter. 'I always knew it was never Reece. It had to be Larry.'

'Larry was about twelve when your mother disappeared,' Blake said. 'Must have been tough on a kid that age.'

'Harder on Reece,' she said. 'It was trouble all the way between him and Dad after that.'

'Do you think that was perhaps because Reece understood what really happened to your mother?'

'Nothing happened. She died, that's all.' It was as if an old tribal allegiance had kicked in. 'Dad put a roof over our heads, food on the table, clean clothes, we all went to school. I may be a mess, but the boys did fine.'

'What?' The exclamation was out before Grace could stop it, but she was mystified by what kind of amnesia could make it possible for Deborah to describe Larry's crimes as *doing fine.*

'Yeah, well, I only meant—' Deborah got up and took her mug to the sink, turning her back on them.

Blake gave her a few moments to rinse out the mug and place it on the draining board before trying again. 'So once your mother was no longer there, we've been told that your father used to offer board and lodging to young women in return for household chores, is that right?'

Deborah's back stiffened. 'I'd left home by then.'

'But you were aware that there were girls in the house who helped out?'

'If that's what you want to call it.'

'What do you mean?'

'Nothing.'

'Did you ever meet a sixteen-year-old named April Irwin?' Blake asked.

She shifted slowly to face them. 'Is she the one who got killed?'

'That's right. Did she ever stay at your father's house?'

'It was someone else who killed her, though,' Deborah stated flatly. 'It wasn't Dad.'

'Did you think it might have been your father?'

'Of course not.'

'Was she ever at the house?'

'I can't answer that,' she said.

'We only want you to tell us the truth, Deborah,' said Grace.

'I can't.'

Grace exchanged glances with Blake. He gave her a little nod of encouragement. 'A young man was knifed to death in South-end the night before last,' she said. 'We think his murder may be connected to the murder of April Irwin.'

Deborah's hand trembled as she shook out a cigarette and lit it. She sat down again at the table, her head bowed. To Grace the sight of the widening line of grey along the centre parting of her dyed hair was heartbreaking.

'What went on at the house, Deborah?' she asked gently. 'When we mentioned housework, what did you mean by "if that's what you want to call it"?'

'Nothing.'

Grace cast around for something that would crack open the familial code of silence. Her eye fell on the rosy cheeks of a curly-haired cherub. 'Did you know that the working girls in Southend call your father the "Guardian Angel"?'

'No!' She looked disgusted. 'No, he can't still be—'

'Still be what?' Grace was becoming exasperated. 'If young women are at risk, then you need to tell us.'

'I can't. I've already caused enough trouble.'

'Was April Irwin ever at Owen Nixon's house?'

'You have to ask him!' cried Deborah. 'Ask him about the girls. It's not fair to ask me. I can't tell you any more. I can't!'

'Please, tell us what you know. Tell us what happened to your mother.'

'Nothing. Nothing happened. Dad did everything for us. We'd be starving in the streets if it weren't for him. We didn't need to know. We just had to get on with our lives. Nothing happened to Mum. Nothing.'

60

Owen Nixon appeared utterly unconcerned when Grace questioned him the following day at Southend Police Station about the whereabouts of his missing wife. 'I know as much as you do,' he said, after they had explained the lack of any evidence that she had died. 'My theory is that she ran off to be with the kid she gave up.' They were in an interview room and he had accepted Grace's offer of a cup of coffee. He smiled at her over its cardboard rim, a malicious glint in his eye. 'You found him yet, by the way?'

'No, and we don't expect to,' Blake said firmly.

'I'm still prepared to testify that Larry has a brother somewhere,' said Owen.

'Then you'd better be ready to produce his birth certificate,' said Blake.

Sensing that Owen was deliberately overriding their agenda to put himself in control, Grace intervened to get the interview back on track. 'If that was your theory,' she said, 'then why did you tell your children that Terri had died of cancer?'

Owen shrugged. 'Pride, I guess. No man likes to admit his wife has left him.'

'You didn't think it was cruel to let them believe their mother was dead?'

'Either way, she wasn't coming back,' he said, 'so what difference did it make? She obviously didn't care much for them or she wouldn't have gone. I could've told them that, I suppose.'

'Is that why you went through the charade of going to a non-existent funeral?'

'Did I?'

'We'd like you to take us through the events leading up to your wife's disappearance, and your subsequent actions.'

'I came home, she wasn't there.'

'Did she leave a note?'

'No.'

'Had you argued recently?'

'Not that I remember.'

'And yet you assumed that her sudden absence was because she'd left you?'

'What other explanation would there be?'

'That she'd met with an accident, perhaps?'

'If that was the case,' he said, 'someone would have told me.'

'Or that something worse had happened to her?'

'Never occurred to me.'

'Do you remember the date she left?' Grace asked. 'Or what day of the week it was?'

'No.'

'What did she take with her? Any clothes, money, documents?'

'Not that I noticed.'

'Why did you never report her as missing?'

'I didn't see the point.' He took a mouthful of coffee. 'If she decided to fuck off like that, I wouldn't want her back anyhow.'

'You weren't worried about her in any way? Didn't become concerned about her safety?'

'No.'

'You still don't seem very curious about her fate.'

'You're talking about a woman I haven't seen or heard from in thirty-five years. To tell the truth, I barely remember her.'

Grace decided to move on. 'So you were left with two teenage boys at home to take care of. How did you manage that?'

'Hired in help when I needed it.'

'In return for board and lodgings?'

He gave her a sly, appraising look. 'Sometimes.'

'Have you stayed in touch with any of the people who stayed in the house?'

'Yeah, we all send each other Christmas cards,' Owen said sarcastically.

'Can you remember any of their names?'

'I don't know. Elizabeth Taylor. Doris Day.'

'Women?'

'Of course. Their job was to mind the house, wasn't it?'

'Young women?'

'You don't have to pay them so much.'

'How many different helpers did you have over the years?'

He gave her a broad smile that was almost gleeful. 'I lost count.'

Owen's look of gratification sent a shudder of distaste through her. 'Do you remember a girl called April Irwin?'

'No.'

'She was murdered in Southend soon after the Marineland fire.'

'Bad luck.'

Grace watched as he drained the last of his coffee and pushed away the paper cup. She longed to snatch it, to bag up the precious evidence of his fingerprints and DNA, but dragged her gaze away from it. 'You don't recall April's murder being reported at the time?' she asked.

'No.'

'You never met her?'

'Not that I remember.'

'Never gave her a lift in your taxi or offered her a bed for the night?'

'Who knows?'

'Where were you on Wednesday night?'

'After I got the news that Larry wasn't coming home thanks to your trumped-up charges, you mean?' he asked nastily. 'At home, drowning my sorrows.'

'Can anybody vouch for that?'

'No.'

'Did you make or receive any phone calls?'

'No.' The sly look was back, as if he was aware of having outwitted them. 'Why? Do I need an alibi for something? Or are you just going to fit me up like you did Larry?'

'You may need an alibi, yes,' said Grace. 'We're investigating the death of a young man named Freddie Craig near Southend seafront on Wednesday night. We're awaiting further evidence, but we may wish to speak to you again on this matter.'

'Suit yourself.' Owen got to his feet, rising unsteadily and putting a hand to his stiff back. He had been upright and robust when he'd walked in, and Grace judged that he was now making a show of being a frail old man who couldn't hurt a fly.

'I'll be going now,' he said, 'unless you're arresting me?'

'You're free to go, Mr Nixon,' she said.

'Good.'

'We'll be in touch.'

'Don't bother,' he said. 'I'm a bit tired of you making life difficult for my family.' He moved towards the door, but then swung back round and scooped up his empty paper cup. He shook the dregs out onto the carpet tiles, crushed it in his fist and stuffed it into his jacket pocket. 'Don't want to leave any mess behind, do I?'

He winked at Grace, the sheer malevolence in his look shocking her into silence.

61

The alacrity with which Dave Clements managed to waylay Grace and Blake as they were leaving Southend Police Station made her suspect he had been watching out for them.

'I'd like a word, if you can spare the time, DI Fisher,' he said.

Blake had been in the middle of checking his messages so she nodded to him. 'I'll catch you up.'

Leaving Blake, she followed Clements to his office, where he closed the door behind her. 'I owe you an apology,' he said. 'I should have made it to you the other day, but, well, male pride, I suppose.'

She smiled. 'I wasn't that quick off the mark to suspect that Larry Nixon was our serial rapist either.'

'Not about that,' he said. 'About DI Jupp. No one likes to air their dirty linen in public, but the truth is that everyone here knows he was as filthy as they get. I'm told it took years to undo the damage he caused.'

'Unfortunately I don't think we're finished yet,' she said. 'We have good reason to think the Freddie Craig murder may be a direct result of his legacy.'

'Because of Jupp's involvement with Owen Nixon?'

'So far, it's all conjecture,' she said. 'Or at least until we see what some DNA results can tell us. Owen's connection certainly makes a compelling story, but then we all know how danger-ously a good story can blind you to the truth.'

'What can I do to help?'

'Tell me everything you know about DI Jupp,' she said.

'Not much, I'm afraid,' he said. 'He'd retired by the time I joined the force and must have died soon after. But, as a junior officer, you knew simply by the way people clammed up the instant his name was mentioned that there'd been serious issues. It was only after most of his generation had departed that people began to admit just how bent he'd been.'

'Can you give me details?' she asked.

'Not really,' he said. 'All I know for sure is that his name had been put on the blacklist.'

Grace frowned. 'The blacklist?'

'Names of officers whose integrity is seriously doubted and who shouldn't be regarded at trial as witnesses of truth. I guess that's why he retired when he did. I heard he slipped on builders' rubble in the station yard, won an injury award and was able to retire early on a full pension.' Clements gave a wry smile. 'Except of course that there didn't happen to be any building work going on at the station.'

'You knew that Owen Nixon was one of his registered informants?'

'Yes, but no more than that.'

'We've spoken to a woman who was a constable around the time of the Heather Bowyer murder,' said Grace. 'DI Jupp warned her off following up on reports that linked Nixon company taxis to the preceding rapes. She resigned soon after.'

Clements rubbed his hand over his face. 'That's bad.'

'We think Freddie Craig's murder may be connected to a case where DI Jupp deliberately secured an unsafe conviction.'

'April Irwin?' he asked. 'I've been listening to the podcasts.'

'Damon Smith had been alibied,' she said. 'DI Jupp knew that from the very beginning, but chose to bury it.'

'So that's why you wanted to speak to Owen Nixon today?'

'Yes. When I told you that the working girls around South-church Park called Owen the "Guardian Angel" you said they must've been pulling my leg. What did you mean?'

'They say he's a dirty old man. He preys on young girls.'

'Girls like April Irwin?'

'I would imagine.' Clements sighed. 'He gets them in his cab and takes them home for sex. Don't think he pays for it, either. The girls gossip and moan but none will come in and make a formal complaint.'

'What are they afraid of?' she asked. 'Is he violent?'

'Not that I've heard, but he's an intimidating bloke and I imag-ine he could make life difficult for them if he wanted to. Tell his drivers not to pick them up or to harass their clients, that sort of thing. We've certainly never had grounds to arrest him.'

'Nor have we,' said Grace, 'but we're beginning to form a pretty sinister picture. His wife disappeared without trace thirty-five years ago. We think he could have been responsible for April's murder and, believing that Freddie was about to take possession of evidence that would tie him to that, has now killed him, too.' A chill ran down her spine as she recalled her careless dismissal of Carolyn's concern about the high tally of girls who had gone missing in Southend. 'Do you think you could review your missing persons files for us?'

'Of course. What sort of time frame?'

'Let's start from when Terri Nixon went missing.'

He looked at her in disbelief. 'Thirty-five years?'

A sense of dread started to pound in her chest. 'Yes.'

'Look,' he protested, 'I've admitted that DI Jupp was corrupt, and probably several of his cronies, too, but from all I've heard he was greedy and lazy, but never this!'

'If he was lazy, then perhaps he never bothered to look too closely,' she said. 'Easier not to know. Or—'

'Or this is all speculation run wild, and Freddie Craig was the victim of a mugging gone wrong.'

'I hope you're right,' she said quietly. 'Believe me, I'd like nothing better.'

She watched him struggle with conflicting emotions as he attempted to make sense of the ideas that even she had only just that moment grasped. Surely she must be wrong?

'I'll collate those missing persons records for you,' he said. 'Get them to you as soon as I can.'

'Thanks,' she said. 'As soon as we've retrieved the DNA profile of April Irwin's unborn child from the original case file we can compare it to the DNA profiles we have from Reece and Larry Nixon. If Owen was the father, there should be enough similarities for us to arrest him.'

'Good. Anything else I can do, just ask.'

Clements escorted her to the front entrance where, with a sombre handshake, he took his leave. Grace found Blake waiting for her under the zigzag portico.

'You OK, boss?' he asked. 'You look like you've seen a ghost.'

'What? Yes thanks, I'm fine.' Still processing her conjectures about Southend's missing girls, she wasn't yet ready to share the full extent of them with anyone else.

He left her to her own thoughts until they were in the car. 'Carolyn passed on a message from Wendy,' he told her, 'about the fingerprint lifted from the cap of the petrol canister from the fire at Reece's house. There's no match to Steve or any other of the people who worked for Reece who would have had reason to handle it. We're at a dead end on that.'

'Right.' She was only half listening.

'Doesn't take Larry Nixon out of the frame, though. Not if he wore gloves.'

'No. Look, do you mind if we park up somewhere, grab a bit of fresh air before we head back to Colchester?'

'Sure.' He had a good sense of direction and weaved the car through residential streets until they reached a wide road bordering a tree-lined slope that overlooked the sea. With a jolt, Grace recognised it as Cliff Gardens. She got out of the car, wrapping her jacket tightly around her and wishing she'd brought a warm scarf and gloves. Blake joined her, but didn't speak and followed her silently into the park.

This was the point she had started from: the search for the elusive DNA link to Heather Bowyer's killer. She had been eager, elated, and rightly proud that her determination had paid off. And now? Could she honestly say that her job – peeling away the layers that hid the ugly truth of what men like Larry and Owen Nixon got up to – was exciting and glamorous? If she believed that, then what was this job doing to her?

She noticed a bench beside the path and sat down, almost oblivious of Blake beside her. Terri Nixon. April Irwin. Other missing girls. Could her earlier sense of dread really be justified? A father and son, both of them sexual predators and murderers?

'Love is a stranger, in an open car . . .' Grace felt she could hear echoes of the Annie Lennox song about temptation and obsession drift towards her on the chill wind off the sea.

'Nothing like the yellow glow of a taxi light on a cold wet night.' Surely Owen couldn't really have been taking girls off the street at will? Not for thirty-five years or more. It just couldn't be possible. But then if, as seemed increasingly likely, he'd enjoyed the protection of a senior local detective, perhaps it was.

She recalled Alison's expressed wish that Grace would find a way of life that wasn't full of such horror and grief. Perhaps her sister's fear that there was something unnatural about dealing with such darkness every day was absolutely right.

'What's wrong, Grace?'

She turned to look into Blake's eyes. They were full of concern and – but no, she couldn't allow herself the luxury of thinking it might be fondness or even love. 'Nothing,' she said.

'Have I done something to upset you?'

'No, of course not.' She gave him her brightest smile. 'It's this case and where it might go. And –' She took a deep breath. 'I wanted to say that I'm sorry I underestimated Carolyn. You were right, she's a good addition to the team.'

'Carolyn?' He looked confused.

'Yes. She's had some good ideas, and I was wrong to overlook them.'

'I wasn't talking about work, Grace.'

She looked at him and laid her hand on his coat sleeve. 'Nor am I,' she said. 'But it's fine. Really. Come on, I'm freezing, let's go.'

'No, wait—'

Unsure if she could bear to hear whatever he wanted to explain to her, she got up and led the way briskly back to the car. Throughout the drive back to police HQ they spoke little, and only of operational matters.

62

Ivo had made sure that the morning's *Courier* carried respectful coverage of Freddie's short career and, given the young man's focus on true crime, the tragic irony of his violent death. It was the very least Ivo could do, yet it bit deep that he'd had to steer so far away from the true reason he believed Freddie had been killed. Not that he minded losing the scoop – he was happy to keep schtum for as long as DI Fisher required – but because it felt like he was covering up for himself, and he was sick of doing that.

At lunchtime he quietly took himself off to a local AA meeting. It was a group he attended fairly frequently. You got all sorts, from City bankers to the woman who had the flower stall outside the tube station. One of the other regulars must have observed that he was more stressed than usual and, as the meeting broke up, came over to make friendly small-talk. Ivo was grateful, but he distrusted the urge to unburden himself. Doing so to Grace had vividly reinforced his disgust that he had left his confession far too late. The recognition that, after years of prevarication, he had been perfectly capable of saying the words without anyone turning to stone only made his previous silence more deeply culpable.

It was odd how you got to know people in AA. Most of them understood that part of being drunk was about fear, about being frightened of facing up to who they were and what they'd done and living with the shame of it all. He'd grown up with people who found themselves unable to speak. His father hadn't been able to tell his ten-year-old son that his mother had died. His parents had not even been able to tell him she was ill. It was cowardice of a kind, he supposed, but nothing like his. Whatever DI Fisher said about inaction not being an offence, *his* silence had been a crime.

Freddie had been looking for a role model. And even if the kid had been kissing the Blarney Stone to get the most out of him, Ivo had allowed himself to lap it up. He'd known the kid was desperate yet, instead of throwing him a lifeline – just landing him a couple of subbing shifts on the *Courier* would have been enough – he'd handed him a grenade with the pin pulled out. And then run away.

It should be he who was dead. That's what he wanted to say now to the friendly bloke – a lawyer, he thought – but couldn't. Instead he made his excuses and left. Trying not to inhale the belch of warm air from the pub on the corner, he went back to his desk.

He was damned if he'd let Freddie's death be forgotten. The kid's attempt to make his mark shouldn't have been for nothing. He needed a good piece for the paper the following day. He doubted his editor would go for a rehash of the April Irwin case and, despite the flurry of headlines about Larry Nixon, now that he had been charged the juicier parts of the story were all *sub judice*, so Ivo couldn't even link the two together. He needed more.

He'd covered hundreds and hundreds of murders over the

years without ever seriously giving the victims or their families a second thought. All that had counted was whether their deaths made good copy. A body, preferably female, young and 'innocent', simply meant more column inches and the satisfaction of elbowing his colleagues off the front page.

Yet it wasn't merely that he'd known Freddie and listened to his young hopes and woes. He wished it were. But he held himself directly responsible for Freddie's death. He might as well have stuck the knife in himself. For years he'd managed to live perfectly comfortably with the guilt of sending Damon Smith to jail, and then, once a day of reckoning loomed on the horizon, he'd simply offloaded the whole sorry business onto an unsuspecting kid. Worst of all, he'd congratulated himself on doing the kid a favour.

He had to put things right. He couldn't leave others to clear up his mess, not even someone as capable as DI Fisher. He had no clear plan, but then he'd often found that hardly mattered. Some of his best stories had emerged from a little creative mayhem. And he wanted a story good enough for his editor to make space in Saturday's paper. He owed Freddie that much.

Ivo picked up the phone and ordered a taxi.

63

As soon as Grace and Blake got back to the office, she called Carolyn into her cubicle.

'I've an apology to make,' she began. 'I cut you off when you wanted to raise the issue of young women going missing off the streets in Southend. I should have listened. Is there anything else you can tell me now?'

Carolyn did a good job of stifling any reaction to her boss's U-turn and sat forward eagerly. 'I've got a list of sixteen names given to me by the sex workers.'

'Sixteen?' echoed Grace, recoiling from the idea that there could be so many.

'Some are from quite some time ago. And these were women who disappeared from the scene without telling any of the others they were leaving,' said Carolyn. 'Some might just have packed it in and gone home or been moved by their pimp to another area. I checked, and seven of them were reported missing by their families, but then that's common for runaways who end up in the sex industry. For most of them there are no indications that anything bad has actually occurred.'

'But not all?'

'No. Two of the sex workers I spoke to have long memories.

Over the years they can name eight girls who spent varying amounts of time living in Owen Nixon's house.'

'Eight whom they say also went missing?'

'Yes,' said Carolyn. 'Although only one of them was among those reported officially.'

'I've already asked Inspector Clements at Southend to review their missing persons files,' said Grace. 'I'd like you to liaise directly with him.'

'Great. Thanks, boss.'

'He told me that the working girls are scared of Owen Nixon. Too scared ever to make complaints.'

'They were pretty cagey with me about him, too.'

Blake tapped on the partition wall. 'Boss?'

'Yes?'

He grinned. 'Results from Wendy on the DNA comparison between April Irwin's foetus and the profiles from both Larry and Reece Nixon.'

'Is there a match?'

'Not an exact one,' he said, 'but Wendy says there are enough similarities for there to be a strong likelihood that Owen Nixon could be confirmed as the father.'

Looking at Carolyn, Grace could see that she, too, was unable to share Blake's elation.

'He killed his own unborn child?' Carolyn's revulsion was clear.

Grace nodded. 'The blows directed at April's belly were particularly brutal. Maybe he never wanted the child, or was punishing April for running away. I don't suppose we'll ever know. But this man is a real danger to women.'

'And if he did kill April,' said Blake, 'then the threat of

exposure in the latest podcast also gave him a motive to kill Freddie Craig.'

'Especially if he has other crimes to keep hidden,' Carolyn suggested.

Grace felt a lead weight descend on her. If her worst suspicions were correct and this was shaping up to be the biggest case of her career, then she was dreading it. 'I'd better set up a meeting with Superintendent Pitman.'

'Want me to take Duncan and go and pick up Owen Nixon?' asked Blake.

'Better wait until I've spoken to Colin,' she said. 'I feel like we could be sitting on top of an unexploded bomb here. If it goes off, then we're going to need extra resources, manpower and the back-up of a solid media strategy.'

Grace was grateful that the communications director suggested she and Colin use her office upstairs for their end-of-day meeting. Away from the busy MIT office, it was relatively neutral territory, and was also far more comfortable. As Hilary invited them to sit on the executive sofas facing each other across the low table where coffee and biscuits had been set out, Colin immediately reached for one and took a large bite. He'd been very upbeat since Larry Nixon had been charged, which was hardly surprising given that the arrest had won him commendations on behalf of the Major Investigation Team from the chief constable and others. As Grace brought him swiftly up to date, she hoped that he'd have the insight to see the full possible repercussions of the latest developments.

'Good work,' he said, reaching for his coffee. 'So where exactly are we up to on the Craig murder?'

'Still working our way through the CCTV footage,' she said.

'Freddie disappeared from view between two camera points near the train station. We know he went into the water very soon after death. There's no sign of the body having been dragged, and no post-mortem lividity to suggest he was killed elsewhere and then transported. But we still don't know at what point along the esplanade he went in. We're examining the routes of all the Nixon company taxis that night.'

'But at this point Owen Nixon is your prime suspect?'

'Yes, sir. I'd like to make the arrest tonight, if only to rule him out.'

'Whatever you think best.'

'There will be issues arising that I thought you might want to consider first,' said Grace.

'Damon Smith's wrongful conviction,' said Hilary.

'Yes,' said Grace, 'and the undoubted police corruption that led to it. If Owen Nixon did kill April Irwin, then all DI Jupp's past misdeeds are inevitably going to go public.'

'Smith's dead, though, isn't he?' asked Colin.

'Yes, but his conviction will have to be overturned. He may have family who will seek compensation. There may be sensitivities around the fact that he came from the traveller community. DI Jupp's corruption will have to be fully investigated.'

'Well, at least Jupp's dead, too, isn't he?' said Colin. 'You're right to raise it, Grace, but I honestly can't see this becoming much of a problem for us. Do you, Hilary?'

'I suspect Grace has more to add,' Hilary said shrewdly.

'I do, unfortunately,' she said. 'Owen Nixon's wife Terri disappeared thirty-five years ago, last seen at the marital home. We've found no proof of life and I think we should be treating it as a no-body murder.'

'Unless we find one, of course,' said Colin.

Grace was glad that he had opened the door for her request. 'Owen Nixon has lived in the same house since his wife disappeared. With your permission, I'd like to use ground-penetrating radar to search the property for her remains.'

'After thirty-five years?' said Hilary.

'A body may not be intact. It may have been dismembered and scattered, burned or disposed of in water. But it may also have been buried somewhere in the house or garden.'

'That's going to attract attention,' said Colin.

'Yes,' she said. 'Particularly as we're also hearing stories from several sources that Owen was in the habit of picking up young women and offering to put them up in return for looking after the house, but in fact for sex. It's possible that's how he first encountered April Irwin. We're checking into how many of them were subsequently reported missing, officially or otherwise.'

'*How many* of them?' exclaimed Colin.

'Inspector Clements at Southend is collating information, but we have word-of-mouth reports of as many as eight women who were not heard from after going to stay at Owen Nixon's house.'

'My God,' he said, 'are we looking at some kind of Cromwell Street scenario here?'

'I don't know,' said Grace. 'I hope not.'

'How prepared should we be?' asked Hilary.

'If I listen to my gut instinct, then I think we should expect the worst,' said Grace as Hilary sat back, clearly shaken. 'However, although it may simply be that records weren't updated, there's also a downside to that. Clements admits there's been a historical reluctance to look very deeply into inactive cases that might shine too bright a light on past police corruption at the station.'

Colin turned to Hilary. 'We can manage any fallout from that, can't we?'

'Yes,' said Hilary, 'although perhaps a vigorously proactive approach might serve us better.' She gave a sideways glance at Grace beside her on the sofa. 'Morally speaking, as well as strategically.'

'Hmm.' Colin frowned as he thought through the implications. 'Take credit upfront for putting things right, cleaning out the stables, even if it turns out that we've cried wolf?'

Grace had to admire Hilary for her ability to keep a straight face. 'It's certainly a line we could take.'

'It depends how big you think this could go,' said Colin, looking at Grace. 'What kind of revelations can we expect?'

'I've no clear idea at this stage, sir. And, as I say, I might be completely wrong about any crimes other than the ones we're already investigating.'

'Even so, we are talking about arresting the father of a serial rapist and murderer,' Hilary pointed out. 'It's going to be a story.'

'The media will have a field day,' said Colin, unconsciously rubbing his hands together at the expectation of fronting such a major inquiry.

Grace was accustomed to her boss's tunnel vision – he regarded even the worst offences solely in relation to his career and the reputation of the Essex force – but she found his reaction profoundly depressing. Was she being excessively naive to imagine he ought to care that it had been police failures that had enabled a man like Owen Nixon to continue doing exactly as he pleased? Admittedly no one who knew him had seen anything, or had turned a blind eye, and his children were too fearful or loyal or collusive to stop him, but it was the job of the police to protect the public when all else failed.

'Perhaps we should delay his arrest until after the weekend,' said Colin.

'He's a dangerous man,' she protested. 'I'd prefer to have him in custody as soon as possible.'

'It's a small delay,' he said. 'And it will give you extra time to get the rest of your ducks in a row. I'd also like to speak to the chief constable and – no disrespect to you, Hilary – take some soundings on how she wants to play this.'

Grace wanted to scream. Did her boss really expect her to time an arrest for the convenience of his media strategy? She reminded herself that he had not yet encountered Owen Nixon, hadn't witnessed the sly pleasure he'd taken in upsetting not only his daughter, but also Anne and Michael Nixon.

The memory of Reece and Kirsty's funerals reinforced her growing conviction that, whether they acknowledged it or not, Owen's children had always known that their mother hadn't died of cancer. Trying to ignore Colin's excited anticipation, she focused instead on Deborah Shillingford. If they were able to confirm that Deborah's mother had been murdered by her father then Deborah would need as much, if not more, support as Monica Bowyer and her son. Grace turned to Hilary. 'Perhaps Colin is right,' she said, 'and we do need to prepare for what we might find.'

64

It wasn't that Ivo required a taxi to pick him up from the station in Southend, but he knew that the father of a man accused of serial rape and murder would never agree to talk to a muck-raking tabloid journalist just because he asked nicely. Ivo's hope was that, if he chatted indiscreetly enough to his driver, word would get back to the driver's boss, Owen Nixon, about just how indiscreet he could be. There were very few people left who could ever have known what really lay behind the cover-up that led to Damon Smith's false imprisonment, but Ivo had to assume that Owen Nixon was one of them. And he hoped that that unwelcome affiliation would make Owen curious enough to rise to his bait.

Accordingly, Ivo made sure to drop three times into his conversation with the driver the name of the pub where he would be found at lunchtime the following day. He also took the precaution of giving a fake destination and made sure the taxi had driven away before he picked up his overnight bag and set off to walk to the modest hotel where he had booked a room for the night. He didn't fancy being ambushed with a knife in his back like poor young Freddie.

It would be Bonfire Night on Sunday, although it appeared that Southend had started its celebrations early. As Ivo walked he heard and saw several rockets tear up into the cloudy sky and burst above the rooftops into showers of coloured light. Once he was startled by some firecrackers going off nearby, followed by a gang of delighted young kids laughing and running off around the corner. Along one side of Prittlewell Square a couple of hoodies had dumped a rudimentary Guy on the pavement. One of them chiselled half-heartedly for donations by rattling a tin with a few coins in it. Their effigy was adorned with one of the grinning black-and-white plastic masks with a moustache and goatee adopted by protesters on anti-capitalist marches. Ivo dropped a fifty-pence piece in the tin, although he suspected from the youths' dull-looking faces that it was more likely to be spent on weed than fireworks.

He doubted either of them knew much about their emblem of four-hundred-year-old sectarian hatred and violence. Not that it mattered. Ivo had always felt that Guy Fawkes Night had survived for so long because it gratified a far more ancient desire; to chase away any evil spirits that were emboldened by the long winter darkness.

The site of the old Marineland complex was not far away. That spectacular bonfire on the night of Freddie's birth had been linked to hidden forces that had violently ended his life. Was that fate, as Freddie would doubtless have spun it, or just bad luck – the same as all Larry Nixon's victims, merely a matter of being in the wrong place at the wrong time?

A rocket whooshed up from inside the square where four adults marshalled a small party of youngsters. A series of falling silver cloudbursts reflected off the water of the ornamental pond and illuminated the upturned faces of the children. Ivo was jolted by a sudden memory of his pint-size daughter, stuffed into a red coat, mittens and welly boots, holding his hand tightly as she watched open-mouthed as her mother lit a spinning Catherine wheel – an even more gruesome symbol of martyrdom. The only other memory of that night Ivo was able to summon up was of how badly he'd wanted to go indoors for a drink.

Relieved to encounter a distraction, he saw ahead of him the floodlit awnings of his boutique hotel – two terraced houses knocked into one, with a couple of silver metal tables for smokers crammed into the narrow paved area between the bay windows and the front railings. He would be glad to find sanctuary inside. The celebration of ancient torture, violence and death, with bonfires and strange lights in the sky, were not good auguries for what he hoped to achieve here in Southend.

He wished that he could spend the evening talking to Grace Fisher, not only because he felt that he was operating in the dark in relation to her investigation, but also because he wanted – he was about to say absolution, but it wasn't that, it was simply the more primal comfort of her company, of feeling less alone on a dark night when evil spirits walked abroad.

He wasn't being fanciful. Freddie Craig's killer was out there, very probably sitting down to an ordinary supper in an ordinary house. Evil wasn't supernatural. It was all too real. All it took to release it into the world was for someone to be in the wrong place at the wrong time.

Ivo hoped Owen Nixon would take his bait and come to the pub tomorrow. He had chosen his lure carefully and named the hostelry in which he'd been drinking that long-ago afternoon in company with four other men, one of whom was Damon Smith. He wondered what he might learn and whether it would make him feel better or worse about his sin of omission.

65

Deborah opened her front door with a paint roller in her hand. She'd tied her hair back with a printed scarf and had splatters of white down the front of the washed-out supersized T-shirt she wore over her jeans. She led them into the box-like front room where one wall of grimy woodchip paper was in the process of being given a coat of fresh paint. Grace glanced at Blake in relief. She had been worried that their visit the previous day would have overwhelmed so vulnerable a woman, and was happy that it appeared to have had the opposite effect.

'Believe it or not,' said Deborah, 'I was on my way to the offy when I saw these tins left on the pavement outside the hardware store, all cut-price. Don't know if there'll be enough to finish the room, but it's a start.'

'It already looks better,' said Grace.

'Thanks. So, what do you want this time?' Deborah spoke lightly but Grace could see the fear and anxiety in her eyes.

'We're not here to ask for information,' said Grace. 'We're here to give you a heads-up that there may be more revelations to come about your family.'

'OK.' Deborah turned her back on them, bending down to push her roller across its tray before applying more paint to the wall.

'We can appoint a family liaison officer if you'd like,' said Grace. 'It might be helpful.'

'No, thanks.'

'You might find it useful to have the extra support.'

Deborah went on pushing the roller up and down the wall. 'Funny the thoughts that come to the surface when your brain is busy with something else,' she said. 'That's what dead bodies do, isn't it? Rise to the surface eventually.'

Grace exchanged shocked glances with Blake. 'Is that what you're expecting to hear?' she asked. 'That we've found bodies?'

'No, of course not,' Deborah said quickly, bending down to coat her roller again.

'We are here to tell you that we're going to arrest your father. It will be on the news.'

'Right, thanks.'

Grace waited, but Deborah continued with her work. 'We're going to search his house for the physical remains of your mother.'

Deborah paused in her movements and then carefully placed the roller on the edge of the paint tray. She looked around, finding what she wanted on the narrow tiled mantelpiece. She lit a cigarette with shaking hands. 'I always felt sorry for Larry.' She blew out a stream of smoke. 'He was the youngest. He missed Mum the most. To begin with, anyway, but then he just grew closer and closer to Dad.'

'Do you know what happened to her?'

'No, not in terms of – I never saw anything. If Dad said she had cancer I wasn't going to argue. But after that, Larry never stood a chance.'

'I don't understand.'

Deborah still did not look at them directly. 'Dad liked him to watch.'

'To watch?'

'To watch Dad with the girls he brought home.'

Grace and Blake stood in helpless silence as Deborah balanced her cigarette on the edge of the mantelpiece and picked up the roller again. She surveyed the half-painted wall, pushing the tail of her scarf out of her eyes with the back of her free hand. 'I suppose that's why people have to have those feature walls that are a different colour,' she said. 'They run out of paint.'

Grace chose her words carefully. 'Larry watched his father having sex with young girls?'

'Yup.'

'Anything more than sex?'

'I wasn't living there then.'

'Did Reece know what was going on?'

'We never talked about it. But I was glad he got out. That was Kirsty's doing. I missed seeing Reece, but I don't blame Kirsty for cutting us all out of their lives.'

'Did you ever witness your father hurting anyone? Any of the young women he brought home?'

'No. They'd be there and then they'd be gone again. I never asked. How could I?'

'Did he abuse you sexually?'

She gave a dry laugh that turned into a cough. 'He couldn't be bothered. Always said I was too ugly.'

'And your mother?' Grace asked. 'What do you think happened?'

'You're going to find out, aren't you? I never believed it, that

Dad – not really, except he was – but I should have been there. I should have helped her.'

'It's not your fault,' said Grace. 'You're not responsible for any crimes your father might have committed.'

'I should've saved her. I should never have let it happen.'

Deborah dropped the roller into the tray, splashing paint on to the stained remnant of carpet, and turned to confront them. 'My mum would still be alive if it weren't for that bastard. I'd still see my kids, too. Probably still be married. He's taken every-thing. You have no idea what a bastard he is! And I've kept quiet all these years. We all did. Even Reece. He knew. He was there.'

'You think Owen killed your mother?'

'Well, she never had cancer. And she could never have run away. But I – you can't – all I thought about was getting the hell out of there.' She retrieved her burning cigarette and took a drag. 'You know, sometimes it's all you can do to save yourself.'

'And that's what you have to focus on now,' said Grace. 'I'm so sorry that chances to stop him were missed. The reasons why that might have happened will also emerge over the coming weeks and months.'

'You won't stop him,' said Deborah. 'You can't. No one could. He always gets his own way. It wasn't never even about the sex. It's about him being able to do whatever he wants. That's what messed Larry up so badly. He tried to be like Dad, even though he's not, not really, not deep down.'

'We will act to stop your father,' said Grace. 'And I can't thank you enough for your help. I realise how hard it must be. Is there anything you want to ask? Anything we can do to help?'

'No.' Deborah looked completely exhausted.

'Just let me know if you change your mind about a family liaison officer. They'd keep you informed better than we can and will help shield you from the media. And you can call me any time.'

Deborah accepted Grace's card. 'You put him away,' she said. 'That'll be a miracle in itself.'

She accompanied them to the front door, barely meeting their eyes as they stepped outside. They were walking towards the car when she spoke again. 'One thing I heard him say once when Larry was upset about Mum. He said we weren't to worry because she wasn't far away.'

She shut the door, leaving Grace and Blake to look at one another in dismay.

'I don't care how Superintendent Pitman and the chief constable want to play this,' she said, 'I want Owen Nixon off the streets now.' She looked at her watch and then at Blake. 'What do you think? Are you up for going over there to pick him up?'

'Right behind you, boss,' he said grimly. 'Sooner the better.'

66

The place hadn't really changed. There was now a soundless flat-screen TV mounted high on one wall to which the barman's eyes flicked constantly, and a slot machine beside the door to the Gents, but otherwise the dingy pub looked much the same as it had twenty-five years ago. Ivo was on his second ginger beer when Owen Nixon entered. Ivo recognised him from the fracas at the funeral, but could see from the way the older man peered around that he was unsure who he was looking for. Ivo allowed him few more moments of uncertainty before raising a hand in laconic greeting.

He was not prepared for the force of the old man's scrutiny. He'd caught the eye of many notorious criminals in his time, but this was like maintaining eye contact with a Great White shark. He was glad he'd taken the precaution of preparing a couple of safety texts on his phone. One covert press of a button in his trouser pocket and he could summon a rescue party. Not that he could come to any harm sitting here watching silent images of football fixtures.

Except that he'd believed that lie twenty-five years ago.

As Owen went to the bar to buy a half-pint of beer, Ivo flipped swiftly through the sturdy card-index of his memory. He failed to come up with a single other occasion when he'd seen this man, and definitely never in company with JJ.

Owen sat down at the little round table opposite Ivo. 'Let's not beat about the bush,' he said. 'How much do you want for them?'

Ivo was taken aback. What did he mean? Ivo hadn't come here intending to sell anything. He had baited his hook in order to talk to Owen about JJ so he could work up a story about the role played by past police corruption in Freddie's murder.

He looked into the eyes of the Great White. Owen meant the letters that Freddie had invented! And if he wanted the letters, then it could only be because— It was all Ivo could do not to jump up away from the table in fright. If Owen had unhesitatingly assumed that Ivo was here to blackmail him over Freddie's fictional letters, it could only be because Owen believed them to be real and thought he knew who was supposedly named in them.

Ivo had unthinkingly supposed that April Irwin's lover, the father of her unborn child, had been someone close to her own age, and surely it was too late now for Owen to worry about covering up for one of his sons? He looked at Owen. He must be nearing eighty, which meant he'd been in his fifties back then. April had been barely sixteen. Perhaps her death had not been the angry panic of a young man saddled with a kid he didn't want. She'd run away because she was frightened, frightened enough to take shelter with a drifter like Damon Smith. And Owen had gone after her.

Just like he'd gone after Freddie.

Ivo thought quickly about how best to respond. 'I don't have them on me.'

'I didn't think you would,' said Owen. 'But you've got them? You've been in touch with whoever had them?'

'I didn't need to,' Ivo lied. 'Freddie had them all along. He gave them to me for safekeeping. We were going to write a story together for the *Courier.*'

'So why aren't you doing the story?'

'After what happened to Freddie?' asked Ivo. 'I'd rather live a few years longer and put something aside for my pension.'

Ivo studied the man as he considered Ivo's words. If he genuinely believed the letters were real, surely he must realise that no amount of killing was going to return the cat to the bag. Was he deranged, and in the grip of some psychotic delusion? Or suffering from dementia? Either way, he was an exceedingly dangerous man with nothing much left to lose.

'I think you should write the story,' said Owen.

Ivo was astonished. 'And say what?'

'All of it.'

Ivo watched Owen smile and decided the man must most definitely be mad.

'It's a good one,' he went on. 'I can promise it'll be worth your while.'

'Why didn't you offer it to Freddie Craig?' asked Ivo.

'I wasn't in command of all the facts at that point,' said Owen. 'I hadn't yet been told the full weight of evidence against my son Larry. Even I can't fix this one. But I can still tell it my own way. So come back to my house and I'll give you everything, tell you about each of my angels. You'll have enough to keep the presses rolling for days.'

Ivo was lost for words. To walk out of here with Owen Nixon could only be a suicide mission. Was he ready for that? But he'd been all too ready to send Freddie out to fight his battles for him, hadn't he? At the very least he owed it to the kid to do absolutely everything he could to bring his murderer to book.

Owen was smiling again. He winked at Ivo. 'You're in the story,' he said. 'Though of course you know that. JJ told me how helpful you were, helping to send that pikey to prison.'

Ivo saw red. But his boiling anger wasn't against Owen so much as against himself. If it hadn't been for his cowardice, his failure to speak up and tell the truth, Owen Nixon would have been put behind bars years ago. If he hadn't been so gullible and pathetically eager to please a man like JJ, Freddie wouldn't be dead. And how many other lives had been ruined by the shameful choice he had made after the long-ago afternoon he'd spent drinking in this very pub? Not just any other young women unfortunate enough to cross paths with Owen Nixon, but some of the people in Ivo's own life. His two wives, his daughter. So many years of hating himself and drinking to blot out the shame; they all stemmed from his decision to help JJ by saving the miserable carcass of the conniving bastard sitting across from him now.

So what if walking out of here now with Owen Nixon meant ending up with a knife in his back? What else could he do to try to put things right?

67

Grace and Blake had not found Owen Nixon at his house and had so far failed to locate him elsewhere. They were on a dual carriageway halfway back to Colchester when Grace received the text.

'We need to turn around,' she said.

Blake glanced at her and then at the phone in her hands. 'What's up?'

'Ivo Sweatman. He's with Owen Nixon.'

'I'll take the next exit,' he said. 'Want to fill me in?'

She read out the text. ' "I've arranged to meet Owen Nixon at the Nag's Head in Southend. If you receive this text, then I'm in trouble." '

'OK,' he said, swapping lanes and indicating left before giving a burst of the siren to clear the way ahead.

As the slip road approached a roundabout, Grace called Inspector Clements to ask him to send an officer to the pub and report back. Once they were on the carriageway heading back towards Southend Blake looked at her once more. 'You want to tell me the rest?' he asked.

'What do you mean?'

'Why does he have your number? He's got all the resources of the *Courier* behind him, so why is he texting you?'

She didn't know what to say. 'Does it matter?'

'You tell me.'

'Ivo's had my back more than once,' she said reluctantly. 'I guess we're friends.'

'He's not only a tabloid crime reporter,' said Blake, 'but he's admitted that he colluded with a corrupt police officer to pervert the course of justice. Isn't that a bit like keeping a rabid dog as a pet and believing it'll never turn and bite you?'

'He hasn't bitten me yet.'

'Doesn't mean he won't.'

Grace longed to explain, to tell Blake the whole story of her various dealings with Ivo, but what would be the point now that it was too late to resurrect their relationship? She stared out of the car window, trying to subdue her feelings. 'Ivo didn't have to come forward and tell us what he did about DI Jupp.'

'So what? He's bad news, Grace,' he said hotly. 'Surely you can see that?'

'He's just given us a lead on where Owen might be,' she pointed out, hoping Blake would let it drop.

They drove for a couple of minutes in silence, but a glance showed her he was still brooding.

'You mentioned once having a kind of safe room,' he said. 'Did you mean him? Did you let our relationship end because of something to do with him?'

'Blake, it doesn't matter now, does it?'

'It does to me.'

'Why? You're with someone else.'

'Really?' he asked sarcastically. 'That's news to me.'

'You're with Carolyn,' she said miserably.

He turned to look at her. 'Carolyn?' He laughed. 'What on earth makes you think that?'

'I thought . . . when I've seen you together . . . you always stick up for her.'

'She's new to the team. I'm her line manager.'

Grace's heart leapt. 'I saw you once, out having a drink. And you came in together one morning. You had an overnight bag.'

'An overnight bag?' He frowned, working out what she meant. 'My sports kit? We go to the same gym. I give her a lift occasionally.'

It was her turn to laugh. 'Serves me right for having a suspicious mind!'

'And Ivo Sweatman?'

'He's given me a lot of help and sometimes offered information I couldn't have got any other way. But it's had to be strictly off the books. If Colin ever found out I'd be disciplined or possibly worse. I didn't tell you because I didn't want you to have to lie for me.'

'Is that it?'

'That's it.'

'All of it?'

'Yes, I promise.'

He turned again to look at her, his eyes warm. 'We're a right pair, aren't we?'

Grace's phone vibrated and she answered the call. It was Dave Clements. A foot patrol who had been near the Nag's Head had visited the pub. Two men answering the descriptions of Ivo Sweatman and Owen Nixon had recently left. The barman was new and hadn't seen either of them before, nor did he have any idea of where they'd been going. Grace thanked Clements and told him that, as they weren't far from Leigh-on-Sea, they would head straight to Owen Nixon's house. With the blues and twos on full blast to clear the slow-moving traffic, they travelled in silence.

As they turned into the web of pleasant, well-to-do residential roads Grace wondered how Owen's neighbours had apparently never noticed Terri Nixon's disappearance. Owen had lived there a long time – long enough perhaps for people simply to accept that every community has its oddball – yet some of them must have waited beside Terri at the school gate, seen her in the local shops or at the hairdresser or doctor. No one had reported any concern. Or, if they had, it had never been followed up.

A taxi with the blue-and-yellow Nixon company logo was parked on the drive. Behind it, the garage doors were closed. Blake drew up outside the house and cut the engine. 'So if he's here, are we arresting him?' he asked.

'Yes,' said Grace. 'Suspicion of murder.'

'Which one?' he asked. 'Terri, April or Freddie?'

'April to start with,' she said. 'Based on the DNA profile of her unborn baby. And Ivo's testimony.' She took a deep breath and put her hand on the door handle. 'I hope Ivo's OK.'

'Hang on.' Blake leaned down and across her to peer through the passenger side window. 'Is that smoke?'

She followed his line of sight to the base of the garage doors where evil-looking grey smoke was curling slowly out into the cold November air. Another fire. Another arson? She looked back at Blake, who was already calling the emergency services, and then was out of the car and running to the garage. The doors gave slightly as she pushed against them, but they were locked and there was no means to prise them open from the outside. She banged on them with her fists. 'Is anyone in there?' She put her ear to the wood, which already felt warm, but could hear nothing apart from the low roar of flames sucking up the air sealed inside.

She ran to the front door of the house, also locked, and rang the bell repeatedly. 'Police! Open up! Now!' The bell echoed inside the house but no one responded.

She remembered the passageway running between the side of the garage and the neighbouring fence. It led through to the back garden, where perhaps there was another door to the garage or a back door to the house. She ran towards it, but Blake was there before her. Motioning to her to stay back, he started down it. He had only taken a few steps when there was a boom and a sharp cracking sound from the small side window of the garage. Orange flames and black smoke shot out as the glass panes were burst apart by the heat, the shards missing Blake by inches.

Grace grabbed his arm and pulled him back from the crackling energy of a blaze that was already scorching the fence on the other side of the narrow path. She was suddenly horribly afraid, and held onto him tightly. He covered her hand with his and gave it a reassuring squeeze. 'Don't worry,' he said. 'Stay here. If I keep really low I can get along the path and through to the back garden that way.'

'No. Wait for the fire service!'

'Stay here.' Pressing her hand once more, Blake dropped to his knees and crawled forward. The fire inside the garage, now fed by the new oxygen supply from the shattered window, roared louder than ever.

Grace knew that the correct thing to do was to remain at the front of the house, ready to direct the firefighters once they arrived. For a moment she thought she'd caught the sound of a distant siren, but if she had, it was drowned out by the loud splintering sound of the double door to the garage breaking open. She moved backwards, expecting any moment to see a figure emerge from the black smoke and fumes, but all that escaped was a shimmering belch of super-heated air followed by more red fire.

Anxious that the intense heat would reach the taxi parked in front on the driveway, she moved further back onto the grass-edged pavement, vaguely aware of neighbours coming out to look in horror at what was happening.

Had Ivo been locked inside the garage? If so, he must be dead. They had responded to his call for help as quickly as they could, but had been too late. Was Owen Nixon in there, too, making sure he went out on his own terms, refusing to bow down to any other authority?

She waited helplessly, already grieving for Ivo, and praying that Blake wasn't being reckless. Finally, she heard the welcome swoop of a siren and within seconds a fire engine turned into the road and drew up outside. Grace ran over to the first crew member who climbed out of the rig. She showed her warrant card and explained what she knew about the situation. By the time she'd finished, the rest of the crew were unspooling hoses and getting down to business.

They were just placing the first hose in position when the front door of Owen's house swung open and Ivo stumbled out, supporting a woman who clung to him, her face half-hidden in his coat. Grace was amazed to recognise Deborah Shillingford. Grace started forward, but was held back by one of the firemen and had to wait while two of his colleagues went to shepherd Ivo and Deborah down the path, demanding urgently if there was anyone else still inside the house.

'Where's Blake?' she cried to them. 'Did you see Detective Sergeant Langley?'

Deborah looked back towards the house. Through the door came Blake, holding Owen Nixon firmly by the upper arm. As they came close, Grace could see that Owen's hands were already cuffed behind his back. Blake grinned at her as he walked past her, leading Owen to their car, where he secured him in the back seat.

'Are you OK?' she asked.

He nodded. 'They were in the house. Owen was threatening to set light to a can of petrol.'

'You were just in time!'

He looked over to where Ivo was helping Deborah to sit down on the low wall which fronted the garden of a house across the road. 'Saved his life for you.'

She touched his arm. 'Thank God you're all safe.' She looked at Deborah. 'What on earth is she doing here?'

'No idea. Let me warn the fire crew that there's petrol in the house and then we can find out.'

The firefighters were now focused on drenching the garage and the side of Owen's house with high-pressure jets of water. The flames still appeared unquenchable, and the swirling smoke and flecks of soot, the noise of fire and water and the smell of charring and steam created a frightening scene. The fire crew remained calm and efficient and thanked Blake politely for his information.

Grace skirted round behind the fire engine to where Ivo

stood protectively beside Deborah, who sat and stared at the ground in front of her.

'You got my message, then?' he asked.

His tone was facetious, but she saw the uncertain appeal in his eyes and smiled. 'Did you have to make it quite so dramatic?' she asked.

'You know me,' he said with evident relief, 'anything for a story. I hope someone's getting some decent snaps, by the way.'

Grace bent down so that she was on a level with Deborah. 'Are you all right, Mrs Shillingford? Would you like to go to hospital to be checked over?'

'I'm not hurt.' Deborah looked up at Ivo. 'He saved me.'

'She was waiting on the front step when we got here,' Ivo explained sheepishly. 'He's got a right mouth on him, her father. Really laid into her.'

'And the fire?'

'Dad wouldn't let us out,' said Deborah. 'He said all of this was my fault.'

'Blake says he had another can of petrol,' said Grace.

Ivo nodded. 'I tried to keep him talking until the cavalry arrived. Only just in the nick of time, I might say.'

Grace looked over to where smoke and steam billowed out of the blackened ruin. 'Why the garage?'

Ivo glanced down at Deborah before replying. 'If half of what Owen said is true, then you'll find out soon enough.'

68

Grace and Blake didn't have to wait long before a prison officer escorted Larry into the small room used for official visits and then went to fetch his solicitor. They sat around a metal table and Blake started the recording of the interview.

'Thank you for seeing us, Mr Nixon,' said Grace. She was struck by how diminished he looked. As a remand prisoner he was wearing his own clothes – black jeans and a grey woollen sweater – but he certainly no longer resembled the confident businessman who had once been the hero of the Marineland fire. Given what she now knew, Grace had to admit that maybe that night had turned his life around more powerfully than she'd ever imagined.

'We're here because I wanted to inform you in person that we will be amending two of the most serious charges against you,' she told him. 'Whether we drop them entirely depends on your cooperation.'

'I don't understand,' said Larry. He looked at his solicitor for clarification, but received only a small shake of the head.

'On Saturday we arrested your father, Owen,' she continued. 'He's been charged with arson, and further charges are pending.'

'I heard about what happened at his house,' said Larry. 'He's OK, is he?'

'Yes. We now have his fingerprints and DNA profile. His fingerprint matches the one found on the discarded cap of the petrol canister used to set fire to the house of your brother Reece.'

Larry closed his eyes, his whole body tensing up.

Grace gave him a moment or two to absorb the information. 'What can you tell us about how your father's fingerprint came to be on that petrol canister?'

Larry licked his dry lips and shook his head, not looking at her.

'Owen and Reece had been estranged for years,' she continued, 'so when might Owen have handled a petrol container stored in Reece's outbuildings?'

'What does he say?'

'Nothing,' she said. 'Was your father at Reece's house that night?'

Larry shook his head again, but said nothing.

'Detective Constable Bromfield, who was with you at the hospital while you were treated for your burn injuries, says that you were terribly upset about your brother's death, that you blamed yourself for failing to rescue him. Would you agree with that?'

'I didn't kill them. He was my brother. He looked out for me when we were kids.' He held out his arms, showing her the reddened scars on the backs of his hands. 'I thought I could rescue them.'

'So you didn't set the fire?'

'I already told you I didn't.'

'Do you know who did?'

He sucked in his lips and shook his head.

Grace tried another tack. 'Reece called you that evening. What did he really say to you?'

'That you'd be coming for me. That you had evidence to prove I killed that girl.'

'Heather Bowyer?'

'Yes.'

'Between speaking to Reece and driving over to his house, you also spoke to your father. What did you say to one another?'

'You'll have to ask him.'

'We already have.'

'What did he say?'

'He said it was all your idea, so that you wouldn't have to go to jail for Heather's murder.'

'He said I killed Reece?'

'That's what he says.'

Larry's solicitor whispered in his ear, but Larry seemed too lost in his own thoughts to listen.

'Did you conspire with your father to commit arson and murder?'

'I didn't kill them. I tried to rescue them.'

'Then here's what I think happened,' said Grace. 'I think you drove over to Reece's house, not because you believed he was going to commit suicide, but because either your father had told you what he planned to do, or you became afraid that he would do something terrible and wanted to prevent it. Does that sound about right?'

Larry stared at her. She was amazed to see his eyes fill with tears, but he said nothing.

'Tragically, you arrived too late,' she went on. 'You tried but were unable to save them, and, to protect your father, agreed to go along with the story he'd concocted.'

Larry nodded reluctantly.

'He took and destroyed the clothes you'd been wearing.'

'Yes.'

'Did he suggest rubbing dirt into your burns to confuse the medical examiner?'

'He did it all to save me. I had to back him up.'

'He murdered one son to save the other?'

'I never thought he'd do it to one of us.'

'On Saturday he threatened to kill your sister, Deborah.'

'She's crazy,' he said. 'You don't want to listen to her.'

'What about your mother?'

Larry put his elbows on the table and leaned his head in his hands. A tear splashed onto the surface and then he laid his head right down, doing his best to cover himself with his hands.

'What can you tell us about your mother's death, Larry?'

Larry sat up and wiped his eyes with the back of his hand. 'She died of cancer.'

'She may have died, but not from cancer.'

'Then I don't know.'

'Did your father kill her?'

'No. Reece said we had to pretend we knew how she died, and about the funeral and everything. He said Dad would kill us if we didn't. Or we'd be taken into care and never see each other again. I just thought, if I did everything Dad wanted, we'd survive.'

It was almost unbearable to have to ask, but she had to. 'And what sort of things did he want you to do?'

'No. No. I was given another chance. Like the phoenix, you know? After I saved those boys from the fire, I told Dad, no more. And he accepted it. After that we kept it straight between us. Father and son, but no more of how it used to be.' Larry looked directly at her. 'Until you came along.'

'Tell me how it used to be.'

'I can't.'

'We believe that he murdered April Irwin. We believe that he may also have harmed other young women who came to help out in the house. Women he had sex with.'

'No. He helped me start my own business. Made sure people used my cars.'

'On Saturday your father set fire to the garage attached to his house. The fire investigators and our forensics team are still processing the scene, but if there's anything to find, we will find it.'

Larry's face paled. He looked frightened.

'What will we find?'

He whispered something, too low for Grace to hear.

'For the tape, please,' said Blake.

'Not Mum,' he said. 'Please not Mum. If she is there, then don't tell me. I don't want to know. I don't believe it. It can't be true. Promise you just won't ever tell me.'

69

With Blake sitting beside her on the sofa in the living room of her house in Wivenhoe as they watched the late evening news, Grace saw herself emerge from the tent-like structure erected over the entirety of what used to be Owen Nixon's garage. Dressed in a white forensic suit, complete with hood and face mask, she would be unrecognisable to anyone else. A drone shot revealed barrier screens around the perimeter of the back garden where two smaller forensic tents had also been set up. As the newscaster detailed how this was turning into one of the most significant murder investigations since Fred and Rose West, the footage cut to the Essex Police media conference held that afternoon.

'Three bodies have so far been retrieved from a former car inspection pit in the garage of 37 Oakville Way, Leigh-on-Sea,' Superintendent Pitman read precisely from the sheet of paper before him. 'One is believed to be that of Theresa Elizabeth Nixon, wife of Owen Nixon, the owner of the house. She was last seen in 1982.'

As camera flashes popped in front of Colin's face, the image reversed to reveal the battery of TV and stills cameras, microphones and scribbling reporters that he faced.

'The remains of two other individuals found in the garage

and another two buried in the garden are those of young women, possibly still in their late teens,' he continued steadily. 'Essex Police are working hard to establish their identities. Anyone with information, or anyone who is concerned about a loved one who may have gone missing in the Southend area during the past thirty years, should contact our incident room. At this stage we do not expect to discover any further remains at the property. A seventy-seven-year-old man remains in custody, already charged with two other murders, that of sixteen-year-old April Irwin in 1992 and twenty-five-year-old Freddie Craig last week.'

'Carolyn told me she saw Colin slip out at lunchtime for a haircut,' said Blake.

'He always keeps a clean white shirt in his desk drawer, too,' said Grace, tucking up her legs and shifting nearer to him. 'But that's OK. At least it shows respect for the families.'

With so little leeway under the rules of *sub judice* for the media to speculate about Owen, the news segment moved on to the background of the April Irwin case and then to a profile of the young podcaster who had lost his life as a result of his one-man crusade for justice, highlighting the tragic irony of his apparent fascination with fate and destiny.

As the newscaster switched to the latest economic forecasts, Blake put an arm around Grace's shoulders to pull her closer.

'My sister Alison would find the idea of us bonding over a mass murderer more than a bit creepy,' she said, looking up at him.

'She won't be the one dealing with the families,' he said sagely. 'For each of the bodies we've seen taken out of that house there'll be at least one person whose ordeal of waiting for the truth is finally over.'

'Even though the truth is so brutal?'

'I'd still want to know, wouldn't you?'

She nodded. 'His angels. Ivo said that's what he called them. All those years of him driving around in his taxi looking for stray young women to pick up and take home, and no one stopped him.'

'You did.' Blake kissed the top of her head.

'Imagine growing up in that house,' she said. 'Almost makes me feel sorry for Larry.'

'Almost.'

'And Reece. Imagine what he must really have been feeling when we turned up asking for a DNA sample.'

'You think he knew the full extent of the horror?'

'He got away, stayed away, wouldn't allow Owen anywhere near his family.'

'So maybe he was relieved to see us.'

'Maybe,' she said. 'You know Ivo has signed Deborah to an exclusive deal to tell her story after the trial? He says he screwed every penny he could get for her out of the *Courier*.'

'Am I supposed to find that endearing?' he asked.

'It'll be more than enough to get her out of Thorpe Bay.'

'I suppose he did grab the petrol can off Owen when he saw me coming in through the back,' Blake admitted grudgingly. 'Might have been a tricky arrest without him.'

Grace was glad that her alliance with the tabloid reporter was no longer in contention. 'Ivo has a knack of being in the right place at the right time,' she said happily.

'Except he's not here now, is he?' asked Blake, turning to kiss her.

ACKNOWLEDGEMENTS

I want to thank Detective Inspector Julie Willats of the Metropolitan Police Service and Tracy Alexander, Director of Forensic Services for the City of London Police. Each gave me generous and patient help, and this book could not have been written without either of them. I am filled with admiration and respect for the work they do. All errors of fact or interpretation are entirely my own.

I also acknowledge the assistance of the Mayor's Office for Policing and Crime.

For background on past police corruption I drew on an impeccably researched book by Michael Gillard and Laurie Flynn, *Untouchables: Dirty cops, bent justice and racism in Scotland Yard*, reprinted by Bloomsbury in 2012.

I also owe thanks to my daughter for keeping me up to speed on podcasting; to Brian Smith for his local knowledge of Southend-on-Sea; and to Carolyn Bromfield, who offered me not only hospitality but also her name.

As ever, grateful thanks to my wonderful editor, Jane Wood, and all the great team at Quercus, especially to Therese Keating and Hannah Robinson for all their hard work. And, last but not least, thanks to my lovely agent Sheila Crowley and her brilliant assistant Abbie Greaves at Curtis Brown, for encouragement and support.